THE ROGUE HEAR⸺

The Suspect's Daughter

Donna Hatch

Books by Donna Hatch

"A highly enjoyable read, equal parts tender and mysterious, with characters you'll cheer for from the beginning to the very satisfying end."
~ Sarah M. Eden, Multi-award Winning Historical Romance Author

Donna Hatch is one of the masters of clean romance with electric tension and smokin' hot kisses." ~
~ Reading is My Super Power Reviews

"No one creates chemistry between Regency Historical characters better than Donna Hatch. If you want a "sweet" read, but with lots of sizzle, you have to read her books."
~ Author Carol A. Spradling

Mirror Lake Press LLC

The Suspect's Daughter original copyright© 2015 Donna Hatch
First Edition Mirror Lake Press, 2015
Digital ISBN 9781311384966
Print ISBN-13: 978-1-5193-9590-0
Print ISBN-10: 1519395906

Cover Art by Lex Valentine
Formatted by Heather Justesen

Published in the United States of America

Dedication

Every book is a combined result of family, friends, and fans, not to mention He from whom all inspiration comes. This makes it difficult to thank people by name who have made an impact on me as a writer, and therefore upon this, my latest book.

However, I would be remiss if I didn't thank Sarah Eden and Janette Rallison, who, when I say "I have an idea but I don't know where to go with it," they help me flesh it out into a story with an actual plot. With them, laughter abounds as well as a few moments of brilliance. And to Joyce DiPastena who has never been tactless to say, "Wow, girl, this is the most worthless drivel I've ever written" but instead suggests how I might revise my rough drafts. Also, a special thanks to Jennifer Griffith who is a voice of reason and loving encouragement when I'm positive I can't write and will never make it as a writer, as well as gently pointing out ways to improve my manuscripts.

A big thank you also goes to my family—sisters-in-law and nieces who proofread and then buy my books, and who constantly reassure me when my confidence falters, my brother David who actually reads my books even though romance isn't his thing, constant encouragement from immediate and extended family, and my children who tell everyone their mom is a real author.

Most of all, to my husband. What I thought was mere tolerance on his part I have recently realized is true support, and always has been. I used to mistakenly believe my husband didn't "get on board" with my annoying writing obsession until I brought home my first royalty check. However, in reality, he was supportive all along. In the beginning, he forked out cash to send me to writer's conferences, retreats, and writer's groups. He carried the load of a young family with six children while I was away at those events, sometimes several days at a time. He never complained when dinner sometimes consisted of pancakes from a mix because I'd spent the afternoon in the throes of creativity—which sometimes felt like captivity by my muse—instead of cooking. He never groaned when during a conversation, or dinner, or in the middle of the night, I suddenly said "Oh!" and rushed off to my computer or a nearby piece of paper to capture a thought before it disappeared forever. There were even a few nights when he went to bed alone because I stayed up late writing. (By the way, I still do most of these.) My husband has always been supportive of me and all my interests. He repeatedly proves that with enough patience, hard work, forgiveness, determination, humility, and commitment, that genuine love and happily ever after is real and attainable.

Chapter 1

London, 1820

Jocelyn Fairley strode toward the drawing room, determined to ensure tonight's ball would be a triumph for her father, and would launch him toward his destiny as the next Prime Minister of England. She'd seen to every detail—chosen flowers and food, hired musicians and chalk artists, and invited all the right people, including a few respectable widows who might catch her father's eye. After all, Mama had been gone three years, and Papa needed a wife at his side.

A single distant violin note sang clear and sweet. Others joined in and then split off, creating the odd cacophony of musical instruments tuning prior to performance. Soon, guests would arrive and Jocelyn's role as hostess would begin.

As she passed her father's study, light glimmered from underneath the door. She checked her steps. She'd left Papa in his room with his valet perfecting the folds of his cravat. Who would be in the study?

Perhaps he'd left a lamp lit. As she entered, the door hinges squeaked. The light instantly extinguished, plunging the room into darkness. Only faint streetlight outlined the windows, one of which, oddly, hung open. Pale fog floated by like wraiths. In the hearth, glowing coals stared like soulless eyes.

Chills ran down her spine. "J-Jonathan?" Her voice quivered like a frightened child's. She took a few cautious steps inside.

Voices and approaching footsteps echoed in the corridor outside Papa's study, growing closer and louder. The faint rustle of fabric provided a second's warning before the door behind her closed. A large hand clamped over her mouth. An unyielding force pushed her back against the wall, while a second hand closed over her throat. Shock waves raced through her.

"Quiet!" The harsh whisper vibrated to her knees.

She struggled against her captor, writhing and clawing at his hands. No effect. The hand muffled her attempts to scream. The grip on her throat tightened, not enough to hurt, but its pressure warned at a very real possibility that her assailant could squeeze the life out of her.

A harsh whisper puffed on her ear. "I said be quiet. I will snap your neck if you give me away."

Oh, heaven above, would this villain kill her? Ravish her? A spasm of fear tore through her. She gulped in tiny, ragged bursts of air that failed to fill her lungs. Her captor's hot breath fanned her cheek. She pushed against a male chest that might have been made of stone. His coat's coarse fabric declared him a member of the lower classes, but he smelled faintly of mint and some kind of citrus like bergamot. The increasing pressure on her throat demanded that she make no further moves. Trapped by the assailant, she stood helpless, her heart clanging against her ribs.

Voices outside the study grew louder, and shadows moved across the floor underneath the door. They passed by and all fell silent. Her captor eased back, but his hands remained fixed on her throat and mouth.

Again came the incisive whisper, "If you say a word of this to anyone, I will return and silence you permanently."

The pressure lifted. For a moment, Jocelyn's only thoughts centered on gasping for air. A shadow moved to the window, and a streetlight silhouetted a male form. The dark figure sat on the window sill, swung his legs over, and disappeared.

Still gasping, Jocelyn put a hand over her mouth. Her knees gave way, and she sank to the floor. Death had paid her a visit. Death had held her in its grip. Death, inexplicably, left her alive and unharmed. A sob caught in her throat. Shaking, she sat and focused on trying to breathe but only managed to gasp. Her own mortality loomed large. She had faced the prospect of mortality when the news came that her oldest brother lost his life in defense of his country, and again when Mama passed. Jocelyn had realized then that life was fragile and short. But she'd never faced her own imminent extinction.

She took several more steadying breaths and fought to pull herself together. She was alive and uninjured. She would not fall apart like some swooning little flower who needed smelling salts to revive. Cool night air crept in through the window. Fog drifted around the streetlamps transforming the light into a spectral glow. Horse hooves clopped on cobblestones, and voices drifted in from the street. Faint strains of music called to her from inside the house and the hall clock gonged. The party. Their guests. Papa needed her. She would not fail him. She must be at his side to greet their guests.

With Herculean effort, she pushed herself to her feet. She took another breath and let it out slowly. Her heartbeat returned to normal and her shaking ceased. The opened window loomed large and threatening, but she forced herself to cross the room and lean out. She peered up and down the streets but no form belonging to her attacker lurked nearby. Reassured, she pulled the window closed and flipped the lock.

After picking up a candle, Jocelyn set it to the dying coals and waited for its wick to spring to life. She shielded the sputtering flame with her hand and cast an urgent glance around. Nothing seemed amiss nor noticeably absent. What had the thief hoped to find? They kept little of value in this room. Perhaps his goal had been another part of the house and Jocelyn had arrived before any real damage could be done.

The front door knocker clanged. Guests had arrived. Drawing on all her inner fortitude, she set down the candle and opened the door. She resisted the urge to look back at the window through which the intruder had fled. Her father awaited.

In the great hall, she paused at the gilded mirror. Wide eyes and a pallid face stared back at her, and combined with the pale blond of her hair and her snowy gown, she appeared ghostly. She pinched her cheeks and bit her lips to force color into them. Though her throat still burned from the attacker's hand, no marks marred her skin. Only her single strand of pearls lay against the ivory of her neck. She froze. The intruder hadn't taken her pearls. This refuted the idea that Jocelyn had surprised a

4

common burglar. Then what had he wanted? His threat to harm her if she revealed his presence rang in her ears.

Now was not the time to dwell on that. Tonight belonged to Papa. Smoothing back a wayward strand of hair, Jocelyn cast a glance over her dress to ensure it remained free of wrinkles. Unfortunately, the gown, however expertly fashioned, failed to transform her figure, which leaned toward plump, into one of slender grace. But wishing would not change it. And she had a task at hand. Filling her thoughts with images of her father's happiness at winning the election, she summoned a smile, and strode forward with all the dignity she possessed.

Her glance fell on a portrait of the loveliest lady she had ever known. Pausing in front of the painting, Jocelyn smiled sadly. "I miss you, Mama." She kissed her own finger and pressed it to her mother's cheek in the painting. "I promise to make you proud."

By all rights, her Mama should be serving as tonight's hostess, but Jocelyn vowed to act in that capacity with her whole heart. The burden to help Papa's rise to fame and glory rested in Jocelyn's hands.

She drew a breath, squared her shoulders, and marched to face the *beau monde* whose public opinion could be so easily swayed for ill, and so rarely swayed for good.

Elegant in his black superfine suit, Papa smiled as she reached his side in the drawing room. Only a hint of silver touched his golden hair, as if to declare him a man of experience and wisdom. An answering smile sprang to her lips.

"You look so pretty, princess." He put an arm around

her and gave her a sideways hug. His scent of bay rum enfolded her along with the tang of mint his valet put in his clothes press to keep away moths.

She smiled, casting off the memory. "And you look handsome as ever."

He sobered as his gaze searched her face. "Does something trouble you?"

Calling on all her courage, she brightened her smile. Tonight she must be at her best. Later she'd decide what, if anything, to tell her father about the intruder. She pushed the last fragments of her fright into a room in her mind and locked the door.

She linked her arm through his. "A bit nervous, I suppose. I know how much this Season means to you."

He kissed her forehead. "The weight of my future does not rest on you, princess."

"I know. But I'm willing to do whatever I can. I am persuaded you would be a wise and strong prime minister."

She glanced around for her brother, Jonathan. After all, the ball had been his purpose in coming home from college for a visit.

"Where is Jonathan?" she asked.

"I haven't seen him in hours." A mild frown wrinkled her father's brow, but the first guests arrived, and he smoothed his expression.

The majordomo announced the Earl and Countess of Tarrington. Emitting understated elegance, and so darkly handsome that her sight of him used to turn Jocelyn into a tongue-tied ninny, the earl arrived with his lovely wife.

The Earl of Tarrington gripped her father's hand. "Fairley, I fear we are unfashionably early."

"Nonsense," Papa said heartily. "You aren't early, only prompt. We rely on your presence to begin the evening." He bowed to the countess. "Lady Tarrington, a pleasure as always."

"The fault for our 'promptness' is ours," the countess replied. "I wanted to see the chalk drawing before dancers mussed it." She gestured to the wood floor where a chalk artist had been hard at work for two days recreating an enormous Fairley coat of arms.

Papa put a hand on Jocelyn's back. "I believe you know my daughter, Jocelyn."

Jocelyn sank into a practiced curtsy. "My lord, my lady."

The countess bathed her in the warmth of her smile. Though she'd recently delivered a baby, her figure had already returned to its former slender grace. "How lovely you look, my dear. I hope there will be an opportunity for you to perform the pianoforte this season. You do play so beautifully."

"It would be my honor, my lady. How is your baby? I understand you were delivered of a son."

Equal pride shone from both faces. The earl spoke. "Indeed. Nicholas Richard Amesbury the Fourth. Lots of dark hair and a lusty cry."

"Lusty, indeed," Lady Tarrington said. "Especially in the wee hours of the morning."

Interesting that a countess would see to her son at night rather than simply turn his care over to a wet nurse. Jocelyn found the idea admirably maternal.

The countess and earl exchanged loving glances. A pain smote Jocelyn's heart. Though she'd had a few suitors during her past four Seasons, none had gazed at her with such open affection. Most only viewed her as a mildly interesting diversion—or as the bearer of a healthy dowry.

Perhaps if she were prettier, or smarter, or more accomplished...but no. She would throw herself into making this a Season for her father and enjoy the adventure of helping him reach his heart's desire. And perhaps she could match him with a respectable lady to help him in his career as well as ease the lingering grief she'd glimpsed in him when he thought her unaware.

Next Season she would apply more effort into seeking a husband. She did want a family of her own someday. The worst part of remaining unwed was the loneliness. None of her married friends resided near any of the Fairley's country houses, nor had further need to attend the London Season. But Jocelyn had her father and Aunt Ruby. That would be enough for now.

"...my support as always," the earl was saying.

"I appreciate that, my lord." Her father bowed.

Jocelyn flushed that she'd been woolgathering when she was supposed to be greeting her guests.

As others arrived, a line formed behind the earl and his countess, so they moved on. Jocelyn focused on each guest she greeted, calling them by name, and asking after their families.

At Lady Everett's arrival, Jocelyn brightened. The titled widow, a brunette about ten years her father's junior, curtsied to her father with just the right amount of respect and grace but with a friendly smile. Attractive enough to be admired, but not so beautiful as to inspire petty envy, Lady Everett bore herself with all the dignity of a queen.

She wore a tastefully simple, elegant ballgown of lilac with blond lace that enhanced her creamy skin.

"Lady Everett, I'm so pleased you are here," Papa said.

Jocelyn watched her father carefully, searching for any indication that he viewed Lady Everett with any interest as a man rather than merely a host. But his features only revealed friendly pleasure.

Lady Everett held out both hands to him. "Mr. Fairley. It's been far too long."

Papa smiled gently. "It has only been since last Season, my lady."

"Yes, as I said; far too long. And I'm sorry you were unable to attend my house party last summer."

"As was I. But it took place at a bad time."

Jocelyn winced at the reminder that Lady Everett's house party had fallen on the anniversary of Mama's death.

"Of course." Lady Everett put a hand on his arm briefly but her expression remained devoid of any coquettishness, only compassion and affection. "How thoughtless of me to have scheduled it at that time. Just know that you were both missed." Her gaze included Jocelyn.

"I hope we will have opportunity to visit in the near future," Jocelyn put in.

"Indeed." Lady Everett inclined her head. "I would be delighted if you both joined me for tea tomorrow."

Papa offered a slight bow. "Tea it is. Thank you."

As Lady Everett stepped away, Jocelyn smiled up at Papa. "She's lovely, don't you agree?"

"Indeed." His impassive voice and expression revealed nothing of his inner thoughts.

She put a hand on his arm. "Am I meddling?"

His face softened. "No, princess. I know your heart is in the right place. We'll speak of this later."

Papa's much younger sister, Aunt Ruby, came next. Though it'd been over a year since Ruby's husband had died, it still surprised Jocelyn to see her aunt without Uncle Arthur at her side. Her aunt, only ten years her senior, often got mistaken for Jocelyn's sister due to her youthful face and figure.

"You've done a lovely job with the decorations, sweeting," Aunt Ruby said with an approving smile and twinkling blue eyes. "I couldn't have done it better. And I am persuaded your guests are enjoying themselves."

Jocelyn basked in the glow of her dear aunt's encouragement even after she moved down the line. Lady Hennessey, sister of the Earl of Tarrington, greeted them. Though she stood next to her husband with her hand resting on his arm, they seemed to stand miles apart.

Lord Hennessey greeted Papa. "Moving speech today, Fairley."

"Oh?" Papa raised a brow. "Did you enjoy it?"

"I found it entertaining, at the least. I wonder at your radical ideals, Fairley. Next you'll have the poor leading the country."

Though Papa stiffened, he kept his voice and expression mild. "I hope, at least, to help the poor find the opportunity to pull themselves out of starvation and obscurity while still observing time-honored traditions."

"Your dangerous views will pull us into a revolution as bloody as the French's."

Lady Hennessey sniffed. "I doubt very much a public

10

educational system will throw us into the embrace of Madame Guillotine."

Her husband turned a sneer on her. "Exactly why women aren't in politics."

"Exactly why they ought to be," she shot back with a lift to her chin. Without missing a beat, she focused her piercing gaze on Jocelyn. "Lovely as always, Miss Fairley. That shade of ivory favors your complexion much better than the unflattering yellow you wore at the Jenison's musical week. I'd wager blue would bring out the color of your eyes."

Jocelyn managed not to recoil at the backhanded compliment and dredged up a pained smile. "Blue is my favorite color."

"Follow your instincts, Miss Fairley. I always regret it when I don't." Lady Hennessey cast a weighted glance at her husband.

Jocelyn wanted to cringe at the obvious disharmony between the Hennesseys and the perfect foil to the love the Tarringtons exhibited—all the more reason for Jocelyn not to rush into marriage simply to assuage her loneliness and feed her thirst for the great adventure of love. She must take her time to ensure her best chances at a union like Lord and Lady Tarrington.

But the closest she'd been to a man in over a year was the one who'd attacked her in her father's study. A shiver raced down her backbone, and her mouth and neck burned where the intruder had touched her.

Again, she pushed away the memory. Papa. Guests. The evening.

Once she saw her father firmly placed as prime

minister, she'd give a thought to her own future. But an edge of loneliness sliced through her consciousness, reminding her of her lack of prospects. Never mind that gentlemen didn't fight for her favor. If wedded bliss remained out of reach, even after another Season or two, she'd embrace spinsterhood and focus her energies on helping manage her father's estates and caring for his tenants. Surely that would suffice.

Chapter 2

Grant Amesbury landed lightly on the sidewalk and flattened his body against the brick building. Keeping to the shadows, he crept away. At the end of the block, he trained his gaze on the window through which he'd made his escape. No face appeared and no cry of alarm sounded. He must have effectively threatened the girl to prevent her from alerting anyone to his presence for the time being.

He swore. He'd committed enough deplorable acts in his life to earn him a place of honor at the right hand of the devil, but he'd never in all his seven and twenty years threatened an innocent woman. Not that any female was entirely innocent. Feminine wiles automatically earned a black mark next to their names from their first coquettish smile to their final act of betrayal.

He traced the scar along the side of his face but refused to indulge in memory.

However, to his knowledge, the one he'd attacked wasn't guilty of any crime. She might have been a maid, of course, but servants seldom smelled as good as the girl he'd briefly captured. Besides, she'd been wearing silk and pearls. A lady. He'd assaulted a lady. He swore again. He pictured her lying in a swoon on the floor. Guilt twisted his gut. He shook it off. A servant would likely attend to the wench and she could raise all the theatrics she desired. As a member of the shallow, spoiled *beau monde*, she'd probably revel in her drama for days, taking to her bed and demanding smelling salts and a bevy of mourners.

He tugged his coat more tightly around him against the penetrating London fog and strolled as if he hadn't a care in the world. He'd have to return to Fairley's house again later to make a more thorough search if he hoped to discover any real proof—beyond informants' words—that Fairley truly was involved in a conspiracy.

Several carriages clattered past him to the Fairley's house. Their occupants got out wearing dancing shoes, and ascended the steps for the party. Grant had counted on guaranteeing no one would be in the study. A serious miscalculation. Tack jingled and hooves clopped on the cobbled streets. The scent of horses mingled with the stench of the Thames and the overruling odor of burning coal in a uniquely London blend.

"Evenin', Mr. Smith." Maggie's smooth alto greeted him in an accent he placed somewhere just outside of London.

Maggie struck a provocative pose on the sidewalk next to her friend and fellow light-skirt. A nearby street lamp illuminated their tattered clothing, exposed cleavages, and legs thrust suggestively out slits in their skirts.

"Evening, girls," he said with a nod. "Business slow tonight?"

"Oh, the night is young," Maggie said, tucking a lock of dark hair behind her ear and eyeing him hungrily. "Are ye lookin' fer womanly company?"

Briefly, the memory of pressing his body against the soft, voluptuous curves of the girl in Mr. Fairley's study flashed into his mind. She'd been soft and had smelled of

14

violets and something comforting like vanilla. And she'd trembled in fear. His right hand burned where he'd silenced her mouth, and the texture of her soft throat created an accusing imprint on his left where he'd threatened her. Regret wormed through him. But he hadn't hurt her, nor would he have even if she had raised an alarm. So why did that annoying guilt remain?

"Come now, it's a cold night," Maggie persisted in a teasing tone. "Let me warm ye tonight." She smiled, revealing remarkably good teeth. She must have bathed recently—she smelled better than usual and none of the usual street grime marred her pretty face.

Grant gave her his customary answer. "The reform house would be warm. Come on, girls, I'll give you a ride to Goodfellow's."

The strumpets giggled and shook their heads. Maggie's companion, a girl barely out of childhood with ginger hair said, "Not warm 'nuff fer us."

With a shrug, Grant strode away. Disreputable they might be, at least they weren't fainting females that flirted in drawing rooms or mysterious beauties who told pretty lies designed to ensnare.

Behind him, Maggie called, "One of these nights, Mr. Smith, you'll show me what you keep all wrapped up inside that coat of yours."

Grant couldn't imagine being desperate enough to share even a few minutes in the intimate embrace of a prostitute. Although, if he did, he wouldn't have to guard his battered, neglected heart.

As he strode in the direction of Bow Street, a carriage clattered past him and pulled to a stop. He glanced back. Maggie stood next to the carriage, speaking to the rider, her seductive laugh ringing out in the stillness. The door swung open and she stepped inside.

Grant gritted his teeth and kept moving. At the rate they were going, those girls would be dead of some awful disease that ate them up from the inside before they saw another year—probably before they were old enough to be "out" had they been born to genteel families. A few months ago, he'd physically picked up Maggie, thrown her over his shoulder and carried her to Mrs. Goodfellow's Institution for the Reformed to learn skills for an honest vocation, but Maggie wouldn't stay there. She'd returned to the streets in two days. He didn't care. Not his problem.

By the time Grant reached the Bow Street Office, the dampness had sunk into his skin. Lamplight through the window guided him like a beacon to the door. Grant pushed it open, nodded to a few clerks who were cleaning off their desks for the evening, and strode to the magistrate's private corner office.

Bow Street's Magistrate, Richard Barnes, sat behind his desk surrounded by stacks of papers and stared into a dying fire. A lamp sputtered, casting shadows flitting in the corners like phantoms. Barnes, a man about ten years Grant's senior, sat in a chair, his head bowed over paperwork, his cravat rumpled.

At Grant's entrance, Barnes brightened and set down his pen. "Amesbury. What news?"

"Nothing," Grant said in self-loathing. "I found nothing incriminating in Fairley's study—I had to cut off my search early."

Barnes waved off Grant's failure. "No matter. I doubted Fairley would leave evidence lying around his London house, anyway. He's probably too smart for that."

Grant threw himself into a worn leather armchair, as disgusted with his failure as much as his means of escape. "I'll try again another time."

"My brother said Fairley made an impassioned speech today." Barnes leaned back and folded his arms. "Won some supporters in the House of Commons. He's certainly making himself *memorable*." He punched the final word with a dark frown.

"Does the prime minister see Fairley as a threat to his position?" Grant asked.

"Difficult to say. It would take a majority vote of no confidence to get Lord Liverpool removed, and for the majority of the House to suggest a replacement. So far, most don't seem inclined to take such a strong stand against Liverpool, but if they did, Fairley seems to be their choice."

This led them right back to Fairley. But it didn't make sense that a gentleman of Fairley's wealth and power would stoop to murder, not even to achieve the position of prime minister. However, people often had hidden motives, as Grant well knew.

If Richard Barnes thought Fairley was guilty, then he was. And the word of two separate informants at two separate times could not be ignored. The magistrate was one of the few people Grant trusted implicitly—and not just because Barnes defied his orders to rescue him, like an avenging angel, from the Corsican Monster's best torturer. But more than that, Grant respected the man's unwavering sense of right and wrong, as well as his instincts.

Barnes continued, "Fairley is ambitious and has shown ungentlemanly conduct in the past. And his wife's death might have pushed him into a state of ruthlessness—enough to murder to achieve his goal."

"We won't let that happen."

Leaning forward, Barnes laced his fingers together on his desk. "We have to handle this delicately. We can't accuse a man with Fairley's standing of plotting such a serious crime without irrefutable proof. And even if we find such proof, we must wait, watch, and learn who else is involved." Barnes picked up his pen and absently sharpened the tip.

"I understand." Grant watched his long-time friend and visualized the gears turning in his head.

Barnes set down the pen and leaned forward. "I need you to go deeper—get invited to the conspirators' secret meetings. The Secret Service is guarding the prime minister day and night, and working to learn exactly when the assassins plan to strike. But if we can discover all the conspirators, we can eradicate them and end the threat."

Grant grimaced. He'd have to make some new 'friends.'

Barnes chuckled softly. "What? You look like I've proposed something distasteful."

"'Going deeper' means I must rub shoulders with a bunch of nobs and dress like a fop and act like I care about politics."

Barnes cocked a brow. "Might I point out that you are the son of a nob?"

"Don't remind me." Grant slumped down in his chair.

Amusement twinkled in Barnes's eyes. "Far be it from me to suggest you spend time with men who are literate and bathe once in a while."

"That's something in their favor. But if I suddenly show up at respectable establishments, everyone will view that as suspicious."

"I'm confident you'll think of something." A smile hovered around his mouth.

Grant resisted the urge to let out a long-suffering sigh. Very well, he'd do the pretty with those who enjoyed worthless pastimes like parties and balls. Few outside his family knew of his involvement with Bow Street, so no one would suspect him of working on a case. If he played the game right, the conspirators would approach him with the suggestion that something ought to be done about the prime minister—something quick and incisive. And Grant would drag the conspirators to justice, one way or another. Those involved would feel the full force of the law.

He took a hackney home. With the aid of his street-urchin-turned-valet, Clark, Grant shaved and changed into something fashionably uncomfortable. That unpleasant task completed, Grant took another hackney to a gaming establishment respectable enough to attract wealthy customers. Grant strode in as if he frequented the place that attracted the idle, bored rich who sought pleasures away from balls, soirees, and the other inane social gatherings of the London Season.

Bright enough to appear honest, yet softly lit to create an ambiance of intimacy, the room hosted a number of tables filled with gamblers throwing away their money on everything from whist to faro. Dark paneling and woodwork from a bygone era adorned the walls, and scarlet velvet decorated the furniture. Grant reminded himself of his role tonight as the son of an earl and relaxed his expression into one of *savoir-faire*.

Out of habit, he noted the row of windows along the street-side wall, and the back door on the far side of the adjoining room, which probably led to an alley. A young man nearest Grant leaned against the wall, too drunk to be a threat. Two next to him shouted at each other and guffawed. Bully boys stood by to throw out any trouble makers. Seasoned players mingled with cocky innocents unaware of how badly they were getting fleeced.

Almost afraid to move his head lest he muss the awkward perfection of his cravat, Grant ambled to a green baize table to observe a high stakes game of faro. Dice rolled to a stop, and cries of triumph and woe exploded as players won and lost money in a vain hope to tempt Lady Luck to smile on them.

Fools. Grant kept his money closely guarded. Even his investments sat with only the most trusted ventures. Lady Luck was unfaithful, and Grant would trust her no more than he'd trust a woman.

Moments later, he wandered to a group playing *vingt-et-un*. Gentlemen at the table sat with guarded expressions and rumpled neck cloths, most of them he recognized as younger sons of aristocracy or nobility, no doubt desperate to add to their allowance. The game ended amid groans. A victor crowed his triumph while one of the losers vacated his spot.

"Too much for me tonight," the gentleman grumbled as he stood and abandoned the game.

A gentleman approached and Grant went on alert. Then he relaxed at the familiar face.

The face from the past grinned. "No, it can't be...Grant Amesbury?"

Grant allowed himself enough of a smile to appear friendly. "James Ingle. I thought you'd have debauched enough maidens to have been chased out of the country by now—or put a period to the end of your life on a dueling field."

James gave a start and drew his brows together, genuinely offended. "I've never debauched a maiden."

"Oh, really?" Grant drawled.

"In truth. And I never touched your sister, I swear."

"I know. I would have killed you if you had. But you broke her heart. For that I should have at least maimed you."

Ingle gave a huff of laughter but sobered at what must have been a deadly gleam in Grant's eye. Shifting from foot to foot, Ingle tugged at his collar and cleared his throat. "Any games catch your interest tonight?"

"I just got here."

"Ah. I prefer Loo, myself."

"I hear that's Prinny's choice of games these days as well." Grant deliberately avoiding calling the former Prince Regent "King." The new monarch title didn't sit any better on the indolent womanizer than his previous one had. Besides, he hadn't yet been coroneted.

Ingle tapped his chin thoughtfully. "I think you're thinking of the prime minister; I hear he favors Loo."

Grant shrugged. "Perhaps. They're both a couple of wastrels, if you ask me. They gamble with the state of the country, as well."

"I can't say that I completely disagree."

"I'd like to throw the lot of them into the sea and put a real leader in charge."

"Maybe we should." Ingle eyed him as if trying to decipher his meaning. "You don't strike me as one of those calling for Parliamentary reform."

"I'm not, really. Just disillusioned." Grant glanced casually around but no one appeared to take any interest in their conversation.

Ingle peered at him. "A disillusioned war hero..."

Grant let out a scoff that went all the way to his toes. "I'm not a hero."

"You served king and country."

Images of war and death crowded Grant's mind—black powder burning his nose, cries of agony echoing in his ears, and soldiers he shot crumpling to lie in their own blood. He sucked in his breath and raced past memories back to the smoke-filled gaming establishment. "I served."

"That makes you a hero." Compassion edged into Ingle's expression and his gaze settled on the scar running down Grant's face that forever branded him.

Grant scowled. "I need a drink."

He moved away from Ingle's pity. After securing a brandy, he sipped slowly, careful to keep his head clear. At the far side of the room, an argument broke out. Grant ambled toward them to be on hand if the argument turned violent. But the bully boys had already noticed and were taking up protective positions.

"How dare you, sirrah!" shouted a fair-haired escapee from college.

The towhead swung a fist at his red-faced companion but his movements were slowed by too much drink. The other youth dodged. The blond missed, but the swing threw him off balance.

Grant grabbed the tottering lad before he fell. "You've had enough merriment for tonight, boy. Time to leave." Fisting his hands in the boy's coat, Grant hustled him toward the door.

"M' mothah wash a lady," the boy slurred.

Grant held his breath at the stench of liquor emanating from the sot, and glanced back at the other youth. If Grant had known the altercation was over an insult to a mother, he would have helped the blond get in a few good blows. No one insulted mothers and got away with it, if Grant could help it. But now was not the time to start a brawl.

To the blond, Grant said, "Indeed, she was. A very fine lady. Come, I'll call you a cab. Where do you live?"

"Mayfair." Then he giggled. "Oxford. But Mayfair for a few daysh till I go back to shschool."

Of course. Most indolent brats lived in Mayfair. Grant hailed a passing hackney cab.

"I'm not a shnot-nosed whelp, either." The young man cast an accusing glare over his shoulder at the door of the building, but the motion threw him off balance. He staggered and fell against Grant.

He put a steadying hand on the boy's shoulder and adopted a soothing, albeit condescending tone used for a stupid child. "No, indeed, and you hold your liquor just fine."

His sarcasm was apparently lost on the boy who grinned at him. "Jush sho." He stuck out a hand. "Jonathan Fairley, at your shervish."

The son of the man Grant had been sent to investigate? Grant recovered his surprise enough to regain the role, however unfamiliar, of a gentleman. He replied without missing a beat, "Grant Amesbury, at yours."

The boy tried to bow but lost his balance again. Grant grabbed the scruff of his neck and held the tottering drunk until the hackney drew up alongside.

Grant called up to the jarvey the address of the Fairleys' residence. Young Mr. Fairley collapsed into a dead weight. Grant swore and considered his options. He could load the pup into the cab like so much baggage and leave it to the driver to deposit him into the care of his relatives. However, perhaps this situation could be used to Grant's advantage. This may be the key to securing the notice, and perhaps even gratitude, of his prime suspect in the assassination plot. Such gratitude might bring him close enough inside the family circle to earn the confidence of the plotters, or at least give him more opportunities to investigate Fairley.

Grant gathered up the gangly lad, loaded him into the hackney, and swung into the seat. The drunk snored as they clattered over the cobbled streets. When they arrived in front of the Fairleys' townhouse, Grant collected his drooling companion, got out with the boy draped over his shoulders, and paid the jarvey. Glancing in every direction to ensure no one lay in wait, Grant carried his snoring burden toward the front of the house.

He paused in front of the steps. If the family were in the midst of hosting a soiree, *sans* one errant son, they might not appreciate a stranger showing up with said errant son senseless and slobbering for their guests to view. Grant smirked. It might be amusing to see stuffed shirts in an uproar over the public return of their wastrel son.

However, such entertainment would not further his purposes.

Grant shifted his burden more comfortably on his shoulders and walked around back to the servants' entrance on the ground floor. A brief rap on the door brought the silhouette of a man holding a spoon in one hand. Grant blinked in the light behind the figure.

"Good evening, my good man," Grant said politely, still immersed in his role. "I have a special delivery." He turned enough to show the face of the lad draped over his shoulder.

The kitchen servant let out a gasp. "It's the young master." He called over his shoulder, "Elwood, fetch Mr. Owen at once, and inform Miss Fairley. Mae, show this gentleman the way to Master Jonathan's chambers." He waved Grant in.

A scullery maid dressed in a plain frock too short for her thin legs bobbed a curtsy. "This way, sir."

Grant followed the small girl up a narrow, steep flight of stairs not unlike the back stairs in his family estate that he'd used as a boy to sneak into the kitchen and steal sweets. He maneuvered carefully so as not to bump the unconscious youth's head, though the pup likely deserved a good head-thumping. Most nobility did at his age. Grant let out his breath in disgust. Useless, bored aristocrats lived for the next pleasure while Grant and other loyal Englishmen spent their youth answering the call to serve king and country. A fat lot of good it did him. But for all he knew, maybe he helped tip the scales toward victory before he was captured. He resisted the urge to let out a healthy snort at the overly optimistic thought.

As he ascended to the family wing behind the maid, a diminutive middle-aged man with the clothes and air of the butler met him in the corridor. "Upon my word, Master Fairley!" His gaze landed on Grant, taking a swift appraisal of his clothes. "Where did you find him, sir?"

"At a gaming...er...establishment trying to start a brawl. I hailed him a cab, but he passed out so I thought I ought to bring him home myself before he came to harm." He almost laughed at the overly concerned tones he adopted for the butler's benefit.

"How very kind." The butler bestowed a smile so fatherly and affectionate that Grant blinked. "I am Owens, sir. If you would be so good as to bring him in here?"

Owens nodded to the scullery maid in dismissal and she scurried away. The butler led the way to a Georgian-style bedroom with an abundance of red and gilt. He gestured to the bed. "Please lay him there. His valet will put him to bed."

As Grant unburdened himself of the snoring youth, the butler said, "My master will wish to thank you, sir. May I give him your name?"

"Amesbury. Grant Amesbury." He retrieved a calling card that Clark had tucked in his pocket since no gentleman of good *ton* would be without one.

Footsteps neared mingled with the whisper of silk. Grant glanced at a young woman wearing a white lace ballgown hovering in the doorway. Her yellow-gold hair was caught up in the kind of ridiculously elaborate style all the husband-seeking females of her class wore, and pearls hung from her ears and neck. Fairley's daughter, no doubt, probably as vain and empty-headed as all high society chits.

"Is Jonathan injured?" Concern wove through her husky contralto. Surprising, that. Most empty-headed chits spoke in thin, high-pitched voices like children about to burst in to peals of giggling, and tittered behind their fans.

Grant tempered the first words that came to his head about how foxed her Jonathan had gotten, and reminded himself that his goal was to ingratiate himself into the family, not to offend the sensibilities of a member of it.

"No, not injured—merely intoxicated," Grant said. "I caught him before he hit the ground when he passed out."

The chit shot a glare at the slumbering sot. But when she returned her gaze to Grant, she smiled with mingled curiosity and gratitude. "That was noble of you, sir. I hope you didn't go to a great deal of trouble."

Grant wanted to smirk at the understatement. "Not at all. It was my pleasure." He almost choked on the words. But if bringing home the sot and earning the appreciation of a villain's daughter led to exposing the plot, then it was worth it. Time would tell.

"We are in your debt, sir," she added.

A sudden thought struck Grant. To his knowledge, Fairley only had one daughter. Had this been the lady he'd attacked in Fairley's study? She, too, had worn pearls around her neck, right below where he'd pressed his hand. Grant gave her a quick once-over, searching for signs of trauma, but she stood composed and clear-eyed. Either she hadn't been his victim, or the lure of a party had the power to pull her from hysterics.

A servant dressed as a valet arrived and set about removing the drunk's boots. The valet nodded to the girl. "I'll see to him, Miss Fairley."

27

The butler headed for the door and Grant followed him out of the room. As he drew near the girl, Owens hesitated, then bowed and intoned, gesturing to Grant, "The honorable Grant Amesbury, miss." Then turning to Grant, he indicated the girl. "Miss Jocelyn Fairley."

Amused that the butler took on the role of introducing them, Grant inclined his head in an aristocratic bow.

She offered a very proper curtsy. "I am the very grateful sister to the young man you were so kind to have aided."

She smiled so brightly that Grant almost shielded his eyes from its sheer brilliance. No doubt, hers was a perfectly rehearsed maneuver designed to ensnare some poor, unsuspecting male in the parson's noose.

The butler discreetly left.

"Mr. Amesbury?" she said. "Brother to the Earl of Tarrington?"

"The same."

The chit knew her book of peerage. Of course she did. All marriage-minded, gold-digging females memorized that book so they could customize their attack plan when they met a man of significance—not that Grant cared to place himself in that category.

The wench's smile deepened and her eyes sparkled. "I cannot tell you how grateful I am to you, Mr. Amesbury for bringing home my brother. And I'm sure my father will share my gratitude. I was growing concerned when Jonathan failed to appear. I'd asked him to come home from Oxford specifically for this night." Her cheer faded as she cast another frown in the boy's direction before returning her attention to Grant's face.

For a society chit, she had a remarkably direct gaze, remarkably bright blue eyes as if lit from within, and a remarkably sunny smile. And she expected something. Conversation.

He seized on the first thing that came to mind. "Jocelyn is an unusual Christian name for a girl."

Her expression turned amused. "My Grandmother's maiden name was Jocelyn so she named my mother Marie Jocelyn. When I was born, my parents reversed her names and gave them to me: Jocelyn Marie." She ended with a bouncy sort of grin.

He blinked. "That explains it."

Some inner joy, or a calculating thought, widened her smile. "We are about to have dinner. Won't you please join us and allow us to thank you properly?"

Grant could hardly resist rubbing his hands together at the thought of so quickly earning entrance into the household where he could continue his investigation. He called upon all his lessons in good breeding, dusty as they were. "You're too kind, but I wouldn't wish to intrude."

"It would be our honor." She hesitated. "Unless you have a previous engagement?"

"Nothing I can't miss. In fact, I'd like to meet your father. I understand he has just announced his intent to become the next prime minister?"

"Yes, indeed."

"I'm sure he'll do a better job than the buffoon in that office now."

She smiled and gestured down the corridor. "This way. I wouldn't call Lord Liverpool a buffoon, but I am persuaded my father will be a brilliant leader if given the opportunity."

As she kept pace with him, she glanced at his arm. Then he remembered his role as nobleman's son in the presence of a lady and offered his elbow. Smiling, she wound her arm through his. Shocked by the long-absent experience of a woman voluntarily touching him, he barely managed to keep moving. She led him to a grand curving staircase overlooking the main foyer with black and white marble tiles. Her perfume tickled his nose, the exact scent worn by the girl he'd roughed up in the study. And she wore pearls, as did his victim. So it had been Fairley's daughter he'd threatened. Grant tried to keep his face benign. His threats repeated in his mind, the threats he'd whispered into her ear as he'd muscled her against the wall and silenced her. Not to mention his grip on her throat. He refused to cringe at the thought. She'd obviously suffered no harm.

He returned his focus to his mission as they descended the stairs. "So you believe Lord Liverpool will be replaced as prime minister?"

"Perhaps. There's talk of casting a vote of no-confidence which will force the House to choose a successor to bring before the king. His will be the final decision, of course." She shrugged delicately. "We shall see."

Grant studied her but saw nothing beyond guileless cheer in her countenance—as if any female could be without guile.

The wench paused to whisper lengthy instructions to a passing footman who instantly dashed away. Returning her cheerful expression to his face, the Fairley chit led him to a drawing room almost as elaborate as the grand ballroom at Tarrington Castle.

The Fairley girl glanced up at Grant, her head not quite level with his shoulder, and gestured to the couples waltzing. "We're just about to begin the dinner set, so we'll dine shortly. I've seated you next to my father. I hope that meets with your approval."

"Perfectly." His gaze darted about the room, noting every door and window, and recognizing many of the nearby guests. He absently noted the intricate woodwork and the paintings on the soaring ceiling illuminated by hundreds of candles.

The finest stuffed shirts, including his brother Cole, the illustrious Lord Tarrington, appeared to be present. His youngest brother, the perfectly perfect Christian and his new wife, Genevieve, whirled by. Even his brother Jared, who'd recently escaped both piracy and death waltzed with his wife, Elise. Jared normally despised social gatherings as much as Grant, but he'd started making more and more social appearances since his marriage to the young widow who'd proved she possessed more than met the eye. A number of other lords and powerful families gathered in the room. Tonight, no lack of pedigree danced at the Fairley's auspicious gathering of nobs.

Grant glanced at the Fairley girl with raised brow. "I see you have a plethora of Amesburys this evening."

She grinned. "You are an unexpected, and might I add, most welcome addition."

Smooth. One corner of his mouth tugged upward. Hopefully, she'd interpret it as friendly and not mocking. And *must* she smile so much? It wasn't natural. No one was that happy. Either she was a desperate and meticulously trained husband hunter, or she had perfected the role of politician's daughter coached to garner goodwill toward her father.

While Grant entertained and rejected every reply that came to mind as being too rude or cutting to fit the part he played tonight, the wench tugged on his arm. "I'll introduce you to my father."

As he and the girl wound through the guests, a few turned curious gazes on Grant. Some stared at the scar running the length of his cheek while other vaguely familiar faces gazed at him in surprise—probably speculating about the arrival of a man reputed to shun polite society. Grant's only appearances at social gatherings since he'd returned home from the war had been his brothers' weddings, events he'd attended out of duty. He'd actually grown to like the women his brothers married. Wonders never ceased.

The Fairley chit led Grant to a tall, fit man with gray fading his blond hair. He stood in a circle talking to two known members of Parliament, and a man whose face Grant could not place.

She touched the blond man on the arm. "Papa, forgive me for interrupting, but I'd like you to meet Mr. Grant Amesbury, brother to the Earl of Tarrington."

Curious, assessing blue eyes swept over Grant only a heartbeat before Fairley offered a bow. "Your servant, Mr. Amesbury."

Fairley's girl rose up on tiptoe and whispered into his ear. Fairley's eyes opened wide, narrowed, and then he quickly mastered his expression. "A great pleasure to make your acquaintance," he said to Grant. "And our thanks to you, as well."

Grant cast off the first flippant response and summoned something that sounded urbane enough for these nobs. "Happy to be of service, sir."

Fairley indicated his fellow stuffed shirts. "Please allow me to introduce Mr. Dawson and Mr. Redding."

Grant returned their bows. He saw nothing overly unusual about either of them except that they were perfect foils, with Mr. Dawson being tall and so thin that a stiff wind might blow him over, and Mr. Redding so short and portly that he appeared almost the same size in every possible direction. And they cast suspicious, almost hostile glances at one another.

This must be Mr. Redding who'd announced his desire for the office of prime minister—Fairley's only contender. For his part, Fairley seemed to have many supporters in the House, but a vote of no seemed unlikely.

However, the current prime minister's death would almost certainly guarantee Fairley's name would be presented to the king. Murder could be a quick path to power.

Chapter 3

Jocelyn stepped back to leave the gentlemen to their discussions and did a quick, visual survey of the room. Guests talked and laughed, couples filled the dancefloor, liveried servants carried trays of drinks through the crowds, and just the right amount of candles burned to softly illuminate the room.

Yet try as she might, she could not keep her attention from wandering back to Grant Amesbury. He was, without a doubt, one of the most savagely handsome men she'd ever seen. With hair as black as a raven, eyes of purest silver, and the chiseled features of a nobleman, he belonged within the pages of a novel by her favorite author. Wearing all black, except for his white shirt and cravat, he gave the impression of severity. Or perhaps he was still in mourning for his father, deceased only five or six months ago.

Judging by his tall, lean but muscular build and the assured grace of his walk, he had to be athletic—probably a fencer and a pugilist. A ragged scar running down the right side of his face as well as his guardedness suggested he bore a hundred secrets. He would have made a perfect pirate or spy. His expertly tailored clothing of the latest fashion revealed his taste in simplicity, yet he wore his hair slightly longer than strictly fashionable as if he often walked just outside society lines.

"Who is that, pray tell?" A gracefully feminine voice drew her focus.

Jocelyn turned to Lady Everett, the lady she hoped to match with her father. "His name is Grant Amesbury, a younger brother to the Earl Tarrington."

"I've heard of him." Lady Everett unfurled her fan and stirred the air.

"Have you? Beyond his family connection, I know little. We toured his ancestral family home, Tarrington Castle, a year or so ago, but the housekeeper who acted as our guide only mentioned him in passing—that he is a returning war hero, and was gravely wounded. What do you know about him?"

"Very little." Lady Everett watched him as if both fascinated and afraid. "A bit of a shut-in, from what I hear. Never attends society gatherings. I can't imagine why he attended tonight, although all his brothers are here aren't they? Is he a friend of your father's?"

"He did our family a great service tonight; he found Jonathan in rather, er, unfavorable circumstances and brought him safely home moments ago. I invited him to stay, and he accepted."

She glanced at him again. Surely the breadth of his shoulders were his own, and not the result of extra padding in his tailcoat. With his unfashionably long haircut and subdued colors of his evening wear, he didn't seem vain enough to alter his shape.

Lady Everett's expression shifted and she watched Mr. Amesbury speak with Jocelyn's father with renewed curiosity. "He's very handsome, but I feel that somehow I should be afraid of him. Yet, if he came to Jonathan's aid, then I must have misjudged Mr. Amesbury's character. Perhaps it's that scar that gives him such a fearsome appearance."

"Perhaps." Hearing the lady mention Mr. Amesbury's scar instilled an unexpected desire to defend the gallant gentleman. "I wonder if his scar is a reason why he doesn't make many social appearances. He might have been the object of stares or unkind comments."

"Oh dear." Lady Everett put her hand over her mouth. "And I just said..."

Jocelyn touched her arm and smiled gently. "You didn't say it to him."

"No, but I..." She straightened. "When I am introduced to him, I will greet him warmly, and make a point of looking only at his face and not at his scar. I will pretend I don't see it at all."

Jocelyn strengthened her determination to help her father see Lady Everett for the kind and lovely lady she was. "That's a good idea. We'll prove to the reclusive hero he's welcome, and he doesn't need to be alone."

The last notes of the current set died down. As the dinner dance began, her father appeared and bowed to Lady Everett. "May I have the honor?"

Lady Everett smiled as if he'd handed her a long-desired gift. Jocelyn almost clapped for joy. It was working. Soon her father would begin to see the lovely lady as a potential wife, rather than a long-time family friend. It would ease his loneliness and could only help his political career.

"I'd be pleased." With adoration clear in her eyes, Lady Everett placed her hand in Papa's.

Papa led Lady Everett to the dancefloor while other couples filled in around them. As strains of a waltz swelled, Jocelyn watched the dancers, recalling times when music and motion had swept her into a realm of bliss. She'd even waltzed with the handsome Duke of Suttenberg once, but he had only treated her with courtesy, not with the adoration of a suitor.

She pushed back looming disappointment that no one had claimed her hand for tonight's dinner dance. It was just as well; as hostess she had a great many responsibilities. This Season was for her father, both romantically and politically. Perhaps next Season she would find her own true love.

A glance about the room assured her that the footmen had ceased serving drinks and gone to help with final preparations to serve dinner. She gave a satisfied nod. The butler, Owens, ran the household servants with the precision of a perfectly wound watch.

Her gaze fell on Grant Amesbury again. He stood, alert and almost wary, with Mr. Dawson. Apparently no young lady at tonight's gathering had caught the handsome recluse's eye enough to tempt him to dance. However, Mr. Amesbury had accepted an unexpected invitation and probably wore boots instead of appropriate footwear for a ball.

Remembering herself, she pulled her gaze from him and murmured a few greetings to some of her nearby guests. Yet once again her attention shifted to Mr. Amesbury. Curiosity about him finally drove her to his side. Surely as hostess, she could be forgiven for approaching a gentleman. Moreover, she'd known Dawson

37

all his life. She threaded through the crowd to reach Mr. Dawson and Mr. Amesbury.

"... went to school together and have watched our children grow," Mr. Dawson said. He greeted Jocelyn warmly. "Ah, Jocelyn, there you are. I was just telling Mr. Amesbury about your family. A fine job you did of putting together the evening's festivities."

"Thank you, Mr. Dawson."

He put an arm around her and gave her a little fatherly squeeze. To Mr. Amesbury, he said, "This girl is the age of my daughter, and I think of her as my own."

Jocelyn tilted her head to look up at Mr. Dawson. "How is Charlotte?"

"Oh, she and Charles are very happy. I don't see them as often as I'd like, but her letters are filled with joy. Still no mention of a grandbaby yet, sadly."

"I'm so glad he returned home safely to her." She glanced at Mr. Amesbury but he only observed them with serious, silver-gray eyes that contrasted sharply with the almost pure black of his hair.

She explained, "They were sweethearts since childhood. When the war ended, they married."

Mr. Amesbury nodded without comment. Something shifted—darkened—in his eyes but his expression remained completely neutral. Had he left behind a sweetheart?

Giving in to her curiosity, she stepped on the edge of politeness and asked him a personal question. "I don't recall hearing whether you're married, Mr. Amesbury."

"No," he said shortly.

Then this handsome gentleman hadn't found his happily ever after, at least, not yet. What was his story?

Perhaps he had not found the lady of his dreams yet. Or had lost her. Regardless, the subject appeared to be sensitive to him. Surely, a lady he preferred hadn't rejected him because of his injuries. Why, that would be tragic.

She scrambled for a change in topic to something less personal and painful for him. "Do you follow horse-racing?"

"A little." Mild amusement touched his eyes, as if he saw through her attempt. Or perhaps he merely thought her silly.

Mr. Dawson took up the subject as she hoped he would, discussing the latest races and his own contender. Mr. Amesbury replied politely but without true interest. Still, he appeared knowledgeable, but not horse-mad, which suited her just fine.

Why she'd thought that, she couldn't imagine. It wasn't as if she had any romantic feelings for the stoic man. No, her idea of a perfect husband was charming, who smiled and laughed easily, who loved dancing and music. Although, after four Seasons, her requirements for a husband simplified to a good man who would love her with his whole heart.

Chapter 4

Grant suffered through polite conversation until the orchestra's final notes died away and dancers left the dancefloor. Mr. Fairley announced dinner, offered his arm to a brunette perhaps a few years older than Grant, and led the way into the dining room. Mr. Dawson excused himself and wound through the crowd.

Miss Fairley smiled up at Grant with an air of expectancy. "Shall we?"

He blinked. Oh, right. He was supposed to escort a lady to the dinner table—her, apparently. "If you'd allow me?"

She smiled that brilliant ray of light that probably dazzled lesser men and took his arm. As they filed into the dining room, Cole caught Grant's eye. His brother's faltered step and wide eyes betrayed his astonishment. Grant shot him a meaningful look, hoping his brother would understand not to make a scene. Cole inclined his head, his expression smoothing over. Grant let out a breath he didn't know he'd been holding. He spotted Christian, but his youngest brother seemed absorbed in conversation with his wife and never glanced Grant's way. Jared's wife, Elise, caught his glance and murmured to Jared, but his middle brother only nodded to Grant, making no visible reaction. His years in the Secret Service had obviously taught him to mask his thoughts.

40

Grant seated the Fairley girl at her end of the table and moved to his assigned seat next to his target, Mr. Fairley.

Once seated, Grant waited until the host had finished speaking to the lady at his side to address him. "Mr. Fairley, I understand it is your desire to serve as prime minister?"

"Yes, it is."

"I admit, I don't follow politics as carefully as my brother. To what policies do you adhere?"

Fairley launched into a well-rehearsed campaign about upholding time-honored traditions while improving the rights and opportunities to the lower classes. As if any politician really cared about any of that. Grant pretended to be totally absorbed while he searched through the man's words, gestures, and expressions for any motives sinister enough to plot an assassination. Nothing obvious presented itself yet, but if Grant spent more time with Fairley, the man might yet reveal himself. If not, perhaps Grant could earn the candidate's trust enough to be invited to join the group avowed to orchestrate the plot. But nothing was ever that easy.

Grant inclined his head. "I am convinced you care a great deal more about the state of this country than Liverpool."

"We have different focuses." Fairley sipped his wine.

"Do you think enough of the House will cast a vote of no confidence?"

"I'm not certain, but that is the hope." Fairley smiled. "Unless Lord Liverpool simply decides to step down."

Grant said very casually, "The world is a savage place. Accidents happen."

Fairley assessed him curiously. "They do. But I think it will take more than a mere accident to remove Liverpool."

"We can hope for that as well."

Fairley had no comment, and Grant let it go, content to let the seed germinate in Fairley's mind.

The rest of dinner passed in dismal predictability, exactly the same reason why Grant shunned such mindless gatherings. Although, he had to admit, the food was better than the fare Grant found at his usual haunts. If only formal dinner clothes could be more comfortable. He glanced down the table at Christian who'd probably snort into his dinner at the sight of Grant so meticulously attired. As fate would have it, at that moment, Christian caught his eye, raised a brow, and gave a maddening smirk before turning his attention to his wife. At least the whelp hadn't made a scene.

As dinner wound down and the guests returned to the drawing room for more dancing, Grant took his leave of both Mr. Fairley and his still-cheerful daughter, accepted their renewed thanks for his aid with their prodigal son, and bade them good night.

In the grand foyer, he paused. The study lay just a few steps away. With everyone so occupied, perhaps he could make another search, this time without getting caught. And if he did, he could use the excuse of seeking a quiet place to have a drink.

He pretended to admire a Chinese vase until the footman at the front door turned the other way. Casually, Grant strolled to the study, slipped in and closed the door. He lit a lamp and explored the room. Gray coals in the fireplace gave off little warmth. A triangle of parchment at the far edge of the hearth caught his eye. He crouched down and picked it up. Most of the parchment crumbled to ash, but a corner remained intact.

rifles will be...

prime minister...

next meeting...

Well, that was promising. He pocketed the scrap. He doubted those words found in a single document conveyed an innocent meaning. After an unhurried prowl around the study, he found nothing else unusual. He would have to find a way to get invited to their meetings so he could expose the conspirators. In the foyer, as Grant sauntered toward the front door, a voice called him.

"Grant?" Cole's voice rang out.

Grant turned and waited for his brother to catch up. The picture of perfect propriety, Cole bore the role of earl with precision. His parents would have been proud if they'd lived to see their heir assume his role so expertly.

Cole lowered his voice as he reached Grant's side. "Should I be concerned?"

Grant shrugged. "Just following up on a lead."

Cole nodded. "Let me know if I can help."

"Wedded bliss and fatherhood too boring?" Grant smirked.

Cole's mouth pulled to one side. "Not at all. I'm not looking for a lark, you cynic; just wanted you to know I have your back if you need me. Jared and Christian, too. You know that."

Sobering, Grant held out his hand and let his brother clasp it. For a moment, he welcomed the human contact and the reassurance that he wasn't completely alone. Still,

Cole had a wife and a baby and the responsibility of the earldom. His other brothers had recently married. Grant would never subject his brothers to the kind of danger they once eagerly faced as bachelors. And Grant never asked for help.

"I'll send you word if I need you."

Cole shook his head slightly. "No, you won't. But the offer still stands."

Grant almost smiled. They parted. Grant hailed a hackney and returned to his bachelor's quarters. Inside, he paused. Complete darkness greeted him. Only the faintest glow burned in the fireplace. He paused, searching with all his senses for signs of habitation. Clark, the boy who helped him with odd jobs, fetched for him and took care of his laundry, must have gone somewhere.

Within moments, Grant had candles lit and a fire popping in the grate, but his rooms stayed empty and cold. At times, his life seemed empty and cold. His heart certainly remained empty and cold.

He shook off the dismal thoughts and focused his energies on stripping off his clothes and getting into bed.

Tomorrow, he would watch Fairley's house for signs of suspicious behavior and follow anyone who left. Briefly, Fairley's daughter's smiling face danced before his mind's eye. Trailing her might not be too much of a hardship. Her voluptuous figure was so much more appealing than those overly-thin figures most girls starved themselves to achieve. Not that he had any interest in her beyond a means to condemn Fairley. Grant's only interest in the Fairleys was to determine their involvement in a conspiracy for treason and murder.

Chapter 5

Setting her quill down on the desk, Jocelyn rubbed her eyes and stifled a yawn. Last night's revelry had kept her up into the wee hours of the morning, and fatigue weighed on her limbs today. Her errant brother still hadn't arisen, the wastrel. She was tempted to dump a pitcher of cold water on his head. But Papa had shrugged it off as the follies of youth, so Jocelyn restrained herself—this time. Next time she wouldn't be so reserved.

She bent her head over the guest list for the dinner party scheduled for next week. The invitations had gone out, and acceptances arrived. She'd planned the meal and reviewed everything with the chef. But how to seat everyone left her baffled. Everyone wanted to be viewed as a guest of honor, and most of the guests were members of Parliament, many of them lords. She did not wish to offend anyone. Jocelyn tapped the end of the pen against her chin as she mulled over the possibilities.

Inexplicably, her thoughts returned to Grant Amesbury. She'd seen her share of handsome men—including his stunning brothers—but no one had created such sizzling awareness in her. His kindness in returning Jonathan home safely piqued her interest; not many gentlemen would trouble themselves over a misbehaving boy, but that didn't explain her reaction to him. Perhaps it was the mystery around him, a virtually unknown man with no apparent use for society. But there was something

45

else about him, an air of sophistication mingled with a supremely masculine intensity that proclaimed him a fearless man of action. If an enemy army invaded, Mr. Amesbury would probably fend them off single-handedly. She could almost swoon at the thought, but she wasn't that kind of girl.

A nearby parlor maid, Katie, caught Jocelyn's eye. Though she moved as quietly and efficiently as usual, frown lines cut creases between Katie's eyes, and the corners of her mouth turned downward.

Jocelyn called softly, "Katie? Is something troubling you?"

Katie started at the sound of her name, and met Jocelyn's gaze. Dark shadows rimmed reddened eyes. She let out a sigh and cast a glance about the room as if to ensure they were alone. "Yes, miss. I'm worried about my sister. She's poorly again."

"Is she ill?"

"Not ill, exactly, but she suffers from the melancholy some'in'—*something* fierce." She slowed her speech and corrected her accent to keep it more genteel. "Some days, she can't get herself out of bed. I don't know how to help her."

Jocelyn set down her pen. "Oh, poor thing. My mother suffered from the same malady on occasion."

"I help her when I'm off duty, care for the little ones and do a bit of cleaning, but lately nothing cheers her."

Jocelyn swiveled in her chair to fully face the maid. "Would she welcome some company? Or would meeting a stranger only make her feel worse?"

Katie paused, her feather duster poised over a

figurine. "I'd been wishing I could give her a change of scenery, but A new face might be just what she needs."

"Then perhaps you and I should pay her a visit this afternoon before I have tea with Papa and Lady Everett."

Katie's eyes shone and she hugged her feather duster. "Oi, miss, you would do that?"

"Of course. You had only to ask."

"Oh, Miss Fairley, thankee—er, *thank you* kindly."

Satisfied with her seating arrangements, Jocelyn sought out the butler, Owens, to inform him she needed to borrow Katie on a personal matter and ordered a basket filled with bread, clotted cream, jam, cheese, and fruit, enough for a good-sized, hungry family. She changed into her plainest clothes and donned an unadorned straw hat. Katie waited for her in the foyer.

Katie bobbed a curtsy. "Miss Fairley, it's so kind of you to do this, but I fear you may not like going to such a poor part of town."

"I regularly visit my father's tenants at our country estates and do what I can to help them. I'm no shrinking violet that I fear meeting your sister in her home."

Katie nodded and tied her limp bonnet under her chin. Though normally Jocelyn would have taken a footman to accompany them, she feared that so many strangers, including a man, would intimidate Katie's sister. They hailed a hackney to take them to a part of town near the riverfront.

Inside the cab, Jocelyn readjusted the basket in her arms, firmly tucking the cloth around the contents. "Tell me more about your sister. How long has she struggled with the melancholy?"

47

"She's had a few bad spells in the past, but never this long or this bad."

"Did something happen to trigger this last bout?"

"Yes, miss. Her husband...died...seven weeks ago, just before her last baby was born. She's been in a bad way ever since, but this last week, she won't get out of bed."

Jocelyn's eyes misted. "Oh, poor thing. She's in mourning, and she probably has the kind of malady that often follows childbirth. No wonder she's been despondent."

"After her husband's death, she took in additional laundry to help feed the li'l 'uns—*little ones*—but now she's too bad off to keep up with it."

The cab stopped and Jocelyn paid the jarvey. He paused. "Do you want me to wait for you, miss?"

"No, that won't be necessary. I will be well over half an hour, I suspect."

Still, he paused. "Shall I return for you in half an hour's time?"

Jocelyn considered. Finding a cab in such a poor part of town could be difficult, and she daren't risk being late to Lady Everett's tea appointment. "That's probably a wise course of action. Yes, please do return for me here. But give me an hour, just in case."

He nodded. "As you wish. One hour."

Leaving the hackney on a main road, Jocelyn and Katie followed twisted alleys between sagging buildings. Jocelyn pressed a perfumed handkerchief to her nose to help filter the stench of refuse swept into piles and left to molder. She gripped her basket, hoping she'd brought the right items to help the family.

48

Katie led her to a battered door, tapped on the rotting wood, and pushed it open. "Lucy? I'm here with my mistress."

Jocelyn followed Katie into the semi-darkness. At the doorway, Jocelyn halted to let her eyes adjust to the gloom. A baby fussed and a child's voice crooned off key. One thin blanket covered the only window, cutting out most of the sunlight but very little of the chill. Clothing hung over several ropes strung across one end of the small room. Piles of clothes lay in a heap next to a peeling wooden washtub. Jocelyn's courage faltered at the stark poverty.

"Katie!" A girl about three years old pattered barefoot to Katie and threw her arms around the maid. The child's ragged, faded frock exposed too much of her thin limbs.

Katie hugged the child before setting her on her feet. "Mary, curtsy to Miss Fairley."

Mary immediately shrank against Katie's skirts and stuck a thumb into her mouth as she stared warily at Jocelyn.

Jocelyn sank down on her haunches to get eye level with the little girl. Rallying her courage, she smiled and said in a soft voice, "Good afternoon, Miss Mary."

Mary only blinked at Jocelyn without taking her thumb out of her mouth.

Katie touched Mary's head. "I brought Miss Fairley to meet your momma."

The baby fussed again, and again crooned a child's voice. Jocelyn followed the sounds to the corner where a girl about five years of age sat on the edge of the pallet on the floor. As she crooned, she bounced a baby wearing only a dingy nappy who slurped on its fist. Behind the girl and baby, a woman lay as if asleep, her arm over her face.

Still encumbered with little Mary holding onto her legs, Katie sat on the pallet. As she picked up the baby, his nappy slid down. The baby nestled against Katie's breast and then let out a lusty cry. While the baby wailed, Katie laid the baby on the pallet and efficiently tied the nappy into place.

Jocelyn wanted to burst into tears at the dirt on his skin. "What a beautiful baby," she cooed when she could say it believably.

Katie nudged the woman in the makeshift bed and said loudly enough to be heard over the baby's cries, "Lucy? When did you last feed the baby?"

The woman moaned without raising her arm. "I can't feed 'im anymore. My milk dried up. I tried all morning but there's nothin' to give 'im."

Standing, Katie turned to the older child who'd been holding the baby. "Flora, fetch Nan. Tell her to come quick. We need her to nurse Johnny."

The child nodded and dashed outside.

Jocelyn had spent enough time with her Aunt Ruby, who was as knowledgeable as a village midwife and apothecary, to know herbs that could help, if administered in time. Though daughters of gentlemen of means and property didn't normally delve too deeply in the healing arts, Grandmother had come from a long line of healers and midwives. Following family tradition, Aunt Ruby's passion followed after her mother's, and she was a sought after favorite at her father's estate before she married and moved to Kent.

Jocelyn gleaned all she could from her beloved aunt, although possessed a fraction of her skill. Whether or not Jocelyn knew enough, or could act soon enough, remained to be seen. She'd have to take command if she were to help this family in need. Jocelyn set down the basket, and removed her hat.

"Who's wit' ye?" asked the woman from the bed. She had to shout to be heard over the baby's screams.

"This is my mistress, Miss Fairley," Katie said. "She wanted to meet you and the little ones."

"We ain't much t' look at." The woman put her arm back over her face.

Jocelyn pressed her hands together and rested the tips of her fingers under her chin. "We need an apothecary. Is there one in the neighborhood?"

Katie replied, "There's one several blocks over."

Jocelyn did a mental count of the money she carried in her reticule. "Do you know an older child who can be trusted to bring some medicine?"

Katie furrowed her brow and chewed on her lip. "I'll get the boy next door." She carried the wailing baby outside. A moment later, she returned with a boy about ten years of age with a mop of curls. He stared at Jocelyn with earnest brown eyes.

Jocelyn crouched down to speak to the lad. "I need you to go the nearest apothecary and bring back fenugreek. Can you remember? Fenugreek."

He nodded. "Fenugreek."

"Come back without delay." Jocelyn handed him several coins.

Katie gasped.

"Yes'm." The boy dashed off with a white-knuckled grip on the money.

"Oh, miss." Her eyes grew shiny. "I didn't mean for you to pay..."

51

"Consider it an extra vail in appreciation for your devoted service to our family."

Katie bowed her head, still bouncing the squalling child. Jocelyn removed the cloth tucked over the top of the basket and spread it out over the rough, dirty table. It rocked back and forth on rickety legs as she removed food and sliced bread, sending a silent thank you to the chef who packed a knife.

Mary overcame her shyness enough to wander to the table and rose up on tiptoe to see what Jocelyn was doing. Jocelyn spread clotted cream and jam on a thick slice of bread. She handed the bread to Mary. Solemnly, the child took it and immediately stuffed so much of it into her mouth that she could barely chew.

Jocelyn smiled when her heart threatened to break. How long had that child been hungry? All of her life? Since her father died, which added to the tragedy of losing him? "Slow down, Miss Mary. There's plenty."

If only she'd thought to bring milk for the children and tea for the adults. Katie had been right when she predicted Jocelyn would be unprepared for her sister's poverty. None of the tenants on her father's estates were so destitute. When Jocelyn returned on the morrow, she'd bring more of what this family needed.

On a badly chipped plate, she put a slice of bread, cheese and half an apple. Bearing the plate, she approached the bed. "Lucy, I hope you don't mind, but I brought you something to eat."

Lucy removed her arm off her face, and leveled an expressionless stare on Jocelyn. "Don't wan' yer charity. Don't matter, no how. We'll all be dead soon."

52

Jocelyn drew nearer. "If you give up and die, who will look after your little ones?"

"No one. They'll all starve, too. Can't feed m' baby. Can't feed m' li'l 'uns."

"No one is going to starve," Katie interjected hotly over the baby's cries, fixing a fierce stare on her sister. "I'll make sure of that."

Jocelyn wanted to hug her. A little pang that she'd never had a sister of her own touched her heart.

Lucy frowned at Katie. "Ye can't keep givin' me all yer wages and doin' your own job and takin' in the laundry fer me, too."

"I can and I will for as long as it takes." Katie stuck out her chin. "But you have to get outta bed and do something for yourself and for them."

"Moa," Mary said from the table. She stood on tiptoe, vainly trying to reach the bread.

After leaving the plate on the pallet next to Lucy, Jocelyn said firmly, "Eat."

Jocelyn went to little Mary and handed her the other half of apple. While Mary stuffed it into her mouth and chewed, Jocelyn scooted a stool to the table, picked up Mary, and seated her on the chair. Absorbed in food, the child offered no resistance to being manhandled by a stranger. Jocelyn spread more clotted cream and jam on another piece of bread and set it with cheese on the make shift table cloth in front of Mary.

The older child, Flora, returned with a young woman. Katie conversed with the woman, who immediately sat on the edge of the bed and put the baby to her breast. Seconds later, only the infant's noisy gulping broke the silence.

Jocelyn beckoned to the older child. "Come Flora. Here's cheese and bread with clotted cream and jam, and apples." She held out a second plate she'd filled.

Flora cast a cautious glance at Katie, her mouth working and her thin body wavering between accepting and fleeing.

Katie nodded at the child. "You can trust Miss Fairley, Flora. She's my lady."

Flora accepted the plate and tucked into the meal. Katie cleared her throat and glanced meaningfully at Jocelyn.

Around her food, Flora mumbled something that resembled, "Thank you."

Katie came to the table, drawing up a second stool and gesturing to Jocelyn. "Won't you please sit, miss?" She waited until after Jocelyn sat before she picked up little Mary, sat in her chair, and plopped her down on her lap.

Jocelyn searched through possible solutions to help the family locked in poverty and despair. Bringing them a basket of food—even if she did it daily—would do little to relieve them of their current circumstances and would only help them temporarily. Jocelyn nibbled as little as possible, encouraging the others to eat their fill, and tried to make conversation.

"Have you lived all your life in London?" Jocelyn ventured to ask Katie.

"Yes, miss. Never left. But I always wanted to see the country."

That was easily remedied. She could speak to Owens about putting Katie on the servants crew who followed her family from their country estate to their city home each

Season. Since many servants preferred not to travel with the families they served, adding Katie to those who traveled should be easy. She made a note to ask Katie about that later to be sure she really wanted to do so.

Lucy sat up and hugged her knees. "I saw the country once. Me John took me ou' there once t' meet 'is grandfather. 'e was a gamekeeper on a fine estate, 'e was. I never saw so many green growin' things in all my livin' life." Her eyes took on a faraway wistfulness that transformed her face into one approaching beauty. "'e was a good man, 'e was. Jes' tryin' t' feed the li'l 'uns." She buried her face in her hands as her shoulders shook in silent sobs.

Katie hugged little Mary and said nothing.

Jocelyn looked from Katie to Lucy's lowered head as tension fell heavily in the air. Almost afraid to know, she asked gently, "What happened to him, Lucy?"

"They 'anged 'im, they did. 'anged! Like a common criminal. John was a good man, 'e was. Looking for 'onest labor." The rest of her words garbled and disintegrated into sobs.

Katie spoke as if from a great distance away. "He was accused of stealing." With a laden sigh, she kissed the top of Mary's head and replaced her on the stool. Quietly, Katie pulled clothes from the lines and folded them neatly.

No wonder Katie was so concerned about her sister, a widow with small children, having suffered such tragedy. Jocelyn bowed her head as her heart ached. The seed of an idea formed in her head of how to help the family, but it was so underdeveloped that she would have to give it further thought before she gave voice to it.

Little Mary slid off the stool, crawled in bed next to her mother, and sucked on her thumb.

The door burst open and the boy she'd sent to the apothecary returned. "They didn't 'ave fenugreek, but 'e said fennel and red raspberry leaves would work jes' as well." He held out a carefully wrapped paper tied with string.

"He's right." Jocelyn inspected the fennel seeds and raspberry leaves. "You did very well, thank you."

He solemnly held out the change from the purchases. Jocelyn took his offering, but in their place, she pressed half a crown. He let out a strangled gasp.

"Oi, miss," he breathed. "Do ya mean it?"

"Yes, I do. I'm very pleased with your speed and your honesty. You're a bright boy."

His eyes shone in mingled disbelief and pleasure, cradling the coin as if she'd given him a priceless gift.

Jocelyn turned her mind to helping restore Lucy's milk supply. "I need to make some tea. Where is the...?" She'd been about to stay stove but stopped herself. This family couldn't possibly own such a fine commodity. "Fireplace?"

Katie shook her head. "Nothing that fancy here, miss."

"How can I heat water to make tea?"

Katie frowned. "We don't drink tea."

No, of course not. When they didn't have the means to provide bread for the children, how could they possibly hope to afford something as expensive as tea?

Flora spoke up, "The Smiths down the way 'ave a 'earth."

Katie shook her head. "A hearth, yes, but they

56

wouldn't be able to spare the coal, and we have none to give them to burn for our fire."

As Jocelyn opened her mouth to offer to buy coal, Flora shrugged. "I'll go mudlarking an' see if I kin find some on th' banks."

"Wet coal won't burn," Jocelyn protested, aghast at the idea of a child scavenging the filthy Thames for coal.

"No, it won't," Katie said, "but maybe we can trade it to for some dry coal."

Flora let out a contented sigh, rubbed her tummy, and heaved herself out of her seat as if she were an aged woman. "Me tummy feels good." She offered Jocelyn a shy smile. "I'll get th' coal."

Katie stood and picked up two bundles of clothing. "I'll go with you, and make these deliveries. Excuse me, miss?"

"Of course," Jocelyn said.

Katie and Flora left together. Jocelyn turned back to little Mary who lay next to her mother blinking as if she could hardly keep her eyes open. Lucy sat stroking her child's hair and munching on bread and cheese. All that remained of the apple was the core.

Jocelyn smiled at the sight. With proper nourishment, and the right herbs in time, Lucy might produce milk for her baby. If not, Jocelyn would see about hiring a wet nurse.

The girl who'd nursed the baby stood and handed him to his mother. A calmer Lucy took him and rubbed his fuzzy head. The baby nuzzled against her, his mouth making little sucking motions in sleep.

Jocelyn turned to the temporary wet nurse and

pressed all the rest of her coins into her hand, leaving nothing with which to pay for her return trip home. If the driver would agree to wait outside her house, she could go inside, get some more money, and pay him then. Or she could walk.

As the young woman gaped at the bounty in her hands, Jocelyn asked, "Will you come back again in a few hours?"

The girl agreed. When she left, Jocelyn crouched next to Lucy's bed. "Go ahead and let him suckle you even if he isn't truly hungry. It might help your milk return."

"As you wish." Her tone resigned, Lucy did as Jocelyn directed.

There was much to do here. Jocelyn rolled up her sleeves and cleaned the room within an inch of its life.

Katie returned and stood open mouthed. "Oi, miss. You've been busy."

Jocelyn smiled, tired but content. "I don't hire you to clean the parlor because I'm helpless."

Katie smiled with the kind of indulgence one might give a defiant child. "No, miss. Here." She held out a battered tin cup filled with steaming water.

Jocelyn crumbled in the herbs to make a strong tea. A few minutes later, she handed it to Lucy and made sure she drank it, as well as made arrangements to ensure that Lucy would have several cups a day.

Aware of the passage of time, and satisfied she'd done all she could for now, Jocelyn took up her hat and pelisse. "I should return home. Papa and I have an appointment."

"Yes, miss." Katie also donned a bonnet and a pelisse, a style of at least five years ago but of high quality.

Jocelyn knelt by Lucy. "I'm so happy to have met you, Lucy. Thank you for allowing me to visit."

Lucy made a strangled noise. "Don't know why ye bothered, but fer what it's worth, I thank ye."

"You are most welcome. I'll visit again soon. Keep drinking that tea and plenty of water, and suckle the baby even if you get nothing out—your milk should return."

As they wound through the alleys, Jocelyn said, "Katie, I want you to make sure Lucy drinks the tea, and if her milk doesn't return, tell me so we can hire a wet nurse for her baby."

Katie bowed her head. "Yes, miss."

Jocelyn turned over the problem of Lucy and her children. How could she help them best? Her stomach hadn't stopped tying itself into knots at their desperate poverty. Katie surely deserved a little help with her family after all her faithful years of service, as her mother had served for years before her. No human should have to endure those atrocious living conditions.

An idea struck her. "When my father and I return to our country home, do you think your sister would come with us?"

Katie's step faltered. "To the country, miss?"

"Yes. She seemed to like the country, and I could find her a position doing laundry or whatever she can do."

Katie's mouth pulled to one side as she considered. "The servants' quarters probably don't have room for children."

"She could live in a cottage near the manor house where her children would have plenty of fresh air and not have to go mudlarking or live in a single room with no heat." Jocelyn's voice rose in both pitch and volume as frustration wove into her words. "I realize there are hundreds like her, and I can't possibly help them all, but I mean to help her if I can."

Katie's mouth flattened and she swallowed. She blinked several times to hold back tears shining in her eyes. "I'd be ever so grateful to you, Miss. Lucy and her wee ones are all I have left in the world."

Jocelyn touched her arm. "We leave in two weeks' time for the house party. With your help, I'd like to have her move with us to our country house. She can live there all year. And you'll come with us to see that she and the little ones get properly settled."

"Yes, miss. Thank you." Katie smiled. "See the country..." her voice trailed off and a dreamy expression overcame her.

"If it pleases you, you can travel back and forth with us so you can see her rather than remaining on the London house staff. We spend most of the time in the country when Parliament is not in session. Of course, if my father gets appointed to prime minister, we'll live in London more, but we'll cross that bridge when we come to it."

They turned onto the nearest street and found the cab. Standing next to the horse, the driver waited, rubbing the animal's neck. He had come, just as he'd promised. Smiling, Jocelyn pressed her hand over her heart. There were so many good people in the world, despite what others may say.

The jarvey's face relaxed at their approach. "I was just about to send someone in after you two."

"I apologize for keeping you waiting."

"No trouble a'tall, miss. I were jus' concerned for your safety, is all."

The jarvey's gaze passed carefully over Katie, a faint grin tugging at his mouth. As the maid caught his open appreciation, she immediately cast her gaze downward and fluttered her hands. Any man would have to be blind not to admire a pretty girl like Katie. If only men would look at Jocelyn like that.

Then she remembered her monetary situation and addressed the driver. "Sir, I fear I've no money for the return trip, but if you'll be so kind as to wait after you deliver us home, I'll pay you then."

"Sure, miss."

The jarvey helped them both into the carriage, and at Jocelyn's direction, turned the hackney around and headed for Mayfair. Outside the carriage window, a shadowy figure slipped along the road, but when Jocelyn peered more closely, it vanished.

Perhaps she'd imagined it due to some lingering effects of her fright in her father's study. Last night's intruder had been all too real. Was it possible the man in the study and the figure she thought she saw were the same? The burglar who threatened her couldn't possibly know whether she'd revealed his presence, so his threat must have been made simply to frighten her into silence.

Well, she was not easily frightened. If the ball hadn't lasted until the wee hours of the morning, she would have told her father about the incident. Then, by the time Jocelyn had arisen, Papa was already gone. She'd tell her father everything this afternoon on the way to Lady Everett's house. And then she'd turn her mind to charming Lady Everett for her father's sake. His happiness was her joy.

Chapter 6

Wearing the clothes of a gentleman of fashion and wishing he were in his usual attire, Grant sauntered casually along the walkway outside the Palace of Westminster. The rain stopped, but clouds hung low in a somber sky in a reminder that moisture could fall again at any moment. Blocked by the enormous building, the unique scent of the Thames failed to reach Grant, but the usual smells of the city remained, held in by the oppressive sky. He glanced at Jackson, one of Bow Street's best Runners, dressed as a shopkeeper, who walked across the street with his head down as if he were really going somewhere.

Members of Parliament vacated Westminster in small groups, some walking together, others waiting for their coaches. Mr. Fairley exited in the company of a familiar-looking lord, their postures relaxed. Grant held back, pretending he admired the impressive, seven hundred-year-old building that housed Parliament, and hadn't noticed the men.

The lord said something Grant didn't catch, and Fairley clapped him on the back. "Well said, St. Cyr."

To Grant's left, a non-descript middle-aged man wearing the suit of a clerk strolled along the opposite side of the street. A few carriages passed and a dog trotted by, but the clerk made little progress. Moments later, the clerk crossed the street, eyed Fairley and St. Cyr, and then rammed Fairley.

As Fairley staggered back, the man steadied him with both hands in a classic pickpocket move. Grant's senses sharpened. So quickly that Grant almost missed it, the man slipped a scrap of something white into Fairley's pocket. He repeated the action into St. Cyr's. Odd. Thieves didn't usually pick pockets in reverse.

"Sorry." The strange thief put his hands in his pockets and strode off.

Intrigued, Grant drew nearer.

"Clumsy fool almost ran me down," Fairley muttered.

"Odd, that," St. Cyr said. "Well, good evening, Fairley." He strode off toward a fancy coach with a coat of arms on the door.

As Fairley headed toward his own coach, Grant called out, "Mr. Fairley. Good evening, sir."

Fairley turned. "Ah, Mr. Amesbury."

Grant caught up and strolled with him. "I enjoyed your party Saturday evening. I don't, as a rule, socialize much, but you and your daughter made me welcome."

"Our pleasure. My Jocelyn sure outdid herself. Planned the whole evening. Her mother would have been proud."

Grant managed a polite smile. "You must be proud, as well."

Fairley grinned. "Indeed I am." He stopped in front of his coach and glanced at Grant curiously as if to ask why Grant had hailed him.

Before the footman reached them, Grant waved him off, grabbed the handle of the door, and opened it. "Here, sir, allow me." He steadied Fairley as he climbed up. As Fairley's back was turned, Grant slipped the note out of Fairley's pocket.

Meeting postponed one day. Same place.

A message about a covert meeting; it had to be. If only it had given the address. Grant slipped it back in before Fairley turned.

Once Fairley had seated himself, Grant shut the door and stepped back. "Have a good evening, sir."

Fairley hesitated. "Is there something I can do for you?"

"No, no. Just waiting around for my brother."

Fairley glanced at the doors of Westminster. "Ah, yes. Of course. Good evening."

Jackson had already started tailing Fairley's coach. Satisfied, Grant turned to the doors as if he really were awaiting Cole. His brother stood watching Grant with an unreadable expression. Perfect. Mindful of Fairley's possible gaze, Grant strode directly to his brother. Cole wore his signature blue colors, stylish enough that less confident men of fashion imitated him, but no one would accuse him of being a dandy.

Cole's brow raised. "What's this new fascination with Fairley?"

"Just following a lead."

Cole's gaze shifted to Fairley's departing coach. "If a majority votes no confidence on Lord Liverpool, I'd planned to nominate Fairley as the new prime minister. Is there some reason why I shouldn't?"

"None at all."

Cole put on a hat and started slowly toward his coach.

"I realize you can't discuss a case with me, but my offer stands. If I can help..."

"I know." Grant turned up his collar against the sprinkling of rain and put his hands in his overcoat pockets.

As they reached the family town coach, Cole gestured. "Can I offer you a ride?"

Considering the excuse he'd given for being here, Grant cast off his usual response and replaced it with, "My thanks."

Inside the Tarrington-crested coach, Grant settled against the upholstered squabs. He'd forgotten the luxury of traveling without getting one's teeth rattled. As the well-sprung coach glided over the normally bumpy road, Grant glanced out of the windows. They left behind the towering Westminster and turned onto St. James Place, passing the green park bearing the same name as the street.

He returned his focus to Cole who watched him thoughtfully. Finally, Grant asked, "What do you know about Fairley?"

"Devoted, hard-working, well-spoken. Honorable."

A description that differed from Barnes's.

Cole continued, "His son was killed in the war. His wife died of some illness a few years ago."

"Who are his closest friends?"

"From what I can see, Lord St. Cyr and Mr. Dawson, among others."

Absently, Grant nodded. He'd met Dawson at the ball. And Lord St. Cyr had been the recipient of a note as well. They must be co-conspirators.

Cole grinned. "He has a pretty daughter. Not the

usual society miss. She reminds me a bit of Alicia—genuine, in possession of substance, truly kind, steady."

Grant scowled. "I'm not interested in his daughter."

Still grinning, Cole stretched out his legs. "I see."

Let Cole believe what he will. Grant's only interest in Fairley's daughter was as a possible means to incriminate her father.

"Do you want to come home with me for dinner? Alicia would be happy to have you join us."

Grant tossed out his usual response without thinking. "No. I'll eat later."

Cole leaned forward and eyed him. "You don't have to wait for a wedding or funeral to come by. Jared and Elise, and Christian and Genevieve are in town for a few weeks. Alicia wants to plan a family dinner. Will you come?"

Grant let out a healthy snort. "And spend the evening with a room full of newlyweds? I'd rather put out an eye."

"Margaret and Rachel would be there, too."

"They aren't enough buffer." In addition, Grant might not be able to refrain from stabbing Margaret's husband to end her misery.

"Is it the abundance of marital affection that bothers you or the fact that you haven't found a loving wife, yet?"

A sharp, bitter laugh leaped out of Grant. "Marital affection turns my stomach. And I have no wife to find."

Cole eyed him thoughtfully, speculatively, so Grant turned his attention back out the window.

"Did she break your heart or die a tragic death?"

That grabbed Grant's attention. "Who?"

"The reason you're so bitter. You've always been aloof and cynical, but since the war...." He shook his head. "What happened?"

As visions of *her*, and the love he'd believed they'd shared mingled with her final act of betrayal crowded his mind, Grant clamped his mouth closed and glared before returning his focus out the window.

When he thought he could speak around his bitterness, he said, "This is close enough. I'll walk the rest of the way." He banged on the roof to signal the coachman.

Releasing a long exhale, Cole dragged a hand through his hair. "Don't leave. I'm not trying to pry; just understand."

"There's nothing to understand." As the coach slowed to turn, Grant opened the door and jumped out.

He strode to the Bow Street Magistrate's office and sat at the back of the courtroom while Richard Barnes processed the latest batch of criminals the Runners hauled in. As Grant sat, he tugged at his cravat until he loosened enough that he could breathe. The whiteness of his shirt and neck cloth made him feel conspicuous in the dimly lit courtroom.

Barnes, wearing the traditional white powdered wig of his station, glanced Grant's way, but stayed focused on his duties as magistrate.

When the last felon was led away, Grant stood. Barnes glanced at him and relaxed his mouth into a tired smile. Grant followed him into his private office. As Grant's former commanding officer removed his wig and fell into a chair behind his desk, Grant took a seat opposite.

"What has you so blue-deviled?" Barnes asked.

Grant looked pointedly at his clothes. "Next time you send me undercover, I'm going as a chimney sweep."

"Your shoulders would get stuck."

"A stable hand, then."

"Cut your hair before you visit the Fairleys again." Barnes scribbled something on a scrap of paper. "Here's my barber. Tell him to give you a...hmmm. I think a Titus style would do well on you—a little longer than the Brutus."

Grant slumped. Great. First clothes. Now a haircut. But Barnes was right; if Grant wanted to fit in with the leaders of society, he needed to look and act the part.

"What did you learn?"

Grant straightened. "I found two clues. Not substantial but enough to suggest a possible connection—encouraging." Grant retrieved the burned corner he'd rescued from the fireplace in Fairley's study and flicked it onto the desk.

Barnes picked it up and read. "Well, well. That can't be innocent."

"I also picked Fairley's pocket and found a note that said the next meeting time had been changed but the location was the same. Jackson is tailing him now."

"Excellent. Put your energies into getting invited to their meetings."

Grant nodded.

"Don't worry. I won't let Fairley and his cronies get away with murder."

More than Grant's reputation was at stake; a life was at risk, and perhaps the safety of England.

Chapter 7

Grant shifted his weight, keeping to the shadows of the narrow alley where tall buildings sagged drunkenly against one another, and the gray sky narrowed to little more than a pinprick above. Emaciated cats picked through moldering piles of refuse, and cloaked forms hurried along broken cobblestones.

For three days and nights he and Jackson had taken turns trailing Fairley, but the suspect attended no secret meetings, unless they took place inside Westminster. Fairley's wastrel of a son returned to Oxford two days ago, which removed him as a lead. Today, Jackson tailed Fairley, so Grant had the duty of watching Fairley's daughter. The most unusual thing she'd done was take a basket of food to a family in the slums. Admirable, that, but futile in the face of so many in need.

He was going to have to try something more direct, like talk to some of Fairley's closest associates, just as soon as he followed Fairley's foolish daughter home. The foolish chit might get herself killed traipsing around the seedier side of London wearing all her finery and fripperies or whatever females called their many layers of clothes that they seemed to change a dozen times a day. Worthless, the lot of them. And in this case, unhelpful in leading Grant to evidence against Fairley. She probably had no involvement in, or knowledge of, her father's plot. Still, Grant liked to be thorough.

Opposite the hovel into which the Fairley girl had entered, another door opened. Two girls, talking quietly, exited together and entered the narrow alley. Grant barely gave them a glance. Yet something familiar about them drew Grant's attention. Maggie and one of the other light-skirts who frequented the streets pulled their wraps around their thin shoulders.

Grant shook his head. He'd tried everything he knew to get them off the streets, but they seemed bent on destroying themselves.

As they approached, Maggie's expression brightened. "So, it's you, Mr. Smith." She smiled but it came out strained.

By way of greeting he said, "Girls."

"You goin' to be me first customer tonight? It's a little earlier than me usual workin' time, but I'll make an exception fer ye." Maggie picked up their usual game of her offering her body, and his offering an escape from her chosen way of life.

"I'll buy you dinner if you let me take you to Mrs. Goodfellow's House for the Reformed."

"Now, ye know we're not wantin' that."

"She helps girls like you find honest employment."

One of her friends said, "Owwoo, we're 'onest. I never stol nuthin'."

"Honest employment." Maggie let out a scoff. "At least I know what me customers want. Employers ain't always so straight up."

In clear defiance, the girls linked arms and launched into a bawdy song as they headed down the street. Grant mulled over her words. Maggie had likely been the victim of unwanted advances from the man of the house. Scoundrel. May he rot in the deepest pit.

A moment later, three figures stepped into the alley from the hovel into which they had disappeared about an hour ago. Grant recognized the Fairley girl, a young girl who was probably her maid, and a handsome woman carrying an umbrella. They all smiled and practically skipped—probably proudly congratulating themselves on their great act of charity and anxious to get home and brag about how wonderfully condescending they were to the poor, and then promptly forgetting the objects of their charity as they dressed for the next ball.

Silently, Grant slipped in and out of shadows and obstacles, keeping his senses tuned to the females. He sensed rather than saw the Fairley girl glance about cautiously. He was almost certain she'd noticed him the first day he'd tailed her. Unexpected, that. But she hadn't gotten more than a glance before he made sure he disappeared from her view. He'd been more careful today.

She relaxed her posture, and they chatted amongst themselves as they turned off the alley and headed to a wider street where they would find a hackney waiting to take them home. The attractive lady, who couldn't have been much more than five years the Fairley wench's senior, walked with the proud bearing of a duchess, perfectly confident of her place in the world. The younger girl exercised more caution, as if she understood she trod on turf belonging to those who viewed her as an aristo and therefore the enemy.

His senses went on full alert as he spied another shadow tailing the women. Some thug had noticed a couple of easy targets. The predator might have only theft and not something worse on his mind, but Grant moved into position to stop him. The ruffian slipped behind the women.

The thrill of the hunt coursed through Grant's veins. The world became sharper, each sound more clear, every color more vibrant. He trotted across the street, reaching for his gun. Knives were less messy and more elegant, but the gun made a better display of threat, and he wasn't in the mood to stick a knife in someone's ribs this afternoon. That might change by tonight.

Grant dodged a milk cart. He wasn't exactly dressed to pay a call on a member of Society, and revealing himself would lead to all sorts of questions, but it couldn't be helped.

The blighter leaped in front of the girls and brandished a knife he'd probably used to chop wood. "Gimme yer valuables and I won't 'ave t' use this."

The maid let out a gasp, her hands flying out to the side. The lady with the umbrella merely drew herself up as if her status alone protected her from harm.

Grant moved closer and to the side as the Fairley chit offered the armed a compassionate smile. "I realize you must be very desperate to threaten ladies. And while I will agree to give you all the money I have on my person, I must tell you that if you'd simply asked, I would have offered it freely."

Grant almost snickered. Oh, that was rich; she was trying to help the blackguard. Grant had to admire her courage, though. She didn't fall apart like her maid. Hesitant to break up the little drama and deprive himself from a moment's entertainment, Grant waited to intervene.

The thug made an inarticulate sound something like, "Ugh?"

"Here." The Fairley wench opened her reticule and drew out half a crown and six pence.

"Jocelyn, no," said the lady with the umbrella.

The Fairley girl ignored her. "This is all I have. Although now you leave me in the difficulty of not having enough to pay for our fare home."

The thug swiped the money out of her hand but then he got greedy and grabbed her by the wrist. "Wha' else ye got fer me, ducks?"

The Fairley girl's cry of surprise rang out. "Let go of me!" She kicked his shin.

The Fairley girl's companion swung her umbrella and landed a solid hit on the thug's shoulder. "How dare you! Let go of my niece at once, you villain."

The cretin grunted in surprise. He jerked the Fairley girl closer to him and put his knife to her throat. The girl sucked in her breath and went utterly still. Grant's thirst for justice sharpened and he got into position.

The thug's mouth twisted. "I'll slit 'er purty neck if'n ye don't shut yer trap, hag."

Grant stepped up into the thug's line of eyesight and cocked the gun. He kept his voice soft and deadly calm. "Let her go, dog."

The attacker's gaze flitted to Grant's gun. "No 'arm done, eh?" In one swift motion, he removed the knife and threw the girl at Grant before dashing down another alley.

The Fairley girl stumbled into Grant and collapsed

against him. He steadied her, torn between going after the lout who attacked ladies and his duty to see them safely home. He let the man with the knife go for now. Grant would hunt him down tonight. It would be fun to catch the thug unawares and thinking he'd gotten away with assaulting a defenseless girl.

The girl in his arms—in his arms?—shivered. Grant put her back on her feet perhaps a bit too roughly. "Miss Fairley? Are you hurt?"

She wrapped her arms around herself and drew two deep breaths. Her enlarged pupils nearly obliterated her irises. She gave a little start as recognition came to her. "Mr. Amesbury? How can I ever thank you?" In a classically feminine gesture, she smoothed trembling hands over her fair hair underneath an old straw hat.

"Did he hurt you?" He looked for a cut on her throat but no blood marred her pale skin. Her gloves and sleeve hid possible bruising on her wrist. Oh, he would enjoy hunting down the blackguard and making him pay for his brutality.

"I'm unharmed." She laughed weakly in the throes of after-battle nerves. "I seem to be making a habit of attracting men who wish to do me bodily harm."

Grant winced at her reference of his own attack in her father's study. He hadn't held a knife to her throat, but he'd threatened her convincingly, and she had no way of knowing his warning had been idle.

She let out a long, steadying exhale and stopped shaking. Gratitude shone in her eyes, and a smile edged through her fright. Her breathing returned to normal and her pupils shrank to a normal size, revealing the clear blue of her eyes, so blue a summer sky would be envious. Which was a stupid thing to think at this time. But indeed her recovery powers were impressive.

She said, "And you seem to be making a habit of rescuing members of our family. We are so grateful to you for your brave assistance."

"Indeed we are," said the attractive lady who resembled the Fairley girl enough to be an older sister. Still pale, she took fast, shallow breaths but her gaze was steady. "We are most indebted to you, sir. If not for your timely intervention..." she cast a glance at the younger woman and put an arm around her. "Please allow me to thank you properly, Mr.—? Do I know you? You look familiar." She eyed him, her eyes resting briefly on his scar.

Raising her chin and summoning a smile from somewhere within, the Fairley girl took over the introductions. "Aunt Ruby, may I introduce Grant Amesbury. Mr. Amesbury, my Aunt Ruby, Mrs. Shaw."

Calming surprisingly fast for a so-called lady of quality, Mrs. Shaw repeated, "Amesbury. Was your mother the Countess of Tarrington?"

Grant added another layer of protection around the velvet space in his heart where his mother's memory resided and inclined his head. "Yes, she was."

The aunt said, "Fine lady, indeed. I don't recall meeting you, so I cannot account for why you seem so familiar."

With a voice growing increasingly steadier, Miss Fairley said, "Mr. Amesbury was in attendance at our ball, Aunt. You might have noticed him at the dinner table next to Papa."

The aunt nodded. "Perhaps that's it." She cast a curious glance over Grant's clothing.

"And this," the Fairley girl tugged on the arm of the pale and trembling maid to bring her forward, "is our parlor maid, Katie Jones. We were here visiting her sister."

Grant concealed his surprise that the Fairley girl included a maid in the introductions. He offered her the same slight bow he'd given to the others. "Miss Jones."

Still openly terrified, the maid bobbed a curtsy but kept her gaze lowered. "Sir."

Miss Fairley smiled more brightly, her nerves visibly stronger every second. Had she recovered so quickly when he'd threatened her in her father's study? The memory of the press of her lush, curvy body against his, the softness of her skin under his hands, her scent of flowers and something warm, like vanilla, the same scent that permeated her now, leaped into his memory. He ruthlessly crushed it.

"We've been visiting Katie's sister and her children," Miss Fairley explained. "I thought my aunt's particular skills would help her."

"Good of you," Grant managed, because they probably expected it.

She smiled again, but she eyed him carefully as if detecting the layer of sarcasm he tried to hide underneath his voice and finding some amusement in it.

He gestured toward a wider street up ahead. "Allow me to escort you to a hackney."

"Thank you," the aunt said. She linked her arm through his as if he were a fine gentleman and had already offered her his arm. Her hand trembled.

Spurred to remember his oft-forgotten manners, Grant held out his other arm to Miss Fairley who beamed, and placed a steady hand on his. All trace of her earlier terror vanished. She certainly had stern nerves, that one. She might have made a decent nurse on the battlefield. Of course, no blood had been spilt today. That was an entirely different matter. Grant shut out all thoughts of war and bloodshed and escorted the two ladies while the maid trailed behind.

Calming every moment, Mrs. Shaw smiled up at him, all warmth and gratitude. "You must come home with us and enjoy a cup of tea and perhaps seedcake or biscuits."

Grant had to hold himself stiff to keep from shrinking at the thought of having tea with two ladies in some frilly parlor. "There's really no need."

"What's this about you making a habit of rescuing the Fairleys?" Mrs. Shaw asked.

Miss Fairley answered, "He found Jonathan carousing in a gaming establishment. When Jonathan got so deep in his cups that he passed out, Mr. Amesbury was kind enough to bring him home."

Mrs. Shaw let out a scoffing noise and uttered something about wastrel and dissipated. She patted Grant's arm. "Not you, of course, dear—I speak of my nephew."

Grant almost choked. *Dear?* He couldn't remember the last time anyone called him by that term of endearment. Not even his Aunt Livy called him dear, and she tolerated him better than most of his relatives. And why would a woman about Grant's age speak to him as if she were thirty years his senior? "Thank you for clarifying, Mrs. Shaw. I was about to feel very scolded, indeed."

Mrs. Shaw chuckled. Miss Fairley's warm, husky laugh rang out and she tightened her hold on his arm. Except for the night of the Fairley's dinner party when Miss Fairley had held his arm, he couldn't remember the last time a woman had done so. Today was a day of many rare events. He darted a glance at Miss Fairley. She grinned as if all were right with the world, not as if she'd been threatened at knife-point only moments ago.

Miss Fairley glanced at him and he could almost swear her expression was that of friendly camaraderie. "My aunt is something of a midwife. She was kind enough to accompany me to help Katie's sister."

"You're a midwife?" He'd never heard of a member of her class in such a profession.

"Not truly," Mrs. Shaw said. "But my mother comes from a long line of midwives and passed her knowledge down to me. She reached far above her station and married the man who later became my father." She smiled ruefully.

"And we're all so glad grandfather did marry her," Miss Fairley said with affection shining in her eyes.

"You've already done well with Lucy, sweeting," Mrs. Shaw said. "I couldn't have done better myself. I have every confidence in you."

"I bow always to your superior wisdom." Again came that smile, joyful laced with a touch of mischievousness. Though a bit playful, Miss Fairley was totally innocent, for a woman, that is. She couldn't know anything about the extent of her father's ambitions or plots, not that he really thought a man would involve his daughter in so sordid a scheme.

As they turned a corner, a hackney rolled up, the same

78

one that had brought them there. Apparently the young Miss Fairley had the jarvey twisted around her finger. Typical female, using men for their own devices.

"You'll be safe now." Grant handed in all three women.

"Oh, no, Mr. Amesbury," the aunt protested. "This will never do. You simply must come with us and take a bit of refreshment. How else can we thank you properly?"

Grant almost choked. "That's really not necessary. I'm just, er, happy you're safe."

"Oh, do say you will come," Mrs. Shaw persisted. "There's plenty of room in the carriage. Katie scoot over, there's a good girl. Come, come, surely your business isn't so pressing that you can't have tea with us."

Did the woman not know when to let up? "I'm afraid it is, but I thank you for the offer."

"Nonsense. Bachelors never eat properly. Come now, we won't bite."

The Fairley girl put a hand on her aunt's arm. "You're making him uncomfortable, Aunt Ruby."

"Oh, he's just being gallant so we won't feel indebted to him, but we do indeed owe him much." The Shaw woman turned a pleading smile on Grant that would have melted ice. She obviously knew men found her attractive and knew how to use her charms to her advantage, the wench. "But you'll be gallant enough to allow us to at least feed you, won't you?"

Grant mentally threw up his hands. How did one fight against such a force of nature? Clearly the woman would have her way no matter what. He climbed inside the carriage while all the females smiled, a bit too victoriously for his taste, he might add, and settled himself in the rear-facing seat next to the maid.

They looked at him expectantly. Right. Small talk. He had no knack for small talk. It was one of the reasons why he avoided social situations. That and he hated the way most people either stared at his scar or made a point not to. But mostly he avoided society because of insipid conversations and vain pretenses.

Sitting next to him, the maid kept her gaze cast downwards and her hands folded tightly in her lap, probably painfully aware of her place among them.

"I understand you were a war hero," Mrs. Shaw ventured.

Grant firmly kept his expression bland. "Hero is a vastly overused term. I went to war. I came home."

"Your mother worried for your safety, you and your brothers," Mrs. Shaw added. "But she was also proud of you all—you in particular. Once, she mentioned a letter she received from your commanding officer praising your valor and loyalty."

"I did what I had to do." He leveled a cold stare at her, while every nerve in his body screamed at him to change the subject. He grabbed his favorite weapon of choice and hurled rudeness at her. "She never mentioned you."

She waved away his attack. "I cannot claim to be one of her bosom friends, but I always admired her and made a point of seeking out her company whenever we crossed paths. She was gracious and kind."

Mama had, indeed, been gracious and kind. Too good for Grant's father.

Miss Fairley studied him so intently that he adjusted

his cloak to cover himself like a shield. He glanced at her with a raised brow to let her know he considered her study of him overly bold, then ignored her to address the aunt. "Do I know your husband?"

Mrs. Shaw winced as pain crossed her features before she drew a breath. She spoke wistfully. "His name was Arthur Shaw."

"A fine man, may he rest in peace," Miss Fairley said. She exchanged a tender glance with her aunt before returning her attention to him. "Mr. Amesbury, my father is sure to want to thank you himself for your assistance today, but he is not often at home in time for tea. Perhaps you would be so kind as to have dinner with us tomorrow evening? We're hosting a very small gathering with some of Papa's closest friends, so it will be an intimate, informal evening."

"Yes, yes, do come," added Mrs. Shaw. "I won't be there myself as I have another engagement, but Jocelyn does a lovely job as hostess. The menu will be very fine, I am sure."

Grant thought it over. Fairley's closest friends would probably include those who supported him politically. They might speak freely enough to drop hints as to the plot. If nothing else, he might get invited to their next meeting.

Miss Fairley said, "It won't be a huge affair, just some of our closest friends—a fine group of gentlemen and their wives. No one will be trotting out their daughters for bid, I assure you." She smiled knowingly.

"Oh, good. Then I'll only bid on the horses at Tattersall's and not on the women at your dinner party," he quipped.

She smiled as if she appreciated his dryness. But there was something more, something soft and almost tender in her expression, as if she suspected he carried painful secrets and she sought for a way to ease his burden. Which was ridiculous. Most gently bred females were either conniving and merciless or silly and vain. This girl simply hid her evil better than others of her gender. She might be innocent of her father's schemes, but no woman was innocent of being a...woman.

She tilted her head to one side, her lips still playing their little game. "Does that mean you'll accept my invitation?"

"Very well. I accept. As long as no silly daughters are present."

"Only this one." She gestured to herself, her smile broadening and taking on a self-deprecating flavor he found almost charming. Oh, she was good. He'd have to be wary of her.

He stretched out his legs. "I suppose I can defend myself against one."

The aunt watched their exchange with that same calculating attentiveness present on the faces of mothers whose daughters had selected the next victim for their game of hearts, or the hunt for a fat purse to marry. The size of his purse, he'd ensured, remained quietly his own business, so no one could accuse him of being a wealthy bachelor and have designs upon him.

He'd have to walk a fine line between getting close enough to the family to covertly investigate the father without giving them any reason to believe he'd be a desirable match for the daughter. He was completely out of his element. He'd have to be polite. It was so much easier to be rude to people so they'd leave him alone, and people generally gave him so many reasons to insult them.

When they arrived at the Fairley's house, Grant stepped out and handed them down, treating the aunt, the girl, and the maid with the same indifference. The maid hurried off while the aunt paid the driver before Grant got out his money.

"Thank you so much for your services," Miss Fairley said to the jarvey. "Will you please come for me at the same time tomorrow?"

"As you wish, miss." He tipped his hat.

Grant stared hard at her. "You're going back there?"

"I am."

"In spite of what happened today?"

She gave him a solemn smile. "I'm going back because Katie's sister needs us. But only Katie will go tomorrow—I'll have to wait for the following day. I must be present for our at-home hours tomorrow."

He raised his brows.

She smiled and lifted her shoulder in a shrug. "It's my duty as the lady of the house to set aside my desires to observe rituals such as at-home hours. It must seem silly to you, though, doesn't it?"

He spoke honestly for a change. "I don't understand much of what ladies do."

She laughed lightly. "I'm sure a great number of gentlemen feel as you do. But if I play hostess with proper decorum, it reflects well on my father. And if the wives approve of me, their husbands might approve of my father and recommend him to the king as the new prime minister."

"You take on a burden of responsibility if you feel your at-home hours are crucial to his victory."

She and her aunt put their arms through his again as he ascended the front steps. "Not crucial, but a factor, perhaps."

The aunt leaned around Grant to speak to the girl. "Your father is very proud of you, sweeting. And your mother, I am sure, would be too." She smiled with a fondness reminiscent of Grant's Aunt Livy.

A hint of sadness shadowed the girl's eyes, dimming her usual sunny exterior. Such a sheltered miss would never have experienced anything like the nightmare of his years at war, but she clearly wasn't untouched by true sorrow. She'd lost a brother and a mother, just as Grant had.

Inside the house, Miss Fairley called for a tray while she removed her hat, revealing a simple coil at the nape of her neck. As her wrap came off, it displayed a plain muslin gown completely unlike the silk creation she'd worn at the ball. He found her unpretentious appearance refreshing.

The butler, Owens if memory served, turned to Grant, to take his hat and cloak. Owens never batted an eye at the coarse, dark clothing Grant wore. The Fairley girl focused on his face and smiled as if she didn't notice his attire, and while the aunt had given him a quick once over at the beginning of their encounter, she refrained from comment.

Grant allowed the women to lead him to a parlor which wasn't as frilly as he'd feared. It retained the Georgian elegance of old money, without appearing overly ostentatious. A maid served the silver tea service and withdrew quietly.

Miss Fairley poured and handed cups all around. "Do you take your tea with sugar or milk, Mr. Amesbury?"

"Plain suits me."

She glanced at him with an expression hovering somewhere between amusement and satisfaction. "Let me guess; you prefer coffee over tea."

He blinked. "How did you know that?"

She smiled, once again shining some brilliant flash of light that left him with the urge to run for cover...except Grant never ran from anything, least of all some unnaturally cheery female. "My father prefers coffee and he wears that same expression when offered tea—polite but resigned."

He'd have to be more careful around Miss Fairley; she was far too perceptive by half.

"Try the seedcake, Mr. Amesbury. It's very moist."

He held up a hand. "I'm not overly fond of caraway seeds."

"The lemon cake, then?"

He accepted and balanced the tea cup in one hand and the slice of cake in the other. Gritting his teeth, he determined to survive the painful ritual of tea with two ladies. He'd faced down enemy soldiers trying to kill him, watched friends die, met danger head-on with his brothers—witnessed one get shot, and one hanged. Grant had even endured torture and captivity. Surely he could emerge unscathed from such domestic tranquility. If he hurried. And if he could burrow more deeply into his role of earl's son who frequented parlors and ladies and tea.

Chapter 8

Jocelyn observed her taciturn guest who looked as if he'd rather jump out a window than have tea with them. Or perhaps he longed to retrieve a myriad of weapons and shout a battle cry. She pictured him fighting off half a dozen cutthroats all at once and dispatching them with ease. He sat stiffly, his eyes darting from the windows to the door, briefly to her, to her aunt, and back again as if he expected to be ambushed. He probably developed that habit during years of war, poor thing.

How odd that a nobleman would dress in such unfashionable clothing. Yet he did so with the practiced ease of a man who wore them as often as the fine attire he'd worn the night he'd brought Jonathan home in an unconscious heap.

At his first bite of lemon cake, he let out a barely discernable sigh of contentment. With the manners of an earl's son born to privilege, he ate as if he sought for an excuse not to speak. Then he outwardly relaxed, even leaning back into the sofa as if he had tea with ladies every day.

Perhaps he'd merely been hungry. Jocelyn smiled. "I'll be sure to tell cook you approve of his lemon cake. He'll be happy to hear it."

He gestured to it. "It's good. Our cook used to make something like this."

"I visited Tarrington Castle once," Jocelyn ventured.

"It's surely one of the most beautiful castles I've ever seen. And the gardens. Ah, I've never seen such lovely gardens."

Something flickered in his eyes, some shadow of pain that tortured him. It vanished as he glanced away. "I haven't been to the gardens in years."

As Jocelyn flipped back through the pages of her mind, a vague memory surfaced of one of the Amesbury boys dying years ago in one of the gardens, but the servant who'd acted as guide refused to elaborate or even allow them to enter the scene of the tragedy. Jocelyn wondered if Mr. Amesbury had been close to the brother who'd died. She had never been particularly close to her oldest brother; he'd left for the war when she was only eleven. But his death in France had torn a gaping hole in her soul that time never fully filled.

Mr. Amesbury added as an afterthought, "The gardens are the product of generations of work."

Aunt Ruby leaned forward. "Doesn't your family title date back to William the Conqueror?"

Mr. Amesbury glanced at her, his expression completely blank. Did he view her as a fortune hunter? "The Baron Amesbury does. The title Earl of Tarrington was only bestowed six generations ago."

"I see. Well, the castle and gardens are, indeed, lovely," Aunt Ruby said, smiling.

"My brother is designing a new garden," he ventured. "Every earl adds a story from Greek Mythology." He shifted and for an instant a chink in his armor slipped, so brittle he might shatter at any moment, before he quickly rebuilt his façade of ease.

His discomfort awakened Jocelyn's need to comfort,

but surely he'd reject any attempt she made to touch him or offer verbal sympathy. She settled for a gentle, "I look forward to seeing the new addition when it's complete."

He sent her a wary stare. What makes a man so prickly that he bristles when offered simple courtesy?

Aunt Ruby asked, "Do you visit your family seat often?"

"Only when some family occasion requires my presence." Again, he added, as if he thought it expected, "I spend most of my time in London."

Jocelyn nodded absently. If she remembered her gossip columns correctly, those family occasions of which he spoke included brothers' weddings, and before that, his father's funeral. "You prefer the faster pace of London?"

"You might say that."

She studied him, searching for the hidden meaning behind his words, but a man so guarded as Grant Amesbury would surely never reveal his thoughts. Instead, she sipped her tea, speculating on whether his failure to spend much time at home centered on his reluctance to face the place that reminded him of all he'd lost, or whether interests in London truly captured his focus.

He sat like a shadow, so dark with his midnight hair and dark clothing. The scar running the length of one side of his face added to his aura of danger. Even so grave and defensive, he was attractive with his more-rugged-than-strictly-patrician features and alert, silvery eyes. When he smiled—*if* he ever smiled—he would probably be stunning.

Aunt Ruby toyed with her teacup. "I'm surprised you don't visit your family home more often. What keeps you here in London?"

Again that darting gaze passed over the room. He sat like a coiled snake, ready to strike at the slightest provocation. As if aware of her observation, he deliberately opened his fists and affected a relaxed stance. "I have varied interests that I'm sure you'd find dull."

"I think you underestimate our interests," Ruby said.

He inclined his head as if conceding the argument. "I ride, fence, shoot, spend time with old friends and occasionally help them with their...endeavors. Lately, I've been following the political arena, what with all the talk of removing the prime minister." He glanced at Jocelyn as if awaiting her reaction.

Jocelyn's heart warmed at his effort to please them with conversation when he so clearly didn't spend his days in such a fashion. "Who knows if it will come to that, but should Lord Liverpool step down or be removed from office, I have every confidence that my father, if he is selected, will be the best prime minister that England has ever had."

He nodded thoughtfully. "Your loyalty is admirable."

Ruby set down her teacup. "Perhaps loyalty guides my niece's opinion, and mine as well, but my brother bridges the gap between the Whigs and Tories. And he has many devotees who'd go to the moon and back for him."

He lifted a brow. "Fanatics?"

Frowning, Ruby shook her head. "No, of course, not—just supportive."

He seemed to turn that over in his mind. And again came that visible rally to make small talk. He glanced at Ruby. "So Mr. Fairley is your brother? You look more of an age to be his daughter."

Aunt Ruby grinned. "Thank you very much, sir. He is twenty years my senior. There are five children between us. I am nearer Jocelyn in age."

He nodded absently.

Jocelyn picked up the plate of lemon cake and held it out to him. "More lemon cake?"

"No, thank you." He stood and bowed. "Really I must be going. But I thank you for the tea and cake."

Jocelyn stood. "I'll see you out."

In the main foyer, she saw to it that he got his coat and hat. "Thank you for coming. I'm sorry if you felt bullied into it. Aunt Ruby can be...forceful."

"It was nothing."

"Will you come to our dinner party tomorrow night?"

He inclined his head, the picture of civility. "I accept."

Surprised he'd agreed to another social gathering, she smiled. "Seven o'clock."

"Until then." He moved to the door but turned back. "Miss Fairley, I hope you'll take today's mishap as a warning and not go to that part of town without protection."

She shivered and rubbed her hands over her arms. Odd, but she'd been even more afraid today than she had been when the man in the study attacked her. Perhaps she simply had a sharper sense of her own mortality now. And the man today had the cold blade of a knife at her throat instead of just a hand.

She rubbed her throat slightly as if to wipe away the memory. "I would have brought a footman, but I feared a strange man would frighten Katie's sister. She's been ill and is quite despondent. But you're right; when I go again, I'll be sure to take protection."

He nodded. "Good. Until tomorrow night, then." The promise almost rang as a threat.

She mulled that over while she returned to the parlor where Aunt Ruby waited. Her aunt exclaimed over the odd visit and the mystery. "I almost wish I could be here tomorrow night."

"Are you setting your sights on Mr. Amesbury, Aunt?"

She smiled. "I haven't yet decided if I want him for you or for myself...or if he's so strange he wouldn't do for either of us. And he carries with him that element of danger. I almost feel as if we should be afraid of him."

"I think if he wished us harm, he would have let that villain with the knife do it for him," Jocelyn said dryly.

"Unless he wanted to do it himself."

"I am persuaded that he's only dangerous to criminals. But he is very tightly wound."

"Yes, I've never met anyone so intense." Aunt Ruby smiled. "He comes from a fine family, but even the best families often have a black sheep. He's nothing like his brothers."

"No, indeed."

"Handsome, don't you think?"

Jocelyn considered. "Yes, but not in the way that his brothers are that make women swoon when they pass by— but he's certainly finely formed."

"Too bad about that scar."

"I hardly noticed it." Indeed, Jocelyn could barely remember a scar, she'd been so entranced with his edginess and that aura of power and danger that radiated from him.

The puzzle of Grant Amesbury hovered around the edges of her mind as she went through her duties. Late that evening, when her father returned home, she related the day's events.

Her father stared at her as if she'd lost her mind. "You went without an escort to that part of town, not once, but twice? Jocelyn, what were you thinking?"

"I was thinking her sister would be terrified if I brought a big burly man to her house."

"He could have waited outside."

"I know, I just…"

"If you were younger, I would take you over my knee." He let out a long breath. "Promise me you won't do anything so foolish again."

She took his hand and gave it a squeeze. "I vow it, and I'm sorry. But Mr. Amesbury was there and everything turned out all right. So I invited him to dinner tomorrow. I hope that meets with your approval. It gives us an even number."

"Of course." He stood and kissed her cheek. "Good night, princess. And for heaven's sake, no more flirting with danger."

"Yes, Papa."

She smiled. Did flirting with Mr. Amesbury equate flirting with danger? She highly doubted a man like him would tolerate a little innocent flirting. Which made her actually want to do it, just to twit him.

Throughout the following day, Jocelyn glanced repeatedly at the clock as she saw to the final details. Strange. She hadn't experienced such nervous excitement since her first season years ago. The knowledge that Grant Amesbury would be present…no, surely that could not be the explanation.

Her maid arranged her hair with great care creating a stunning effect and picked up the evening gown laid out on the bed. After agonizing over her attire, Jocelyn had decided to accept Lady Hennessy's advice about wearing blue. The wintery blue evening gown with silver netted overskirt brought out the color of her eyes, and the hem kissed the tops of her new kid slippers in royal blue with silver shoe flowers. A blue and silver band in her hair made a pretty final touch. Avoiding the pearls, she chose instead a sapphire broach and earrings. White elbow-length gloves completed the ensemble. She stood and drew a steadying breath. Tonight was just another dinner party. Nothing more.

When the hour of the dinner party arrived, Jocelyn stood at her father's side and greeted the guests as they gathered in the drawing room before dinner. She made sure everyone had something to drink and was conversing comfortably. Mr. Amesbury had yet to arrive. He'd given her no reason to believe he was attracted to her, and he clearly disliked social gatherings; perhaps he'd changed his mind. Disappointment dimmed her enjoyment.

But he didn't seem the kind of man to break his word. She wouldn't give up on him.

She glanced back at the doorway. He had arrived. With hair as dark as a starless night, a tall figure clad almost entirely in black strode toward them. Something shifted inside her and she took a step back from his presence of power. As he neared, his air of deadliness swept ahead of him like a giant clearing the path. Piercing gray eyes set in his fearsomely handsome face caught and held her gaze as he drew nearer.

She chided herself. Grant Amesbury had protected her. Why everything about him seemed so deadly tonight, she couldn't explain, but she surely had nothing to fear from him. Firmly wearing the role of hostess, she moved to welcome him. He was dressed in beautifully tailored clothing, as fashionable as the clothes he'd worn the night he'd brought home Jonathan. His new haircut and style gave him Town polish.

"Welcome, sir." She sank into a curtsy.

He inclined his head. "You look lovely." The words fell awkwardly from his lips as if he'd rehearsed them. She doubted he often paid compliments to anyone.

"How kind of you to say."

He paused and focused on her. Something changed in his expression. He studied her in a way that sent heat from her face clear down to her toes. Oh heavens, if these were the kind of looks he was capable of giving, he clearly was dangerous to ladies, but not in the way she'd thought.

Her attention zeroed in on his lips, and hers tingled in response. Powerless under his stare, she wrenched her gaze from his and nervously touched her brooch as if to assure herself it remained in place, anything to restore her good sense, which had quite literally failed her for a moment.

Softly, his voice ringing with sincerity and an unaccountably sultry quality, he said, "You are beautiful."

The simple complement, and his delivery of it, dried her mouth. With an expression she could only describe as surprise, he swallowed and took a step back. She moistened her lips and focused on the floor to give herself a moment to compose herself.

When she raised her gaze to him, Mr. Amesbury's gaze had shifted to her father as if searching for a valuable bit of information. She'd love to pretend he wondered if her father would approve of him as her suitor, but didn't dare flatter herself, despite that world-tilting moment that came and went too quickly.

"Sir." His greeting carried some hidden meaning, but she was at a loss as to decipher what.

Her father extended a hand. "It appears I am, once again, in your debt, Mr. Amesbury. Indeed, I can never repay the service you rendered to my daughter and my sister yesterday."

Mr. Amesbury took the hand, his features schooled into perfect impassiveness. "I'm glad the outcome was not more serious."

"It would have been, if you hadn't come to their aid. How can I thank you properly?"

Mr. Amesbury blinked as if unaccustomed to such an outpouring of gratitude. "No need. Their safety is enough. I enjoy administering a bit of justice now and again."

The corner of his mouth twitched and an unholy gleam shimmered in the hardness of his eyes. For a fleeting moment, a vision of Grant Amesbury hunting down the criminal who'd attacked her and exacting some form of vengeance upon him flashed through her mind. He was like a rogue knight with his own code of honor and his own methods of justice. But that was a silly fantasy. Men like that lived in the Middle Ages, not in today's world.

Papa tilted his head as he regarded Mr. Amesbury. "We are having a house party next week. We'll have archery and fencing tournaments as well as riding, fishing, shooting. Perhaps a little cricket. We may have a few political discussions as well. We'd be pleased if you'd join us."

"It sounds like a pleasant diversion," Mr. Amesbury replied. This time he was all courtesy. "I accept."

"Grand. I thought you the type who would enjoy such activities. Nice to get out of London for a while, too."

They discussed details while Jocelyn mentally worked out the sleeping arrangements for next week. She could put Mr. Amesbury in the west wing, in the green room. He might appreciate the masculine décor, and she doubted he cared that it failed to offer a view of the gardens. She'd move Doctor Blake to the red room—smaller, more ornately decorated, and a view.

"I look forward to it, sir," Mr. Amesbury said.

Jocelyn led him to other gentlemen in attendance. "And you remember Mr. Dawson from the ball, of course."

Mr. Amesbury seemed to grow even more alert, and his darting gaze probed deeper into Mr. Dawson's face. He inclined his head in a brief bow. "Yes, of course. You are advocating for Fairley to be the best prime minister, if I recall."

"Of course I do." Mr. Dawson sniffed. "He'd do a better job than that monkey in the seat now."

Mr. Amesbury asked casually, "You don't view Mr. Redding as a candidate?"

Dawson waved off his question. "Not at all. He's not strong enough to get our country back on track after the war."

Mr. Amesbury digested that information. "I agree the current prime minister should be removed posthaste. It's a wonder we've put up with him for as long as we have."

"It is my hope after the king's coronation we can recommend Fairley to His Majesty."

"How likely do you think that is?"

Dawson straightened. "It's not all in my hands. If it were, there would be no question."

Jocelyn studied Mr. Amesbury's profile, fascinated with his cautious probing. He was so solemn, so intense. If only he'd smile. But no, perhaps it was best he didn't. He'd probably be so handsome she would be rendered unable to utter an intelligent word.

When the butler opened the door to announce dinner, she said quietly, "I hope you don't mind, Mr. Amesbury, but I've seated you next to me."

He blinked as if he'd forgotten she stood next to him. "Why would I mind?"

She huffed out a self-deprecating laugh. "You seemed a bit ill at ease yesterday when you came for tea."

His pale gray eyes passed over her. Again came that intensity. His hard edges softened. "Not because I object to your company, Miss Fairley."

It was ridiculous, really, the warmth that wrapped around her like a blanket at his words. She probably grinned like some kind of silly schoolgirl. His crusty, protective barrier returned in his posture and his expression. How long would it take her to break open his emotional armor and find the real Grant Amesbury?

Dinner passed uneventfully with conversation that shifted between politics to gossip to the growth of America. Mr. Amesbury ate silently, alert as a watchdog but offering very little comment. He moved his hands beautifully as if performing some kind of dance as he ate and lifted his glass to drink, each motion a study in seamless grace. His posture remained utterly still as if he were encased in a bubble and any sudden movement might pop it, yet poised to leap to his feet if necessary. Years of war must have made wariness a part of life.

Jocelyn tried to imagine the kind of danger he must have endured, but all the stories she'd heard were likely transparent echoes of the true horrors brave Englishmen faced. The thought tugged at her heart, urging her to offer him comfort, a gesture he would, no doubt, soundly reject.

Once the guests finished dessert, Jocelyn stood and raised her glass. As the assembly followed her lead, she said, "A toast to my father. With a little luck, the future Prime Minister of England."

A chorus of, "Hear, hear" rang out and all glasses raised to her father.

They drank and she held up a hand of entreaty. "Ladies, if you'll follow me?"

As she stepped away from her chair, she nodded to Mr. Amesbury. For a second, she faltered under his focused stare. Was that desire in his gaze? Admiration? Or did he find her no more important than a vase? She longed to ask him what he was thinking but doubted he'd be open enough to tell her. He returned her nod briefly. Remembering herself, Jocelyn led the ladies out of the room to leave the men to their brandy. All the while, she puzzled over the mystery of the intriguing Grant Amesbury and his many secrets.

Chapter 9

Seated at the Fairley's dinner table, Grant sat back and toyed with the stem of his glass, leaving it largely untouched so as not to cloud his head. With the ladies gone, conversation turned to politics. As far as Grant could determine, all tonight's guests served in Parliament. He watched Fairley work the room using the right balance of charm, humor, and intelligence. Based on the nods, smiles, and thumping on the table with the occasional 'hear, hear,' gentlemen liked Fairley and agreed with the points he made. Dawson, in particular, supported Fairley enthusiastically.

Despite the condemning evidence against him, Fairley didn't seem desperate enough to want to kill the prime minister so he could take his place. But one of the informants had named Fairley in connection with the conspiracy—not to mention Barnes' famous instincts—so Grant had better not make the mistake of allowing his opinion to distract him from his mission.

As conversation waned, Fairley spread his hands. "Gentlemen, shall we join the ladies?"

A chorus of agreement accompanied the scraping of chairs as men stood and followed the host out of the dining room toward the drawing room.

Grant sidled up to Dawson. "I must admit, I'm convinced Fairley is the man for the job. Too bad there isn't a way to guarantee his success."

Dawson's gaze slid to Grant. "Too bad, indeed. But I have every confidence the best man will win this one."

"I hope you're right. I only wish I had the power to help you make that come to pass."

"As do I. He's like a brother to me; there's no length I wouldn't go for him—and for his family."

"He's fortunate to have such a loyal friend."

Dawson inclined his head. Grant let the subject drop, content to let the seed germinate in Dawson's mind that Grant might be a possible candidate for their secret club sworn to remove the prime minister and make way for Fairley to step into the role. If Fairley were part of the conspiracy, surely his closest friend was, as well.

The men joined the ladies who sat chatting comfortably. Miss Fairley sat next to an attractive woman he recognized from the ball a few nights' past—Lady Everett, if he remembered correctly. Fairley went to the woman's side immediately, and they conversed in low voices, their postures intimate. A love interest, possibly.

Fairley turned to address the group. "Ladies and gentlemen, shall we begin a game of whist? Ladies, choose your partners."

Dawson called to Grant. "Come, Amesbury, do join us." He introduced Grant to the couple present as Lord and Lady St. Cyr.

Grant inclined his head and took a chair. As the cards were dealt, he surreptitiously observed the men, St. Cyr especially, since he'd also received a covert message outside Westminster.

Lord St. Cyr cast a glance at Grant over the top of his cards. "Mr. Amesbury, I don't recall seeing you at many social events."

"I don't often attend them," Grant said.

Lady St. Cyr eyed him, her gaze pausing only briefly on his scar. "Not much interested in frivolous social functions?"

"Nothing that involves girls looking for husbands." Grant allowed a wry smile.

While the others chuckled appreciatively, Dawson nodded toward the host's daughter sitting at a table with three other ladies. "The only unmarried girl here is Fairley's daughter, and she's absorbed entirely on helping her father, not searching for a husband. At least, not this Season."

"No?" Grant asked, in case any useful information about Fairley arose.

Dawson placed his bet. "She's focused on being the perfect hostess and daughter. If I had a son old enough to wed, I'd send him her way. She's a fine girl, very fine girl. Her head isn't stuffed with all that nonsense like so many her age."

Lord St. Cyr let out a sigh. "I have three daughters, and they do nothing but chatter about dresses and boys."

Lady St. Cyr raised a brow and said defensively, "And sew and study French and play music and dance and draw..."

With a nod and a gesture of surrender, Lord St. Cyr acquiesced.

Dawson's gaze flicked to Grant. "I'm well acquainted with your eldest brother. He's a fine man, and his political views seem well aligned with Fairley's."

Lady St. Cyr put a hand on her chin. "Your brother is Lord Tarrington, is he not?"

"He is." Grant nodded. Quickly, he added, lest the lady verbalize ideas about his eligibility for her afore mentioned daughters, "I don't get into political discussions much with him, so I don't know who he favors as prime minister."

Dawson leaned back in his chair. "Have you ever thought of running for the House of Commons, Mr. Amesbury?"

"No, but after making your Mr. Fairley's acquaintance, I'd almost be tempted to do it so I could take a seat and vote for him."

"Politics is not for the faint of heart," Lord St. Cyr said with a slight grimace. "It takes a strong constitution to endure all those speeches without falling asleep."

Grant allowed the corners of his mouth to curve upward. Confident that his bait had been taken if these were indeed the conspirators, he played out the rest of game, then made an excuse about an early appointment tomorrow and bade his farewells.

Miss Fairley rose to escort him to the door and saw to it that he got his hat and coat. Her smile was part teasing and part sympathetic, as if she sensed Grant's discomfort in social gatherings. "I hope you enjoyed yourself, Mr. Amesbury."

"More than I expected." He faced her fully. "You really believe in your father, don't you?"

Her eyes shone with undisguised admiration and affection. "He is the finest man I've ever known. Our country needs him. Besides," she paused, "he is so much more alive since he decided to run. When Mr. Dawson first approached him about the office, my father was still so deeply grieving my mother's death that he had faded away to a mere shadow of himself." Her brows pulled together and some of the light left her eyes. Then she visibly brightened. "But when he found a new purpose, he became himself again."

Grant turned over her words and explored them from all angles. "Every man needs a cause, something to live for."

"That's exactly right."

"So it was Dawson's idea?"

"Yes. He's been such a devoted friend, always buoying up my father when he doubts himself." She smiled, that persistent sunshine returning like a ray spearing the clouds. He'd seen her frightened and sad, but always quickly recovering to a state of joy.

Grant bowed. "Good night, Miss Fairley."

He turned to go, but she touched his arm, a light touch, no more than the feathering brush of a butterfly. Still, he stiffened at the contact and withdrew. She blinked down at the thwarted contact as if searching for the source of his abruptness.

"Yes?" he prompted.

She faltered but seemed to draw from that endless well of happiness, and managed a sincere smile. "I look forward to seeing you at our house party."

If Miss Fairley knew her father was his prime suspect, she wouldn't be treating him with such kindness and familiarity. Her devotion to her father was clear. She'd be devastated when he brought her father to justice for conspiring to murder and treason. That Grant might play a part in dimming that ray of sun felt a tragedy. But better that than allowing a group of radicals commit murder.

"I look forward to it as well." He inclined his head in farewell and left.

The touch of her hand still burned through his sleeve to his skin. A great pit of loneliness opened up inside him. He would never find joy to shine light into all the dark places of his soul.

No matter. He had work to do, and that required he become a creature of darkness.

Chapter 10

Jocelyn's heart started an odd thumpity-thumpity when Grant Amesbury arrived at their country manor for the house party. It wasn't as if she had any designs on him. In fact, he'd make a terrible husband—dark, closed, unfriendly, solitary, and he clearly didn't like to be touched judging from the way he jerked out of her hand at the end of their dinner party. But she wanted to peel away the protective layers around him and determine whether he were truly as dark as he seemed, or if his heart were so tender that he kept it carefully locked away to protect it.

That was an interesting notion: he didn't *not* feel; he was afraid to feel. She would consider that later. For now, she'd settle for trying to make him smile. She could make it a game. And it certainly wouldn't hurt him. Very well, she'd go to any lengths to make the overly serious man smile.

He had cast off his all-black attire in favor of fawn breeches and a bottle-green coat. He stood in the doorway shouldering a large bag, glaring fiercely at a footman who visibly shrank from him.

Jocelyn drew a breath and called upon all her happiness, letting it bubble up to the top, and hurried forward to Mr. Amesbury, smiling as if he were her dearest friend. "Mr. Amesbury, I'm so happy you've arrived. I trust your trip was pleasant?"

"Tolerable. Thank you." He raised a brow as if he

105

found her mildly amusing, the way one views a puppy's antics.

"Wonderful! Where are your trunks?"

He jerked his chin toward the bag on his shoulder. "This is everything I brought."

She raised her eyebrows. "A man who travels light. How refreshing." She gestured to the nearest footman. "Westley, please take Mr. Amesbury's bag to the Green Room. I hope you like it," she said to Mr. Amesbury. "It doesn't have a fine view but it's very comfortable. And the fireplace doesn't smoke, so that's an advantage." She smiled brightly.

Mr. Amesbury paused. Had she been babbling?

"Thank you." He surrendered the bag he'd been easily supporting on his broad shoulder.

The brawny footman let out an *umph* as he took the bag and practically staggered away with it.

"Are your horses and coach being seen to?"

Her taciturn guest nodded. "I rode on horseback, but the groom is seeing to my mount."

"Shall you take some refreshment first, or would you like me to show you to your room?"

"My room, please."

She swept an arm out and offered a welcoming smile. "This way. I hope you aren't afraid of ghosts, Mr. Amesbury, because we reportedly have one."

"Oh?" He kept pace with her as she led the way up the large curving staircase.

"Yes, it haunts naughty children who get out of their beds. Or so my nursemaid told me." She smiled, watching for signs of amusement in him.

One corner of his mouth twitched. Not exactly the

smile she'd hoped for, but it was something. "A tale born of necessity, no doubt."

"I hated bedtime. There was always something to do instead."

"Such as?" He studied her as if he truly wanted to know.

"Oh, look at the stars, listen to the nightingale, search for signs that the dolls and toys really come alive at night. I used to lie so very still, hoping they'd think I was asleep, and then open one eye to see if I could catch them moving. When that proved fruitless, I'd go to the window to watch the gardens for signs of fairies. They come out in moonlight, you know."

"You have a vivid imagination." His voice wavered between amusement and disapproval.

"Didn't you play make-believe as a child?" She pictured him as a little boy with black curls and serious gray eyes. Surely, he'd been more talkative and more inclined to smile as a child.

"I did."

She waited.

His eyes softened. "I used to play in the gardens with my brothers. One tree in particular often served as a lookout tower or a ship." He broke off and the hardness returned to his eyes. One hand curled into a fist. "It was a long time ago."

The gardens. He must be thinking about the brother he lost in the gardens. How old had he been when tragedy struck?

She led him to his room and peered in, content to see a fire crackling in the grate and his bag resting against a clothes press. No valet had unpacked his things. "You didn't bring a valet?"

"I brought a boy who does odd jobs, cleans, fetches dinner, does my laundry—that sort of thing. He isn't really trained as a valet. He has only been with me for about a year, and my needs are simple. He's probably still belowstairs."

That was the longest monologue she'd heard him utter. "He's your only servant? You don't live with family?"

He shook his head. "I live alone."

"It sounds lonely."

Though he shrugged casually, he avoided eye contact. "It's peaceful. If I want company, I know where to find it."

Facing him fully, she admired the lines of his handsome face and the shine of his midnight hair. His gaze darted about the room as if searching for danger, or perhaps to avoid hers. Very gently, she asked, "Do you? Want company, I mean?"

He huffed a harsh laugh. "Usually I have more company than I can stand."

Her smile faltered. How could anyone get close to such a prickly character? Or was that a defensive move? "If you feel you're being overwhelmed by unwanted company while you're here, no one will badger you if you leave the group." She stepped back a pace. "I'll let you get settled in. We have tea at four, and dinner at seven." She withdrew.

"Miss Fairley," he called when she'd only taken a few steps.

Jocelyn turned back, her smile in place.

His gray eyes were solemn. "If you can spare the time after you've seen to your guests, I'd appreciate a tour."

She could hardly contain her surprise that the solitary, reserved Grant Amesbury wanted her company. Or maybe he wanted to survey the area the way he always visually surveyed every room he entered. "Of course. After tea?"

He dipped his chin in a brief nod.

She smiled. "I look forward to it, sir." Probably more than she should. He'd said nothing, done nothing, to express any sort of interest in her. But the idea of spending more time with the handsome, mysterious gentleman added a bounce to her step.

He nodded again. Leaving him to settle in, she turned her attention to the other guests as they arrived. Once they were settled, she donned her pelisse and bonnet and left the house to check on Katie's sister, Lucy, to see if she and her children were settled into their new home here at the country estate. As she walked, she put the intriguing Grant Amesbury out of her mind. She had plenty of other concerns.

Breathing in the clean country air, Jocelyn strode across the back lawn, hopped off the ha-ha, the low wall that served as a barrier between the lawn and the open fields where sheep grazed. She strolled over wild grasses down a shallow depression in the land. Ahead lay the creek and a cottage with new residents. The small stone structure, nestled near a grove of trees, had once belonged to the caretaker in generations past before the Fairley family made this estate their permanent residence. The caretakers had long since gone, and now it housed her four refugees from London.

Laundry hung from lines near the house and voices carried to her. Children laughed, chasing each other around in the grassy clearing near the house. Beyond the house, a creek bubbled bringing fresh clean water.

"Miss Fairley!" Flora ran up and threw her arms around Jocelyn's legs. "The country is so big and so green!"

Jocelyn laughed at her exuberance. "Yes, indeed."

Little Mary toddled over to Jocelyn and raised her arms. "Up."

Jocelyn picked her up and put her on her hip. "Where's your momma, Miss Mary?"

The child pointed behind her.

"Getting water," Flora supplied. "We can 'ave all the water we want. That's called a creek and it brings new, clean water all th' time."

Jocelyn chuckled at the child's delight. "Yes, it does."

Lucy trudged up the slope from the creek, carrying buckets full of water that sloshed with each step. Baby John rode on her hip, tied snugly inside a sling made up of clean linen.

The young mother actually smiled. "This is a righ' pretty place, Miss Fairley."

Jocelyn could hardly believe the change in the woman. Judging from the healthy glow to her cheeks and her confident walk, a change of scenery had already done her a world of good. Of course, plentiful food and a safe place to raise her young children had probably added to the improvement. Jocelyn let out a happy sigh.

Gesturing to the lines of clothing, Jocelyn said, "I see you already have work."

Lucy adjusted her hold on the baby. "Th' other laundress gave me all the bed sheets and linens to do. But I'm nearly done and it's not even dark yet."

Jocelyn smiled. "The job and the cottage are yours for as long as you want them."

The young widow set down the bucket. "Thankee kindly, Miss." She hesitated. "I can get ye some tea?"

"No, thank you. I must return to my guests soon. I merely came to check on you and the children to see if you were settled."

Lucy nodded and spread her arms. "It's heaven."

Overjoyed to have been of some help to this sweet young mother, Jocelyn turned to the two little girls. "Have you rolled down the hill, yet?"

"Rolled, miss?"

"Oh, yes. It's great fun. Watch." Jocelyn walked to a place where the grassy ground angled down toward a hollow. Ignoring the threat of stains, she lay on the grass, and with her arms over her head, rolled down. It had been too long since she had done that.

Laughing and a little dizzy, she sat up at the bottom and gestured to the children. "Try it."

Flora went first. She, too, was laughing by the time she reached the bottom of the little hill. Mary hung back, too afraid to try it until after Jocelyn and Flora had rolled down the hill several times. Mary finally braved it, screaming all the way, but at the bottom hopped up and said, "Again."

They rolled again until Jocelyn was too dizzy to continue. She laughed out of pure joy. If any of her guests suspected their hostess was rolling down the hill with children, they'd disapprove. Good thing none of them frequented the laundress' cottage.

She got up, brushed off her pelisse and waved. "I must go. Goodbye."

They waved. Lucy finished folding the last sheet she'd removed from the lines, picked up her bucket of water, and shepherded her children inside for an early supper. If only Jocelyn could help everyone in need. But at least she'd aided Lucy, and by that she'd helped not only the children, but Katie, too. Maybe she couldn't help the stoic Mr. Amesbury, but she would try to prove to him that his face wouldn't crack if he smiled.

As she strolled back to the house, the object of her thoughts paced along the ha-ha edging the back lawn. Sheep grazed on the lower side of the barrier like fluffy clouds floating in a green sky. Mr. Amesbury's focus remained fixed on the house as he glided like a phantom, barely stirring the grass. She'd read of ninjas of the far off Orient and how they'd been trained to move with undetectable stealth. She'd never seen a real ninja, of course, but easily pictured Grant Amesbury as one of their kind—silent, precise, deadly.

Acutely aware that she'd been rolling down the hills and probably presented a shockingly disheveled appearance, she veered off to the kitchen entrance. As if sensing her presence, Mr. Amesbury turned in a half crouch, his hands reaching for something at his side. He straightened quickly, and moved toward her as if he'd been out for a casual stroll. Now that he'd seen her, there was nothing for it but to greet him. She rounded the end of the ha-ha and climbed up the steep rise.

"Do you always expect someone to attack you?" she asked lightly as she reached him, hoping to tease him.

He regarded her gravely, not looking the least bit shocked at her mussed appearance. "Years of training don't vanish the moment the war ends."

She sobered. "No, I suppose not. But you're home now. Safe."

"Safe." He tested the word.

What would make Grant Amesbury feel safe? She glanced at his side and made out the rough outline of a small gun inside his waistcoat. Most waistcoats didn't have pockets, but his did. He'd probably had his tailor add it. She almost asked him if he carried knives in his boots or up his sleeves. She probably didn't want to know.

Softly she asked, "How long were you in the military?"

"Twelve years."

"You must have been young when you joined."

He nodded.

More time as a soldier than as a child. How sad. "Were you infantry?"

Again that consideration of how much to reveal. "No. I was a sharpshooter at first. Later, I was assigned to work as an assassin."

She put her hand to her throat, fascinated. "Truly?"

His mouth twitched. "You don't seem as shocked as I expected."

"Was that your goal? Shocking me?"

Again came a twitch. "I believe so."

She shrugged self-consciously. "A moment ago I was thinking how you could be a ninja."

"A what?"

"In the Orient, they have highly trained warriors who are taught to be totally silent. They slip in, kill their target, and slip out undetected."

He said nothing for a moment as he carefully erased every emotion from his face. "It isn't the great adventure you imagine. And the costs are high." Probably without realizing he was doing it, he raised his hand and touched the scar on his face.

Jocelyn bit her lip to keep from asking prying questions. She settled for touching his sleeve. "No, probably not. But as you pointed out, I have a vivid imagination."

"I wouldn't expect someone like you to understand what war is like."

Letting her hand fall, she studied the ground. "I know what it's like to be home praying for the safe return of loved ones." She started walking and he fell into step. "My oldest brother never came home from the war."

Before he felt obligated to utter his condolences, she rushed on, "When he was sixteen, he received his commission. He was seven years my senior, and we were never close, but it was torturous to wait for his letters, hoping and praying he'd come home safely."

So much for trying to make Grant Amesbury smile. Instead, she'd stepped into his darkness. She straightened. "I'm going inside to change and serve tea, but afterwards, I'd be delighted to take you on that tour."

Dryly, he said, "I'm not sure I can stand the suspense."

She glanced up at his sarcasm. One corner of his mouth pulled off to the side. He wasn't smiling, but appeared to be darkly pleased in some way. Surely he hadn't meant to be rude.

She cocked her head to one side sassily. "I'll try to make it worth the wait. Perhaps we can scare up a ghost or two."

"That would be interesting."

She grinned. Something in his face shifted and lightened. Not a smile, but a start.

Chapter 11

Grant endured tea with all its asinine small talk—although the food was good—and breathed a sigh of relief when the other guests dispersed for an archery tournament on the back lawn. Miss Fairley gave him a nod and waited until they were alone in the room.

She gave him a smile that seemed strangely intimate. "Still interested in that tour?"

He nodded. Prickles of awareness skittered over his skin but he mentally flicked it off like a speck of dust. The tour would probably be a complete waste of time, but she might say something to give Grant an idea of where to begin searching for evidence; she may have unknowingly observed something that could help Grant's investigation.

She gestured around the room. "You already know the drawing room. It's partitioned off so we can close it into smaller sections for intimate gatherings or open it up to make a ballroom. The far end is where we keep the musical instruments." She led him out the door. "We have both an old harpsichord and a new pianoforte, as well as a one hundred year-old harp. My mother played the harp." Her expression clouded. "But I don't, so now it sits idle." She opened a door to let him see the music room.

Grant saw nothing unusual in those rooms, so he kept his features schooled to polite interest. Acting polite always took more effort than being rude and cynical.

She led him to the far end of the room, her usual

smile that always hovered on her lips ready to spring to full bloom at any thought, remained in place. He'd never met anyone with such a perpetually sunny disposition. He couldn't decide if he found it charming or annoying.

"Down here are the library and my father's study." She opened the door to the library. Two curving staircases twisted along each end leading to both upper levels. "I love this room, and I love to read." She sighed contentedly.

Grant tried to remember the last time he'd read for pleasure. He read the newspaper, but it had been too long since he'd indulged in a good book.

An impish expression lit her face. "Although as a child, I played as much as I read." She stepped on a sliding ladder, pushed off with her foot, and rode the ladder as it slid along one book-lined wall.

Alarm shot through Grant. Reaching around her, he grabbed the ladder's sides with both arms and stopped it. "You're going to break your fool neck," he growled.

She twisted her head around, bringing their faces just inches apart. Then he realized his error; he now had both arms virtually around her back. Yet, unable to move, he stood, drinking in her nearness. Her creamy skin, smooth and free of blemish, begged to be touched. Her lips parted and their moist softness called to him.

His own mouth opened in response, and his breathing rasped in the stillness of the room. Her scent curled around him with invisible fingers, drawing him in closer, closer. Powerless to resist, he leaned in. He could almost taste the sweetness of her mouth. Years of consuming loneliness rose up and begged him to end the isolation, if only for a few moments, in those sweet lips.

But he'd sworn years ago never to place himself under the power of a woman.

And she was the daughter of his prime suspect.

Stepping safely away, he folded his hands behind his back and ordered his heart to stop thumping like a running horse. Miss Fairley drew a shaking breath and rested one hand on her chest. Carefully avoiding his gaze, she stepped down from the ladder and cleared her throat. A smug pleasure that she'd been as affected by their closeness curled inside him.

But that was stupid.

Her voice came out breathy as she turned her back to him and gestured to the room in general. "There are a number of books on any kind of subject you could possibly want—art, philosophy, history, nature, animals, law, even some novels."

Her voice grew steadier as she spoke. Her recovery powers were really quite remarkable. Not trusting himself to speak, he nodded. She strode toward the door as if fleeing both the room and that moment that might have changed everything.

"Down here is my father's study." She opened the door. "It never ceases to amaze me how such a fastidious man could always have such disorganized clutter all about his desk."

Grant stepped inside, pretending to examine the paintings on the wall. Then he took a closer look. Two seemed likely to conceal a safe, and the ornate desk probably had several secret compartments. He'd return later tonight and make a search. A wise man never left incriminating evidence lying around, but Grant would leave no stone unturned.

"That's my mother." She gestured to the portrait of a woman with the same yellow-gold hair as Miss Fairley's.

"No wonder you're blond," Grant commented. "Both of your parents are."

Her lips curved upward. "My mother's ancestors hail from Germany, and my father can trace his all the way back to the Vikings."

"I have one brother who is blond like my father was, but the rest of us have our mother's dark hair." Why he volunteered that useless detail, he couldn't guess. He pressed his mouth together and vowed not to make any more unnecessary personal comments.

"I've met your brothers. Delightful, all of them."

He bit back every comment that came to mind.

She glanced at him as if expecting a reply, but when he said nothing, she added, "I met Jared and Elise for the first time this Season, although it seems odd to use their Christian names, but I can't very well call them Mr. and Mrs. Amesbury, can I?"

Jared. Who'd nearly lost his life for king and country last year. Grant still couldn't shake the image of his brother hanging from a noose, nor the frantic and almost failed attempts at reviving him. Grant clasped his hands behind his back and stepped into the corridor.

She led him to the gallery with red walls covered floor to ceiling with paintings. "People who appreciate art like this room. But I like it best for one reason."

She moved to a life-size painting of a proud man wearing a ruff around his neck common in Elizabethan fashion. She pulled on the right side of the frame. It swung open like a door on a hinge revealing a doorframe with darkness beyond.

118

"It's a secret passageway. My great, great grandfather had this made as an escape route in case his Catholic wife fell under the eye of the queen."

Intrigued, Grant peered into the hidden room, but only black met his eyes. "Where does it lead?"

"To the far edge of the village." The excitement shining in her eyes and her hopeful smile bathed him in light. "We could explore it sometime if you want."

He lifted a brow. "Unchaperoned? I'm shocked, Miss Fairley."

She grinned as if they were old friends. "It's only indecent if someone sees us and thinks the worst."

"And what if I turn into a monster and suddenly attack you?" Again. Something akin to shame edged into his consciousness that he had already attacked her once but for an entirely different reason.

Her gaze lowered to the gun he kept in a pocket he'd had his tailor add to his tailcoat. What would she think if she knew he had two other knives secreted away? "I don't know much about you, but I have a pretty good idea of your character—enough that I know you wouldn't hurt an innocent person."

"You shouldn't be so trusting."

"I only trust people worthy of it."

He let out a half-scoff, half-laugh. "Which is why you went into a seedy alley in London without protection and got attacked by a ruffian with a knife."

She bit her lip as her cheeks pinked. "I admit, that was a lapse in judgment."

"If you assume everyone is out to do you harm, and take precautions, you stand a better chance."

"Is that what you do?" Her gaze probed deeply into his eyes as if trying to discover his secrets. "You assume people are out to hurt you?"

"Always."

"You are a very lonely man, Mr. Amesbury."

He took a step back. "Why do you say that?"

"You won't let anyone near you. I suspect you're so afraid that they'll hurt you that you won't let them love you."

He laughed harshly. "There's nothing to love." He turned away, desperate to escape her probing and all the emotions she might stir from their safe hiding place. "I believe I'll retire to my room until dinner. Thank you for the tour." He strode to the open doorway, deliberately pacing himself so as not to run.

"I haven't shown you the wings or the tower."

"Perhaps another time."

He left her alone and headed toward the stairs to his room, fully aware that he'd literally run away from a girl rather than face emotions and memories best left undisturbed.

The rest of the day passed uneventfully. Neither dinner nor the gentlemen's conversation nor the musical entertainment revealed anything of interest to his case. Miss Fairley played the pianoforte with a great deal of precision and passion, and other guests performed as well. During the evening, Grant spoke to Miss Fairley no more than anyone else present so as not to arouse suspicion.

When at last the guests retired for the evening, Grant made a point of bidding everyone good night, seeking out St. Cyr, Dawson, and Mr. Fairley in particular to remind them of his presence in case they decided to invite him to any meetings. They extended no such invitation.

Alone in his dark room, he waited until all noises ceased before creeping out of his room into the corridor. Moonlight spilled onto the floor from a far window at the end, but all else remained in darkness.

A door opened nearby and candlelight shone on the carpet, illuminating the face of one of the guests. Grant flattened himself against the wall, his adrenaline sharpening his senses. The man holding the candle glanced both ways then moved to the room directly across from his. He scratched lightly on the door. Grant crouched ready to spring. A woman opened the door wearing only a dressing gown, her hair spilling over her shoulder. She smiled at her guest and motioned him in. They threw themselves into each other's arms as the man used his foot to push the door closed.

Grant straightened, wishing he could rub the sight from his eyes. A fleeting instance of envy for the joy they were finding in each other's arms flashed through his mind. But that sort of tryst always led to heartbreak, as he well knew.

He waited a beat, then stole forward, relying on his night vision to maneuver around sideboard tables and chairs along the corridor walls. After descending the darkened stairway, he paused, but no lights and no drowsing footman became visible. He crept toward the study. Light shone underneath the door. He paused. Voices murmured, coming from the study. As he drew nearer, the voices became distinct.

"—you said he wasn't considered a contender." Fairley's voice remained low as if to avoid being overheard.

Grant almost rubbed his hands together in glee.

"He's starting to gain some support. Some fear your views are too progressive. They aren't convinced your solutions will really help a recovering economy." Was that Dawson's voice? They spoke so softly, Grant couldn't be sure.

"How can we overcome this?" Fairley asked.

"We discredit him."

"How?"

"Find a weakness, any weakness, and exploit it."

The door next to him opened, and a figure in a gown stepped out. A feminine gasp propelled him into action. He moved to the woman, pushed her against the wall, and clamped a hand over her mouth.

"Shhh," he hissed.

The woman made a tiny sound of distress and went still. Her heart hammered against his chest.

"What weaknesses does he have?" Fairley said. "He's the most boring, perfectly upright man I've ever met."

"Then we make up something. Suggest that he might be having an affair with an actress, or that he might have some involvement with the crime world. No outright lies, just enough to throw doubt on his character."

"I don't know..."

"Look, you and I both know you are the best man for the position. And you have numerous supporters. We only need to convince the rest that you're the best man by showing how perfect you are, and suggesting some tarnish on Redding's character."

The woman moved, but Grant held her tighter, one hand on her mouth, the other across her collarbone area to pin both shoulders. He tried to focus on the voices in the study, but the womanly soft curves divided his attention. And she smelled heavenly—violets and vanilla.

Oh, no.

He studied her face. Wide eyes met his. Even in near-darkness, he recognized Jocelyn Fairley. He almost swore out loud. That was twice he'd attacked her. And this time, she'd know him; if he could make out her features, she'd made out his.

He removed his hand from her mouth and placed a finger on her lips to shush her. If she cried out, he would have no way to extricate himself. She blinked and kept silent.

The voices in the study broke the silence. "I don't like it," Fairley said. "We should stay focused on how my policies are an improvement on the prime minister's, and leave Redding—"

"Trust me, whatever doubt we throw on him will be harmless and short-lived. I'll take care of it. You just keep being charming and wise and pretend we never had this conversation. Later, we'll discuss our plan to deal with the prime minister once and for all."

"Very well. Then I'll bid you good night."

"Rest well."

Footsteps tapped on the floor from inside the room, growing louder. Grant grabbed Miss Fairley by the wrist and dragged her into the library with him. He pushed the door almost closed behind him, not daring to risk the noise of the latch. The same instant, the study door opened, and footsteps and candlelight passed by.

Grant waited. To her credit, Miss Fairley held her

peace. Moments later, a second set of footsteps and candlelight passed by. The house fell into silence.

Miss Fairley let out her breath in a huff and whispered tersely, "When are you going to tell me what's going on?"

"I'll let you draw your own conclusions." He reached for the door, but her voice stopped him.

"Then I'll have to tell my father you were eaves-dropping on what was obviously meant to be a private conversation. And then I'll tell him you attacked me. Twice—the last time while you were searching his study in London." She offered a tight smile. "And here I was starting to think even burglars put mint in their clothes presses and use bergamot-scented aftershave."

Grant cursed silently. She knew. He swung back to her. "Then I might have to silence you." He put his hand on her throat, not squeezing, but enough to let the threat be clear.

Standing motionless, she looked him steadily in the eye, no cringing or trembling or whimpering. "You aren't an evil man, Grant Amesbury. You won't hurt me, despite your threats. But your actions are suspicious, and I demand you tell me what you want with my father."

Taken aback, he removed his hand, but stared her down, hoping to cow her. She didn't flinch or blink. If anything she raised her chin. What the devil was he to do with the wench now?

He made a loose gesture toward the study. "You heard what they said. What do you think is going on?"

"They always discuss ideas of how to gain supporters, especially in the House. I admit, Mr. Dawson's tactics sounded a bit...extreme, but..." She peered closely into his face. "What do you suspect?"

He turned away and paced the length of the room. He'd never been good with people, women in particular. Hunting down and administering justice to criminals, like that lout who threatened Miss Fairley and her aunt with a knife, came naturally. At times, it was almost fun. But this sparring with words left him scrabbling for footing.

He fisted his hands. "Nothing. They're obviously two upright, honest citizens." He moved to the door.

She stepped in his way. "What are you looking for?"

"A little peace and quiet and no meddling females."

She folded her arms. "What did you hope to find in his study in London?"

"The name of his tailor."

She laughed sharply and shook her head. "I can help you if you'll tell me what you think is happening."

He let out a caustic laugh. "You? Help me?" He shook his head. He pushed her aside and stepped around her.

"Then I'm telling my father everything you've been doing."

Angrily, he lashed out. "What if I suspect your father of a murder plot?"

She jerked back as if he'd struck her, her arms falling limply to the sides. She moistened her lips. "Then we'd hunt for clues together, and I'll prove to you his innocence."

"You'd get in the way."

"I'll get in the way regardless, but at least we can both search in the same places for the proof we're each trying to find." Confusion and hurt mirrored in her eyes. "What makes you think he's involved in a murder plot?"

"I didn't say I thought he was; I only asked what you'd think."

"I see." Her mouth pressed into a firm line. She straightened and tugged a sash more tightly about her. Only then did he realize she wore nothing more than a shift and a dressing gown, scant covering that taunted his imagination and revealed all too well her delicious curves. Her pale hair hung down her shoulders, framing her face—a foolish thing to notice at a time like this.

She opened the door. "Come. Let's search his study. You'll see there's nothing incriminating."

Grant cursed. Then cursed again. That blasted female was going to ruin everything.

She turned back and beckoned to him. He threw up his hands in surrender and followed her in. As he entered, she lit a lamp from the spill at the fireplace, every move jerky, indignant. Leaning over, she reached her hand underneath a drawer. A click sounded and a side panel on the desk swung outward. With swift, sure, angry motions, she opened the panel and retrieved a strong box. From another drawer, she retrieved a key she used to open the lock. She removed a stack of papers and dropped them on the desktop in front of Grant.

With her arms folded, she glared at him. "There you are. All his most important papers. If he were involved in any sort of conspiracy, he'd keep them hidden here."

Grant shook his head. "If you know how to find it, he wouldn't keep it here."

"He trusts me not to go through his things, a trust I am now breaking. But if this will help clear him from whatever illegal act you think he's involved in, then it's worth it."

To appease her, Grant picked up the stack of papers,

sat at the desk chair, and held them in the lamplight. The girl perched at the edge of a chair with her arms folded, sending visual daggers through his chest.

He read the copy of Fairley's will, all his financial information, the state of his properties, and the inventory of the family jewels. Grant learned more than he ever hoped to know about anyone. But nothing to suggest illegal activity.

When he finished reading the final document, he handed the stack of papers to Miss Fairley. "You can return these."

She rose, took the papers, and replaced everything. After shooting him a murderous glare, she moved to another drawer, opened it, and removed another box. This, too, she opened. "He keeps his letters here."

Her jaw clenched. Anger and hurt rolled off her in currents. He couldn't blame her. She obviously adored her father, and Grant had accused him of being a villain.

He indicated the letters. "There wouldn't be anything condemning in an unlocked drawer."

"He has no reason to hide anything."

Grant capitulated. Sometimes people left things in plain sight, thinking no one would notice them. So he read the letters. When he got to the third one on the stack, he paused and re-read it.

At our next meeting we'll discuss how to deal with the prime minister. He's not as safe in his ivory tower as people suppose. Others are willing to help us.

Your servant,

D

He held it out to her. She snatched it out of his hands.

With a glance over the letter, she let out a huff. "This could mean anything."

"It could mean they're plotting to kill the prime minister."

"No, of course it doesn't. Why would they?"

"So Parliament would have no choice but to choose another candidate to recommend to the Prince as Prime Minister and First Lord of the Treasury. Since no one thinks Redding is a viable alternative, especially if they smudge his reputation so he has no support in the House, they'd only have your father's name to bring before the crown."

"That's preposterous. You're reading too much into this." But her brows pulled together, forming a tiny pucker.

"Am I? Are you willing to risk standing idly by and watch the prime minister get murdered?"

"But..." she waved her hands helplessly, "this letter is dated a week ago and nothing has happened."

"They are setting the stage. Plots of this kind take time."

She lowered the paper and stared straight into his eyes. "Who are you?"

At that moment, it didn't seem to matter anymore what Jocelyn Fairley knew. For the first time in his memory, secrecy and isolation and loneliness bore down upon him in an unbearable weight. While one part of his mind screamed at him to be silent, the larger part craved to unburden itself. To her.

He leaned back in the chair. "I'm investigating your father as a favor to Bow Street. They got wind of a murder plot and have reason to believe your father is involved. My task is to determine if your father really is part of the conspiracy. We must expose and stop those involved."

She stared at the paper in her hands and let it fall onto the desk. "This isn't proof."

He leaned forward and stared her in the eye. Her desperation touched his heart and he gentled his voice. "Miss Fairley. If your father is innocent, I will be happy to clear his name. But if there really is a plot, I must discover everyone involved and bring them to justice. You wouldn't want an innocent man—the prime minister—to be murdered, would you?"

Her eyes opened wide. "The prime minister?" Her brows wrinkled and she drew a long breath. "No, I certainly don't wish anyone to be murdered, least of all the prime minister." She chewed her lips, an action that captivated him. Full, and shapely, they promised sweetness.

Her voice dragged his thoughts back where they belonged. "If there is a plot, I vow my father is not involved."

He admired her devotion to her father but he'd already seen how clouded a woman's judgement could be regarding parents. "Miss Fairley, I trust you will keep this conversation strictly confidential."

She nodded soberly. "I give you my word I won't breathe a word of this to anyone—not even my father. And I will help you find whoever it is so you can protect the prime minister."

He resisted the urge to swear. With her underfoot, hampering his investigation, he might learn very little. Still, if she were willing to help him gain access to places like this locked desk perfect for hiding papers, he might discover something. If Fairley really were as guilty as the evidence he'd gathered so far suggested, Grant would ensure he faced justice in spite of the consequences to his innocent daughter. Grant squelched any thoughts of Jocelyn Fairley devastated and alone and branded the daughter of a traitor.

Chapter 12

The morning after Grant Amesbury's startling revelations which led to a sleepless night, Jocelyn picked up her favorite hat she always wore with her plum riding habit and handed it to her maid. The older woman fastened it over her chignon nestled against the nape of her neck. Despite the fitted jacket of her riding habit, Jocelyn shivered, chilled right through to her heart.

The idea that someone would suspect her dear father of anything as evil as plotting to commit murder, especially of a government leader, left her icy. All night, she wrestled with the implications. Grant Amesbury was wrong—perhaps not about an assassination plot—but certainly about her father being involved. This morning, a renewed determination seized her to prove it to him. Not only would that serve the purpose of protecting her father, but the sooner the authorities ruled out her father, the sooner they would search for the real conspirators.

She thanked her maid and left her chambers to meet her guests. As she swept down the stairs, her gaze flitted over those gathered in the great hall. Grant Amesbury drew her attention. He stood like a shadow between Mr. Dawson and Lord St. Cyr, eyeing everyone with the alertness of a watchdog, his head tilted as if dissecting every word that passed between those assembled.

Several current members of the cabinet made up the house party, but that meant nothing. Most of them were

131

long-time family friends. Certainly they all knew each other from their association in the government. Wanting to gain their support enough to bring her father's name to the new king for his approval had nothing to do with any conspiracy. Her father certainly didn't want the position enough to kill to attain it. He was a good, honorable man who would never commit murder.

Amesbury's gaze flicked to her face and traveled down the lines of her habit. His handsome but hard face remained as impassive as stone. No recognition, no appreciation, no emotion of any kind. Perhaps she'd been wrong, and he had no heart and therefore no emotions.

She lifted her chin. She would prove her father's innocence and remove all doubt. If the Amesbury bounder wouldn't listen to reason, she'd take the matter to the magistrate of Bow Street and make him see the truth before it went as far as any formal questioning. She would do whatever it took to remove all doubt from Grant Amesbury's mind as to her father's innocence.

Stepping off the bottom stair, she gathered her riding habit's short train and draped it over her left arm. As she approached her father standing next to Lady Everett, he turned.

He pressed a kiss to the back of her gloved hand. "You look as lovely as ever, my princess."

She smiled, locking away all her troubles. "Today is an ideal day for a ride."

"The weather wouldn't dare ruin your plans for our guests."

She sniffed with mock snobbishness. "Certainly not. Today will be perfect." With her hand looped through her father's arm, she smiled with false sweetness at Amesbury—the scoundrel!—and walked past without speaking to him.

She felt rather than heard him sigh behind her. Good. Let him stew, the unfeeling cad.

The guests mounted horses that grooms and stable hands held ready for them, and they set off as a group.

Amesbury rode next to Lord St. Cyr, engaging him in conversation. Jocelyn had to admit that even so focused and serious, Grant Amesbury was a handsome man. But she'd do well to think of him as the enemy. Well, no, perhaps not the enemy. After all, he was trying to protect the prime minister against any possible threat. With King George III dead and the prince not yet officially crowned king, the murder of the prime minister during such a transitional phase could cause panic.

Very well. Not her enemy. Instead of fighting against Amesbury, she'd help him—help him understand that if any such threat truly existed, her father was not involved. There. That helped. Now she didn't have to expend so much energy disliking Mr. Amesbury.

In fact, perhaps she should do all she could to help win his confidence in her father and prove to Amesbury what a good man her father was. She'd kill Amesbury with kindness, even help him find a direction to focus his investigation so he could find the real conspirators.

With a lighter heart, she chatted with her guests and enjoyed the gorgeous day. The clear sky arched overhead like a canopy, turning fields to a glorious emerald. The river crossing the land sparkled like a thousand diamonds. Yes, today was perfect. She'd win over Mr. Amesbury somehow. As they rode, the distant song of the sea serenaded them.

Jocelyn reined her mount and pointed to the ruins crowning the hill. "Over there we see the ruins of Westbrook Castle, built during the time of King Richard the Second."

"It looks like it's haunted," Lady St. Cyr said with a shiver.

"Oh, indeed it is," Jocelyn said with an exaggeratedly solemn tone of authority she normally reserved for playing make-believe with a child. "But I have it on good authority that these ghosts only come out at night. We are safe as long as we are gone before the sun sets."

The lady took her words at face value, nodded her head, and relaxed her posture. "Oh, good."

"But the pixies come out during the day and cause all manner of trouble." Jocelyn just couldn't help herself.

Lady St. Cyr gave her a motherly smile. "Pixies aren't real."

Jocelyn kept a solemn expression. "I assure you, pixies are as real as ghosts. I've seen evidence of their mischief."

Lady St. Cyr peered more carefully around her. "Really?"

Jocelyn glanced at Mr. Amesbury whose mouth tugged off to one side in a smothered smile. Her father's gaze slid her way, and he let out a suppressed laugh, shaking his head over her harmless prank.

They passed under a crumbling arch where a portcullis had once stood and entered the courtyard. Stones the size of carriages lay strewn about with matching gaps in the stone walls which stretched heavenward. Grasses and flowers carpeted the enclosed area. Silence reigned in this fallen castle.

Jocelyn dismounted and patted Indigo's neck. Her horse *wuffed* in her ear, the long whiskers on his nose tickling her skin. She let the reins fall so he could graze where he wished and sauntered to her father's side. Guests began exploring the ruins. Grant Amesbury watched everyone with the same quiet, restrained energy that he used to visually examine the ruins. Remembering her vow to make peace with him so he would see reason where her father was concerned, she sidled up to him.

"Shall we explore the upper tower?" She motioned to the one tower that had stood against the ravages of time and neglect.

He passed a cool gaze over her. "Oh, now you're speaking to me?"

"I forgive offenses easily." She gave him an overly bright, somewhat mocking smile. By the narrowing of his gaze, he clearly saw her true opinion of him in her expression.

She reminded herself he was a good man whose efforts were misguided, not evil. "The tower?" she repeated.

His eyes flicked briefly at her father before he nodded. "As you wish."

"Jocelyn, I'm not certain it's as solid as it appears," her father called.

Amesbury paused, and his gaze passed over the tower. "I'll go first, and test each step to ensure it holds."

Papa held his lip between his teeth, clearly torn.

Quietly, Mr. Amesbury said to him, "Perhaps you'd like to go with us to be sure it's safe."

A brief, apologetic smile twitched Papa's lips. "It's not that I question your judgment, Mr. Amesbury, but I fear where my daughter is concerned I am perhaps a bit overprotective."

"Of course. We must protect those we love."

Hearing the word "love" on Grant Amesbury's lips sent a shiver through her. She had the distinct impression he seldom used the word, and never lightly. A guarded man like him probably chose carefully those he let into his heart, and no doubt loved them with a power she could only guess he possessed.

Mr. Amesbury's focused, intense stare passed over her father again, and from the minuscule relaxing of the man's shoulders, Jocelyn suspected he'd just made some sort of decision about her father—not a grand decision, but perhaps a tally on the side of his being a good man unworthy of the accusation against him.

Mr. Amesbury stepped into the doorway of the tower, and the darkness swallowed him up as if it found him a familiar companion. Papa followed, leaving Jocelyn to trail behind. The stone tower's uneven, winding stairs took all her attention. Her companions' soft footfalls and breathing echoed in the narrow space. They moved cautiously, and she pictured Mr. Amesbury testing each step before he put his weight upon it. Jocelyn passed a tiny window carved in the stone walls and took a moment to catch her breath as she gazed over the landscape already far below. At the edge of the horizon, a cloud-bank puffed up like a mound of Devonshire cream.

Returning her attention to her task, she continued climbing in darkness. As she reached the top of the stairs, she stepped out into the sunshine, blinking against the brilliance. Both men stood waiting. Her father held out a hand to lead her out of the dark. Mr. Amesbury held back. His hand twitched as if to offer aid to her, but he held himself in check, no doubt unwilling to have unnecessary contact with the daughter of a man he suspected capable of great evil. His eyes met hers and something akin to pain passed over his expression. He flicked his gaze away from her to flit around their surroundings, and the moment passed.

He stepped to the crenellated edge and braced his arms on it, gazing out. "Nice view."

"This castle survived wars," her father said. "Assaults, sieges, battles...but lack of a living heir made the land revert back to the king who never saw fit to bestow it upon another lord, so it stood forgotten for generations." He toed the stone brick. "And now it crumbles, not because it wasn't strong enough to withstand an enemy assault, but because it had no defense against neglect."

Mr. Amesbury said nothing, merely studied his surroundings. Whether he pictured it in its former glory, or mourned its unnecessary fall, or even engaged in idle curiosity, she couldn't say.

She folded her arms on top of the wall and leaned on them, admiring the view. A cool breeze tugged at her hat. "Nothing will last if it's unloved."

The enigmatic gentleman eyed her as one corner of his mouth lifted in mocking smile. "Stone walls only need a mason to keep them in repair."

She stood resolute. "A master won't spend money required to keep up a home he doesn't love."

"Anyone with half a brain will maintain his house if he doesn't want the walls to crumble," he said.

His grim denial of the need for human love left her poised between pity and contempt. She waved her hand in frustration. "Yes, but he takes care of his property in order to protect those he loves."

Amesbury shook his head. "You're speaking of two different matters. Men can love their homes and lands without loving their families."

She folded her arms. "Then it is a misplaced love."

Her father said from behind her, "It is, indeed. Power and money are empty without a loving family to share it."

Amesbury's gaze flitted to Papa. "Some believe power and money are all that matters."

Her father seemed to take Amesbury's measure. "It is a counterfeit happiness. I would give all my wealth and power if it would make my family happy." He added quietly, "Or bring back my wife. And my son." His voice hushed.

Mr. Amesbury leaned on one elbow and eyed Jocelyn's father more intently. "I'm sure your wife would be proud if you became the next prime minister."

"Perhaps." Papa's expression shuttered to block the pain that must have been churning in his heart.

"How likely, truly, do you think your chances are of convincing Prinny~er, the new king~you're the best man for that position?" Mr. Amesbury asked.

Her father straightened and Jocelyn held her breath. His answer would weigh heavily in Mr. Amesbury's determination as to whether her father could be involved in the conspiracy.

"I have many supporters in both Houses." He shrugged. "Whether or not it's enough for him to choose me is anyone's guess."

"But you're confident," Mr. Amesbury pressed.

"I'm confident."

Jocelyn put her arm through her father's. "Of course he's confident. Any man of ambition ought to be. And I'm sure time will prove him to be the one best suited for that position."

Mild irritation shadowed Mr. Amesbury's eyes that she'd interfered. "So all that remains to be seen is to remove Liverpool."

Footsteps and voices rang out from the stairway. A moment later, Lady Everett arrived, followed by several others.

Lady Everett checked her step, her gaze darting between them as if asking if she were interrupting. "Oh, we didn't realize others were up here."

Papa held out a hand to her. "This is the best place to enjoy the view."

While other guests leaned over the edge exclaiming over the view, Papa tucked Lady Everett's hand into the crook of his arm and led her to the opposite corner to point out something in the landscape below.

Left to stand with Mr. Amesbury, Jocelyn resisted the urge to lift her chin and shoot him a challenging smile. Her task was to win him over with kindness, not gloat every time she thwarted his attempt to find something incriminating. Still, the man could be infuriating the way he kept trying to set verbal traps for her father.

She lowered her voice. "I apologize if I have been uncooperative, Mr. Amesbury. My goal is not so much to throw off your investigation as to help you find the real criminals involved."

A hint of a derisive smile lifted one corner of his mouth. "You still want to help me."

"Of course. If we can figure out who is really involved, then you'll have no doubt about my father's innocence."

"There is no 'we' in this. You shouldn't even know about it."

"Oh, pish, I won't tell anyone." She waved away his words.

"Perhaps, but the more people know of this, the more likely someone might destroy evidence. Or even plant evidence against someone innocent."

As the implications of his words sank in, she let out a gasp and only at the last second remembered to keep her voice low. "Destroy or plant evidence? Are you suggesting that I would be dishonest enough to actually try to throw suspicion on an innocent man to throw off your investigation?"

He spoke softly but in flat lines. "It's clear you would do anything for your father."

She pressed a hand over her tightening stomach. How dare he accuse her of being so underhanded? "I would never stoop so low as to deliberately use someone like that, and I can't believe you'd think that of me. Only a scoundrel would say such a thing."

Blindly, she whirled around and ran. The narrow stone stairs of the winding tower came sooner than she expected. As she plunged into the darkness, she put out a hand to guide herself down the stairs. Her foot slipped. She reached out to catch herself but met only empty space. With a scream, she pitched forward, bracing for a fall.

Chapter 13

Grant moved without thinking. He leaped, his hands outstretched into the inky stairwell where Jocelyn disappeared, her scream reverberating in the stone passageway. As his fingers brushed cloth, he made a frantic grab and fisted his hands. A weight jerked his arms, and he yanked inward to his chest. A soft body met his. In the dark, he landed hard on his knees but his forward momentum and the weight of her body pulled him down the stairs further. Still falling, he twisted to shield the girl in his arms from the unyielding stone. Pain exploded from his shoulder as he landed. A second explosion on the side of his head left him stunned. How much time passed, he could not say, but he lay dazed, unable to think or move.

The image of Jocelyn Fairley tumbling down repeated in his mind. Another, older, infinitely more painful memory superimposed itself over the memory of her fall—his brother Jason falling down, down, down, away from him, more slowly in his recollection than it had really happened. Jason, standing on a tree limb far from the ground, had tried to jump from one limb to another far above the ground. But he'd missed the limb. He'd fallen. Grant had sat on a branch higher up, helplessly watching his brother's body plunge downward and disappear through the leaves. A sickening thud from below had shot through him. He'd known from that sound, even though he'd tried to deny it, that his brother, his closest friend, the

141

only one who'd ever understood him, was dead. Consuming grief chipped at what was left of his soul.

Voices shot through his skull, indistinct, nonsensical. The warm body in his arms shifted. He held on tighter, terrified he'd drop whomever he had dived to save. His head throbbed with every beat of his heart and the pressure built. Surely any moment his head would explode. His shoulder burned. Light blinded him and he squeezed his eyes closed, still holding on to his precious bundle of warmth and softness.

One distinct voice, soft and feminine and nearby, cut through the raucous. "Mr. Amesbury."

It wasn't Jason he'd caught. It was her. Jocelyn Fairley. Not Jason. Never Jason. His brother was gone and Grant was left to carry on alone. Alone, always alone. The one woman who'd made him feel alive for a short, blissful time, had proven false—her words of love broken and empty. In the end, he'd always be alone.

A small, cool hand touched his cheek and again came the feminine voice. "Grant. You can let go of me. We're safe."

His senses cleared and he relaxed his hold on her. He tried to lift his head but nausea and pain held him captive. She moved out of his reach, leaving only cold in his chest where she had lain against him.

"Lie still," another voice ordered. Male.

The light neared, bringing searing pain. Grant squeezed his eyes closed against it. His stomach lurched and he gritted his teeth to try to keep from getting sick. Someone leaned over him bringing the scent of bergamot. Strong hands probed his neck and limbs.

"Wiggle your fingers."

A doctor, then. One of the guests had been introduced as Dr. someone—Blake, wasn't it? Grant raised both hands and moved his fingers. White-hot pain shot through his arm to glower in his shoulder.

"Now your feet."

Again, Grant obeyed, grateful he could.

"Can you sit up?"

He tried to open his eyes but a candle blinded him. He squinted against it. "I think so."

He lifted his head. A masculine hand reached out to aid him. Grant grasped it and used it to pull himself up. Pain knifed through his shoulder and he let out a moan despite his clenched jaw. Hands helped push him up from behind. Only then did he realize he'd been lying with his head down and his feet up on the stairway. That explained the excruciating pressure in his head. As he sat up and pulled his knees in close, he cradled his still-aching head. His shoulder throbbed. He rubbed it but the pain only intensified.

"Your shoulder?" asked the doctor who had ordered him to move his hands and feet.

He didn't dare nod. "Yes," he managed through gritted teeth.

Again came those probing hands, manipulating his shoulder. Grant hissed in his breath between his teeth and clamped his jaw down tighter.

The memory of the girl falling forward flashed through his mind. She'd spoken to him, but he needed to know for sure. "Jocelyn—Miss Fairley...is she...?"

"I'm here. You saved me." Her voice, roughened

with...what? tears? awe?...vibrated through the stone passageway.

"Are you hurt?" He resisted the urge to reach for her again, to touch her, to assure himself of her safety.

"No, I'm not hurt." Again that hoarse quality laced her voice. "You caught me and cushioned my fall."

He braced his elbows on his knees and pressed his hands over his head. Again came a probing on his shoulder and ribs. Searing pain rippled through him with every touch. Still, it fell short of what he'd experienced as a prisoner.

The doctor's voice broke into his thoughts. "The good news is; it doesn't feel broken."

Grant shook his head and instantly regretted the motion as dizziness and pain closed in. "It doesn't hurt enough to be broken."

"Oh? You've broken several bones, have you?"

"A few." He firmly shut his mind to memories and gulped in several steadying breaths.

"The bad news is; it's dislocated."

Grant winced. He'd seen a man get his dislocated shoulder put back into place. He didn't envy him.

"I can't reset your shoulder in here—it's too tight. Can you stand?" The doctor's voice, echoed in the narrow stairwell.

Bracing himself with his uninjured arm, Grant tried to push himself to a stand but fiery pain burned one knee. The weight of dizziness bore down on him and he crumpled. Indistinct voices echoed and strong arms supported him on both sides. With a groan, he stood and leaned on them as they led him out into the sunlight. He walked unsteadily but managed to keep upright. Shielding his eyes from the glare, he squeezed his eyes closed again. His knees buckled. At least two sets of hands lowered him to a stone floor.

A hand gently probed his head. Pain shot through his skull and he sucked in his breath. "It's not cut, but a bump is already forming," said the doctor. "How do you feel? Dizzy? Nauseous?"

"Both."

"You probably have a concussion. We'll have to keep an eye on you. Let's set that shoulder. Lie down flat."

Grant swallowed, remembering how the soldier in the medical tent had screamed when his shoulder was reset. Grant took a bracing breath and eased himself down on his back. He almost asked for something to bite on to avoid screaming but clamped his mouth closed, determined to bear it silently. The doctor straightened his arm and gently tugged it away from Grant's body, keeping the pressure even. The tugging increased. Pain radiated in waves from his shoulder.

"Try to relax," the doctor said.

Grant focused on controlling his breathing and relaxing his body. The ball joint popped and the doctor relaxed his hold on Grant.

"All done," the doctor said.

Hardly daring to hope, Grant opened his eyes. "That's it?"

A surprisingly young man with warm brown eyes smiled. "That's it. I try not to torture my patients when I treat them. I charge extra for that, of course." His eyes twinkled.

Grant let out his breath. Then, horrified that he

might have revealed his dread, he grunted at the doctor, "My thanks."

"You'll be badly bruised, I'm afraid." He looked carefully into Grant's eyes. "And I want you to rest for the next few days to give your head time to recover. That was an impressive fall."

It was a stupid fall. Where on earth he'd left his brain when he'd decided to take a leap head-first down a stairwell to save an empty-headed female was beyond him.

Said empty-headed female sat nearby, watching him with enough gratitude shining in her eyes that he had to avoid her gaze lest he convince himself she was worth saving or risk allowing any of her light to reach his shriveled, neglected heart and give it false hope.

With the doctor's help, Grant rose to a seated position. His head spun and his stomach threatened to embarrass him in front of everyone. He pressed his hands over his head and clamped his mouth shut, both to avoid moaning in pain and to tell his stomach who was in control. Wind cooled perspiration on his face and sun shone as if it had no thought for useless mortals below.

"Papa." Miss Fairley's voice slipped over his senses. "I think we ought to take him home where he can rest."

With his eyes still closed, Grant made a dismissive wave. At least, he hoped it appeared dismissive. "I'll be all right. Just give me a moment." He took several bracing breaths and then pushed himself to a stand.

Fairley said, "I don't think you should stand up so soon, son."

"I'm fine, no need to fuss." Grant pried his eyes open and blinked. The pain receded, but his stability remained questionable and he sagged against the wall.

Jocelyn Fairley stood with her hands over her heart, her gaze darting over him, her mouth twisted into something between disbelief and concern.

He fisted his hands to keep himself from touching her. "Are you sure you're unharmed?"

"I'm well, thanks to you." Her voice quivered.

And thanks to him and his accusations, she'd run headlong to escape him. If she hadn't felt the need to run away, she wouldn't have fallen in the first place.

"I'm glad you're safe." He rubbed a hand over his head. He was beginning to sound like a lovesick puppy, curse him for a fool. "Clumsy wenches shouldn't go racing down stairs."

She blinked in disbelief. Then, one corner of her mouth lifted as if she saw through his defensive measure. "Boorish oafs shouldn't go down stairs head-first." She smiled. Was that fondness in her eyes? Sobering, she placed a hand against his cheek, the heat spreading outward to warm his entire body. "I can't believe you saved me like that. You could have broken your neck."

He must have hit his head harder than he thought; why else would he have that idiotic, almost irresistible desire to turn his head and press a kiss into her hand? He fought it.

About a dozen people stood on the roof, staring at him as if he'd committed some kind of unforgivable *faux pas*. Scowling at them, he pushed off from the wall. But before he took more than two steps, dizziness overcame him and the floor tilted so violently that he fell into darkness.

Chapter 14

Jocelyn stood next to Dr. Blake in the doorway of Grant Amesbury's room, uttering another prayer for his safety. Dr. Blake had checked on him several times since the fall but could offer no prognosis beyond the assurance that patients with head injuries such as Grant's usually made a full recovery. Usually. The idea that this brave, if somewhat grumbly, man might die or suffer long-term side effects because he'd saved her left Jocelyn with the urge to weep. If she thought it would do any good, she would have shed a waterfall's worth of tears.

With a sigh, Grant turned his head. His eyes opened a slit, and he went very still. His gaze fastened on her as if he'd never seen her. "You can't be one of the devil's minions; you have the face of an angel."

Relief left her weak. She smiled, her vision turning suddenly watery. Despite his quite understandable disorientation, he seemed well enough, if a bit delusional. No one had ever compared her face to an angel's. But the hope that he might actually think that of her in truly unguarded moments flamed in her heart.

She offered a smile. "Welcome back."

His silvery gaze studied her another moment before surveying the room. He moistened his lips. "Have I been somewhere?"

She let out a cross between a sob and a laugh. "You went wherever the sandman takes people when they sleep.

But don't worry—you've only been in and out, not truly unconscious, and it's only been a few hours."

His brows drew together. "What happened?"

Doctor Blake leaned over to examine his eyes. "You hit your head. I'm checking on you to be sure you're not suffering any lingering effects."

"Effects?" Mr. Amesbury frowned and pressed a hand to his head.

Jocelyn cast an anxious glance at the doctor. Was a lack of memory about that fall sign of serious injury? "Effects from your fall."

He frowned as if he thought them both mad. "What fall?"

"Well, actually you threw yourself down the stairs to save me."

His scowl deepened, and he turned his head, then hissed in his breath. He reached up and felt the side of his head, his expression turning thoughtful as his fingers no doubt encountered a lump.

Dr. Blake passed his hand over Grant's eyes. His pupils were so enlarged that his irises became only a fine silver circle around the black. "Do you remember falling down the stairs?"

"The stairs...." Grant squeezed his eyes closed.

"Of the castle ruins?" Jocelyn supplied.

He opened his eyes and focused on Jocelyn. "I remember. You fell, and I ... are you all right?"

That was thrice he'd asked after her safety. The man clearly had a more tender heart than he let on. Mutely, lest she give in to her urge to bawl like a child, she nodded.

His features relaxed. For a moment, he appeared

149

young and handsome and carefree. He shifted and grumbled, "No need for tears."

She squared her shoulders and swallowed her emotions since they made him so clearly uncomfortable. "You are remarkably chivalrous, Grant Amesbury. Whenever I need you, you always come to my rescue."

He tried to glare, but it looked forced. "I'll be sure to restrain myself in the future."

She smiled at the adorable way he struggled in discomfort at her gratitude. He wasn't as rough and grumpy as he appeared—he had a tender heart that he disliked revealing. If she weren't so indebted, she might have tried harder to express her appreciation just to watch him squirm, but that would be sorry repayment for all he'd done for her. And when he'd been delusional, he'd called her an angel. How lovely.

Jocelyn took a step back. "I'll leave you to examine him, doctor. Please send word if there's anything you require."

The doctor thanked her and turned his attention to Grant Amesbury, her dark, grumpy knight. She smiled. Surely a man so diligent about putting others' safety ahead of his own would be fair in his investigation.

Upon receiving word that her rescuer appeared to be resting comfortably, she spent the remainder of the evening with their guests having dinner and playing several rounds of charades. As the hour grew late, the guests dispersed to seek their beds. Jocelyn reviewed the next day's menu with the cook. That task completed, she headed across the great hall toward the stairs.

Hushed voices caught her attention. The furtive quality of the voices raised the hairs on her arms.

Stepping lightly on her soft-soled slippers and hoping the rustle of her skirts wouldn't give her away, she crept toward the conversation occurring on the far side of the curving grand stairway.

"...Lord Liverpool."

A bolt shot through her and she held her breath.

"I understand that sacrifices must be made but I can't like the rest of your plan. Even if it works, the king might appoint someone else. And you're talking about destroying innocent men..."

"As you said, sacrifices must be made. Then he will be the only suitable candidate for the king to consider once our plan plays out in its entirety."

As Jocelyn drew nearer, the floor under her shoe squeaked. The conversation halted. The blood rushed out of her head. They must know she was there. Her first impulse was to find a light, discover the speakers' identity, and demand answers. But if they were plotting murder, they were capable of anything. Thinking fast, she started humming and walking up the stairs as if she had been walking a steady pace with no knowledge anyone stood in the shadows. Gliding up the steps with her head high, she continued to hum, keeping her focus fixed on the portrait at the head of the staircase. The back of her head throbbed as if someone had a gun pointed at her. Perspiration trickled between her shoulder blades.

Sacrifices...destroying an innocent man...Good heavens! Could this be a conversation over ruining someone's reputation? Or did someone in this very house plot to assassinate the prime minister as Bow Street and Grant Amesbury suspected?

But who were the men she'd overheard? The words "our man" suggested they spoke of someone not present during that discussion. She refused to think Papa would be party to such evil. Possibly it meant some of his supporters were acting without his knowledge. But which of her father's supporters were zealous enough—and ruthless enough—to want him in that position badly enough to commit murder?

Upon reaching the top of the stairs, she turned immediately toward her room. At the last second, she stepped into the shadows, glancing downward toward the conversation she'd overheard. It was too dark to make out anything of the forms below. She waited, but no one approached. No sound broke the silence. She let out her breath, releasing pent-up fear quivering in her stomach.

She resumed her path toward her room but checked her steps. Surely she ought to check on Grant Amesbury. As a guest in their home, he deserved her attentiveness. As her rescuer who'd injured himself in the course of his brave and selfless act, he deserved her undying gratitude and an extra measure of care.

In the guest wing, she stopped in front of his door and tapped softly.

"Come."

At least he sounded stronger. She entered and found him sitting on the floor next to the bed, hunched over with his head in his hands, wearing only trousers and a shirt.

"Mr. Amesbury?"

He lifted his head.

At the sight of his pallor, she rushed toward him. "Did you fall?"

He scowled. "I tried to get up...."

She kneeled in front of him. "Didn't the doctor tell you to stay abed for at least a day?"

"Can't. Have work to do."

"Your work will have to wait. You won't get anything accomplished if you injure yourself again." She pressed the back of her fingers to his forehead, checking for signs of fever.

He went very still under her touch, his eyes wary. Her fingers tingled. A shiver of awareness ran the length of her whole being. Remembering she was supposed to be checking for fever, she cleared her throat. His skin remained cool. The utter stillness about him and that sharp intensity in his gaze left her breathless. His unbuttoned shirt only opened to a slight V at his throat, but as an unmarried miss, she certainly should not view his state of dress. Heat flushed her cheeks.

She lowered her hand. "You don't feel feverish, thank goodness, but you belong in bed."

He growled. "I don't have time for lying about."

Clearly the man felt none of the same physical reaction to their closeness that currently zinged across her skin. She moistened her lips. "I'll call a footman to help you up."

"No. I can manage." But his pallor and the tightening around his mouth betrayed his pain.

She huffed an exasperated laugh. "I don't think you can, not today. I'll help you." She lifted his arm to put it around her shoulder but he hissed in his breath, his face twisting in pain. The she remembered. "Oh! I'm so sorry. That's your sore shoulder."

She moved to his other side, ducked under his other arm and placed it around her shoulders. With her arms wrapped around his waist, and after tucking her feet under her body and bracing her back against the bed, she said, "Up you go, then."

She stood, groaning under his weight. It was like trying to lift a horse. Her muscles strained and shook. Leaning on her, and using his other hand to steady himself, Grant pushed himself up enough to get back up into bed. As he lowered himself onto the mattress, she placed a hand behind his head and guided him back onto the pillow. She pulled up the counterpane on the bed and covered him with it.

He pushed it back. "Leave it off. It's too warm."

To assure herself no fever had developed, she touched his face again and relaxed when she encountered cool skin. She gave into the urge to brush a strand of hair away from his face. Dark as midnight and as soft as a child's, his hair obediently moved under her fingers. Pale gray eyes with enormous pupils watched her steadily.

Heat rushed to her cheeks at the familiarity she took with him. She cleared her throat. "I'll leave you, then. Good night." If he had any sense, he'd stay abed tonight. Her skirts swished as she stepped toward the door.

"What troubles you?" His voice halted her.

She stopped, meeting his gaze. "What do you mean?"

He rolled over onto his side and folded his elbow underneath his head. "You've learned something. About your father?"

She caught her breath. Grant Amesbury was too perceptive. "No."

Under his probing stare, she studied the ground and

wrapped her arms around herself. In an attempt to appear nonchalant, she shrugged. "It's nothing. Nothing at all."

Very quietly, he said, "You can tell me."

"No, I can't. You'll twist it around to make sure it fits what you've already decided is the truth."

His stare remained fixed upon her. Was it her imagination or were his pupils still too large even for the dim lighting? "I admit when I first started investigating your father, I had something of a bias."

She sighed and nodded.

"But I give you my word, I will carefully examine every clue and be fair. I am not on a witch hunt; I seek justice."

She huffed and sank into the nearest chair. "Who believes this of my father?"

"Bow Street."

"And you believe my father capable of something this heinous?"

"His name is linked to the plot."

She waited but he didn't elaborate. "So, someone said my father is guilty and your task to prove it." She cocked her head to the side. "What if you find that he's innocent? Or what, even, if you cannot find any evidence of his guilt?"

"Then I will report back such and work to discover the real conspirators." But his words lacked conviction and something of a struggle revealed itself in his expression. His gaze refocused on her face. "What have you learned?"

She hesitated. "I don't remember their exact words."

"Whose words?"

She'd heard nothing condemning for her father; only a confirmation that a plot existed. Still, she hedged. "I didn't see them."

He said nothing, only focused those pale eyes with

155

their too-large pupils on her, stripping away her defenses. Was he so formidable in matters of love, as well?

Heat returned to her face at the unbidden thoughts and her words tumbled out. "They were in the dark and speaking barely above a whisper. But I heard something about Lord Liverpool, and sacrifices, and destroying innocent men."

She stopped. She wanted to confide in him about such a serious matter but feared how he'd react. Still, she had to tell someone; an innocent life was threatened.

She drew a breath and revealed it all. "And they appeared to be having some kind of disagreement. One of them mentioned 'our man' being the only suitable candidate once they made their move."

His eyes took on an even deeper intensity as he mulled over her words. "'Our man' meaning whom?"

"My father was not one of them," she said desperately.

He sat up and draped an arm around one knee. "No, I doubt he'd speak of himself as 'our man.' But that doesn't mean he is unaware of the plot."

"It doesn't mean he is aware of it, either."

"True, but you'd never admit it even if we found irrefutable proof." He pressed his fingers against his temples.

She stiffened. "He's my father. Wouldn't you defend your father to your dying breath?"

He let out a snort. "My father was a tyrant."

She stared, shocked at the venom lacing the harsh words.

Unlike his usual stoicism, he added, "He made it very clear that Cole and Christian were his favorites and the rest of us were expendable."

"Surely not."

"Neither one of them could do any wrong. But if the rest of us stepped out of line, he was all too quick with the cane. I got sneakier, Jared got more outrageous, but Jason..." He swallowed hard. "Jason tried so hard to please him, but he never gave Jason the time of day except to express his displeasure." Grant sank his head into his hands and drove his fingers through his hair. He sat hunched over, his fingers still in his hair, and took labored breaths.

"Is your head causing you pain?"

"Some." He swayed a little.

She jumped to her feet and went to his side. "Are you dizzy? Lie back down. You need rest. Such a blow to the head is nothing to trifle with."

Unresisting, he lay down and squeezed his eyes closed. She ached to smooth back that strand of ebony hair laying over his brow and soothe him. But she'd been too bold already. "Rest now. We'll talk more in the morning."

He said nothing, only pressed his lips together.

"Good night." She stepped out and closed the door.

Resting her forehead on the door, she pictured a dark-haired child desperate for attention and approval, but instead receiving the wrong end of a cane. With such highly protective instincts, he must have suffered seeing his beloved brother receive the same treatment. And then that brother had died. No wonder Grant had closed up. The inner wounds he carried from childhood had probably multiplied during the war until his only defense from pain came from layers of emotional armor. Some people grew gentler with adversity and tragedy; others grew into hardened men like Grant.

Her childhood home had been filled with love and laughter. She'd never been physically punished and couldn't imagine her parents using force as a means of discipline. Tragedy had struck when her eldest brother died in the war serving king and country. And then dear Mother was gone. But despite the aching hole in her heart at their loss, she'd never doubted their love.

Grant wasn't truly hardened. She'd seen too much evidence of his goodness. But he protected a soft heart behind a hard barrier. What did he hope to keep out? Pain? Unfortunately, that same barrier probably also kept out love.

She pushed away from the door and continued down the corridor toward her room. A boy of perhaps fifteen sat slumped in a chair, dressed in the tailored, if subdued, clothing of a valet. He sprang to his feet as she approached, and he trotted toward Grant's room.

As they passed she said, "Are you his valet?"

He checked his step and blinked large brown eyes at her. "Yes, ma'am."

"Your name?"

He glanced around wide-eyed. Perhaps he was unaccustomed to being addressed by ladies of her social status, or perhaps by women in general. "Clark."

"Is that your first name or your last name?"

He paused. "It's the only name I have."

She stared, startled by his answer. Compassion overcame her for the child that must have grown up all alone in the world struggling to recall the name his mother had given him. "Clark, have you been with Mr. Amesbury long?"

He cast a glance at the door. "Since the war."

"You were in the army together?" Her attention fell to his missing ear and the spider web of scars splayed along the side of his neck.

"No, ma'am. We met after he came home."

She nodded, tempted to press him for information but suspected he would prove as taciturn as his employer. He proved her wrong.

"He caught me trying to pick his pocket. He grabbed my hand and told me I could either go to the constable or find a way to improve myself." His mouth twisted in attempted suppressed humor.

Leaning forward, she waited for him to elaborate. An image of a stern Grant Amesbury issuing an ultimatum to a street urchin formed in her imagination.

His mouth lifted faintly on one side and he spoke carefully, as if practicing polished words rather than using the accent of a London street urchin. "He fed me, asked me lotta questions about the streets—thieves, flash houses, others who lived on the wrong side of the law. Then he told me he'd pay me to give him information. So I did. I had food in my belly, I did—for the first time in a long time. Eventually, he hired me to be his valet."

"I'm sure you do an outstanding job." She smiled and nodded, hoping she appeared interested and encouraging. It must have worked because he kept talking.

"But I'm not a real valet, not according to what the other valets tell me they do. I fetch his dinner, take his clothes to the washerwoman, keep my ears open on the streets for anything that might help him when he needs information."

"I'm sure that's exactly what he needs of you." She lowered her voice, "Clark, for the next few days, he needs rest to recover from his head injury."

"Yes, miss. The doctor, he explained that to me."

"Try to get him to stay in bed."

"I'll try miss. He's powerful stubborn."

"I know. Do your best. Goodnight, Clark."

"'night, miss."

Smiling, she went to her room and prepared for bed picturing the very tough, unapproachable Grant Amesbury rescuing a street urchin. Despite his grumbly exterior, he was proving to be a surprisingly complex and kind man.

She could only hope he'd be fair enough to see her father's innocence.

Chapter 15

Grant took a few cautious steps forward, steeling himself against the nausea and dizziness that plagued him the previous day, but his stomach stayed in place and the ground remained level. Doctor Blake had warned him that he'd have dizzy spells and headaches, possibly even difficulty concentrating, over the next few days or weeks and to get plenty of rest. But Grant had work to do. And at the moment, he felt well enough. Truth be told, his body ached all over from the fall, but he never let a little thing like pain stop him.

"Are you sure you should be up?" Clark asked, rubbing absently at what was left of his ear.

"Don't be a mother hen."

"The doctor, 'e, I mean, *he* warned me to keep you abed—"

Grant waved his hand to cut off the boy's words. "I need to get to work. This house party is my best opportunity to investigate our prime suspect, and no little bump on the head is going to stop me."

He wiggled his toes as he pulled on his boots. With a longing glance at his trunk where one set of comfortable clothes lay, he tugged at his fashionable tailcoat and let Clark wrestle his cravat into submission, all the while wordlessly cursing the investigation that had thrown him into gentleman's clothing and amid polite company. He'd rather be in the streets. Creeping along alleys in search of

161

cutthroats suited him so much better than wearing fancy togs and doing the pretty with the brainless, boring members of the *beau monde* who swore by honor but lived for pleasure. Only a murder plot kept Grant at the house party.

He chose not to give Jocelyn Fairley a single thought. Nor did he consider the way her eyes glittered and her cheeks pinked when she defended her father with her admirable loyalty. He most certainly did not recall the softness of her hands when she helped him back into bed last night after he'd fallen, or the way she'd combed his hair away from his face. And he refused to recall the lure of her mouth or the fullness of her lips.

Generally, he made a point not to think of females at all. They were either empty-headed twits or conniving, treacherous serpents complete with fangs and venom. No. He didn't think of her even for a second.

"Before you ask," Clark's voice brought him back to the present. "I've been keeping my eyes and ears open, but the only scuttlebutt in the servants' hall is about your heroism in saving Miss Fairley." His mouth twisted into a wry grin.

"I think they mean 'stupidity,' not 'heroism,'" Grant corrected.

Clark's grin widened. "None o' them are talking 'bout politics or prime minister or plots."

"Stay sharp."

Clark shot him a frown as if he'd just insulted the boy's honor. "Always."

Careful to hold his head level lest he cause another dizzy spell, Grant left his bedchamber and strode into the breakfast room. As savory scents called to him, his stomach complained at his neglect yesterday when he'd been too nauseated to eat.

He paused in the doorway, noting the position of the men present. Mr. Dawson sat next to Dr. Blake with an empty chair at his other side. Perfect. As a loyal supporter of Fairley, Dawson would likely be involved in a scheme to assure Fairley's rise to power. And he could be the 'D' who signed the letter he found.

After serving himself eggs and a scone with jam, and pouring a cup of strong, hot coffee, Grant seated himself next to Dawson.

The doctor leaned forward. "Up and around already, Amesbury? How do you feel?"

Honestly, he felt like he'd gotten into a fight with a gang of angry trees. "Well enough."

"Don't over exert yourself. A concussion is nothing to take lightly."

Grant sipped his coffee and said wryly, "Then I'll be sure to avoid challenging anyone to fisticuffs over the next few days."

The doctor remained sober. "I caution you to avoid anything that strenuous for the next few weeks."

Dawson glanced at him. "Quite the hero, Mr. Amesbury, the way you leaped after Jocelyn."

Grant shrugged. "I didn't think about it. I just acted."

"Her father and I are in your debt."

Grant waved it off.

Dawson lifted his brows and eyed Grant. "Have you developed an attachment for her?"

Grant choked on his coffee. "No, sir. I make it a point of avoiding those kinds of attachments."

"I hope you haven't raised the lady's expectations."

"Not at all. Nor does she show any particular fondness for me." Surely her attention last night had been the act of a dutiful hostess. Nothing more.

The doctor eyed him. "A girl could do worse than the son of an earl."

Grant stuffed a piece of scone into his mouth to avoid having to verbalize an answer, and only shrugged again, making a mental note to spend less time in Miss Fairley's company. The last thing he wanted was a protective father, or family friend, insisting marriage to his daughter because of raised expectations—not that Grant cared about the feelings of a possible murderer, or his daughter, however desirable, but that sort of complication would interfere with the investigation.

Dr. Blake's gaze turned searching, clearly tracing the scar down the side of Grant's face. Grant carefully scooped up a forkful of eggs, resisting the urge to touch his cheek where the scar served as a constant reminder of his life as a prisoner—not that he was in danger of forgetting—nor the reason he'd found himself in such a predicament.

"You don't think a mere scar on such a strapping man would deter the affections of a young lady, do you?" Dr. Blake asked.

A 'mere scar,' no, but a shriveled black heart, not to mention the scars crisscrossing his body, would send any woman fleeing for shelter. More importantly, he wanted no woman. Ever. He'd live and die alone. He coolly crushed the emptiness that tried to follow on the heels of contemplating such a future. He was better off without the schemes and lies and false promises of a woman.

He said as dismissively as he could manage, "I haven't given any thought as to how to gain or deter the affections of ladies." He chewed his eggs and studied his plate as if breakfast required all his conscious thought.

"What do you do in your spare time, Mr. Amesbury?" Dawson asked.

He almost smiled at the expression that would have appeared on Dawson's face if he answered that he preferred to bring cutthroats to justice and to assault young ladies in their fathers' studies. "Oh, the usual—riding, fisticuffs, fencing." How could he turn the conversation to politics? "Lately, I've considered running for parliament. There's a rotten borough in one of my brother's parishes, and he's asked me to consider filling the position." Which was an outright lie, but it created the perfect segue.

Lord St. Cyr entered, nodded a greeting at them, and served himself.

"Your brother is Lord Tarrington, is he not?" Dawson asked.

"Yes, he is, but I'm new to politics. I've been following the discussions in the papers, and asking a lot of questions to those who already serve, but I'm not sure that's my calling."

"Politics is not for everyone," Dawson said.

Grant leaned forward and lowered his voice. "I'm mostly hearing about the hot debate over who the better candidate for the next prime minister is, and whether that position needs a change."

Dawson smiled. "Obviously, I favor Fairley. But others think no one can usurp Lord Liverpool."

"Many seem unhappy with how slowly we've

recovered economically from the war," Lord St. Cyr added as he joined them.

Grant nodded and waved his fork in St. Cyr's direction to emphasize his point. "With good reason. But honestly, how likely is it for the House to cast a vote of no confidence?"

St. Cyr shook his head. "Who knows? Some of us would, but are we enough? That's anyone's guess."

"If that happens, will they select Redding?" Grant asked him.

"Oh, he's a good man," St. Cyr said. "But he doesn't have as many supporters in the House of Commons as Fairley."

Dawson picked up the dialogue. "No one expects Redding's name to be brought to the king while Fairley has so many who have vowed to choose him. The only real barrier is Lord Liverpool himself." He sipped from his cup as his eyes glittered thoughtfully.

So the evidence pointed straight back to Fairley. The only one who benefited from assassinating Lord Liverpool would be Fairley, who would almost certainly take his place.

Grant glanced around. "I'm not in the House, but I have enough reason to wish Liverpool out of office. Who knows, maybe someone will take him out another way and pave the way for either Fairley or Redding." He smirked as if he jested and glanced at all three men listening to gauge their reactions.

"Another way?"

"He might take ill, have an accident, or..." Grant shrugged.

St. Cyr jerked back, but huffed a laugh. "Yes, well, last I checked, assassination was illegal in England, not that a little thing like that would stop everyone."

"If everyone respected the law, the gaols and gallows would be empty," Grant said.

"The end justifies the means, Amesbury?" St. Cyr tilted his head at Grant.

Grant shrugged. "I suppose that depends."

Dawson leaned forward and laced his fingers together on the tabletop. "Depends on what?"

"On the end, I suppose." Grant let the subject drop, hoping he had planted a seed in their minds that he might be a supporter of their cause.

Jocelyn Fairley entered the room, her usual disgustingly cheerful smile in place. Only today it didn't seem disgusting. Her cheer lightened the dark shadows in the corners of his soul. She turned his direction. When her eyes met his, her smile softened and became more intimate, almost...affectionate. His heart tripped and stuttered.

He focused on his breakfast. Surely the blow to his head caused this unwarranted reaction to her.

She sat next to Dawson. "Good morning, gentlemen."

They greeted her and she asked them how they were enjoying themselves. Small talk erupted with all the predictability of growing grass, but Miss Fairley's focus fixed on him again and again. She smelled heavenly. And her pretty face was like a ray of light. He sipped his coffee, trying not to let her gaze throw him into a state of chaos. He failed.

She turned her face his direction. "And how are you feeling, Mr. Amesbury?"

"Confused." He clamped his mouth shut, horrified he'd uttered the first word that came to his mind.

"Understandable after your injury," Dr. Blake said. "You asked me a dozen times yesterday what happened. You may be disoriented on and off over the next few days."

Grant nodded as if the doctor's explanation had merit and vowed not to make any confessions where Jocelyn Fairley was concerned.

Chapter 16

Jocelyn sat at her writing desk in the back parlor, pouring over the dinner menu for tomorrow evening. Since it would be the final dinner of their house party before returning to London, it needed to be perfect.

A pattering of footsteps drew nearer. "Miss Fairley!" One of the younger footmen, a boy of perhaps fourteen or fifteen, burst into the room, breathless and red faced.

"What is it, Johnson?"

"My momma needs you. The baby is coming and the midwife is ill; she can't come. We need you to deliver the baby."

Alarm shocked Jocelyn into full alert. "But I'm not a midwife. I can't deliver a baby by myself. I've only helped other midwives."

"My brother is riding for another midwife, but she's a fair ways away. Please, miss, I beg you to be with my momma until the midwife can come."

Jocelyn hesitated. She had only helped deliver three babies, and each time the midwife had been in charge; Jocelyn had only assisted. She'd helped foal mares, too, but that didn't exactly qualify her as an expert. But if a midwife were on her way, Jocelyn could at least offer comfort to the woman.

"Very well. I'll do what I can to help her until the midwife arrives."

Relief overcame Johnson's face. "Thank you, kindly."

If only Aunt Ruby were here. She had actually

delivered babies and would know better what to do during the labor. "Have my horse ready to leave as soon as possible. Pack as many clean towels as you can carry. And clean sheets. Tell Cook to prepare a substantial basket."

Hopefully she'd only need to hold the mother's hand and tell her everything would be well. After dashing upstairs to change into her oldest riding habit and boots, and to tie on a large, heavy pinafore, she sent a message to her father to let him know where she was bound. Outside, as she descended the front steps, Grant Amesbury approached from the opposite direction. He walked with remarkable steadiness after taking such a bad fall yesterday.

He made a visual perusal of her attire. "Going for a ride?"

"One of the tenants is having a baby, and the midwife is miles away."

His brows shot up. "You deliver babies?"

"I've only helped Aunt Ruby and the local midwife deliver them. I hope to offer comfort until the midwife arrives."

A curious light she could not identify entered his gray eyes. "I've never heard of a maiden delivering babies."

"Yes, well, my dear aunt comes from a long line of midwives and healers, so I'm keeping with family tradition. And Aunt Ruby doesn't see any reason to shelter me from something I'll go through someday. Maybe." Not that her prospects for finding a husband to father her babies looked too promising.

"Maybe? Does delivering babies make you question whether you want to go through that?"

She scoffed. "I'm not a coward." Although, he had a point. She'd lived, in detail, every moment of the woman's pain. But seeing the mother's joy when she beheld her tiny child made Jocelyn ache to have a child of her own someday.

His voice rumbled, "No, I would never dare accuse you of cowardice."

She glanced sharply at him, expecting his usual mocking expression, but the light in his eyes bordered on approval. She tested it. "You're probably shocked I'm not a dainty little lady who faints at the mention of blood."

"The world could use fewer of them, and more women with spine."

His validation sent happy little twirls through her. Still, she could not help tweaking him a little. "Why, Grant Amesbury, I think you just paid me a compliment. Perhaps all you needed to sweeten your disposition was a good rap on the head."

"I'm sure it's temporary." One corner of his mouth turned up.

She stared at the closest thing he'd come to smiling. A smiling Grant Amesbury was almost too beautiful a sight. And it caused a sudden weakness in her knees. "Let us hope so. I had just become accustomed to your usual grumpiness."

He frowned. "I'm not grumpy...I just don't like most people."

"Ah, that's different." She smiled. "If you'll excuse me, I must go to the mother in labor." As she headed to the stable, he kept pace with her. She glanced at him, puzzled.

He met her gaze. "I'll accompany you. You shouldn't be traipsing all over the country alone."

She smiled again. Could it be possible he actually wanted to spend time with her? "This is my home; I know all our tenants, so I won't be alone. And you probably shouldn't be riding so soon after your fall."

"I didn't fall; I dove after a foolish woman who fell."

"Yes, indeed." Sobering, she stopped walking and turned to face him fully.

He also stopped, a question in his eyes.

Every second of her fall, the terror of plummeting into the darkness, the strength of his grasp, the warmth and safety of his arms, the cushioning of his body as they hit the stone steps, his injuries, her horror and fear that he'd been seriously hurt, the bravery with which he bore the pain, all came tumbling over her. As she gazed up at him, she pictured him as a rogue who fought for justice with his own code of honor.

She spoke barely above a whisper. "I still can't believe you did that for me."

He blinked. A reply poised on his lips, but it fell away, and he stood, so serious and focused—focused on her—that she took a step toward him. A wrinkle formed in his forehead as he watched her, wary and silent. She moved in so close that their bodies almost touched. He held his breath. Raising up on tip toe, she put her cheek so near his that he warmed her skin, an intimate position.

"Thank you," she whispered directly into his ear. "Thank you for catching me. You probably saved my life. And I am in your debt." Her eyes stung with tears at his valor.

A second passed. She didn't step away. Neither did he.

He whispered a reply, "You're welcome."

With a flash of unaccountable boldness, she kissed his cheek and then strode away so quickly that she had almost broken into a run by the time she reached the stables.

Johnson led two horses, saddled and ready to go. One was her horse, Indigo, and the other, a gelding past his prime.

"We're ready to go, Miss." Johnson said. "I have the sheets and towels you asked for, and the basket." He gestured to the bundles affixed to both horses' saddles.

She took the reins from his hands. "We? No, you aren't going; a lying-in is no place for a boy."

Scowling as if she'd insulted his honor, he drew himself up. "I'm sixteen."

She almost smiled. "Yes, well, it's no place for boys who are almost men, either."

A hand reached around her to take the reins for the second horse. "She's right." Grant's voice rumbled next to her ear. "You don't want to see your mother now. I'll escort her."

She whirled around and almost bumped her nose into Grant's chest, startling Indigo who whinnied and pranced. Placing a soothing hand on Indigo's neck, she glared at Grant. "A lying-in is no place for men, either."

"I'll only see you safely there. I won't go inside." At her hesitation, he moved to give her a leg up. "Don't keep the poor woman waiting. Up you go now." He laced his hands together.

With a sigh of exasperation, she placed her foot in his hands and let out a little gasp as he boosted her up effortlessly. "I really think this is a bad idea."

"I'll stay out of the way."

"Dr. Blake will ring a peal over my head if you faint and fall off your horse." She settled herself in the sidesaddle and arranged her skirts.

Grant stiffened. "I won't faint," he grumbled. "You make me sound like a weak old woman."

Softening, she smiled gently. "Of course you aren't. But your head injury could have lasting effects."

With a nod to Johnson, Grant took the reins and swung onto the saddle of the other horse with practiced grace. "Lead the way."

Honestly, the man was so stubborn! But she didn't waste time arguing. Besides, half of her supplies were strapped to his mount. Without much of a choice, she clicked to Indigo and they were off. With Grant Amesbury at her side, they rode through the countryside. He rode like a shadow, silent and watchful. Jocelyn enjoyed the lovely day and the beauty of the countryside in spring. Moments later, she turned her attention to her silent companion.

"Are you feeling well?"

His gaze shifted to her. "Fine." He resumed his visual scan of the area.

She smiled. "I doubt very much we're in danger of attack out here in the open."

"I'm sure we aren't." A mildly patronizing tone touched his voice.

They rode silently through the village, Jocelyn calling out greetings to everyone they saw, and stopped at the Johnson's cottage. She glanced at the thatched roof, pleased to see that it had been recently replaced, and dismounted. Two young girls played outside next to a line of laundry dancing in the wind. Jocelyn peered at them, trying to remember their names.

"Miss Fairley!" one of the girls called.

"Good afternoon, young miss," Jocelyn replied.

"Momma's gonna 'ave a baby!"

"Yes, I know; that's why I'm here." At the girls' questioning stare at Grant Amesbury, she gestured to him. "This is Mr. Amesbury. He's...a friend," she finished, wrinkling her nose at the lame explanation. But how to categorize the man lay completely beyond her.

Grant took the reins. "I'll see to the horses. Go."

"You should return home. I may be a long while."

"I'll wait."

She shot him a grateful smile and, after tapping on the door, pushed it open. "Mrs. Johnson? It's Jocelyn Fairley."

"Oh, thank heavens," a voice called out. "Momma, she's here."

Inside the cottage, Jocelyn took off her hat, gloves, and pelisse, and laid them over the back of a chair drawn up to a kitchen table already set with dishes. A pot of stew bubbled over a dying fire.

"In here," called the voice from the only other room.

"Oh, Miss Fairley," came Mrs. Johnson's voice. "Hurry. I think it's coming soon."

Jocelyn tied on her pinafore before she stepped into the bedroom of the modest cottage and into almost total darkness. Shutters covered the window, and rags stopped up every crack. Knowing of the custom to keep out possible bad air, a practice Aunt Ruby soundly discounted, Jocelyn paused to determine how to proceed.

175

Tear-filled moans reached her ears, spurring her to action. She called out, "It's too dark in here. I need some light to see. Quickly, open the shutters."

"Oi, miss, it's bad for the baby," said the young girl's voice.

"I don't know how to help her if I cannot see what I'm doing. Hurry now."

With a patter of bare feet, the shutters flew open. Mrs. Johnson sat propped against pillows in bed, her hair loose and pain twisting her face. A birthing chair sat nearby. Her eldest daughter, Beth, stood wringing her hands.

A neighbor younger than Jocelyn, Mrs. Black, sat next to the laboring mother. Mrs. Black turned worried eyes to Jocelyn. "I've never done this. I don't know what to do."

Jocelyn sat on the mattress. "How close are they?"

Mrs. Johnson let out a wail, her face scrunched in pain.

Mrs. Black shook her head. "So close she can't hardly catch her breath."

That close? Oh, heavens. What if the midwife didn't arrive in time? Shutting down her fear, Jocelyn focused on the mother. "Mrs. Johnson, don't hold your breath. Breathe in and blow out your breath hard."

Jocelyn knelt and placed her hand on the tightened abdomen. Once the labor pain passed, she pressed gently with both hands, feeling the outline of the baby with its head low in the womb.

"Do you feel the urge to push yet?" With her hands still on the abdomen, she felt the next labor pain tighten the stomach.

"No," the woman gasped. "Just hurts."

Trying to sound cheerful and competent, Jocelyn said, "You've done this what? Five times now? Six?"

Drenched in perspiration, Mrs. Johnson cringed. "Six."

Jocelyn nodding, remembered that one of the woman's children had died as an infant; another died as a toddler. She couldn't imagine anything more heart-breaking than losing a child.

Rallying, she focused on the present and kept cheer in her voice. "You're an experienced mother. You know what to do. When you feel the urge to push, tell us and we'll move you to the birthing chair."

Teeth gritted, Mrs. Johnson nodded again. The pain passed, and she relaxed into the pillows.

"Everything is going to be fine," Jocelyn said. "You're doing very well. Keep breathing; don't fight the pains when the next one comes."

From the front room, Grant called "Miss Fairley? Do you want these bundles?"

"Yes. Can you bring them inside?"

"They're here."

Jocelyn turned to Mrs. Black. "I need the bundle. Leave the basket of food on the table for the children." To Beth standing off to the side, she said, "Bring me a rag or sponge and a cup of clean water."

They ran to carry out her instructions. Within a moment, Jocelyn had her needed supplies. Beth stood nearby, anxious and pale-faced, a girl barely out of childhood who didn't appear strong enough to witness such a difficult event.

Jocelyn gave her a task to get her out of the room. "Feed the gentleman who is waiting for me, and make sure the children eat. Boil enough water for a bath. Then pick a big bouquet of wildflowers for your momma."

Beth nodded, cast another frantic glance at Mrs. Johnson, and left the room.

Jocelyn waited until the next pain passed before pressing the cup of water to the mother's lips.

"Take only a sip; don't drink too much," Jocelyn cautioned. Dampening one of the cloths she'd brought, she wiped the mother's face and brow.

Several agonizing moments passed with Jocelyn and Mrs. Black each holding one of Mrs. Johnson's hands, bathing her face and murmuring encouragement. Finally, the mother felt the urge to push. Jocelyn and Mrs. Black helped move the surprisingly calm woman into the chair. With the next pain, she pushed. She pushed, and pushed, and pushed. But nothing happened. Six children should have speeded up the process. A slow fear built up in Jocelyn that something was terribly wrong.

She carefully washed her hands, and knelt in front of the mother. "Mrs. Johnson, listen carefully. I need to check the baby. I'll try not to hurt you."

Mrs. Johnson nodded and gritted her teeth. Trying to imagine she was helping birth a horse instead of touching a woman in such an intimate way, Jocelyn reached in and felt for the baby. Her fingers encountered the baby's head. She ran her fingers around it, searching for something amiss. There. The cord. The umbilical cord shouldn't be on the top of the head. She slid a finger around it, and pulled it off. Just as another tremor of pain tightened the abdomen, Jocelyn slid her hand out.

"There. That should do it."

178

The mother pushed, letting out a hard groan. A tiny baby entered the world into Jocelyn's out stretched hands. Mrs. Johnson let out a sigh of relief, her body going limp and her head falling against the back of the seat.

Jocelyn gazed down at the baby, still blue from not having taken a breath yet. A miniature, perfect little human. How amazing. What a miracle!

"It's a boy," she breathed.

Wait. What was that? Peering closer, she found the umbilical cord wrapped several times around the baby's neck. Cold dread spread through her. With trembling fingers, she carefully removed the cord and massaged the baby's delicate skin. Jocelyn held the wet infant upside down, rubbing its back to encourage it to take its first breath. Nothing. She patted the baby's back. No response. She swatted his bottom. Again, no breath. No sign of life. Shockwaves ran down Jocelyn's spine and her limbs turned icy. She smacked his bottom so hard her hand hurt. Nothing.

"Bring me a bowl of warm water and one of cold. Hurry!" Her panic colored her voice and Mrs. Black raced to obey.

"What is it?" Mrs. Johnson stared down at the silent child in Jocelyn's arms. "Hasn't he started breathing yet?"

"Not yet." Jocelyn continued working to get the baby to breathe. When the water arrived, Jocelyn dipped the infant first into warm water then cold in an attempt to shock him into breathing. Nothing. She rubbed him hard with a towel, turned him over, and rapped hard between his shoulder blades. No response.

This child would never take a breath. Never feel his

179

mother's arms, her kiss, her love. Never feel the sun on his face, see a rainbow, smell flowers. Never take a step. Disbelief crept over Jocelyn in a slow current, leaving her cold and empty.

Moving like an automaton, Jocelyn wrapped the small, lifeless form in a blanket. "I'm so sorry." Her voice caught. "The cord..." tears cut off her words and she sat mute and shocked.

Staring, Mrs. Johnson demanded, "What are you saying?"

Steeling herself against the truth, Jocelyn steadied her voice. "I'm sorry. I'm so sorry. He's gone."

The mother shook her head, her voice growing in volume as she repeated, "No. No! NO! Give him to me!"

Wordlessly, Jocelyn obeyed. Sorrow left her stunned. She couldn't think of what to do next. What would Aunt Ruby do? Drawing on some inner reservoir of strength, she ran through the after-birth process in her mind. She squared her shoulders. She had work to do.

She fell into a numb, afterbirth routine, moving automatically, emotionlessly, her ears almost deaf to the mother's cries and attempts to get her baby to breathe.

The mother continued wailing, hugging the lifeless little body frantically. Her friend sat with her arms wrapped around the mother, weeping tears of sympathy. Jocelyn gently but firmly moved the mother from the birthing chair to the bed and urged her to lie down.

Beth stood in the doorway, holding a bouquet of wildflowers. Her eyes were wide and her mouth slack.

Jocelyn could think of nothing to say to her. Numb,

bereft, Jocelyn removed her stained pinafore and wrapped it up with the soiled linens into a bundle. She stood staring down at the floor, forcing herself to listen to the mother's grief.

Bleak sorrow pushed back through her carefully constructed stoicism, and the impassivity that had insulated her during the last few minutes crumbled. Failure rose up and condemned her with sharp cruelty. Had she done all she could? Was there more she should have done, or should not have done? Had she failed this sweet mother, and this perfect, innocent babe?

Grief bored a hole through her, leaving wreckage in its wake. The image of the still baby lying in her hands superimposed itself over her vision like an apparition. Outside, all sound hushed. No birds sang, no children played, no workers' song broke up the deathly silence. Anguish and loss reigned as cruel monarchs. Distant thunder rumbled as clouds cast a pall over the land.

"We need to go. There's a storm coming." Grant Amesbury's voice reached her.

His voice nudged her to action. And there was nothing she could do here.

"I'm sorry," Jocelyn whispered one last time to the family.

Still grappling with her own helplessness, she headed to the door with the bundle of soiled linens under her arm. A tall frame blocked her path. Grant Amesbury stood in the doorway, his broad-shouldered form silhouetted by the gray sky outside.

She made a vague gesture behind her. "I..." she

couldn't finish. Tears stung her eyes and a sob wrenched its way out of her. Clutching the bundle, she pushed past the enigmatic man in her path and rushed outside.

In the fading sunlight, she stood holding the bundle, her head bowed while silent tears slid down her cheeks, cooling in the breeze.

Another form approached, whistling. "Ah, Miss Fairley."

Jocelyn pressed her hand to her chest as she recognized Mr. Johnson's voice. How would she break the news to him that his infant son was stillborn? She wiped her tears and raised her chin, determined to face the father with courage.

"I just got word my Mary is about to have the baby..." his voice trailed off and his cheer faded to concern. "Is she...?" His gaze flitted over her, resting briefly on her gown.

Following the line of his stare, Jocelyn lowered her gaze to the stain spread over her gown; her pinafore must not have been large enough nor thick enough to protect her clothing.

"Mary?" he asked hoarsely, paling.

She cleared her throat. "Your wife is alive and ..." she stopped herself from saying *well*. No woman who lost a baby would be well. "She came through the birth unharmed."

His color returned at news of his wife but he waited, clearly sensing her news.

She cleared her throat again. "But I'm afraid the child was..."

His jaw went slack.

"I'm so sorry, Mr. Johnson."

He clamped his mouth shut. The muscles of his face worked for a moment. Fisting his hands, he swallowed and drew himself up. "What went wrong?"

"The cord was wrapped around his neck. It probably happened hours, or even days ago. There was nothing anyone could have done." Yet she could not shake off the distress eating through her, the suspicion that an experienced, competent midwife could have saved the baby.

Weeping coming from the cottage reached their ears, and Mr. Johnson turned his head toward it. In soft monotone, he said, "Thank you for your help, miss. We're obliged."

"I'm only sorry I couldn't do more." She gestured toward the cottage. "She needs you now, very much."

He nodded and moved heavily inside. Sniffling attracted her attention. Two little girls huddled together next to the cottage, staring at her as if she were a monster. When she made eye contact, they both ran inside. Jocelyn stood hugging the bundle, her inadequacy crushing her. She sank to the ground. She'd been helpless to save the child, helpless to offer comfort, helpless to prevent tragedy.

Horses' hooves clopping on the ground grew louder behind her.

"You cannot save everyone, Jocelyn." Grant held Indigo's and his horse's reins.

She shuddered. "No. But I try to save the ones in my power to do so."

"That one wasn't."

She almost snapped at him that he wasn't a doctor—

how did he know if that child could have been saved. But she didn't have the energy.

He took the bundle from her and tied it to Indigo's saddle. She remained motionless, staring over the fields ripe with summer harvest, a mocking contrast to the bereft family inside the cottage.

Grant pulled her to her feet and guided her to Indigo's side. After boosting her up, he stood solemnly eyeing her. "It's something I learned in the war; you can't save everyone. You just do what you can and hope it's enough. Sometimes it isn't."

The setting sun fell below the cloud bank and cast a warm glow over his grim features, softening the harsh lines. He tilted his chin toward the cottage. "You were very brave and calm in there. Army doctors weren't always as collected."

She wiped the tears leaking out of her eyes. "Not so calm now."

"You're human. You have a heart."

Her gaze dropped to her hands. Blood crusted around her fingernails. She probably looked like a ghoul, blood-stained and drained of life. A breeze blew a strand of hair over her eyes, and she pushed it back with shaking hands.

"You're exhausted," he said softly. "Let's get you back."

She nodded, grateful to let him take the lead. What a relief to rely on someone else for a change instead of always being the responsible one. She cast a sideways glance at Grant Amesbury, surprised to find in him a source of comfort.

Each time she thought she understood him, she discovered a new facet of this remarkable man.

Chapter 17

Grant guided the silent, pale woman home, checking to make sure she didn't fall from the saddle in her exhaustion. Her inner strength surprised him. No gently bred maiden of his acquaintance could have accomplished what she'd done, nor even tried. His sisters, Margaret and Rachel, were no wilting lilies, and Margaret had spent much of her youth in the stables helping foal horses, but he couldn't imagine her delivering a baby.

The efficiency with which Jocelyn dealt with the situation, including such a crushing blow, left him in awe. She rode next to him in silence. No hysterics, no wailing, just quiet, compassionate grief for one of her tenants who'd lost a child. She probably knew every tenant by name. They clearly loved and relied on her.

This remarkable lady was no simpering weakling whose interests centered on finding a rich husband. Here was a woman of substance. And heart. The lucky man who won her love would have no fear of lies, no fear of deceit, no fear of betrayal.

The sun set and the clouds darkened as he guided them back to the manor house. They reached the stables as the first raindrops fell. At the entrance to the stables, he lifted her down. Head bowed, she stood so close that the warmth of her body reached him.

"Are you...feeling well?" he asked softly. Which, obviously was a pathetic question, but the right words eluded him.

She took several deep breaths and let her head drop against his chest. Silent weeping shook her shoulders. He acted without thinking. Wrapping his arms around her, he pulled her in closer. She wept, still noiselessly, while he held her. An unfamiliar contentment stole over him. He excelled at hunting down criminals and took savage delight ensuring thugs and thieves got their due; it helped satisfy his thirst for vengeance. He couldn't strike back at the one who had nearly destroyed him, but he could strike out at others who deserved to face the consequences of their wrong doings. Even the thrill of the hunt made him feel alive. Another part of him, a small, mostly unacknowledged part, prided himself on the knowledge that he protected the innocent from evil.

But this offering of comfort was entirely new. And yet, it seemed familiar and necessary, as if he'd been missing a key gear to the mechanics of his life.

She nestled in against him, all warmth and softness and that sweet fragrance. He rested his chin on top of her head and closed his eyes. It wouldn't last, but he'd be a fool not to enjoy the long-absent moment of a woman in his arms or the uniquely powerful position in which he'd found himself—not the power to destroy or subdue, or even protect, but to comfort.

Several rather satisfying moments he should not have enjoyed so much passed before she lifted her head. "Forgive me."

"Nothing to forgive."

She studied him. "You're a complicated man." Without explaining her cryptic comment, she stepped out of his arms, strode to the house, and disappeared inside.

Grant spent the afternoon snooping around the house, half-heartedly searching for evidence of Fairley's guilt.

In the study, he found the desk left open and a stack of papers on top, which meant Fairley would probably be back in a moment. Grant quickly sifted through the papers. The bottom page caught his eye—a bill for the purchase of twenty-five rifles, dated two days ago.

Twenty-five rifles. Why would Fairley need so many rifles? It didn't sound like a single assassination; it sounded like a battle.

Dread sank into him. He was beginning to like Fairley. He seemed a decent man. If he hadn't found such condemning evidence against him, Grant would have believed Jackson's informant had lied.

He rubbed his hands over his face. Jocelyn would be devastated. All of society would turn against her.

He replaced the bill and left the study, cold down to his core. As he stepped through the doorway, he nearly collided with a surprisingly pretty maid.

"Beggin' yer pardon, sir." With her gaze lowered, she sank into a curtsy.

Grant mumbled to her and headed to the drawing room. As he crossed the great hall, he glanced back. With her dusting cloth in hand, the maid slipped into the study. Wasn't she one of the parlor maids? Apparently, she had more duties than the parlor.

Alone inside the drawing room, he pushed back his unaccountable disappointment in this latest evidence of Fairley's involvement. He had a duty. And he still didn't know when or where the conspirators planned to strike.

Which brought him back to his task of getting invited to their meeting.

Following voices, he stepped out onto the terrace and joined the group for a game of lawn bowls, listening in on conversations that might suggest a co-conspirator or at least give him further evidence of people's characters. However, the more he interacted with the guests, the less he believed any one of them to be guilty. They had no clear motive. They were wealthy, powerful families with nothing apparent to gain from the death of the prime minister. None of them—not even Fairley—seemed the type to risk losing everything simply for the goal of putting Fairley in office. If they were involved, they'd have to have a compelling motive. Settling a grudge, perhaps?

He'd found written evidence—several pieces, and there were overheard conversations as well. And Barnes believed the informant who named Fairley as the leader of the conspiracy. Surely a motive existed; he just had yet to find it. More importantly, he must learn of their plans.

When the game ended, Grant went to his room to change. Clark arrived, grinning. "Ready to dress for dinner?"

"I suppose," Grant grumbled. "I've never changed so often in one day in my life."

"At least you don't have to deal with all the laundry."

"Feeling overworked, are you?"

Clark scoffed. "No, 'course not. A bit more carrying is all, but the work here is light enough. And lots of pretty girls."

"Clark, I'm amazed. Are you actually talking to girls?"

Blushing, Clark stammered, "N-no. But some are right pretty."

"They're all vipers, mark my word. Look your fill, but don't be foolish enough to let them get their fangs into you."

"They're not all like that," Clark protested.

Grant frowned. "Yes. They are."

Try as he might, he could not quite make his tone as convincing as usual. In good conscience he could no longer label Jocelyn Fairley a viper. She surprised him in many ways. But he chose not to dwell on that.

He scribbled a hasty note to Barnes outlining his finding as well as his own thoughts in discreet language lest it be intercepted. After sealing it, he gave it to Clark. "See to it that this is sent by messenger immediately. Tell the messenger to wait for a reply."

Clark tucked the message away and initiated his system of genteel torment, known as assisting Grant as he dressed for dinner.

Dressed and tied and tucked like a man of, well, not of fashion, exactly, but at least a respectable member of the *haute ton*, Grant left the safety of his room and ventured downstairs. As he passed the library, soft voices pricked his ears. Stealing forward, he unabashedly listened at the partially opened door.

A male voice was speaking. "...what you did was brave and selfless. And no one blames you."

"I know." A feminine voice, thick with tears, replied. "It was just so horrible. Such a tiny, perfect baby, looking for all the world as if he were sleeping, except for the cord wrapped around his neck and the bluish color of his skin. He was so silent. So still. I keep seeing that image over and over."

Grant peeked in. Jocelyn Fairley stood next to her father, using a handkerchief to wipe her face.

Fairley took her into his arms and held her tenderly. He kissed the top of her head. "My brave girl. I'm so proud of you, princess. Your grandmother would be, too, if she were here."

In her father's embrace, Jocelyn broke down and sobbed. Murmuring words of comfort and love, Fairley held her, his face pained in compassion he so clearly felt for his daughter.

How could a man so tender with his daughter be so evil as to conspire to assassinate his own country's prime minister? It didn't make sense. Nothing about this case made sense.

Grant crept away like the guilty intruder he was and went to the drawing room to await the others. An unaccountable desire to be the one comforting Jocelyn struck him with such force that his steps faltered. That was her father's job. Grant's job was to find the plotters and protect the prime minister. Mooning over a female did not fit into his plans. Not now, not ever.

At dinner, Jocelyn Fairley sat in her usual spot, her smile in place and her posture ramrod straight, speaking easily with the guests and asking them thoughtful questions. But the light had gone out of her eyes. From across the table, she offered him a sad smile filled with kindness and something soft that he couldn't quite identify, but it created a melting sensation inside him. He made a point to keep his attention off her for the remainder of the meal.

Once dessert had been served and consumed, Jocelyn stood and led the ladies out. He watched her as she walked, her delicious, voluptuous curves, reminded him that he'd held her only a few hours ago.

The men's conversation failed to capture Grant's attention. Nothing of interest came up, and Grant's thoughts continued to circle back to the host's daughter. He couldn't convince himself that she harbored any of the usual feminine evil.

It wasn't just that she was pretty; he'd certainly seen plenty of pretty girls. It wasn't only her lush, full figure; lots of women had that as well, although most girls in the upper classes were too thin to be truly appealing. Could it be her annoying perpetual cheer? Today's events had dimmed that, and oddly enough, he missed her smile, the glow in her face, and the light in her eyes. At least she was capable of a full range of emotions besides continual happiness. But that thought gave him no pleasure. At the moment, he'd do almost anything to see one of her smiles.

She was sincere and resourceful and brave and kind. He admired her devotion to her father, her concern for the downtrodden, and her strength as she faced danger and tragedy.

But surely, if he spent enough time in her company, she'd reveal something that would restore his unshakable knowledge that women were chock full of wicked schemes, and intelligent men should avoid them.

Even as he formed the words, he knew he was lying to himself. The fact was, he only had proof that one particular woman was full of wicked schemes. In his bitterness, he'd lashed out at all females to punish them for the actions of one.

Perhaps he'd been wrong.

He almost swore out loud. The plot. How could he get invited to the plotters' meetings? What of the conversation he had heard two nights past when he'd attacked Jocelyn again and he'd told her of his investigation? And what of the conversation Jocelyn had overheard? Someone here knew something.

A chorus of voices reached a crescendo. "Dance? Oh, yes, let's dance."

Grant groaned out loud. No. Anything but dance.

Jocelyn appeared at his side. "You don't enjoy dancing, I presume?"

"No," he said flatly.

"You did learn how, didn't you?"

"A long time ago."

She eyed him with a solemn gaze shadowed by her heartache over today's loss. "Do you not wish to dance because you don't remember how, or do you not enjoy it?"

"Both."

She nodded slowly. "Just as well. You probably ought not engage in anything quite so vigorous as dancing so soon after injuring your head. As it happens, I'm not in the mood for dancing, either. But I'm willing to play the pianoforte so the guests can do so. Would you turn the pages of my music for me?"

He nodded and followed her to the pianoforte. She settled on the bench, carefully arranging her skirts, and patted the seat next to her before leafing through books and sheets of music. After a moment's hesitation, he sat next to her on the narrow seat that forced them so close together that her body heat warmed his thigh. Her feminine, subtle scent invited him to lean closer and take a deeper breath. He resisted. Still, his focus drifted to the fine hairs that grazed her cheek.

Fairley headed up the line with Lady Everett whom he'd been favoring throughout the house party. He turned a fond gaze on Miss Fairley. "A Cotillion, I think, princess."

She opened a thin book of sheet music, and placed her graceful fingers on the keys, running a grand arpeggio. Her small hands, so unmarred and scrubbed free of stain, gave no indication that they had given so much to help a tenant.

As she played, the guests performed complex formations that tickled the back of Grant's memory, the same steps he'd so blithely danced with *her*, before he knew her true identity, her true desire. Her mocking, spiteful words tore through his head and conjured searing pain in his face, a foretelling of what he would yet suffer as a prisoner...

"Turn the page, please," Jocelyn said softly.

Her words brought him back to the drawing room. A light breeze blew in through a nearby open window, cooling perspiration on his brow and down the sides of face. As he released his breath, he turned the page with a shaking hand. He was safe in England. War and prison and all their horrors fell behind him. Breathing in through his nose and deliberately relaxing his hands, he watched the music notes, trying to follow Jocelyn's progress. The tightness in his chest eased. As she reached the bottom of the next page, he turned without her prompting.

Out of the corner of his eye, he caught the curve of her mouth. Without missing a note, she said, "You read music."

"A little."

A few measures later, she asked, "Do you play?"

"I did as a child."

Her smile formed fully. "That surprises me."

"I'm sure you think me completely without culture."

Her smile turned rueful. "I never said that. Did you enjoy it?"

"After a time, I did. I started because my mother wanted all of us to play. My older brothers complained so often she finally gave up on them. But I continued—mostly to please her, but also to show up my brothers. Then I learned to like it. For a while."

"What changed?"

"My baby brother Christian took to it. I couldn't stand to do anything he did; he was so smugly virtuous about everything. Such a mama's boy. So perfect." He glanced at her. "That probably sounds childish, doesn't it?"

"It sounds like normal sibling rivalry. I would love to still have that with my oldest brother James. But he never came home from the war. I already told you that, didn't I?"

"You did." The words *I'm sorry* poised on his lips, but they didn't help. He'd learned that first-hand. Nothing helped. No trite phrases or brief epitaphs such as "he was a wonderful person," or "my condolences" or even "I'm sure you miss him" helped.

If she were a man, he would have gripped her shoulder. But he couldn't touch her, not like that, not again. That he wanted to do so just proved what a sentimental idiot he was going to become if he continued to spend time in her company.

"Were you close?" he asked.

194

"No." Sorrow and regret weighed her words.

He waited to allow her to talk about it if she wanted to.

Apparently, she did. "I wish we had been close, because then I could hold onto fond memories of him, but he went away to war when I was so young that I barely knew him. He came home for holidays sometimes, and he was a lively, vivacious young man, but—" She played a wrong note and fell silent for several minutes while she focused on playing. Then, "I understand you lost a brother, too."

"Jason. We were close. He died right in front of me." He clamped his mouth shut and tried to focus through suddenly blurry vision.

Why in Hades he'd revealed so much, he couldn't explain—perhaps all the talk about music lessons and his brothers—but revealing that much came as a surprise. He swallowed, found his place in the music, and turned the page just in time.

Softly, in almost a whisper, she said, "I heard about that." She glanced at him, and understanding and compassion caressed him in an almost tangible touch.

He wanted to scowl, utter a sarcastic rebuff, anything to shake off her offered sympathy and free himself of the threads of affection she wove around him like a soft blanket. It would surely turn into a perilous net that would hold him fast until a great, ravenous predator consumed him.

But he couldn't seem to muster any alarm. Or sarcasm.

They sat in comfortable silence, her playing and him turning pages, for the duration of the evening.

Comfortable. In the presence of a woman. Clearly the blow to his head caused long-term side effects.

As the evening waned, the guests called a stop to dancing and began games of whist. A few said their good nights. Grant glanced at Jocelyn. She gave him a soft, intimate smile. He almost returned it but pressed his lips together instead and settled for a brief nod.

As he stood, the base of his head started to ache. Perhaps a good night rest would restore his sanity.

As Grant headed for the main staircase to seek his bed, the butler, Owen, hailed him. "Mr. Amesbury, this just arrived by special messenger. He said it was urgent."

"My thanks, Owen."

He broke the seal. Barnes's writing raced along the page.

Motives are often unclear. Also consider that we were misled. Evidence can be planted. However, I'm certain our informant was truthful. Proceed as you see fit.

B

Grant folded the note and tucked it in his coat breast pocket. As he headed down the corridor toward the stairs he turned it over. Deliberately misled. Planted evidence. If someone deliberately misled Bow Street, they would assume Fairley would be under investigation. He hadn't found anything in Fairley's words or character, nor in those of his friends, except possibly a conversation taken out of context, to suggest these men were conspiring to assassinate the prime minister...except the partially burned note in his London study, and the note someone slipped into his pocket—possibly without his knowledge.

If some other person or group wanted to assassinate the prime minister, and decided to blame Fairley, they could have left incriminating evidence knowing Bow Street would send someone to investigate. Grant had made enough arrests that a few members of the seedy side of the law might know him and might be leaving it for him to find.

A pounding in his head and sudden dizziness sent him staggering against the wall. He fought for balance. Pushing through the pain and light-headedness, he waited for the room to stop spinning. He closed his eyes. Steadier, he returned his thoughts to the case, searching for a solution.

Fairley. Was he really a member of the conspirators as Barnes believed? Or could someone else, someone both ruthless enough and smart enough, have planned not only a conspiracy but to blame Fairley? In order for this kind of plot to work, the two criminals who'd named Fairley were involved and were devoted enough, or fanatical enough, to allow themselves to be arrested. It also meant the man outside Parliament who'd passed the notes was one of them. And someone inside Fairley's house was helping. That took a plot of a grand scale.

But who? And more importantly, when did they plan to strike?

Chapter 18

Jocelyn bade goodnight to her father who partnered Lady Everett in whist, and to the guests still playing the game, and left the drawing room. Normally, she'd remain up until the last guest went to bed, but her emotional day had sapped her strength. Of course, sitting next to the ever-surprising Grant Amesbury as she played pianoforte had an unexpectedly restorative effect on her.

Just outside the drawing room, she stopped short. The object of her thoughts stood leaning heavily on one arm braced against the wall, his shoulders slumped and his head bent.

She went at once to him and touched his shoulder. "Grant? Are you unwell?"

He snapped to attention. "I'm fine." He swayed and leaned his shoulder against the wall.

She slipped a supporting arm around him and guided him to a chair. "I am persuaded you are not as fine as you suppose."

He sank into the chair and pressed his hands over his eyes, leaning forward and resting his elbows on his knees. "A little dizzy."

"Shall I summon Dr. Blake?"

"No. It comes and goes. He said it would."

She knelt in front of him, suppressing another desire to stroke his hair—such thick, black hair, shining in the lamplight like the glossy wing of a raven. But she should not be so familiar with him again.

Softly, she asked, "Can I bring you anything? Water? Tea? Brandy? Coffee, if you prefer?"

"Nothing," he murmured. "I just need a moment."

Aching to offer comfort without making him uncomfortable, she touched his sleeve. He lifted his face and met her gaze. Silently, he studied her. She returned his stare, admiring the lines of his handsome face, noting every shade of gray in his eyes. He would be remarkably attractive if only he'd smile, a true, genuine display of mirth or pleasure. And she just might fall under his spell. What would it take to win a smile from the cynical Grant Amesbury?

A faint scent of mint and bergamot wafted to her. She almost smiled as she recalled that evening when he'd threatened her in the father's study that first night, she'd noticed that trace of upper class even when he was in disguise.

In the soft lighting, the scar on the side of his face barely showed. She ached a little more at how much pain he must have suffered. Softly, slowly, she reached up and touched his scar with one finger. He held his breath but didn't pull away. She traced the raised smooth pink line from the corner of his eye down to his jaw. What would make such a ragged injury? It looked like it had been torn rather than cut with a blade.

Her attention focused on his mouth. Would a man like him kiss roughly, like his hard exterior, or would he be gentle, like the soft heart she'd seen in brief glimpses in between the chinks of his emotional armor? She'd been kissed before, stolen kisses when chaperones weren't watching. Such kisses had been pleasant but empty and disappointing.

199

No doubt Grant's kiss would be worlds different. Her face warmed in embarrassment, for thinking of him by his given name, and for craving his kiss.

Aching loneliness crossed his features and settled into his eyes. Then something inside shifted, and wariness took its place. He said huskily, "You aren't just being kind to me because you're trying to convince me to stop investigating your father, are you?"

Stunned, she dropped her hand and sat back. A rush of cold hit her face. "I can't believe you'd think that of me."

"I don't know what to think of you." He parted his mouth as if to speak again but stopped and swallowed hard.

With a growing pain in her heart, she climbed to her feet. Clearly, he felt none of the attraction for her that quickly grew inside her for him. He was so closed up that he probably felt nothing.

She motioned to the young liveried footman at the other end of the great hall.

He hurried to her, tugging the jacket of his livery into place. "Miss?"

"Mr. Amesbury is unwell. Please accompany him to his room—make sure he doesn't get hurt. And find his valet."

"Yes, miss."

She strode away before the stinging in her eyes turned into tears. Stupid, stupid, stupid. She should never mistake moments like the one they shared at the pianoforte for true fondness. A man as prickly and wounded as Grant would not yield his affections so easily. Surely he'd always question or reject her attempts to reach his heart.

Jocelyn almost stumbled. Is that what she wanted? To reach Grant's heart?

She would not think of reaching anyone's heart now—least of all, his. She had to clear her father's name, match him with Lady Everett, and help him win the election. In addition, she had guests to entertain and tenants who needed her care—far too much to do to make wild and unwise investments of time and heart on a man incapable of accepting or returning love.

Yet as she sought her bed, his words echoed in her head so much that by morning, she felt little more rested than when she'd retired the previous night.

What had happened to make him so hard-edged? Surely something besides war had caused it. How tragic that a fine man like him, one in possession of a tender, valiant heart, might never give or accept love.

Before she and her father returned to London on the morrow, she had errands. Though the sun had barely risen, Jocelyn sent a note to the kitchen asking cook to prepare a basket for a family of five, and another message to the stable master to saddle Indigo. She could take the secret passageway to the village, but the lure of a bruising ride called to her. And she'd rather not carry such a heavy basket all that way.

After she broke her fast with fruit, bread, and chocolate, she dressed in her riding habit and stepped into the corridor. A maid slipped out of her father's room and hurried down the hall. Jocelyn paused. Wasn't that the new parlor maid?

"Are you lost? Emma, isn't it?"

The maid gave a start. "Oi, you gave me a start, you did." In her fright, her accent crumbled from Queen's English to something closer to Cockney. She cleared her throat and drew herself up. "Yes, miss; I'm Emma. Just running a quick errand for Owen, miss."

Since when did the butler send parlor maids on errands to the master's bedroom? "I see. You may go."

The pretty maid bobbed a curtsy and hurried toward the servants' stairs.

How odd. Jocelyn went to her father's room and peeked in. He had arisen to take the gentlemen on an early morning shoot, and his room stood vacant. Nothing seemed amiss. She opened the box containing his cuff links and rings, and found no obvious pieces missing. Again, she glanced around but all appeared normal.

With a shrug, she left and descended the stairs. A scullery maid trotted to her and handed Jocelyn a large basket covered with a cloth. Basket in hand, Jocelyn went to the stables where Indigo waited, saddled and ready. She secured the basket and mounted.

Each step her horse took seemed to pound directly into her chest as she drew ever near the scene of the tragedy. Would the mother be upset to see her? Or blame her for the baby's death? Outside the humble cottage, Jocelyn fortified her courage and rapped on the door of the Johnsons' cottage. Even the sunrise was subdued under gray clouds hanging low.

A solemn Beth opened the door. She dropped a hasty curtsy. "Miss Fairley."

Jocelyn held out the basket. "May I come in?"

The girl held the door open for her. Jocelyn entered, set out the food, and made all the proper inquiries. In the bedroom, she checked on the mother who lay in bed as if asleep but opened her eyes when Jocelyn entered.

Nervously, she smoothed her skirts. "I came to see how you were feeling, Mrs. Johnson."

"A little tired. I never thanked you for coming yesterday."

She let out a shaking breath. "Not that I did any good."

A sad smile curved the woman's mouth. "Not your fault. I've birthed enough babies to know the midwife would've done no better. 'Twas God's will. We don't have to like it."

Jocelyn huffed a soft laugh. "My mother used to say something like that."

"I know. Fine lady, your mother."

Gesturing over her shoulder, Jocelyn said, "I brought a basket of food."

"Thankyee."

Jocelyn made sure the mother had no signs of the fever that often struck mothers recently delivered of babies, changed her linens, and gave her a strong herbal drink to help suppress the production of milk, as well as made sure she ate something. Once Mrs. Johnson settled in and went to sleep, Jocelyn instructed the children to send word if she developed any sign of fever or unusual pain. She left additional herbs to help the mother's milk dry. Jocelyn swallowed down a lump in her throat.

After visiting other tenants, Jocelyn turned back home. On the lane, another horse approached bearing Grant Amesbury's familiar form. He slowed as he reached her.

His now-familiar voice greeted her. "I thought you'd be here. How is Mrs. Johnson?"

"Better than I feared." At least Grant wasn't accusing her of having ulterior motives.

He nodded. "It will be worse in a few days after the shock wears off."

She glanced at him in surprise.

Seeing her expression, he said gravely, "My sister Margaret lost several babies. She was bad off right away and then went numb. Later, she truly grieved."

Jocelyn nodded. "I felt that way, too, when Mama died."

He rode next to her, strong, silent, enigmatic, and yet safe and familiar in a way she never would have expected. He used to frighten her a little with that deadly quality to his every movement. Now, his lethal presence reminded her of an armed guard, poised to protect her from every threat.

She glanced sideways at him. "How's your head?"

"Better. Not dizzy today."

She nodded. "And your shoulder?"

"Little sore. Nothing to fret over."

What went on inside that head of his? Was he thinking about the lovely weather? How much he enjoyed being with her? No, he probably gave little thought to anything but the case.

"Is the shoot over?" she asked him.

His gaze slid her way. "No, I came back early. The others are still out." He paused as if deciding how much to reveal to her. "I wanted to conduct another search in case I'd missed something."

Cold raced through her core. "You found something, didn't you?"

"I found something." He retrieved two papers from his inside pocket and handed it to her.

A bill of sale for twenty five rifles glared back at her. On the second paper she found a note which read:

Expect the delivery of your rifles on the evening of the twenty second day of the month at your warehouse.

No salutation, no signature.

She sought answers in his eyes. "Twenty five rifles? I don't understand. Why would he buy that many guns?"

"Could be used in a full on assault, charging into a meeting with guns blazing. Although that seems extreme to use on one man. And see the address to be delivered? It's a seedy part of London next to the waterfront."

She frowned. "I'm not familiar with that address." She turned imploring eyes on him. "You don't really think this means he's involved with that plot? Surely you don't."

Just as she took a breath to challenge him to ask her father about the bill, he replied, "I am beginning to suspect that someone is trying to implicate him. The evidence is almost too neatly stacked against him. And it feels wrong. He doesn't seem like the kind of man capable of this."

"He isn't; I vow it. He doesn't want the position badly enough to murder someone."

He nodded slowly. "He has too much to lose and too little to gain." He turned his gaze her way. "Both of these were laying out in plain sight where they would easily be found. That suggests they were planted—the conspirators are deliberately leaving evidence against your father."

Pulling Indigo to a stop, she searched Grant's expression for the truth. "You don't think he's involved."

"No."

She let out a breath she didn't realize she'd been holding for days. "I can't tell you how relieved I am to hear that." Then his words sunk in. "But someone wants him blamed?"

"That's the only explanation that makes sense."

"Who would do this?"

"I'd hoped you might know. Does your father have any enemies? Anyone who might hold a grudge?"

"Not that I know of. He's respected even among his rivals."

"His rivals," Grant repeated slowly. "Mr. Redding is vying for the position of prime minister. With your father out of the way, he'd be more likely to gain his end."

"Badly enough to commit treason and murder?"

Grant shrugged. "It does seem extreme. But I don't know Redding's character enough to judge. Something is clearly going on. And whomever is responsible wants your father blamed." He urged his horse forward, and she kept pace with him, her mind turning over the possibilities.

Who would want her father implicated in such a horrific plan? He was the most amiable of men. As far as she knew, no one truly disliked him. Of course, Mr. Redding might, but surely not so badly. Still, the conversations she'd overheard implied something amiss.

"What if there isn't really a plot?" she ventured.

He turned her way with raised brows.

"What if it's all an attempt to discredit my father—that no one really plans to kill anyone, but wants to get him in legal difficulty? The scandal alone would disqualify him as a candidate."

He nodded slowly. "That's a plausible theory."

"Remember the conversation I overheard?—Not the one we both heard, but the one between people I couldn't identify?"

"Remind me. I wasn't quite myself."

"Something about destroying an innocent man and sacrifices. And that their man will be the only suitable candidate."

He stared straight ahead, deep in thought. Fascinated, she watched the way his eyes darted while his mind worked.

He finally spoke. "But didn't they name Liverpool?"

"I can't remember for certain. But yes, I think you're right. I think there was mention of getting rid of Liverpool."

He let out his breath slowly. "That coincides with our sources that there truly is a plot against the prime minister."

"Could getting rid of Liverpool simply mean casting a vote of no-confidence?"

His brow wrinkled. "I suppose."

"What exactly do you know?"

To her surprise, he answered. "One of Bow Street's best Runners, a man named Jackson, arrested a high profile criminal who wanted to make a deal to lessen his sentence. He said there was a plot to assassinate the prime minister, and it would happen during this Season. He didn't know, or wouldn't divulge any more than that. Later, a pickpocket also spoke of that plot and named Fairley as one of the masterminds."

"I can't tell you how relieved I am that you no longer suspect my father."

His mouth pulled to one side. "I'm sure."

The idea that her father was now safe from suspicion created a cushion of comfort around her. And Grant could no longer question her motives for offering him gestures of kindness.

He paused. "It's possible the informants were paid to provide false information to throw us off the trail of the true criminals. Or they are part of a fanatical group willing to face prison to pass information to Bow Street. If your father were arrested and imprisoned, the authorities would believe they had prevented the murder, and the real perpetrators would be left to carry out their scheme."

A chill settled in her bones and she shivered. "That would be horrible."

"With the king not yet crowned, the prime minister murdered, and no one to take the prime minister's place, it would create panic all over the country until a new leader could be chosen."

As the bigger implications sank in, the chill in her bones turned to solid ice. "What can we do?"

He offered her a grim smile. "We?"

"Well, I'm involved, whether or not you like it. And you did come to me with the bill and the note."

A small, half smile curved one side of his mouth. "If I'm right, someone planted these and others I found in London, so I would find it. Can you think of anyone, either a guest or a servant, who might be party to such a plot?"

She shook her head. "If I thought someone in our household capable of such a thing, they would not be in our employ."

"No, but now that you know of the possibility, review

208

everyone in your mind and think of possible motives. Or possibly even someone who might be willing to do it on a bribe?"

"Most of our servants have been with us for years and are loyal. But perhaps someone new..." Owens had hired a number of new servants in preparation for the house party, and Jocelyn didn't know them all. They also had one or two new servants in London. "I'll have to give it some thought." At the moment, the only servant she could recall was the new parlor maid who traveled with them to both houses. But when Jocelyn had checked in her father's room, nothing had been amiss.

As the house came into view, Jocelyn glanced at her silent companion. "Before I go back, I'm going to pay a visit to the new laundress."

He quirked a brow. "Not doing her job properly?"

"No, not that—she's the widow with children I brought with me from London, the one I was visiting when you saved me from that terrible man."

"I'll accompany you."

She smiled, grateful for his presence. They paid a brief visit to Lucy and her children. All wore healthy smiles and had color in their fattened cheeks.

Grant hung back, saying nothing, except a nod when Jocelyn introduced him. As she spoke to Lucy, Grant picked a tiny wildflower, crouched down, and presented it solemnly to little Flora. She took it, just as solemnly, and curtsied. His expression softened. Flora smiled. Two year-old Mary approached shyly, and did a little twisting kind of dance, chewing her lip and eyeing Grant expectantly. Kneeling to get eye-level with her, he offered her a flower as well. She beamed and accepted his gift as if he'd handed her a treasure.

His eyes softened and his mouth curved. A smile.

Jocelyn's heart turned into the consistency of warm pudding. The crusty Grant Amesbury was gentle with children. And he'd smiled.

Lucy watched the exchange. "He's a right handsome man, miss," she said softly.

"He is." Jocelyn agreed wholeheartedly. And this new, softer side she'd discovered in him over the last few days only added to his appeal. One day, Jocelyn would be the reason he smiled.

As if feeling their gaze, he glanced in their direction, wiped away all traces of his smile, and stood.

Jocelyn grinned at Lucy. "I bid you all a fond farewell."

With their goodbyes and well wishes ringing in her ears, she left with Grant at her side. After riding in comfortable silence, they arrived in front of the stables. Grant quickly dismounted and turned to her with upraised hands. She released her reins and reached out to him. As his hands closed over her waist, a tingling sensation left her breathless. He carefully lowered her to the ground. Though he'd helped her down only yesterday, she had been so overset by the day's events that she hadn't experienced such awareness of him. Yesterday, she had even stood in his arms as she'd cried. Then she'd been only vaguely aware of warmth and comfort. Today every nerve vibrated as they stood inches apart, upper bodies almost touching, his hands lingering on her hips.

He cleared his throat and stepped back, folding his

hands behind his back. She'd touched his hair, kissed his cheek, and cried in his arms. Last night she'd touched his scar, and now...he must think her unladylike and forward. She blushed. Even a man who walked a darker path than most members of the upper classes would have scruples about the kind of lady with whom he spent his time. If only he wanted to spend time with her for reasons other than his investigation. Of course, if he did, that would present a whole new batch of problems, foremost being; did she want to be courted by a man who was so emotionally closed?

A loud crack shattered the silence. Grant moved in a blur. In an instant, Jocelyn lay face down on the ground with a weight pressing on her back. Distant cheers rang out as spectators and players enthused about a game of cricket.

The weight moved and then lifted. "Sorry." He grabbed her elbows and pulled her to her feet.

"What is it?" She fixed her whole focus on the man standing in front of her.

His mouth tightened to a hard line.

"Grant?"

He shook his head, his breathing hard and unsteady. His jaw muscles clenched.

"What happened just now?" She touched his arm.

"I...thought..." He took several more breaths and didn't pull away from her touch.

Another crack sounded. He flinched but remained still. From the back lawn came more cheers as the game continued, innocent of its effect on Grant.

She waited. Perhaps he'd confide in her if she were patient.

He finally spoke. "Loud sounds remind me of gunfire."

She squeezed his arm, warming all the way to her toes that his immediate reaction always was to protect her from danger, whether real or imagined. Then the implications sank in. She'd heard of men coming home from war suffering similar problems, loud noises making them believe they were back on the battlefield, surrounded by death and danger. How horrible it must have been for them, probably far and away exceeding her worst nightmares, to have caused such lasting effects even years after they returned home.

She studied the face of this handsome, tortured gentleman. "Does it happen every time you hear a loud noise?"

"Not every time. Less now than when I first came home."

"You were injured," she said softly.

He closed his eyes.

The word "injured" couldn't begin to describe what he'd suffered. The scar on his face probably paled compared to other wounds not visible to her. Anger at Napoleon, at all the suffering he had caused, renewed in her heart. Banishment was too good for the Corsican Monster.

An aching longing arose to embrace Grant and offer him the comfort of her touch. She slid her hand down his arm and grasped his hand. It had curled into a fist. At her contact, he opened his hand and squeezed hers. She sank into the joy of Grant holding her hand, needing her, opening up to her.

It didn't last long. As if catching himself, he released her hand and glanced about. His mouth quirked. "I wouldn't want anyone seeing us holding hands and think ill of you."

She tried to lighten the mood. "Oh, well, I suppose if they did, you'd just have to marry me to save my reputation."

He let out a harsh, wounded laugh. "You don't want a monster like me."

"You aren't a monster!"

"I'm the very devil, Jocelyn. I've killed more men than you've probably met in your lifetime."

She grappled with the harsh truth of his past and what pain it still caused him. What he'd done in the line of duty didn't make him bad. She shook her head. "Soldiers in the—"

"I wasn't a soldier." His words came out sharp, angry. "I was a sharpshooter. I have a good eye. And an uncommonly accurate rifle. I became an assassin—hunted down targets and killed them from a distance. They never knew I was there. They had no way to defend themselves against me." He turned away and stood with his back to her.

Images of Grant slinking through darkened buildings like the ninjas of the Orient and coldly killing men edged into her mind. But he wasn't cold. His targets weren't innocent men, they were enemies. And he wasn't a murderer, he was a loyal Englishman following orders during a long, brutal, bloody war. If he hadn't taken out his "targets" the war might still be going on, and a lot more of other people's brothers would have died—be dying still. Always Grant's first instincts were to protect.

She moved to face him, standing closely to him to let him know she wouldn't reject him, no matter what he told her. "It was war."

"Not just in war. I've killed since then, too."

"Working with Bow Street?" The thug who had threatened her and Aunt Ruby flashed through her mind. She valued life, but criminals intent upon harming the innocent deserved to face justice. She'd just never thought of those who dealt with such matters, had never considered the cost to their souls.

Grant nodded once. "Mostly. But worse, last summer I shot a man in cold blood."

Her breath caught and a chill settled in her limbs. There had to be more to the story. Grant was not a monster. She waited to give him the opportunity to tell her what clearly weighed on him.

He stared straight ahead as if reliving the past. "He brutalized his wife until she finally left him. He terrorized her after she thought she'd escaped him, threatening to kill her and her parents. He tried to kill my brother—repeatedly. When I had him in my sights, I took careful aim, cold as ice. And I put a bullet right between the eyes." He placed a finger on his own forehead.

Sickened by the news, and cursing fate for putting him in such terrible situations, she wrapped both hands around his upper arm to let him know she was there.

Revulsion twisted his expression. "My life was not in danger. I could have shot him in the leg, I could have rushed him and held him at gunpoint, forced him to surrender—anything. But I didn't give him that chance. I was his judge, jury, and executioner. And I don't regret it—

not really." Finally, he turned tortured eyes upon her. "I am a monster."

She placed a hand on his cheek, the texture of his dark stubble and the puckered edges of his scar rough against her palm. "No. You are not. You are a defender, a protector, who constantly places himself in danger to save others. You might not wear armor, but you are as brave as any knight of old."

His brittle laugh rang out. "I'm no knight."

She allowed herself a small, sad smile and let a drop of humor into her voice. "A *dark* knight perhaps, and completely lacking in courtly manners..." She sobered and put her free hand on the other side of his face, holding his head steady, and gazed directly into his eyes. "I would gladly put my life into your hands. I trust you to do the right thing because you are a man of honor and integrity."

Eyeing her as if he didn't believe he'd heard her correctly, he went very still. Without thinking, she moved, rising up on tiptoe. She placed a soft kiss directly on his lips. He froze. But his lips were anything but frozen. Warm and pliant, they moved against hers, returning the kiss. Shockwaves arced through her, awakening every nerve with new life.

She lowered herself back down on flat feet. His expression defied description. Whether he was aghast at her boldness, or terrified at the new path on which they'd taken a step, or simply shocked that she'd want to kiss him, she couldn't say. Before she had too long to agonize over his reaction, he gathered her into his arms, kissing her over and over and over, a ravenous man setting upon a feast— no words of affection, no gentle touches, he simply devoured her in raw, true need. In return, she consumed him, all his darkness, all his wounded anger, all his defensive barriers. She took all of that from him and offered her acceptance, her genuine affection, her hope, pouring into her kiss what she didn't dare vocalize yet, not when he wasn't ready to hear it.

And she knew then two things that she'd been afraid to explore or admit to herself: Grant Amesbury was a man of extraordinary passion, and she loved him.

Chapter 19

Grant kissed Jocelyn as if his very life depended upon it. Her sweetness, her softness, the exquisite pleasure he'd discovered with her, transcended anything he'd experienced. He craved, no—needed, more. She met him with equal ardor, devouring him as hungrily as he devoured her. For the first time in years, wrapped in her arms and consumed by her kiss, he felt alive. And safe.

Dormant, primal desires raced through him. But he couldn't act on them.

He ended the kiss before he did something they'd both regret. Pulsating with energy he hadn't possessed in years, he set her back and took a step away.

He shouldn't have done that, shouldn't have opened a door he knew he couldn't step through. Years ago he'd sworn off women once he realized they held the power to destroy him. He'd vowed he'd rather live and die alone than open up his heart to complete desolation. Alone and angry, his heart had closed up so tightly that it had shriveled and blackened.

But she'd seen inside his heart, breathed life into it, and filled it with light and acceptance. He held onto that sensation for a moment, the hope and joy, before throwing it out and slamming the door. Better to hurt her now than lead her on and hurt her later. He wasn't capable of loving. Too many years of bitterness had leeched out that possibility.

Her lips, plump and moist, curved into a delicious, lazy smile.

Breathing as if he'd run several city blocks, he focused on a point over her shoulder and said woodenly, "I'm sorry. I shouldn't have done that. We both know there can be nothing between us."

Undaunted, she continued to smile. "That was not 'nothing' and you know it."

"It was just two lonely people sharing a kiss." He turned and stalked away.

With each step, he reminded himself why he didn't want an entanglement with Jocelyn Fairley. He was safer alone. And he had nothing to give. Eventually, she'd want more. And he wouldn't be whole enough to give it to her.

He strode to the house. Tomorrow he'd return to London. The very thought of London brought a conflicting mix of relief to have no further need to associate with Jocelyn, and an unexpected sense of loss. But he could resume his investigation better in London.

At dinner, Grant tried to avoid Jocelyn without appearing as if he were doing so. Then he went to bed early.

Sleep teased him, and he relived the beauty and glory of kissing Jocelyn—assaulting her, was more like it. Of course, she'd kissed him first, soft and warm as the curl of steam from a cup of hot coffee, tantalizing and inviting. The second their lips had touched, something had sprung to life in him, something best left dormant and untouched, and he'd lost control. Then he'd attacked her. She should have stepped away in righteous shock and reprimanded him for taking such liberties when all she'd meant to offer was sympathy. But she'd responded with equal vigor. She'd taken all his dark hunger and replaced it with healing light. For a moment, he'd felt...whole. Safe.

But that was insane. He knew better than to go down that path, tantalizing and fleeting and made only for the lucky few. Not for Grant.

The following day, as they made ready to return to London, Grant glanced at Clark. "You heard nothing below stairs?"

"No, sir. Most of the servants like their employers and don't say nuthin' bad about 'em~them."

"Anyone new?"

"A few."

"Any of them say something odd, something about the country's leaders, or the rich in general?"

"Nothing."

No, that would be just too easy for one of them to announce he wanted to kill the prime minister.

Downstairs in the great hall, the guests made a great commotion as they prepared to leave. Though tempted to skip all the inane pleasantries, and an awkward last scene with Jocelyn, he made a point of bidding farewell to the host and any guest who crossed his path.

"Glad you came, Amesbury," Fairley said. "I hope to see you again. Call on me any time."

Grant bowed and said goodbye, keeping his face composed so no part of his encounter with Fairley's daughter would be apparent.

Jocelyn appeared, smiling as if nothing unusual had happened between them. If anything, her smile beamed brighter and her eyes danced wickedly. "Papa, since Mr. Amesbury is recovering from a recent head injury, don't you think we ought to offer him a ride back to London in the town coach with us? I'm sure it will be more comfortable."

Grant almost choked. "No, thank you. That won't be necessary."

"But if you should suffer any pain or dizziness—"

"Clark will be there to assist me. I really must be off— urgent business in Town. But thank you both." He bowed and all but fled.

He strode as quickly as possible without running outside to where Clark waited. "Let's go," he barked.

Clark, accustomed by now to Grant's moods and mannerisms, made no comment. They traveled quickly and without incident to London. During the journey, Jocelyn's kiss tormented him, tempting him to seek more.

They reached London that evening. Dusk fell as he rode into the familiar streets. Fog hovered over the Thames and stretched lifeless fingers into the surrounding neighborhoods. Grant returned the horses and left Clark at home. Unwilling to let the case rest overnight, Grant immediately went to see Barnes. The magistrate often kept late hours and would likely still be in his office. Grant wound through the streets until he reached the Bow Street Office.

Lamps burned in the building, a pale defense against encroaching darkness. Grant entered and passed through the entryway and reception area toward the magistrate's private office, led by the soft murmur of male voices.

Inside Barnes's domain, he found the magistrate with Connor Jackson. Both men brightened.

Barnes motioned him in. "Amesbury, what news?"

Jackson eyed him speculatively, his eyes glittering in

the lamplight. "You survived polite company at the house party, I see. Nice haircut." He smirked. "Find anything useful?"

Grant threw himself into a chair. Weariness from the journey tugged at his strength. "I believe we can eliminate Fairley as a suspect."

Barnes leaned forward. "What do you mean eliminate?"

"Not only is there nothing in his character that leads me to believe he or his supporters are capable of it, but they have little to gain by it. And the evidence is too neatly stacked, too easy to find out in the open. My instincts tell me it's not him. I'm certain."

Jackson's brow crinkled. "But the two informants who bargained for a lighter sentence—"

"Could have been bribed," Grant said. "Or could be part of the conspiracy. Some men are desperate or fanatical enough to die for their cause. We've seen that before."

Jackson lifted his brows and nodded. "Like the Luddites." Shaking his head, he cursed. "I believed the informants were telling the truth."

Grant held out his hands. "They honestly wanted you to think Fairley is involved."

Barnes turned pensive. "Or they actually believed it. They might have been fed information."

A wall clock ticked and the lamp on the desk shone brightly, holding the darkness at bay. Outside, men's voices raised in a drinking song.

Barnes shook his head. "I know I said evidence could be planted, and it still might, but I really believed Fairley was involved."

Grant shook his head. "I'm telling you; we're looking in the wrong place."

Barnes let out a long breath. "I was sure. But I trust your instincts. They've never let us down before." He grimaced. "To tell you the truth, I wanted to believe it of Fairley. We have a rather...unfriendly history."

Seeking an explanation, Grant glanced at Jackson, but he shrugged.

The magistrate continued, "But being unwilling to be a gentleman and step back when we were both vying for the favors of a lady—a lady, I might add, who was betrothed to me—doesn't make him a traitor. It appears I allowed my judgment to be clouded."

Grant's world tilted. Barnes had been wrong; led by his own prejudice. Grant never thought he'd see the day. But at least Barnes was man enough to admit it.

"I could be wrong..." Grant began.

Barnes waved him off. "I don't think so. Deep in my mind, I had this little niggling doubt that anyone of Fairley's wealth and power and standing would risk it all for a political position, with so little to gain. But I wanted to believe any man who'd steal my girl..." He offered a tight smile. "Just to be sure, I want you to continue to dance attendance on him. Keep planting little seeds of discontent in case he, or anyone near him who might be leaving you a trail, decides to invite you to their meeting. Meanwhile, the rest of us will look for other possible leads."

Grant tugged at his cravat until the knot untied. "If it didn't happen at the house party, I don't think it will but I'll keep up the game."

Barnes rubbed his chin absently, and his eyes half closed the way they did when he went into deep thought.

Jackson toyed with his ring and glanced at Grant. "Are you in danger? If the plotters know you are working with us—"

"Nothing I can't handle. I'll let them think they have us fooled until I find out who is leaving me a breadcrumb trail. Then I'll wring them for information." He glanced at Barnes. "And if it really is Fairley, I'll wring him, too."

Even if it meant breaking Jocelyn's heart. His first duty was to England. The thought of bringing her sorrow put a weight on his shoulders. But it wouldn't come to that; Fairley was innocent and Bow Street was being played.

They discussed more about the case—what they knew and what they only thought they knew. Finally, Barnes eyed Grant. "Go home. You look like you're ready to fall out of your chair."

Jackson raised his eyebrows but Grant scowled and waved him off. "I'll watch the warehouse and see if anything shows up. If I weren't already known at Fairley's, I'd try to get hired on as a servant so I could investigate the staff as one of them."

Barnes glanced at Jackson. "You up for that?"

"Always. I'll go right now and inquire about a position."

Grant said, "Fairley's daughter will help us get you placed in the house."

Barnes steepled his fingers. "Why would she do that?"

Grant paused. There were so many ways he could answer that question, and none of them appealed. He settled with, "She appears to have developed a fondness for me."

The other two men exchanged glances of surprise. Barnes finally said, "That isn't your style."

"No, it isn't." He steered the conversation away from that topic. "I'll discuss it with her when she and her father return to London." He bade them goodnight and left before they could question him.

Outside, lamplighters set street lamps aglow like sentinels against encroaching darkness. A ship's bell clanged and dogs barked. Fog swirled around his legs. As he walked along the street, he hailed a passing cab and climbed in. Leaning back against the squabs, he closed his eyes.

He would see Jocelyn Fairley again. He didn't know whether to curse or smile. For sanity's sake, he should avoid her presence for a long time, perhaps indefinitely. But, of course, the wretched whims of fate would throw him back into her presence. A dark place in his heart actually lightened in anticipation. What a disheartening revelation. Soon he'd turn into some kind of sonnet-spouting, flower-picking, pathetic fool. Or worse, he'd waste every moment searching for signs of treachery until he crushed all hope of a future with her.

He'd tell her what he needed, bid her good evening, and walk away from temptation, from stupidity. From failure.

The following evening, he took a hackney cab to the Fairleys' house. Within minutes, he stood in the foyer awaiting Miss Fairley with anticipation and dread.

He cursed under his breath. She was a mere girl. Nothing he couldn't handle.

Silk rustled, drawing his attention. A voluptuous figure clad in a simple pink evening gown entered the foyer. Smiling, her eyes wide in surprise, she drew near.

Her animated expression, her unpretentious smile assaulted his protective armor.

"Grant Amesbury. What a lovely surprise. We will be dining shortly; won't you join us?"

"I need to speak with you." He spoke a bit more harshly than he'd intended, but the sight of her, and the thrill of awareness that shot through his veins, put him on the defensive.

Her smile faded a shade but she nodded. "Of course." She stepped closer, and her sweet, warm aroma of violet and vanilla tickled his senses. In a lowered voice, she asked, "Did you find something?"

"We want one of our Runners to pose as a house servant here."

She nodded. "Good idea. He might overhear something that only a servant would. I'll tell the head butler that we need a...what shall I tell him we need? I don't suppose he could serve as a footman, could he?"

Grant nodded. "He's done it before."

"Perfect. We lost a footman just yesterday. I'll inform the head butler I know of an experienced footman seeking employment and to give him a chance. Tell your colleague to come to the back door tomorrow. Can he bring references?"

"He can." Not that they'd be legitimate, but he'd have something convincing-looking. Barnes would see to that. "His name is Jackson."

She smiled, her expression soft. "I'm glad you knew you could trust me."

Trust. He shied away from the word. And yet, it didn't seem impossible with her.

225

"My thanks." He offered a curt bow.

"Are you sure you don't wish to dine with us? We're only having a simple family meal, but we welcome your company."

"No." Then, in an afterthought, added, "Thank you."

She stepped closer to him. A teasing light gleamed in her eyes, and she said softly, "You don't have to avoid me, you know. I won't bite you now just because we kissed."

He choked. No demure little miss here. A refreshing change, actually, except that she was probably deliberately trying to provoke him. Her lips drew his gaze, tempting, taunting.

Her smile turned wicked. "Or are you trying to refrain from dragging me to the nearest dark corner and repeating your performance?"

Her shot hit too close to home and left him with the urge to squirm. He didn't know whether to laugh out loud or scold her. Audacious girl. "Good night." He turned to leave.

"Grant."

He froze, glanced over his shoulder.

The flirt vanished and in her place stood a friend. "You can count on me. Come to me for anything you need."

He dipped his chin in a brief nod. She saw him out. Her smile imprinted in his mind and remained before his eyes all the way home. It took all his self-control not to race back there and claim another kiss to feel more alive than he had in years. Giving into that urge would make himself vulnerable to pain. He should never let down his guard in the presence of a woman. They were conniving. Deceitful. Treacherous.

Yet, none of those words stuck to Jocelyn Fairley. She was everything sweet and lovely.

Besides, he needed to stop blaming all women for the actions of one. Even his jaded mind recognized his bitterness was slowly devouring him.

Chapter 20

Jocelyn sent for the head butler immediately after dinner and informed him of her desire to hire a friend of a friend. Owens, with little choice but to heed his mistress's request, agreed. Curious about the man who worked with Grant at Bow Street, she made a point to happen along when the new footman would be shown around. A tall young man built like a prize-fighter, with dark hair and patrician features stood with the butler, listening intently at Owens giving him directions.

She paused deliberately. "You are the new footman, I presume?"

"Yes, ma'am. Jackson, at your service." He bowed.

On a whim, she said, "I am going on a brief shopping expedition this morning, Jackson. I wish for you to accompany me."

If her sudden interest in the footman surprised Owens, his years of conditioning kept his expression impassive.

Jackson bowed again. "As you wish."

Jocelyn sent a message to Aunt Ruby, inviting her to join her for a morning of shopping. If she couldn't, a maid might serve in a pinch but wouldn't really qualify as a true companion. Fortunately, Aunt Ruby replied that she needed new gloves and shoe flowers, so she would be delighted to join Jocelyn.

At the appointed time, Jocelyn donned her hat,

pelisse, and gloves, and went outside to the waiting carriage. Jackson stood nearby, resplendent in the family livery.

She smiled. "I'm impressed they found livery that fit you so well in such short time."

Looking down, he ran a hand down the front. "The housekeeper altered it for me."

"Thank you for coming with me. I know you must think it odd that I'm taking you away from the house, but I wanted to have a moment to speak with you and didn't know how to do it without appearing odd."

"I understand."

As she climbed into the carriage, she took his hand and slipped a folded paper into his palm. "A list of servants we've hired in the last year. I thought you might start with them."

"Good idea." As soon as she got settled, Jackson closed the door.

After a brief ride to Aunt Ruby's house, Jocelyn danced up the stairs and raised the door knocker, anxious to tell her aunt about everything that had occurred and to seek her advice about Grant.

Inside her aunt's house, Ruby tied on her hat. "How was the house party, dear?"

Jocelyn smiled. "Lovely. And eventful. But that's not why I'm here."

Aunt Ruby's eyes glittered. "Eventful? How promising. Do tell me all about it."

"In the carriage."

Moments later, Jocelyn and Aunt Ruby swept out the front door and into the coach outside. Jocelyn offered

229

Jackson a smile of camaraderie. He, in return, adopted the perfectly respectful mien of a footman. Jackson helped them in, closed the door, and took his perch at the back of the coach.

Inside the carriage, Ruby turned to Jocelyn expectantly. "Well?"

Jocelyn drew a breath. "First, the bad part. And it's bad." She studied her hands.

Aunt Ruby placed a hand over hers. "You can tell me."

Amid tears, Jocelyn told all about delivering the Johnson's baby, her failure, her sorrow. With an arm around her, Aunt Ruby listened. All the while, the carriage clattered over the streets.

As Jocelyn's narrative wound down, Ruby embraced her. "Oh, my sweet girl. You did nothing wrong. Some things are out of our hands."

Jocelyn took out a handkerchief. "I know, but—"

"No, sweeting, no 'but.' You did as well as any midwife or doctor. There is nothing anyone could have done about the cord. There is no blame, no failure. It just is. As your mother always used to say, 'Bad things happen. We don't have to like it.'"

Jocelyn laughed sadly. "She did used to say that."

"Now. Tell me the rest—the part about Mr. Amesbury."

"Well, I raced headlong down a flight of stairs at the ruins, and he leaped in and saved me. He got hurt—rather a frightful head injury. But he seems to be mostly recovered."

"Ah." Ruby smiled knowingly. "And now you've lost your heart to him, have you?"

Jocelyn returned her smile. "I'm afraid so, but that's not the only reason. We've talked, shared some very personal things. And he's kind to children."

"And does he return your regard?"

Jocelyn hesitated. "He seems to have some affection for me. But he's very wary."

Ruby nodded. "Closed up tighter than a drum, that one is. Consider that it might be due to his heart having been broken."

"Do you think so?"

"It could be. 'Once bitten, twice shy.'"

Jocelyn turned over that thought. The carriage swayed as it turned a corner. "I thought it was because he was in the war and saw too many terrible things."

"That could be part of it. I have heard of men feeling unworthy of love after seeing and doing acts of violence. But not everyone comes home from war broken. Everyone copes with it differently."

Sorrow for all he'd suffered ate away at her. "What do I do?"

"Prove to him that he can trust you. That will take time. And perhaps some persistence. Did he kiss you?"

A hot blush heated her face. "I kissed him first. But then, yes, he kissed me." She let out a lusty sigh. "And what a kiss. I have hardly slept since."

Ruby chuckled and squeezed her shoulder. "Men like him don't give their hearts easily, and not without good reason. You're a good reason. You just need to make sure he sees that."

The carriage rolled to a stop on Bond Street, and they turned their attention to shopping. First, they paid a visit

231

at a Glover for riding gloves and evening gloves, and then at a millinery where Aunt Ruby ordered a hat to wear with her new walking gown. Lastly, they shopped for shoe flowers and hair ribbons. Jackson followed unobtrusively behind, carrying their parcels while they added to his burden.

Inside the shop, after an apologetic glance at the Runner posing as a footman, Jocelyn selected three pairs of shoe flowers that coordinated prettily with her ballgowns. Aunt Ruby desired several of different colors.

While her aunt deliberated over the selection, Jocelyn sidled up to Jackson and leaned against the wall near him. Keeping her gaze casually flitting over the wares in the shop, she said softly, "We're almost finished. She's just getting her shoe flowers and then we'll return home so you can resume your investigation."

"Shoe flowers?"

"Ladies wear them on dancing slippers. They're pretty. And it's unseemly not to wear them, you know."

Jackson let out a small huff and shook his head. "Ladies and their fripperies."

Jocelyn smiled. "I blame it on fashion. Perhaps it's a secret agreement between fashion designers and makers of shoe flowers."

Then, with Ruby still occupied, Jocelyn brought up the main reason she'd asked Jackson to accompany her. While keeping her focus on items on a shelf nearby, she asked Jackson quietly, "How long have you known Grant Amesbury?"

"Since before we went to war."

"That long? How did you meet him?"

"We attended Cambridge together."

A new curiosity seized her about Connor Jackson, a man who worked as a Runner and yet attended the university while most men of his social class lacked money for a formal education.

But she stayed focused on learning about Grant. "Do you know what happened to him during the war?"

"No details."

She waited, but he didn't elaborate. Finally, in an enormous breach of etiquette, she said, "I don't mean to pry, but if there is anything you can tell me to help me understand him better, I'd be very grateful."

"You're going sweet on him?" He chuckled darkly. "I wish you luck. I don't think he has much use for women, beggin' your pardon, miss."

"You can drop that servants' speech with me, Jackson. But yes, at times, I think he is developing an attachment for me, but other times, he questions my motives as if I have some hidden agenda."

"Most unmarried girls do, don't they?" He grinned.

"He doesn't think I'm trying to drag him to the altar, he thinks...well, I'm not sure what the thinks, but he scrutinizes any act of kindness as if there is an evil reason behind it."

Jackson said nothing for so long, that she had almost given up on learning anything about Grant. Finally, he said, "All I know is that a woman he loved betrayed him and delivered him to the French."

All sound inside the shop and street hushed as if the entire district gasped and then held its breath. What kind of heartless creature would betray a man and hand him over to the enemy? A spy? That was no excuse for toying with his heart.

Poor Grant. No wonder he viewed women with mistrust. Fate had dealt him a brutal hand. All the shoppers suddenly seemed shallow with vain and silly purchases, ignorant of the suffering of brave men like Grant, and her brother James, who fought for freedom in lands far away.

She searched Jackson's face for more detail, but he shook his head. He either didn't know more or refused to say. In little more than a whisper she asked, "Was he a prisoner of war long?"

Jackson straightened suddenly and said to someone over Jocelyn's shoulder, "Allow me, ma'am."

Ruby had approached with several parcels. With a smile, she handed them to Jackson. Though she cast an appreciative glance at the footman, she addressed Jocelyn. "Such a pretty selection today. I could hardly make up my mind."

With effort, Jocelyn tried to hide her sorrow from her aunt by forcing a smile. "My, that's a lot of shoe flowers. How many balls are you attending this season, Aunt?"

"Oh, one never knows. Invitations arrive almost daily, you know, and it's best to be prepared. Not that I'm seeking another husband, but socializing is a nice diversion and I do so love to dance."

Jocelyn nodded and turned her face away to give herself another moment to compose her expression. After enjoying an ice at Gunter's Tea Shop, they returned home.

Inside the foyer, Jocelyn nodded at Jackson. "Thank you for taking time away from your other duties to accompany us."

Jackson touched his hat and strode away. She waved farewell to the hope that she would learn more about Grant through his associate at Bow Street. She'd have to get creative to reach Grant's protected heart.

Chapter 21

Keeping to the twilight shadows, Grant made yet another pass around all sides of the decrepit wooden warehouse looking for signs of life. All remained quiet. No one had entered or exited the building in the hours that he'd been watching the place. He tried the door but found it locked. No matter. Grant picked the lock and crept in. Birds perched in the rafters, flapping at his intrusion. A few high windows let in what was left of the fading light, revealing the leavings of what appeared to be a vagrant's abandoned camp beside a broken down desk. In one of the desk drawers, he found a copy of the rent, clearly listing Fairley as the new lessee, and a copy of a shipment of guns scheduled for tonight.

Someone had gone to a great deal of work to ensure Fairley appeared involved. Grant went back outside to await the shipment, if it ever arrived. Mist crept down the street, dampening Grant's face. A ship bell clanged and dogs barked. Carts rolled past and dockworkers whistled as they strolled. The buildings seemed to crowd together as daylight waned. Sunset faded into the haze of fog and gathering darkness.

Through the swirling mist, a feminine form sauntered down the street, passing from one pool of lamplight to another. Grant frowned. Was that Maggie? The prostitute didn't usually frequent this part of town. He tucked his hands into his pockets and strolled to her.

She straightened, and veered toward him. Her teeth flashed white in the semi-darkness.

"Maggie?" he said quietly.

"Well, well, fancy meeting ye 'ere, Mr. Smith. I hain't seen ye in days. What brings you to me side o' th' street?" She gave him an openly flirtatious smile.

"I didn't know you worked this street."

She shrugged. "Sometimes, when it gits too quiet down th' other way. Are you finally going to share yer night wit' me?" She took a provocative step closer. Did he imagine her face had gotten thinner?

"I'll share my evening taking you to Goodfellow's."

For the first time since their strange friendship began almost a year ago, she paused as if considering it. Then shook her head. "Not fer me. An' ifn ye take me there, I'll leave agin like I did 'afore." She tugged her ragged shawl around her shoulders and raised her chin in a challenge.

Perhaps her resolve was weakening and she would eventually leave the streets. With any luck, she'd do it before she caught a fatal disease.

"If you change your mind, take a cab to Mrs. Goodfellow's Institution. Tell her that Mr. Grant sent you. She'll pay the jarvey for your cab fare and she'll take you in and treat you well."

Maggie grinned triumphantly. "Mr. Grant, is it, then?"

He nodded. It was the name by which most of the Runners and street contacts he'd made knew him, so he'd left that name with the reformer as well, just in case.

"And here I thought I'd always have to call you Mr. Smith." She reached out and brushed light fingers over his hair. "You cut your hair."

For a quick, mad second, he wished it were Jocelyn touching him so intimately. She'd done it so gently, and he'd wanted her to do it far longer than she had.

Maggie giggled. "You look like a real gentleman, Mr. Grant."

Giving up on trying to rescue the light-skirt for the moment, he pointed his chin toward the warehouse where the shipment of guns was supposed to arrive, if the planted receipt were to be believed. The ramshackle building leaned against its neighbor. "Do you happen to know anything about that place?"

"Never seen no one there, at least, not th' hours I'm out. But I think someone new bought th' place. 'Bout a fortnight ago, a new lock 'ppeared on th' door. "

A fortnight ago—the time Bow Street learned of the plot, and that Fairley might be involved.

She cocked her head to the side. "Did you follow me 'ome, is that 'ow ye knew where I live?"

He scrambled to keep up. "I don't know where you live."

"Ye jes 'appened to be there last week when I saw ye?"

Oh, right, the week he'd been tailing Jocelyn, he'd also happened upon Maggie and her friend. He'd forgotten about that. "I was there on an errand, of sorts. I didn't know you lived there."

"With my friends. We share the rent." She nodded and her face clouded over.

"Is something wrong?"

She shook her head and tried to smile but sorrow showed underneath.

He peered into her thin face. "Maggie, are you in trouble?"

"Naw, jes a bit worried 'bout my friend. Ye know her— ginger hair? She's taken ill, is all."

"Has she seen a doctor?"

She let out a mirthless laugh. "Don't got no blunt fer the likes o' them."

Of course. Few people of her income level had money for an expensive doctor. "Apothecary, then?"

She nodded. "I got medicine fer 'er this mornin'."

"I hope it helps."

She quirked a sad smile. "Me, too."

"Are you working here tonight because you spent all the money on medicine and now you need money for food?"

She let out a sigh and nodded. "Me usual street ain't paying well 'nuff these days."

He reached into his pocket and withdrew half a crown. "Will this help?"

Her eyes lit up as if he'd handed her a whole bag of gold instead of a single coin. Then she took a step back and held up her hands in rejection. "Don't take no charity. I work fer me blunt." She turned an imploring gaze upon him. In the soft dusky light, she looked young and pretty and vulnerable. "Don't ye think I'm pretty, even just a little? I can please ye, I can."

"I'm not the type of man who pays for favors, and you know it."

She slumped. Nearby, a cat crept by, crouched, and sprang on a rodent. The small predator carried its meal into a hole in a nearby building. The strong always preyed upon the weak. But not if Grant could help it.

He returned his focus on the girl. "Maggie, we're friends, aren't we?"

She looked doubtfully up at him, her mouth still turned down in disappointment. "I s'pose."

"And just like you're helping your sick friend by going hungry so you can pay for her medicine, I'm helping you by paying for your food." He held out the coin to her.

She still hesitated.

He tried again. "Consider it payment for the information you gave me."

Softly, resigned, she nodded.

As she reached for his coin, he fisted his hand over it. "Buy some food and go home. Don't work tonight. Understand?"

She nodded, still resigned but with a touch of relief in her eyes. "Sure, sure, whatever ye say. Wit' this, I won't have t' work for a week."

"Good. Now be off with you."

She walked with sure steps down the street and disappeared into the gathering fog.

The clattering of wheels and the clopping of hooves announced the approach of a cart. The shipment, perhaps? Grant slunk into the shadows to watch. A cart stopped in front of the warehouse, and a swayback horse stood with its head drooped. The driver leaped down from his seat and banged on the door. No reply. He paused, then banged again. He squinted at a paper in his hands.

The driver went to the horse, a nag really, and patted its neck. "Well, Nell, this 'ere is the right place. But no one 'ere to take me delivery. What do you say about that?"

The nag whinnied.

"Lor' luv ye, yer right. I got mesself keys, I do."

Grant stepped out of the shadows and began

whistling a drinking ditty. As he reached the front door, he stopped and looked pointedly at the driver. "Ah, yer 'ere, are ye?" he said in his best Cockney.

"Aye, right on time." The driver hesitated. "I didn't know anyone was gunna be 'ere. Why'd they give me keys, then? Are ye Master Fairley?"

Grant sniggered. "Lor' luv a duck! Do Oi look like a nob to ye? No, Oi ain't Fairley. 'e's 'ome 'avin' a noice, juicy beefsteak while Oi'm out 'ere working me bones. You got me shipment, mate?"

The man nodded sympathetically and gestured to the cart. "All 'ere."

Grant helped the man hoist a large, wooden crate and carry it inside. Good thing he'd already broken in or it would have appeared suspicious if the employee had to pick the lock. They carried in several cases, staggering under the weight.

The man handed Grant a crowbar. "Wan'ter check th' goods?"

Grant took the crowbar and pried open one of the lids. Inside, nestled in straw, lay shiny new guns. As if he were doing a thorough job, he checked them all.

Grant nodded and said to the driver, "Buy ye a pint, mate?"

"Temptin', but I gotta be on me way. Oh, a'most forgot. 'ere. I s'pose I should give you these back, since you're in 'is employ." He held out the keys.

After Grant pocketed the keys, they parted. Grant waited until the cart clattered away before slipping out and locking the door. Full darkness had fallen before his replacement arrived. The Runner, Connolly, nodded in greeting as Grant crossed the street to him. Briefly, Grant filled the Runner in on the developments.

Connolly listened intently and nodded. "I'll follow anyone who shows up for the guns."

"Good man." Grant clapped him on the back. "Here are the keys to the warehouse the deliveryman gave me."

Connolly tucked them away and virtually disappeared into the shadows. Bow Street was lucky to have Runners like Connolly.

A nearby pub provided dinner, after which Grant walked a circuitous route home. In an alley, he came across a footpad robbing a terrified young buck who should have been at a gentlemen's club instead of out in the streets alone. Grant wrestled down the footpad, took his knife, and cuffed his hands before delivering him to the nearest magistrate's office. The entire encounter didn't even raise his pulse. When had such activities failed to feed his thirst for action, for teaching criminals a lesson?

Still on foot, he passed the Fairley house on his way home. Against his will, he stopped across the street. Yellow lamplight shone out of the windows, casting light onto the darkened street. Jocelyn probably enjoyed a nice after-dinner chat with her father right now, or perhaps read aloud to him or played a game, all the while bestowing those easy smiles on him. Even Jackson was in closer proximity to Jocelyn than Grant. He envied the Runner.

Grant cursed. Fool! No female was worth mooning over. Not even her. Besides, she deserved a conventional man with a whole heart who wanted a warm hearth, a quiet home, a nursery full of children, and maybe a dog for good measure—not a dark, hard-hearted scoundrel who lived in the shadows, befriended women of ill-repute, and chased down thieves.

He jammed his hands in his pockets and strode home, firmly removing from his mind a genuine lady with soft eyes and softer lips and fiery kisses. Long ago he'd vowed never to make the colossal mistake of falling in love again. He'd given his heart freely and foolishly once; fate had stabbed him through the heart.

Chapter 22

Every time Jocelyn went out or glanced outside a window, she half expected to find Grant. It was an unreasonable expectation, of course, since the only time he'd followed her was when he viewed her father as a suspect. Still, she expected to see him in the shadows. Or at her door with news that he'd discovered the conspirators. Or even with a request for help in his investigation. And in her wildest daydreams, he'd present himself to her in her parlor with a bouquet of flowers and an invitation to go with him somewhere so he could kiss her witless again.

Clearly, she was still witless.

An unbending man like Grant Amesbury pliable enough to declare himself? Not likely. Of course, she never expected him to kiss so passionately, either. Maybe he'd claim her and demand, just as forcefully, that she marry him.

His defensive words after their kiss returned to her...*nothing between us...just two lonely people sharing a kiss.*

Nonsense. No other kiss she'd experienced came close to the intimate heat she'd shared with Grant. He cared for her. Desired her. But he denied it. He either didn't trust her with his heart, no thanks to the horrible woman who betrayed him during the war, or he thought she existed too far out of his world to share it with him. Well, she would gladly go into the darkness to find him and bring him into the light. Or at least, twilight. Moonlight. Firelight.

Her lips tingled and desire curled inside her.

Good heavens, she was acting like a tart. First, she had to find a way to reach Grant and show him that they belonged together. Then she could explore these very adult longings he awoke in her.

"It's your turn, princess." Her father's voice interrupted her musings.

Jocelyn blinked and refocused on the chessboard in front of her. "Sorry," she murmured. She searched the board for a possible move that wouldn't leave one of her pieces vulnerable.

"Woolgathering?"

"I suppose."

He leaned back and waited for her to move.

She captured one of his pawns with hers. When he made no move, she glanced up at him.

He studied her with fondness shining in his eyes. "What's on your mind?"

She shrugged. "Oh, nothing much."

He smiled gently. "Out with it. Is it perhaps that young man who rescued you from the fall?"

She focused her gaze on the chessboard as heat spread over her face and neck. "How did you know?"

"You looked pretty cozy each time I saw you with him—especially when he turned pages for you at the pianoforte."

She pretended to study the chessboard without really seeing it. "Yes, I'm sure we did."

She took one of his pawns with her knight, and he took her knight with his bishop. She winced; she should have anticipated that better.

As she contemplated her next move, he broke into her thoughts again. "Pray, what, exactly, do you feel for him? Do you see him as some kind of brave rescuer now?" He leaned back in his chair.

"It's more than that. We've had some very telling conversations. He's a good man. Did you know he fought in the war?"

"Yes, I know. I called in a few favors and made some inquiries about him when he first showed up here."

"Oh." Of course her father would be cautious with gentlemen who came into contact with her. When her first suitor turned out to be a fortune hunter, Papa had grown more cautious with other suitors.

"As to his service record," Papa said, "he served heroically—earning several medals. He was a member of a special force, was captured, tortured, rescued..."

"Tortured?" She wrapped her arms around herself.

"Apparently he bears scars on more than his face. The war ended before he had recovered enough to return to the field."

She nodded to show she was listening, her interest in the game waning.

"No one knows much about him except that he keeps to himself and is rumored to aid Bow Street with specific cases from time to time."

She nodded again. "Yes, I was aware of that as well."

"And now he suddenly takes an interest in our family."

She said nothing. He waited. What could she tell him that would still keep Grant's confidence?

"I believe I have formed an attachment for him," she admitted softly, unable to confess that she loved him, not when they hadn't properly courted. "He's...different. He has great depth."

He rested his elbows on the chair arms and clasped his hands together. "My child, I would be the last man to deny any measure of happiness to a returning war hero. But you must know, some men return home so broken that they cannot give or receive love."

"I do not doubt that he has suffered much, and that he is careful with his heart. But I have seen great kindness in him—the way he helped me when I was so distraught about the Johnson baby, for one. Did you know his valet used to be a street urchin who tried to pick Grant's pocket? Instead of turning him over to the authorities, Grant gave him a job. He's unconventional, but goes around doing much good."

His eyes glittered in the lamplight. "So now he's Grant, is he?"

She smiled guiltily. "He hasn't given me leave to call him by his Christian name." But he was Grant in her thoughts.

"And you view him as a dark knight?"

She smiled that her father had chosen the same title she had. "In a way."

Her father rubbed his chin with his thumb. "Dark knights are rogues, following their own code and not always trustworthy."

"I trust him. I've seen into his heart and I know he is a man of honor."

"Does he return your esteem?"

A myriad of moments they'd shared flickered through her mind, his small touches, and his instinctive rescue of her, his tenderness when she'd been distraught over the stillborn baby, his quiet understanding when they'd spoken at the pianoforte. His indescribable kiss.

"Yes, I believe he does."

"Am I to expect a visit from him soon, then?"

She let out a sigh. "No, I think you are right that he finds it hard to give or receive love. But I hope, perhaps, I may one day earn his trust."

He said nothing more and they returned to their game. A few moves later, he called out, "Check."

Jocelyn rallied but she'd lost too many pieces and had nothing well placed. Three moves later, he placed her in checkmate.

She smiled ruefully. "Well played."

As they set up the pieces for a future game, her father said, "Do you recall that your aunt's dinner party is Friday?"

"Yes, I look forward to it." She lined her pawns up in a neat row.

"Ruby asked me if I wish to invite Lady Everett as well, but that would give her an uneven number. Shall I encourage her to invite Grant Amesbury?"

She paused. "I don't think he's very comfortable in social settings."

He continued setting up his pieces. "That matches with what I heard about him. But he seemed to do well at our house party."

"Yes," she said slowly. He'd been investigating then. Would he accept an ordinary social setting? "She can certainly invite him, but I cannot promise he will accept."

"Nor should you answer for him."

She smiled and kissed her father good night.

248

He said, "Jocelyn, most men are reluctant to let go of their independence and marry. I remember being intimidated by that prospect, but also at the daunting idea that my actions would result in the happiness or misery of the lady I was growing to love. If your Mr. Amesbury is truly the one for you, it will take some patience and persistence on your part."

"I know." She leaned on the doorframe. "I'm just not sure how to go about it without appearing overly forward. Or desperate."

"I have complete faith in you."

She went back and hugged him. "I love you, Papa."

"And I love you. Always." He held her close, the safety of his arms and the scent of his jacket transporting her back to childhood, if only for a moment.

Haunted by dreams of trying to find something elusive and always out of reach, Jocelyn woke cold and tired, despite the glorious sunny day, and with a burning need to talk to Aunt Ruby. She hurried through her morning routine and arrived on her aunt's doorstep earlier than strictly proper for a social call. She found her aunt poring over papers on her desk, her faithful dog, Max, lying at her feet.

The collie mix raised his head at Jocelyn's entrance and barked a quiet greeting.

Aunt Ruby beamed. "Good morning, sweeting."

"I hope you don't mind my coming so early."

"You know I don't."

Jocelyn leaned down and scratched Max behind the ears. "I haven't seen you in a while." Time had turned his muzzle white, but he looked at her with bright eyes and thumped his tail.

"What brings you here so early?" Aunt Ruby set down her pen and capped her inkwell.

Suddenly unsure of what to say, Jocelyn hesitated. She pretended to make a study of the sitting room and admiring the flowers in the vase.

Her aunt peered into her face. "Are you well?"

"Yes, Aunt."

"And your father?"

"Oh, yes."

Ruby nodded slowly, thoughtfully. "Chocolate is just the thing, I think—with sugar and cream?"

Jocelyn smiled. "That would be lovely, thank you."

Her aunt called for a tray and they found a spot on a gold and cream striped settee near a window where they might enjoy the beautiful spring morning in the diminutive Town garden. Max moved to lie at Aunt Ruby's feet once again.

"Now then, sweeting, tell me what is on your mind. Or shall I guess: Grant Amesbury?"

Jocelyn's words came out in a rush. "I'm in love with him."

Aunt Ruby nodded, gesturing for her to continue.

"I'm certain he returns my regard, but he is very cautious, and even denies there is anything between us."

Jocelyn told her everything except events related to the murder plot. Aunt Ruby nodded, listening without speaking. A maid entered with a tray laden with chocolate, sugar, cream, scones, and fruit.

In between sips of chocolate, Jocelyn related Grant's reaction to sounds resembling gunfire and what he told her about himself, and how the deaths of the men he'd killed haunted him. She described her kiss. Then his.

She clasped her hands in front of her. "It was the single most glorious experience of my life. Everything we shared led up that perfect moment. He was so passionate. And the heat in his eyes afterward...I cannot begin to describe it. Then it all went wrong. I might have imagined it, but for an instant, he looked almost afraid. And then it was as if he put on a mask. He backed away and he tried to tell me it was meaningless. But I don't believe him. He's just not ready to accept what is between us yet."

"Perhaps he needs time."

"And it gets worse. One of his friends told me that Grant was in love during the war but that the woman betrayed him to the French."

Aunt Ruby let out a gasp. "Oh, that poor man. So that's what it is about him. He probably views women as deceitful." She set down her cup and saucer and wrapped her arm around Jocelyn's shoulders.

Jocelyn whispered, "Papa said that after he was captured, they tortured him."

A sob broke free as Jocelyn ached for all he'd suffered. A renewed resentment arose within her for Napoleon—the greedy devil who dared call himself emperor, who'd waged war for so many years, causing such loss and pain to so many. Captivity was too good for such a monster.

Aunt Ruby sat silently, simply holding her for several

long moments. Finally she spoke gently, "Oh, sweeting, you have chosen a very hard man to love. He has many wounds that have not healed. And if he's bitter, they may not ever heal."

"I love him, all his strengths and all his hurts. I have so much love that I want to give him, if he'll only let me."

"I know. And I can't blame you. That vulnerability inside, combined with such a tough exterior, is very appealing, isn't it? And it doesn't hurt that he's so handsome." A sad playfulness touched her tone.

Jocelyn let out a half-sob, half-laugh as she pulled a handkerchief out of her reticule and dried her tears.

Ruby held her tighter. "We must make him see that he needs you and loves you."

"I don't know how." Jocelyn sighed. "He came to the house a few days ago on business but he wouldn't accept my invitation to stay for dinner. He hasn't come since. I don't know if he'll ever come back. I wish it weren't unacceptable for ladies to call upon gentlemen."

Still holding her, Aunt Ruby rested her head on Jocelyn's. "Sweeting, are you sure about him? I know why you love him but I must tell you that a relationship with him will be extremely difficult. He's like a wounded animal; he will strike and retreat at any sign of perceived danger."

"I can't help myself, Aunt. I love him, all of him. Besides, I have never backed down from a challenge."

Aunt Ruby laughed softly. "No, you certainly have not."

Max shifted positions and lay his head on his feet. Outside a bird sang with all its heart while a breeze ruffled the curtains, bringing the scent of roses climbing the wall outside the window.

"When I was thirteen," Aunt Ruby said, loosening her hold on Jocelyn. "I found a wounded dog. His fur was matted and filthy, and he was half-starved. Life had not been kind to him. He snarled and growled and wouldn't let me near him, though he was gravely injured."

Jocelyn shifted and gave her aunt her full attention.

Aunt Ruby's gaze seemed to look into the past. "My father would have put a bullet into the poor animal to end his suffering but I felt compelled to save him. I could have gone to my mother. As an experienced healer, she certainly could have helped him. But I wanted to do it myself. So I got some herbs that my mother used to help patients sleep when they were in pain, and I stuffed them inside some fresh meat. Then I took it to him and left it where he could reach it, along with some water."

Jocelyn watched her aunt, curious as to where the story would take her. Her gaze flicked to the collie dozing at her aunt's feet.

"He snarled and snapped at me as I left the food and water, and I had to leap out of his reach. I waited. He watched me, wary, and reluctant to accept my offering, but he finally lapped up the water and ate the meat. When he was too drowsy from the herbs to fight me, I cleaned and treated his wounds."

Jocelyn listened silently, absorbing the story and the emotion her aunt wove into it.

"The next day, I brought him more food and water. I returned every day. Eventually he stopped growling at me, and started wagging his tail when I came. He became my staunchest friend. When he had healed, he followed me everywhere, and guarded me so closely that my mother considered him an acceptable chaperone. He has been my friend and companion for fourteen years—one of my best sources of comfort after your uncle passed." She leaned down at patted the dog's head. He opened his eyes and thumped his tail.

"I never knew that's how you got Max," Jocelyn said.

"It was hard to win him over at first. It took a lot of time and patience and persistence, but he is worth it."

Jocelyn nodded, admiring the beautiful collie mix who'd been such a staunch friend to her aunt after her act of kindness to him. "How do I win over a man? I can't exactly put herbs in his meat."

Aunt Ruby huffed her amusement. "No, but we can invite him to our events. I suspect small, informal gatherings would be more appealing than grander affairs to a recluse like him." Aunt Ruby looked her in the eye. "It will be up to him to partake of our offering, just as Max had to decide to eat and drink what I brought him. And he'll have to choose to trust you with his heart. All you can do is prove to him you are worthy of his trust."

"Well, he did trust me with some of his past."

"Then you are on the right path." She smiled. "I am proud of you, niece. I wouldn't have thought you were brave enough to kiss him. You might have to continue to be bold to reach him. Bold and persistent."

"I know. I don't mind. He reciprocates well." She grinned unrepentantly.

Aunt Ruby gave a lusty laugh. "When I got your father's note, I sent an invitation by special messenger inviting Mr. Amesbury to tomorrow night's dinner party. And I'll put some thought into what else we can do to entice him to join our company so you can ply your charm on him. If that doesn't work, maybe I'll just hit him over the head and tell him he's an idiot if he doesn't see you for the wonderful young lady you are."

Jocelyn chuckled. "Thank you, Aunt. I appreciate your support, but I believe his poor head has been battered quite enough—he got a concussion when he saved me from falling down the stairs."

Ruby winced. "Quite right." She laid a hand on Jocelyn's shoulder and gave it a little squeeze. "I'm sorry your mother isn't here to guide you through this, sweeting, but I'm so happy that you knew you could confide in me."

"I am, too."

They put their heads together and planned several small social events that either Aunt Ruby or Jocelyn's father could use as an invitation for Grant Amesbury to join them. If he chose to decline them all, Jocelyn would have to get more creative, and less conventional, to win Grant's trust.

Chapter 23

Standing in the main room of his bachelor's rooms, Grant glared at the invitation in mixed distaste and disbelief. "I've been invited to a dinner party."

Clark laughed. "You lived through all those other social events. A dinner party won't kill you, eh?"

"Those were for a case."

"So? Pretend this is a case."

"Why?" Grant snarled.

"Food will probably be good. Pretty girls will be there."

Grant grunted. Ruby Shaw had specified that her brother, Mr. Fairley, and her niece, Jocelyn, would be present at the 'small, informal dinner aboard her boat.' As if a dinner party aboard a boat could be informal.

Jocelyn would be there. For a split-second, he toyed with temptation. No. Best to avoid her evermore. He'd cleared her father of suspicion at least in his own mind and Bow Street was exploring other leads. Grant had no further reason to associate with her. In fact, he thought of a dozen reasons why spending time in her company would be foolish, despite what Barnes would say. Besides, every member of the *ton* declined invitations once in a while.

Grant tamped down the part of him longing for another evening in Jocelyn's presence. Instead, he scribbled a note, expressing his regrets and handed it to Clark. "Take this to Mrs. Shaw."

The boy paused, eyeing Grant doubtfully. "You sure?"

Grant bristled.

Clark held up a hand. "I know it ain't my place to say, but what I heard about Miss Fairley belowstairs, and what I saw for myself, she's a right lady."

"Clark."

The boy threw up his arms. "All right, all right."

All morning, Grant wrestled with memories of Jocelyn and dreams of the future, what they might have together if he dared. Would trusting her—loving her—be an act of courage, or of supreme stupidity? One moment, thoughts of a future with her enfolded him in a warmth and contentment. The next moment, he broke out into a cold sweat.

A few hours later, a second invitation arrived. This one came from Mr. Fairley inviting him to a family dinner with no mention of boats. Grant deliberated longer. Should he? Could he?

No. Even if Jocelyn turned out to be as genuine and loving as she appeared, she needed a whole man with a whole heart.

Yet, this party would be at the Fairley residence. Barnes would want Grant to accept an opportunity to earn an invitation to the meetings. If someone close to Fairley were involved, this might give him another chance to learn the truth.

Someone knocked. A messenger handed a small note to Clark with the type of stationery Barnes favored and sealed with his stamp. Clark grew sober and handed it to Grant immediately.

Inside, heavy, angry writing scrawled across the page. *Connolly dead. Shipment gone. No leads.*

B

The news hit Grant like a fist to the gut. They'd killed the Runner he'd left to watch the warehouse and had taken the guns. Grant cursed and rubbed his eyes. Connolly. A strong life, full of purpose, snuffed out. If Grant had watched the warehouse instead of leaving the task to a Runner, would Grant now be dead? Or would his instincts have protected him? Either way, the young Connolly with the reflexes of a seasoned veteran, would be alive.

Lust for justice and vengeance ran though Grant's veins. He would punish Connolly's murderers.

The best way to punish the killers was to solve the case. He drew several steadying breaths and cleared his mind before focusing on what he knew. The assassins planned to attack the prime minister, armed with twenty-five guns, and he still had no idea when or where they intended to strike. The prime minister had three full-time body guards, but such small protection would not hold out long against at least two dozen armed men.

"Clark, I'm accepting Fairley's invitation for dinner tomorrow. And you're going with me. You can tell anyone who recognizes you that you double as a footman." He penned a note of acceptance and handed it to Clark. "Take this to the Fairley's and then hang about the kitchen. Flirt with the maids, make a negative comment about the government, and try to find Connor Jackson. If you can get a moment alone with him, let him know the shipment is gone and Connolly is dead. Tell Jackson we're running out of time. If he has any leads, he needs to act now."

Clark nodded solemnly. "I understand." He hesitated. "Can I still have tonight off?"

Grant made a dismissive wave. The boy disappeared,

258

and Grant paid a visit to Barnes. Silence and the Runner's grim faces transformed Bow Street into a funeral. Some of the Runners paced, their fists clenched with pent up energy of bloodlust, waiting for the word to wage war against whomever had killed one of their own. A few members of the mounted guard who patrolled the highways leading out of London lined the walls of main room like sentinels, clearly as thirsty for justice or revenge as Grant.

Grant waited while Barnes finished processing a stream of criminals. When the last one was taken away, still proclaiming his innocence, Barnes glanced at Grant and jerked his chin toward his office.

Inside, the magistrate removed his white wig and collapsed into a chair. "I may start having Runners go out in pairs so they can watch each other's back."

"Connolly shouldn't have needed a partner."

Barnes let out his breath and ran a hand over his face. "Tell me you have a lead."

"Not yet, but I'm having dinner with Fairley tomorrow night. I sent my boy to deliver a message and instructed him to speak to Jackson if he can. One of us will get a moment with him."

Barnes relaxed. "I can always count on you."

Grant shifted.

The magistrate eyed Grant and the light of friendship shone in his expression. "You don't owe me anything, you know."

Grant's gaze snapped to his.

A smile touched Barnes's face. "You don't need to help me out of obligation."

Silently, Grant waited for him to elaborate.

"I didn't pull you out of that chamber of horrors because I wanted you indebted to me your whole life."

"I know."

That his commanding officer had defied orders and assembled a team to rescue Grant from the French prison spoke volumes about Barnes's commitment and concern over his men, and about his loyalty as a friend. Barnes had never asked for Grant's help with the assumption that any debt was owed, but the burden weighed on Grant anyway. Besides, whatever Barnes needed usually satisfied Grant's need for danger and the thrill of the hunt—a thrill that had waned lately.

Barnes leaned forward and eyed Grant soberly. "I appreciate your help—always—but you must know that if you find that your life takes you in a new direction, a better direction, you have your freedom to take it."

"If that happens, I'll let you know." Not that it would, but his answer seemed to satisfy Barnes. Grant shut Jocelyn Fairley's face out of his mind.

"For now, let's get those cretins who killed Connolly."

Grant could have used a few more vulgar words to describe the conspirators, but refrained from voicing his thoughts. He returned home to find Clark shaking out evening coats and trousers Grant would need for the dinner party tomorrow. Grant frowned but didn't experience the same revulsion that once came with the knowledge that he'd have to dress for a dinner party. It brought his thoughts to a halt. He would explore that reaction later.

Grant peeled off his coat. "Did you speak to Jackson?"

Calmly, Clark said, "I did. He has two suspects in the

household and is investigating further. And I met a pretty maid. Calls herself Emma. But the scullery maid told me Emma has a lover and won't be interested in me." His expression turned wistful.

"Just as well. Don't let a girl get her claws into you, lad."

Clark shook his head. "I don't understand you."

"I learned years ago not to trust a female who claims to care. They all want something."

"Surely not all."

"All," Grant snapped.

Obviously Jocelyn didn't plan to lead him to an ambush, or bring some other harm to him, but sooner or later, if they continued their association, she'd want something from him that he couldn't give, and he'd let her down.

Clark's tone returned to one of deference, as if fearing he'd overstepped his bounds. "Do you want me to bring you a plate from the tavern down the way before I leave, sir?"

"Leave? Oh, right. You asked to have tonight off. No, don't bother. I'll go get something. You'll need to wear livery for the Fairley's dinner party tomorrow night."

"I've already found something and pressed it. Good night." Clark left, whistling.

Grant read the newspaper and set it down. The walls seemed to close in around him and the silence that Grant normally greeted as a friend, became stifling. He had to get out.

A gray drizzle greeted him outside. His gaze strayed toward Pall Mall and unbidden thoughts of home and

261

family came to him. A thread of desire to seek the company of his family wound through him. Perhaps a few minutes with Cole would help his gnawing emptiness. Besides, he needed to use a coach to convey him to dinner. Even Grant wasn't so far gone that he'd arrive at a dinner party, even a quiet family affair, in a smelly hack. He'd either need to rent one, or borrow a coach from Cole. It also gave him a reason to need a footman at the Fairley's dinner party. He might as well ask for a coach in person.

The butler who responded to Grant's knock actually smiled before he recovered his aplomb. "Master Grant. What a delightful surprise."

Grant spared a kind glance at the aged servant who'd been with the family for as long as he could remember. "Is my brother at home?"

"He's in his study, sir."

"I know the way." Grant strode to the study and paused outside. The same swirly pattern in the wood grain that reminded Grant of a nightmare version of the hooded Grim Reaper remained on the wooden door, much lower than Grant remembered, but still there. For an instant, Grant was a young boy standing on shaking limbs and staring at the distortions in the grain, loathe to enter and put himself in his father's presence, yet knowing that to dally would further incite the earl. The only time Grant, or any of the boys in the family, were allowed in the study was when their father commanded them to present themselves for punishment.

The ghostly voice of his brother Jason urged him, *Don't be so stubborn. You know he'll stop sooner if you'd just unbend enough to cry. After only two or three lashes, I bawl like*

262

a little girl and he stops pretty quickly. One of these days, he'll cane you so hard you won't be able to walk at all.

But at an early age, Grant developed a stubborn refusal to cry when his father caned him. Oh, he'd wept aplenty after it was over and he had climbed the highest tree, or crawled inside the old Roman grotto on the far side of the lake. But he refused to shed a single tear in the earl's presence. He wouldn't give the tyrant the satisfaction of thinking he'd broken Grant's will.

When Grant had returned home from the war to recover from the talents of his torturer, he'd paid his father a call. The old man had glanced at Grant's scarred face, nodded, and said, "Well, you lived. You always were a tough nut." That was the last time Grant paid a visit to the earl.

Still, perhaps the old bully had instilled in Grant the ability to withstand all the horrors he faced in the war. And at the hands of torturers. Not that those thoughts instilled any desire to thank the old earl.

Shattering the vision, Grant threw himself inside the room. Cole sat at the desk, every inch the Earl of Tarrington from his impeccable clothing to his signet ring, and even the Amesbury seal nearby. Cole's head bent over a stack of papers.

"You really should paint that door, you know," Grant said.

Cole lifted his gaze with raised brows and blinked rather owlishly. "You hate that pattern, too, huh?" He glanced at the door in question. "I had it sanded and painted but it still shows. I suppose I could replace the door, but honestly, I don't even notice it anymore." A lazy smile curved his mouth. "Alicia helped me create better memories in this room."

Grant let out a snort to convey exactly what he thought about wifely charms, and sat in the nearest chair, one that didn't used to be there. In fact, most of the furniture was different, as was the paneling and draperies. The colors had been changed from greens and browns to every shade of blue. Maybe Cole couldn't stand to spend time in this room until he erased a few reminders, in more than one way.

His brother sat back and toyed with his pen. "What's amiss?"

"Does something have to be amiss for me to pay a visit?"

"I don't know. I don't recall you ever doing it before unless our family was facing a crisis." Cole softened his words with a one-sided grin. "Drink?"

Grant shook his head. "Lend me the town coach?"

Cole cocked a brow. "Really?" he drawled.

"I need a reason to bring a footman to a dinner party."

Sagely, Cole nodded. "So your boy can go belowstairs and snoop for some case you're working on?"

Grant covered up his surprise with a caustic, "You aren't as thick as you seem."

"My wife would disagree." Cole grinned.

"She's not as empty-headed as most women."

"I'm speechless at your outpouring of affection and praise. What has you in such a charitable mood?"

"The fine weather."

Cole chuckled. "So, a dinner party, huh? At Fairley's again?"

"As it happens, yes."

"Is this case the only reason you're having dinner with them again?" Cole cocked his head and studied Grant's face.

"Of course," Grant answered blandly.

"Uh-huh. And it has nothing to do with his attractive daughter?"

Grant scowled. "No."

"But she's the reason they've invited you back?"

"How should I know?" Grant growled. "Maybe Fairley just likes me."

Cole's eyes twinkled. "I'm sure. People love spending time with men who have the charm and manners of a rabid dog."

"Woof. Are you going to lend me a coach or not?"

Mildly, Cole said, "I'll have the driver pick you up tomorrow night."

Grant nodded. "My thanks."

The door opened and Cole's wife, Alicia, bounded in wearing a butter-yellow gown he was pretty sure wasn't formal enough for an evening out. "Cole, darling, we—" Her gaze fell on Grant. "Oh, Grant, I didn't know you were here."

Grant inclined his head. Despite getting his brother shot a year and a half ago, the wench seemed to be making Cole happy. Grant had eventually stopped glaring at her whenever they met.

She settled into Cole's lap. "I was very surprised to see you at the Fairleys' ball a fortnight ago. Did you enjoy yourself?" she asked.

"Tolerably," Grant said.

"I like your hair cut like that." She smiled again, and Grant couldn't tell if she was mocking or patronizing him.

She turned her focus onto Cole. "You're not dressed for dinner."

"Grant and I were chatting."

"Oh?" She darted a glance at Grant and he could almost hear her say, *Grant never chats.* But instead she said, "Is something amiss?"

"No." Grant stood. "I'll leave you to your evening plans." As he passed through the doorway he glanced back.

Cole and Alicia spoke softly, their heads close together. Cole grinned and tapped the tip of Alicia's nose. She kissed him.

Grant toed the carpet as memories tumbled over him of Jocelyn's kiss. Every inch of his body craved another taste of her. But one wouldn't satisfy. He ached for dozens, hundreds, a lifetime.

But kisses and embraces were no guarantee of happiness.

As he turned to head toward the front door, his sister-in-law's voice stopped him. "Grant, won't you please stay for dinner? It's just a simple family meal, no company and nothing fancy."

His refusal died on his lips. He could eat at a pub, alone. Or he could go home and eat, alone. His solitary lifestyle had become suffocating, rather than liberating.

He eyed her. "I might be bad for your appetite."

Cole watched him as if trying to discover Grant's meaning, but Alicia smiled. "You always provide stimulating conversation, and that's good for the appetite."

"Stimulating?" Grant raised his brows.

"I find it stimulating dodging the verbal blows you aim at women in general."

Grant almost smiled. His sisters-in-law, all three of

them, had proven they were remarkably human. He glanced down at his clothing. "I'm not changing."

Her smile widened. "I think you already have, a little."

Grant chose not to comment on that cryptic comment. "I accept."

Cole practically gaped at him for a moment until he recovered his aplomb. "Excellent."

"I'll make sure another plate is set for dinner." Alicia breezed past him as she left the room.

They had a surprisingly enjoyable evening, and the food certainly surpassed the fare Grant usually ate. By the end of the night, which lasted far longer than he would have suspected, he wondered why he hadn't accepted more dinner invitations from his brothers. Of course, they'd stopped inviting him years ago.

Perhaps Grant should adjust his aloof demeanor enough to allow the occasional family gathering that didn't include crises like murder attempts, funerals, hangings, or weddings.

As he departed, Cole clapped Grant on the shoulder. "Stop by any time. You don't need an invitation."

Gratitude almost choked him until he could only mumble, "Thanks."

The evening of the Fairley dinner party arrived and Grant glared at his reflection. A true gentleman glared back—clothes, hair carefully styled, a perfectly tied cravat— a real slave to fashion. Only his expression and the scar running the length of his cheek resembled the real Grant.

His two worlds, his real self and his cover for the investigation, fought against each other. He couldn't seem to bring Jocelyn's world and his world to the same place.

Dressed in footman livery, Clark called from the open door, "A fancy coach is here."

Grant tucked a compact pistol into the flat pocket he'd had sewn into the inside of his tailcoat, and a knife into a sheath under his sleeve. "Do you know what to do?"

"Flirt with every maid and help Jackson find someone with a reason to off the nobs up at the top."

"But don't be too obvious."

Clark returned and stuck his head in, frowning. "Don't insult me."

Grant smirked. The boy had been hanging around him too long. "Then, at evening's end, you go fetch the coachman."

Outside, Grant settled inside the town coach. An uncommonly clear night revealed a half moon peeking over the rooftops, giving off almost as much light as the lamps along the roads. The coach turned into Mayfair and arrived in front of the Fairleys' house.

Grant allowed Clark to open his door, although he chafed at the ridiculous idea of being waited on this way. Clark trotted around the side of the house to the servant's entrance, and the coach drove away.

At the front door, Grant's courage cracked. A social event. With Jocelyn's family. A quiver of excitement and dread ran through him. But this was for a case. While Grant tried to appear to enjoy himself, Clark would be downstairs keeping a watch on the servants and offering his aid to Jackson. Grant shored up his determination and lifted the brass knocker.

The butler, Owens, took Grant's hat and gloves, "Good evening, Mr. Amesbury. Please follow me, sir."

In the drawing room, closed off to create a more intimate setting, Jocelyn stood next to a round table, leaning over a bouquet of flowers. Her delicious figure filled out her blue gown nicely, and a smile curved her lips—lips that had awakened a yearning within him for more pleasure, lips that breathed new life into his dying soul.

That yearning returned full force, spreading over him like heat from a blazing hearth. As she straightened, her gaze fell on him, and her smile turned warm, intimate. The longing for her, for more of her smiles, more of her kisses, more of her attention, multiplied.

Grant swallowed. This was a bad idea. Spending more time in Jocelyn's company would only weaken his resolve to stay a bachelor, to stay sane, to stay safe—and to protect her from the pain he'd surely cause her. What demon had possessed him to think he could put himself in her presence and escape unscathed?

Chapter 24

Standing in the drawing room Jocelyn stared at Grant, stunned by her awareness of his presence. A half-frown turned down his mouth, a now-familiar defensive move. If only she could get him alone and kiss him again, maybe she could break through to the passionate man underneath all those barriers. Maybe she could coax him to smile.

"Mr. Amesbury," Owens announced.

Her father turned from his conversation with Lady Everett. "Ah, Mr. Amesbury, welcome. I believe you've met Lady Everett, and my sister, Mrs. Shaw."

"Yes, sir." Grant nodded to them. "Good evening."

"And my son, Jonathan, who is home for a brief visit."

Standing in the corner, Jonathan stared at Grant. Apparently he either didn't remember or didn't want to meet the man who'd found him in such a disgraceful state of drunkenness. At least the boy wasn't three sheets to the wind this evening. He stood on steady feet, and the eyes through which he regarded Grant were clear, but guarded.

"Mr. Fairley." Grant crossed the room and greeted the lad as if he were an adult.

"Apparently I owe you my thanks," Jonathan said, still wary.

Grant waved it off. "Not necessary."

Standing at Grant's elbow, Jocelyn supplied, "Jonathan is attending Oxford."

"Which college?" Grant asked.

"Brasenose," came Jonathan's reply.

Grant nodded as if he didn't find the one word answers impertinent. "Do you row?"

Jonathan softened. "I do. Did you attend Oxford?"

"No, we are a Cambridge family, and I left for the war before getting my degree."

Jocelyn watched his expression but no emotion revealed itself. Grant had been young, too young, to face such violence. Not that a man of any age should face that kind of horror. She resisted the urge to take his hand.

Jonathan's eyes lit. "You fought in the war? Which branch?"

"Army."

"Which battles were you in?"

"Many." Grant glanced at Jocelyn with sort of a desperate plea.

She smiled chidingly, "Jonathan, why don't you tell us about that professor you said was so fascinating?"

Jonathan's shoulders slumped and his mouth set into a mulish line. "Not fascinating. Just entertaining because he's so easy to distract."

Mr. Dawson strode in. "Good evening, all. Forgive my tardiness."

"Not at all," Papa said.

The late arrival greeted everyone, and they enjoyed a few moments of small talk. Grant remained silent and alert as if he expected them to start a fight or ask him questions he did not wish to answer.

When Owens announced dinner, Papa led the way with the radiant Lady Everett. Mr. Dawson walked with Aunt Ruby, and Grant offered his arm to Jocelyn. Jonathan

271

strode in alone. Grant's tension from his arm vibrated through her gloves to her skin. The urge to hold him close, assure him he was safe from the demons that haunted him, zinged through her.

He glanced at her inquiringly. She slowed her steps. Eyeing her expectantly, he matched her until they fell behind the others.

"I'm glad you came," she said softly. "I didn't think you would."

He opened his mouth but closed it without speaking. A brief twitch in his brows told her all she needed to know; he was here because of the case, not because of her. Disappointment stung her, but she rallied. She must stay focused. Persistent and bold. She would win him over eventually.

She moistened her lips. "Jackson wants to speak with you. He will meet us in the conservatory after dinner. Aunt Ruby will accompany us as a chaperone, but she will withdraw briefly. We can speak candidly then."

"Why would she do that?"

"She doesn't know we need to speak with Jackson, only that I want a few moments alone with you. I think she is trying to make a match of us." She tried to keep her tone lighthearted as she told her half-truth and snuck a glance.

His forehead creased in a poorly suppressed wince. Doubt edged in, doubt that his passionate kiss had been filled with the first seedlings of love. It might have been momentary lust. No. She must not doubt. She loved him enough to believe they had a future together, even if he didn't see it yet or was too afraid.

She offered him a consolatory smile. "Don't worry.

I'm not trying to trap you into something you don't want."
Only convince him that he wanted her in his life.

He stared hard at her, but she focused straight ahead.
As they reached the table, he held her chair out for her,
and she made a production of sitting and removing her
gloves.

Jonathan behaved himself, acting and speaking like a
gentleman. Papa and Lady Everett spoke often, sharing
glances of admiration. Jocelyn nodded. Lady Everett could
make him happy. And she'd be a fine prime minister's wife.
Aunt Ruby and Mr. Dawson's friendly banter had everyone
laughing. Even Grant unbent enough to smile—not a true
smile, but his mouth pulled to one side. Occasionally,
Grant offered intelligent comments as topics ranged from
hunting to the upcoming coronation of King George IV
scheduled for July, followed by the biggest, most
ostentatious celebration the country had ever known.
Eventually, the subject of reformers arose.

Mr. Dawson said, "While I applaud the concept, I
don't believe people really change. Most don't truly wish
to."

Ruby shook her head. "But we cannot see into a
person's heart. It's not our duty to judge, only offer
opportunities to help people who want to improve their
lives. I think people like this Mrs. Goodfellow and her
institution are to be commended. Indeed, I make annual
contributions to her cause."

"That's all fine and good, but would you really allow
a former pickpocket into your home? What's to stop him
from stealing all the silver, or your jewels?" Dawson tapped
the tabletop to emphasize his point.

Ruby gazed back at him almost primly, "If that person

has reformed, his own will and conscience would stop him."

Dawson nodded. "Perhaps. But rounding up every street urchin, thief, and disreputable person and delivering them to the doors of such institutions will not ensure that a transformation has occurred in their hearts."

"No," Ruby said slowly. "I suppose not."

Grant spoke. "A person has to be willing to go, has to want to reform, or they won't change. They will return to the life they know." The grimness in his tone suggested he knew this truth first-hand. Another layer around the mystery of Grant Amesbury became visible. "But without reformers, those who want to change will have no help, no opportunity."

Lady Everett said soberly. "I agree that no matter how much we want someone to improve themselves, he or she will not do it unless they truly desire it. Some, it seems, simply cannot help themselves."

Papa put a hand over hers in understanding of whatever private sorrow Lady Everett suffered.

Grant fingered the stem of his wineglass. "So it seems."

Of whom did he speak? Grant had saved a street urchin who became a loyal friend under the guise of a servant. But as someone who dealt with criminals on a regular basis, Grant must see humanity at its worst. Still, just as Jocelyn reached out to Katie's sister and to her father's tenants, Grant also reached out to the downtrodden, lifting those who allowed it. A new kinship for him dawned.

The silence that followed seemed to draw too much

attention to Grant, who valued his privacy. As Jocelyn scrambled for a change of subject, her aunt came to the rescue.

Aunt Ruby waved her hand in the air. "I hear Princess Caroline, er, Queen Caroline, is returning from the continent soon."

Jocelyn shot a grateful smile at her aunt for effectively redirecting the conversation as they debated on whether the king would receive his scandalous desire to annul his marriage and strip the queen of her title before she'd even been crowned.

As everyone finished dessert, Jocelyn stood. "Ladies."

As the hostess in lieu of a mother, Jocelyn walked confidently to the drawing room to leave the gentlemen to their port and after-dinner conversation. A servant had built up the fire against an uncommonly cool night.

Lady Everett took a seat nearest the fire and smiled at Jocelyn. "It was a lovely dinner, Jocelyn. You are always an outstanding hostess. Your future husband will be a lucky man, in more than one way."

"How kind of you to say." Jocelyn admired Lady Everett for a moment. In the soft firelight, her skin took on a delicate, flawless quality. But more appealing was that glow of inner radiance and that elegant, gentle demeanor she bore. "As will yours."

Lady Everett smiled almost girlishly. "I'm not certain I am to remarry. I hope to, but..." she shrugged delicately.

So, Papa had not yet made his intentions clear. But at least their relationship appeared to be progressing at an encouraging rate.

Aunt Ruby spoke. "I always knew our Jocelyn would

grow up to be a fine young lady. Will you provide a little music for us, sweeting?"

"Of course." Whether Ruby wanted to speak with Lady Everett alone, or she merely wanted Jocelyn to display her talent as a pianist when the gentlemen, including Grant, joined them, Jocelyn could not say. But she went to the pianoforte and played from memory, beginning with her favorite sonatas, to provide soft background music that allowed easy conversation.

The two older ladies spoke, getting on famously. Of course, Lady Everett had been a family friend for years. Did Aunt Ruby know of Papa's interest in the lady?

As Jocelyn concluded a prelude by Mozart, the gentlemen arrived. The very air vibrated with Grant's presence. Jocelyn ended with a flourish and joined the others.

With uneven numbers, whist would be impractical, so Papa suggested a game of Twenty Questions. Everyone took a turn. Sitting close enough to set her nerves all aflutter, yet properly distant, Grant consumed her attention to the point where Jocelyn could hardly hazard a logical question to ask. Some of the others posed such outlandish questions that by the end of the game, everyone was laughing—except Grant, of course, but he actually smiled a few times—on both sides of his mouth. Oh, my, he was handsome when he shook off his darkness enough to smile. Aunt Ruby noticed and exchanged an appreciative glance with Jocelyn each time.

"I believe you are the last person to have a turn, Mr. Amesbury," Papa said.

Grant paused. "Very well. I have it."

"Is it an animal?" Lady Everett asked.

The game continued, with Grant answering only yes or no, a supremely smug light glinting his eyes, until Mr. Dawson guessed, "A book."

Grant's mouth curved and he appeared almost sheepish. "A book."

Jocelyn's mouth dropped open. A book seemed such an ordinary word for Grant to have chosen. "Really?"

He tilted his head. "Disappointed?"

"No, I just...do you like to read?"

"I do."

"I do too, I just didn't think that'd be a pastime you'd enjoy."

"I like libraries, too." Pleasure gleamed in his eyes.

That moment in the library, when he'd stood so close to her on the ladder, came to her mind. His magnetic pull had been so strong, she'd almost leaned in and kissed him.

But he liked to read? He hadn't mentioned that. She couldn't picture him doing anything as ordinary as reading. But then, she'd never imagined he'd kiss with such knee-weakening passion. Her imagination drifted out of the room. She visualized another parlor, small and peopled by only Grant and Jocelyn. She sat on a settee, reading, next to a fire. Closely enough for their thighs to touch, Grant also read. But after only a few minutes, he grabbed her, dragged her onto his lap, and proceeded to remind her how well he kissed.

"A shark!" Jonathan exclaimed.

Jocelyn started. Horrified that her daydream might have revealed itself on her expression, she darted a look at Grant. He watched her, the corners of his mouth lifted, and an air of smugness surrounded him. She pressed a hand over her cheeks. He knew somehow.

At the game's conclusion, Aunt Ruby stood. "I believe I'll take a turn about the room. Or better yet, I haven't visited the conservatory in some time. Do mother's orchids still grow there?" she asked Papa.

"They do." He raised his brows.

Ruby nodded. "Jocelyn, Mr. Amesbury, do accompany me. My mother used to grow an extensive herb garden outside, mostly for healing purposes, but in the conservatory she cultivated orchids the likes you've probably never seen. Do allow me to show them to you."

"I'd like to see them," Grant murmured as he rose and offered an arm to both Jocelyn and Aunt Ruby.

They left together while the others started a new game. Aunt Ruby glanced at Grant as if planning her next move, but she chatted with them in apparent ease. Jocelyn hoped her aunt's zealousness to help Jocelyn earn Grant's affection would not have the opposite effect.

The conservatory housed not only a plethora of exotic and native plants, but a variety of birds as well. While many conservatories resembled parlors with a few plants, Grandmother's conservatory always reminded Jocelyn of a garden with a gathering of furniture in the middle. Overhead, the night sky provided a backdrop to the warm, botanical paradise. Jocelyn's instructions to light the lamps in this seldom-used area had been carried out, with candles and lanterns casting a soft glow over the flora gracing the room.

Aunt Ruby gestured to a raised planter filled with orchids of every color. "Here are the orchids. Aren't they lovely? Pity they don't smell as good as they look."

Grant made a show of examining them as if he were truly interested. "Yes, it is."

"Oh, dear," Ruby said. "I just remembered something I must see to. You two stay here and enjoy yourselves. I'll be back in a while—I'll leave the door open, of course—and then we can all return to the others together." With a conspiratorial smile at Jocelyn, Aunt Ruby hurried away.

Jocelyn pressed a hand to her forehead. "Oh, dear, that wasn't very subtle, was it?"

"You did warn me." One corner of Grant's mouth lifted and amusement lightened his silvery eyes.

"With any luck, Jackson will be here soon."

"I'm already here, miss." Jackson stepped out from behind an orange tree.

Grant's transformation was so profound that it left Jocelyn breathless. He all but snapped to attention, his expression grim, and his eyes so alert, they seemed to leap from his face. He glanced at Jocelyn, but instead of bidding her give him a moment's privacy to speak with Jackson, he asked, "What have you found?"

"A few possibilities. A footman leaves in the middle of the night every few days. I tried to follow him last night but lost him. Also, a stable boy seems to hate everyone who isn't a member of the working class. They are my best leads so far. I'm also keeping an eye on a parlor maid. She's skittish and has snuck out on occasion, too."

Jocelyn mutely watched the exchange. If only she could do something to help. But these smart, capable men obviously knew their roles.

Jackson continued, "Your boy Clark flirted with the parlor maid, but she told him she'd already given her heart to another. Gave him a right good set down. It's possible she sneaks out to visit her lover."

Grant nodded. "Do you need assistance?"

"No. I'll follow her the next time she leaves." The Runner paused. "I heard about Connolly."

Both men sobered. Jocelyn waited for the men to explain, but they seemed lost in their private thoughts.

Looking from one man to the other, Jocelyn asked, "Connolly?"

"A Runner," Grant told her. "He was guarding the warehouse to see who came for the guns."

Jocelyn frowned. "The shipment of rifles? You mean the ones shown on the receipt you found?"

Soberly, Grant nodded. "Connolly was assigned to follow whomever showed up for them." His jaw clenched. "They killed him."

Gasping, Jocelyn put a hand over her mouth. If there had been any doubt that the plot was real and deadly, this removed it.

Jackson glanced at Jocelyn. "Your butler suspects me of something. He keeps showing up to check on my work."

Jocelyn considered how she could help. Speaking to the butler about leaving the new footman alone would only appear strange and even more suspicious. "Let me know if you need to go somewhere you aren't assigned to be, and I'll make an excuse to send you there."

Jackson nodded. Grant's gaze rested on her, his mouth relaxing and his eyes softening. Little thrills of pleasure ran down her spine at his expression.

"I'd best get back," Jackson said, "before anyone realizes I've spent longer than necessary lighting the lamps in here." He exchanged glances with Grant before nodding to Jocelyn and leaving.

One of the canaries allowed to fly free in the room landed on a lemon tree behind Grant and began trilling. Nearby, a fountain kept up a steady song of splashes. The noises and smells of London seemed far distant inside this miniature paradise. Orange blossoms mingled with jasmine and other exotic flowers to create a bouquet of fragrances.

Jocelyn drew in a long breath. "I should come in here more often. It's really beautiful."

Grant nodded, his focus intense on her face, a small, half smile tugging at his mouth. Her lips ached to press against his, and her whole being craved to enfold herself in his arms.

Trying to keep her voice steady she asked, "What is it?"

"You surprise me, sometimes."

"Only sometimes?"

That half smile deepened into a three-quarter smile. She almost fanned herself.

With what she could only describe as a sultry quality to his voice, he said, "Quite a lot, actually."

"Do you care to explain?" She admired the shape of his mouth, the silver light in his eyes, the breadth of his shoulders.

"This case. You've been surprisingly calm. Helpful, even."

She couldn't resist twitting him a little. "For a girl, you mean?"

That three-quarter smile almost reached a whole smile. "For a girl."

"I'm happy to have been a pleasant surprise." She grinned at him and he almost, almost grinned in return. Her legs wobbled.

Grant almost grinning. She'd have to record this in her journal. Maybe it could become a state holiday, although she'd rather throw herself into his arms to celebrate.

In order to keep from collapsing into a pile of mush at his feet, she gestured to the center of the room where several chairs had been drawn together to make a conversation area. "Shall we sit?"

But he didn't move. He remained fixed, focused on her. His gaze lowered to her mouth. Warm tingles buzzed across her lips and spread outward. He leaned toward her. She lifted her chin, silently pleading, *kiss me. Kiss me. Kiss me.*

With no apparent reason, his eyes sharpened, all traces of that magical grin vanishing like the pop of a bubble. "Is she supposed to return and 'catch' us together?"

Such suspicions shouldn't have surprised her, but it hit like a slap. Her breath rushed out of her, leaving her deflated. "No." Her tone came out wounded, defensive, but she didn't care. "This isn't some kind of ruse to claim you've compromised me so I can try to force you to marry me."

"Good. Because it won't work," he snapped.

She turned away to hide the hot tears burning her eyes. "Why must you always assume the worst of me?" She knew the answer but hoped he'd tell her something, anything. It might take the sting out of his words.

"Women always want something—money, power, status." More quietly, he added, "Revenge."

She turned around. "Always?"

For a second, uncertainty revealed itself in his expression and posture. After a quick, military turn, he strode to the fountain and stood staring at it, clenching and unclenching his fists.

Jocelyn stood at a crossroads with so many possible paths toward hidden destinations that she simply couldn't choose one, especially with her heart wounded from his latest attack. His was a self-defensive maneuver, of course, but it smarted.

Or did he truly find her so undesirable that he couldn't bear to consider a life with her?

Chapter 25

Grant stared at the ripples on the surface of a decorative pool below a fountain in the Fairleys' conservatory, battling against the magnetic pull of Jocelyn, the comfort she offered, her sweetness, her obvious affection.

Why would a nice girl—a genuinely unselfish, kind girl—care about a cynical, fragmented man like him? Either she truly didn't care, and he had not yet discovered her motive, or she was naïve enough to believe he had anything to offer her. A name. The status of marriage. Which, despite appearances, might be all she sought. Surely she hadn't run out of suitors and had set her sights on him out of desperation.

His very core screamed at him to return to her and immerse himself in the beauty and grandeur of a woman's touch. Of her touch.

But he'd sworn off such pleasures.

He strode to the far end of the room by the door leading back to the house proper. Perhaps a little distance would diminish temptation. It didn't work. Jocelyn's intake of breath shot through Grant, even at this distance.

Her skirt rustled as she approached. Very softly she said, "What happened to you? Who hurt you?"

He squeezed his eyes shut, grappling with the desire to tell her everything, to show her his wounds. She might pour her healing warmth over them. Was he willing to take that chance? Then what?

A gentle hand rested on his back, so warm, so long-absent, so welcome. "Who was she?"

Clenching his fists, he focused on trying to breathe.

Her voice rippled over him. "You can tell me anything. Your secrets are safe with me."

Safe. With her. Was he really?

She stepped closer and lay her head and both hands against his back. The warmth created an ache deep in his core, and yet, also as a calming sensation.

"Tell me," she whispered. "What was her name?"

"Isabel." He swallowed. The name burned his tongue.

"Where did you meet Isabel?"

He clenched his jaw but it came out anyway. "At an officers' ball."

"Was she beautiful?"

"She was more than beautiful—she was mysterious and exotic. Every man there practically threw themselves at her feet, but she smiled at me. Me."

He bit back the rest. The story remained his alone. No one knew the full truth. To share that much of his soul with another person, especially a woman, left him shaking in fear. Fear. Grant, who'd faced war and death and danger, who scrabbled in the streets with cutthroats, was afraid. Afraid of revealing his worst pain.

Jocelyn stepped closer until the full length of her rested against his back. Heat seeped into him, bringing with it a sensation he could only identify as safety. Fear dissolved. He wasn't alone. Years of loneliness faded away as if it had guided him to this single moment.

Still softly, as if applying balm on an open wound, she asked, "What happened at the ball with Isabel?"

He sawed his teeth together, but the story fought its

way out and the last of his defenses crumbled. "We danced and laughed and I thought I'd never found a more perfect woman. I wanted to marry her that night, but as a lieutenant, I didn't have much financially to offer her. And I didn't want to rush her." A caustic laugh tore out of his core. "I begged her to let me see her again, and she agreed. I courted her, and her father—or at least the man I thought was her father—encouraged me. I thought she loved me. And I loved her. I was happier than I'd ever been." Again came a laugh—harsh, angry, wounded.

He took several breaths but they failed to still the rage shaking him. The lush foliage around them filled with life and beauty mocked the cold bleakness inside him as memories stabbed at him, turning every tender, passionate moment in Isabel's arms to the sinister lies they had been. But she'd appeared to love him so convincingly, that even when he sifted through the memories, seeking clues, none appeared. Either she'd been perfectly focused on her role of seductress to devastate his heart and soul before she led him to his death, or he was completely unlovable.

Jocelyn's arms wound around his waist as she held him from behind. He rested his arms on top of hers and found his voice again.

"One day, she asked me to meet her in the woods that night. I thought she'd prepared another lover's bower. I was so giddy I could hardly think. I got permission to go on a personal errand and left. Alone." Whistling and practically skipping his way to meet her, he'd been so sure of himself, so sure of her love. "She was waiting for me. With friends."

Men stepped out of the shadows to beat him nearly

senseless while she watched, smiling coldly. Isabel's beautiful face, twisted in hatred, haunted his memory. Even then, he couldn't believe she'd used him, couldn't believe she'd betrayed him—worse, couldn't believe she'd lied about loving him.

He swallowed. "After they overpowered me, she leaned over and said, 'This is for my father, General Lavier.' Lavier was a target I'd eliminated two months prior to that. She'd hunted me down to take revenge. But killing me wasn't enough; she had to destroy me first by cutting out my heart as effectively as if she'd used a knife."

He stopped, overcome by memory, by the desolation that arose each time he thought of it. Jocelyn stood motionless against his back, her arms around him, her head resting on him, sniffling softly in the silence.

"She cut my face with her father's ring. They dragged me off to prison and delivered me to their torturer..." Devastated by Isabel's duplicity, sickened by the knowledge that she had never loved him, he'd nearly succumbed to the welcome embrace of death. He tried to swallow but choked. "If Barnes hadn't disobeyed orders to search for me, I would have died there."

Finally, Jocelyn spoke, her voice rough with emotion. "I'm so sorry, Grant." She shuddered.

Footsteps neared, along with loud, off-key humming. "Jocelyn, sweeting," Jocelyn's aunt, Mrs. Shaw called out.

Jocelyn stepped away and turned her back, wiping her cheeks.

"We should get back to the others now." Mrs. Shaw pushed the door open the rest of the way and entered, beaming. Her smile dropped as her gaze flitted between them. She reached for Jocelyn but dropped her hand.

Grappling to restore his composure, Grant refused to look at Jocelyn. Swiftly, he rebuilt his casual façade to eliminate traces of any undesirable emotion. He offered Mrs. Shaw a tight smile. "Yes, we should."

Aunt Ruby's gaze darted between Grant and Jocelyn, her expression collapsing as if years' worth of planning had failed. "Is everything all right?"

"Fine. We should return." He held an arm out to Jocelyn. "Miss Fairley?"

Still facing away, Jocelyn drew a shuddering breath and turned, her expression serene but her gaze focused on the floor. Her hand rested on his arm so lightly that he glanced down to be sure it was actually there.

In silence they left the room. In silence, they walked along the corridor. In silence, they returned to the drawing room. During that long walk, Grant almost cursed out loud. He'd revealed the most personal part of himself. No one needed to know that much about him. He'd be less vulnerable if he were naked. Every muscle screamed at him to run, to escape, to find safety in solitude.

Clark hovered nearby and Grant gestured to him. "Send for my coach."

As the boy rushed off, Grant escorted the ladies to the drawing room and strode directly to the host. With each step, he forced all those memories back into their prison and locked the doors.

He approached Mr. Fairley who was still engrossed in the game. "Sir, thank you for the invitation. Good night."

Fairley turned to him in surprise. "Leaving so soon?"

"Yes, sir. But I...enjoyed myself this evening." And then it hit him; he truly enjoyed dinner with the Fairleys, surprisingly so. "I appreciate your hospitality."

Fairley stood and offered a handshake. "Then I bid you good night. I hope you will call upon us again in the future. You are always welcome here." Warmth and sincerity rang in both his eyes and his expression.

This man was no murderer. If Grant had any doubt, the certainty hit him now.

"Thank you, sir." Grant sketched a bow. Though his muscles bunched to run, to make a quick escape, he bowed to Jocelyn. "Good night, Miss Fairley."

All the blue in her eyes resembled shattered marbles. "Good night, Mr. Amesbury."

He collected his coat and hat, and strode as evenly as possible to his waiting coach. Outside, a crow took flight. Perfect. That's all he needed, a little morbid mood-setting and he was ripe for a stupid gothic. He must be the brooding hero. Only he was no hero.

As Clark opened the coach door, he said, "I found out that one of the footmen Jackson caught leaving was just going to visit his mother who is ill. He goes to see her twice a week and takes her medicine. And the pretty maid he wondered about? When she sneaks out it's to meet her lover. He'll follow her the next time she leaves, just to be sure. So that really only leaves the stable boy as a possible suspect. Jackson will keep a closer eye on him."

Grant nodded, only half listening. Jackson would send a full report to Barnes so Grant didn't need details. What he did need was a good stiff drink. Or to go bang his head against a wall. Repeatedly.

Cole might know what to say. Loathe as he was to accept Cole's advice, perhaps that was exactly what Grant needed. Besides, his brother had a well-stocked wine cellar.

"Take me to Tarrington House," he called up to the driver.

"Yes, sir."

Grant stared out of the coach windows, but the darkness, broken only by the occasional lamp, created a mirror. He eyed his reflection. His mother wouldn't have recognized him. Oh he looked more like her son in his present clothing and with his new haircut than he had in years, but everything else about him had changed. The scar. The darkness in him. The attitude he'd adopted toward the world in general and women in particular—until recently. Even the way he moved.

Would she be saddened by his changes?

Inside Cole's house, the butler informed him that the earl and countess were out but were expected to return soon. Grant wandered to the drawing room. A harp stood in the corner. The pianoforte sat in the other. He ambled to the pianoforte and ran his fingers along the keys. Memories of lessons ran through his mind, the way his mother's eyes shone when he played. Then, a new image, one of sitting next to Jocelyn as she played, the comfort of her closeness edged into his thoughts.

She'd listened to him as he described his reaction to loud noises, as he'd confessed his acts of violence. She never withdrew, or shuddered, or expressed revulsion. She simply accepted him, his darkness. She'd even held him, from behind so he could accept her touch, as he revealed all the horror of Isabel's betrayal. But now. Now, he felt revealed, exposed, defenseless.

He strode to a sideboard table and poured himself a port.

Cole's voice rang out from the foyer. "He's here?"

Grant turned as Cole appeared wearing full evening wear and dancing shoes.

"Grant." Cole crossed the room and poured himself a cherry brandy. Then settling in a leather armchair, he eyed Grant. "Sit."

Grant drained his glass, refilled it, and sat. "Thank you for the use of your coach and driver."

Cole waved it off. "I have more than one, you know. Any of them are at your disposal."

Sinking into a chair, Grant sifted through possible ways to discuss his thoughts, casting off everything that came to mind.

"She's gotten to you, hasn't she?" Cole's remarkably gentle voice drew his focus.

Grant went still.

"She's a fine woman, Grant. And yes, love was scary and it made me feel extremely vulnerable. But it's worth it. The more deeply you love her, the more deeply you let her in, the happier you'll be."

A terrifying concept, but he'd experienced a taste of what Cole said. Since Grant had started a habit of speaking openly, a sickness he hoped would cure itself soon, he voiced his deepest fear. "But what if I can't make her happy? What if I don't have enough to give her?"

"Give her what you can and trust her to accept you as you are. Then, the next day, give her more."

Grant studied his hands, turning over the possibilities. Did he dare? He stood. "It's late."

"Can I offer you a ride home?"

Shaking his head, he said, "Walking helps me think."

"Good night."

Within moments, Grant collected Clark and started the walk home. Whistling, Clark trotted along next to him. As they turned a corner, someone moved in the shadows. Grant stepped in front of Clark, putting his hand out to keep the boy behind him. He reached for the pistol he'd tucked into the inside pocket of his evening coat. The shadowy figure stepped into the circle of lamplight and took on a feminine form. Maggie.

Glaring, he approached her. "I thought you said my half crown was enough that you wouldn't have to work for a week."

She bit her lip provocatively and smiled. "I'm waiting for you, Mr. Grant. Oooh." She eyed his clothing. "Why Mr. Grant, yer all dressed up like a fine gentleman. Shall I pretend I'm a fine ladybird, savin' meself for ye?"

Clark's curiosity about the girl almost burned a hole in the side of Grant's head, but he ignored the boy. "The offer stands. I'll bring you to Mrs. Goodfellow's."

"I'm not going there."

"Didn't she treat you well?"

"She was kind. But I ain't goin' t' work fer no rich man in 'is house."

"Why, Maggie?"

She let out a sound of derision, and then turned it into a bitter laugh. "'Cause I jes love what I do now. And I won't stop until I've had ye." She touched his arm, stepped closely and put a hand on his chest. She lifted her chin up. "Kiss me, and I'll give you a little taste of what I have for you."

292

Wordlessly, he shook his head.

She whispered, her eye imploring, "I'll please ye, I will."

He whispered, "No."

"I'll make a special for ye, only five bob."

He touched the side of her cheek. "I'll give you fifty bob if you let me take you to Mrs. Goodfellow's. And stay there until you get a job."

"Fifty?"

Grant peered down into her young, but world-weary face. "Fifty."

She chewed her lip.

He gripped both of her thin shoulders. "Did you used to work in a big house, Maggie?"

She nodded.

"Did the man of the house hurt you?"

Head lowered, she nodded again. Grant suppressed a savage urge to hunt down that man and tear him apart. He kept his voice as steady and gentle as possible. "So you left? And now you let other men hurt you like that?"

Defensively, she said, "I tried to find another job but I 'ad no references. I tried to work in a shop but they all turned me 'way. I got so 'ungry and I didn't know what to do. A gentleman offered to take me 'ome and...it wasn't so bad—better than when the master...." She trailed off, swallowed, and continued. "The gentleman, 'e fed me and gave me money so I could eat th' next day. It's easier than workin' my fingers to nubs all day and getting chilblains, all the while knowin' come nighttime, the master might..." Her face crumpled.

Fisting his hands, Grant held onto his rising temper

293

and focused his energy on sifting through possible solutions. "What were your assignments at the big house?"

"Lots o' stuff—washin', cleanin', but mostly I was the cook's assistant. I can cook—I'm right good at it."

Grant glanced at Clark who stared at him with open-mouthed shock. "Cook for me, Maggie. I usually eat at a pub, but there is a small kitchen in my rooms. I'll hire you. But no more whoring, do you understand? I'll dismiss you if you do."

She opened and closed her mouth. Then, seemed to draw herself up. "Yes. I understand. I will serve only you—not other men, too."

Firmly, Grant said, "I am only asking you to cook for me. Nothing else."

She studied him warily but nodded. "Sure, sure." She shrugged. "I already offered meself to you anyway so if you change your mind, I've no right to complain."

"I won't change my mind. You're safe with me. Come." He tugged her elbow and started walking.

She went willingly with him. Every few steps, she turned a searching gaze his way. Moments later, she said, "I thankee."

He shook his head at the absurdity of fate. "First pickpockets, now prostitutes."

"Sir?"

He gestured to Clark who followed, smiling. "This is Clark. He works for me, too. Clark, Maggie—our new cook." He looked Clark in the eye sternly. "Don't even think about touching her."

"I understand." Clark gave Maggie a toothy smile.

She nodded in return. Grant went home with his

ragtag entourage. He couldn't save them all, but he'd saved these two. For now.

They stopped by Maggie's room, which she shared with two other girls, so she could get her personal items. Grant gave her an advance on her salary so she could pay her share of the rent for the rest of the month and give her former roommates more money to pay for medicine, not that it would matter. No doubt her friend ailed with the kind of fatal disease that often claimed women of their profession. Grant waited outside the room while she gathered her things and said goodbye to her friends.

When they arrived at Grant's apartments, Maggie gazed around in open-mouthed appreciation. "Ye really are a fine gentleman, ain't ye?"

Grant glanced around his rooms, sparse by Amesbury standards, certainly small and plain compared to the house in Cornwall he'd bought when he'd first returned to England, but luxurious to someone like Maggie. "Don't tell anyone."

She nodded. "Is your name really Mr. Grant?"

"Grant Amesbury."

"I always knew there was more to ye than you let on, Mr. Grant Amesbury."

With Clark's help, he got Maggie settled in a nook behind the kitchen. What would Jocelyn think if she knew he'd just brought home a prostitute to be his cook? He almost smiled. Actually, she'd probably approve, considering the help he'd seen her give to the downtrodden.

As Grant stripped off his clothes to prepare for bed, Clark entered. "Message for you. Urgent. From Jackson."

Jackson's surprisingly elegant handwriting penned a brief note:

Suspect found. Will interrogate tonight at Fairley's.

J

Jackson was not going to do it alone, not after what happened to Connolly. Without hesitating, Grant donned his usual garb for prowling the streets, including a few lengths of cord, a pair of handcuffs, two loaded handguns, and three knives. As he strode through the main room, Maggie peeked out. Her hair was down and recently brushed giving her an innocent, childlike appearance.

He paused at the door. "Don't mind me, Maggie. I come and at go at all hours."

She nodded as she perused his change of attire. "Yes, sir."

"If you need anything, call Clark. Keep the door locked and don't leave these rooms."

"Yes, sir."

He left his apartments and headed to Mayfair. To Fairley's house. Where Jocelyn would be. The thought of seeing her again sent fissions of excitement and dread straight to his heart where they swirled like a hurricane. With any luck, she'd be asleep in her bed, unaware of Grant and the ever increasing difficulty of resisting her. And the embarrassment of having bared his soul.

Chapter 26

Jocelyn tossed and turned in her bed, alternating hot, then cold, then simply uncomfortable. Her bed seemed too lumpy, her pillow too full, the fire too bright. Wind in the eaves howled like ghosts. Images of Grant haunted her. She visualized him as a young officer, his silvery eyes bright with hope and love, in the arms of a beautiful siren who'd seduced him only to crush his heart before delivering him to torturers.

Tears streamed down her cheeks, wetting her pillow. How he must have suffered, knowing the woman he loved—probably the only woman he'd ever loved—had used him, lied to him, betrayed him.

Finally, Jocelyn tossed back the counterpane and got out of bed. She fell to her knees at her bedside and prayed. She had begun praying more since her mother's death, seeking and finding comfort. But tonight she poured out her desires as never before, asking that Grant's wounded heart would be healed and that he would find peace. Most of all, she asked for guidance in knowing how to help him and reach him and love him in a way he could accept.

No inspiration came to her but at least her mind quieted. She sat staring at the red coals.

He'd been so quiet after he'd told her about Isabel. And he'd left immediately. Did he still wrestle with the painful memories of the past? Or did he regret sharing such a personal part of himself with her?

She dried her tears. It was late and she needed to

sleep, but despite her weariness of soul, sleep remained far away. Perhaps tea would help. Normally, she'd ring for her maid, but it was the middle of the night. No one deserved to be dragged out of bed at that hour.

For modesty's sake, she donned a dressing gown over her shift. Taking up a candle, she stepped into slippers and stole downstairs. The pale candlelight illuminated a lone footman dozing in a chair. He started at her approach and scrambled to his feet but she waved him off.

Inside the kitchen, a stove sat cold, but a few embers still glowed in the hearth. Within minutes, she'd stirred the fire and nestled a cup of water amid the tiny flames. She settled at a wooden table in a corner of the kitchen to wait for the water to heat.

A step outside caught her attention. The kitchen door swung open and a figure entered, closing the door softly behind.

"Who's there?" Jocelyn called out softly.

A feminine yelp broke the stillness. "Oi! You scared me."

Jocelyn stood and held her candle aloft to see better. One of the parlor maids, Emma, stood with her hands crossed over her chest and gasping.

The pretty girl stared back at her with wide eyes. "Miss Fairley?"

"Emma? What are you doing out at this hour?"

The girl cast a frantic glance behind her. "I...I was jes...ah..."

"The truth now, and be quick about it."

For a second, so quickly that she might have imagined it, pure loathing crossed the girl's features. Then her expression dissolved into true fear. "Oh, please, miss, don't sack me. I was out...er...visiting a friend."

"A friend. In the middle of the night."

The girl wrung her hands together. "Yes, miss."

Jocelyn wrapped her dressing gown more tightly around herself and folded her arms. "A man," she guessed. "A lover, then."

"Yes, miss." She took a few steps toward Jocelyn, her gaze pleading and her hands clasped together. "Please, please. I need the work. He wants to marry me, but we don't have the money. Soon, though. We've both been trying ever so hard to save what we can. Please don't send me away in disgrace."

The butler and the head housekeeper had no qualms about dismissing servants caught engaging in unseemly behavior. Yet Jocelyn couldn't bring herself to do it. To create a moment to think, she gestured to the other chair. "Please sit."

The maid obeyed and sat with her head lowered. With a cloth, Jocelyn fished her tin cup out of the burning embers and added loose tea leaves, sugar and milk.

As she set her cup on a table and took her seat, Jocelyn asked. "What is his name?"

The maid hesitated. "Peter."

"How do you know Peter loves you, really loves you?"

The girl raised her head. "He tells me. And sometimes he brings me little gifts, not much, mind you, but now and again a flower, a bit of sweets, a ribbon for my hair—little tokens that tell me he thinks of me. He took me to the country to meet his ma. But most of all, I feel it in his touch, in his kiss."

Jocelyn absently stirred her tea. Grant never brought

her anything, never spoke words of love. However, he protected her from a cutthroat and saved her from a fall. He touched her tenderly. He'd even opened up to her about deeply personal hurts. His kiss...well, if that wasn't an outpouring of something very close to love, she couldn't imagine what it was. But it wasn't enough. He didn't want her in his life. Not yet. Perhaps not ever.

"I envy you," she whispered.

"Me? You have everything."

Jocelyn's vision blurred and cleared and blurred again. "I would give it all—if only he loved me." If only he cared enough to love her, enough to want her as his wife.

The truth of her words shot through her. She wanted to be his wife. She longed to share his life with him, to be at his side for all he would face, his joys and sorrows, and all that tormented him. If only he would allow her in. But tonight he'd shared a very personal part of himself with her. He'd taken a huge step. That was a good sign, right?

Emma murmured, "Love is all I'd 'oped it would be, but it don't fill an empty belly."

The girl's frankness took Jocelyn by surprise. She countered, "Food doesn't fill an empty heart."

"No, I s'pose not." Emma's mouth worked. "Am I sacked?"

"No, you may keep your job. I won't say anything as long as you continue to be discreet."

"Yes, miss. Thank you, miss." But for some reason, she didn't appear as grateful as Jocelyn would have expected.

"Good night, Emma."

"Good night, miss."

Jocelyn sat in the darkened kitchen and drank her tea alone with her thoughts.

Once again, a step at the door roused her. The door swung open. This time, a large, distinctly male figure entered. He stopped short.

"Miss Fairley?" Connor Jackson came closer. "What are you doing up so late?"

"Drinking tea and having chats with maids."

"Emma White. What did she tell you?"

"She was meeting her lover."

"Yes, but not how you think—at least, not tonight. They, and several other people went into the basement of a pub for some kind of meeting."

"What kind of meeting?"

"I don't know yet. But I mean to find out—they were very secretive about it. I'll question her." He drew nearer, as grim and determined an expression as she'd ever seen on Grant.

"Now? It's the middle of the night."

"Now. We must act quickly if we are to save lives."

"You think this meeting means she is involved?"

"Maybe. All I know is that someone in your household is helping to plant evidence to implicate your father. And her activities tonight are suspicious."

"Very well. I'll go with you."

"That's not necessary. I've already sent for aid in case she puts up a fight."

At that moment, a soft tap sounded before the door swung open. A familiar figure crept in, silent as a shadow.

Jocelyn leaped to her feet. "Grant."

He stopped short. "What are you doing up?"

"Having a cup of tea." She folded her arms, trying to appear as if having tea in the kitchen wearing her shift and dressing gown, and engaging in conversation with a Bow Street Runner in the wee hours of the night were everyday occurrences.

Grant and Jackson exchanged glances. "The maid is spirited," Jackson said. "She'll probably put up a fight."

"Lead the way."

"No." Jocelyn put herself in their path. "I will not allow two men to barge into her room and terrorize her."

Grant's eyes narrowed and his tone was defensive. "We aren't going to terrorize her—just ask her some questions. She's less likely to run or fight if she sees she's outnumbered."

"Fine. But I will talk to her first. You two wait in the corridor and block her path if she tries to run." She stood with her hands fisted at her sides, ready to do battle if she must.

Grant's mouth softened in...admiration? He glanced at Jackson who shrugged.

"Agreed," Grant said. He picked up the candle burning on the table and gestured for her to proceed him.

Leading the way up the servants' stairs to the maids' rooms, Jocelyn glanced ruefully down at her dressing gown and pushed self-consciously at her hair. If only she'd had some inkling of the company she'd keep tonight, she certainly would have gotten dressed and tied back her hair. Of course, Grant had seen her clad thusly once before so her state of *dishabille* wouldn't be new to him.

Close on her heels, Grant held the candle up so its light would illuminate the stairs well enough to navigate them. His breathing sent tingles down her spine. Her nerve endings reached toward him, urging her to turn and throw her arms around him and kiss him until he responded with that same urgent hunger she'd discovered in him. Her lips burned at the memory.

At the top of the stairs, she strode down the corridor and took the attic stairs to the maids' rooms. Though most young ladies never ventured to the servants' quarters, Jocelyn had explored every inch of both of her houses when she was a youth, and she knew the way well. The air got progressively colder as she climbed, but by the time she reached the top, her leg muscles had warmed in exertion.

In the rough, wooden corridor, she hesitated. Which room was Emma's? There. A faint glimmer of light between the cracks of the door and frame. Before she took a step, Grant gestured to the same door. Nodding, she took the candle from Grant. He met her gaze. The steadiness in his eyes reassured her. She could talk to the maid, coax her into telling the truth about where she'd been and what she knew. With a quick gesture for the men to stay back, she proceeded forward.

She knocked softly. "Emma? I must speak with you."

The parlor maid opened the door and peered out. "Miss?" Her face creased in alarm. She probably assumed Jocelyn had changed her mind about dismissing her and had come to tell her she was throwing her out on the streets.

"Emma, I need your help," Jocelyn said barely above a whisper so as not to wake the other maids sharing her room, nor those sleeping nearby.

Emma glanced behind her before she stepped out into the corridor and closed the door. "Yes, miss?"

Aware of the thin walls, Jocelyn whispered, "Someone has accused my father of being involved in some kind of terrible conspiracy."

The maid's expression turned instantly guarded. "Oh."

Her mien confirmed Grant and Jackson's suspicions about her. But if Jocelyn could appeal to her humanity, get her to help them, they might avoid a great deal of unpleasantness. "I'm trying to prove that he's innocent before the authorities take action. I love my father very much. He's a good man. You know that, don't you?"

"Er, yes, miss."

"He has a reputation for treating those in his employ well, doesn't he?"

She blinked. "I s'pose."

"We think someone who works in this house has been placing documents where an investigator could find them to make it appear as if my father is involved in a murder plot. Have you seen anyone do something suspicious?"

"Er, no. Sorry miss, but I must be up early. We can talk later, can't we?"

Irritation wove through Jocelyn. She'd caught Emma out with her lover, forgiven her instead of sacking her, and now Emma attempted to dismiss her?

Firmly she said, "No, it can't wait. Someone followed you. They saw you and a young man go into a meeting at a pub—a meeting where others were not invited."

Emma's mouth opened and closed and she shifted from one foot to another. "Oh, that." She offered a sickly smile. "That was jes some friends tossin' back a few drinks."

"It's a group of people who plan to assassinate the prime minister, and you're helping them."

Pure fear twisted the maid's expression. With a leap, she rushed toward the stairs and pushed Jocelyn so hard that she stumbled and fell. Scuffling and a cry of alarm came from behind her. Jocelyn glanced back. At the top of the stairs, Grant and Jackson had a hold of Emma. She kicked and fought in a tumble of limbs as the two men tried to subdue her.

"Don't hurt her!" Jocelyn cried out as she climbed to her feet.

The moment she uttered the words, shame wagged its finger at her. Grant and Jackson were not brutes who'd hurt a woman. She should not have insulted their honor. The maid got off a few good punches but they finally captured all her pummeling limbs and held her fast, clearly trying to treat their captive as gently as possible.

Emma bucked and twisted one last time as if to test her captors before she finally relaxed. She stared at the three of them with open hatred.

Nearby doors opened and faces peered out. Jocelyn turned to them. "Return to bed. All is well." To the men, she said, "Let's continue this in my father's study. Perhaps it's time to tell him what's really going on."

As Grant and Jackson hauled the angry, silent prisoner down the stairs to the study, Jocelyn tapped on her father's bedroom door. "Papa?"

Dressed in only his shirt and trousers, he peered out. A lone lamp burned in the room behind him. At least she hadn't awakened him. "Jocelyn? What's amiss?"

"Trouble. Please come with me to the study." She headed to the stairway.

He caught up with her. "What's this all about?"

"Bow Street has uncovered a conspiracy to murder the

prime minister. The conspirators have named you the leader, and have even gone so far as to place evidence in the house that implicates you. It appears one of the parlor maids, Emma White, is involved. Grant Amesbury and a Bow Street Runner have her in the study and are questioning her."

Her father said nothing for a moment. Then, "How long have you known about this?"

"I learned of it a few days after the House Party began."

"And Grant Amesbury. He's been investigating me all this time?"

"From the beginning."

He let out his breath. "The scoundrel. He's been using you to get to me."

The words hit too close to the mark. Still, Grant had never led her on, had never made any pretenses about how he felt. He even denied his feelings now.

"He never used me or pretended to court me. He did try to ingratiate himself to you so he could learn if you were truly involved in a murder plot. But he is satisfied you are innocent."

He glanced at her. "You seem to be taking this very well."

"His reasons for befriending our family do not change my feelings for him. I knew the truth before I gave him my heart."

"You never saw fit to tell me about this conspiracy or Amesbury's intentions?"

"I gave my word I'd say nothing."

He stopped walking and turned to her, leveling a stern

gaze on her. "Never keep secrets of this kind from me, Jocelyn. This is dangerous business. You might have been hurt."

She touched his arm, gave it a squeeze. "Grant would never allow me to be harmed."

"What else have you kept from me?"

"Nothing, I give you my word."

After a deep, probing stare, he gave her a rough embrace. "I don't know what I'd do if you ever got hurt." Without waiting for a reply, he resumed their pace, until they reached his study.

"I'm not tellin' ye," Emma's voice rang out. She sat gripping the arms of a chair, glaring at the men.

Papa stopped up short at the scene.

Jocelyn gestured. "Papa, meet Connor Jackson, a Bow Street Runner."

Jackson's gaze flicked to her father and he nodded.

Her father glanced at her in mild reprimand. "New footman, huh?"

She offered an apologetic smile. "He has been watching the servants, searching for suspicious behavior. The only way to really do that was to be one of them."

Grant walked behind Emma's chair and leaned in over her shoulder. "How did you know I was part of the investigation?"

She folded her arms. "I have nothin' to say."

"So you left evidence for him to find which would further implicate Mr. Fairley?" Jackson asked.

She pretended to examine her fingernails.

Her father strode to Emma and stood over her. Grant and Jackson backed off a few steps as he glowered down at the girl.

"Is it true? You've been leaving evidence here to convince the authorities I was plotting against the prime minister?"

She studied the floor.

"Why would you betray your employer in such a terrible way?"

No reply.

Papa continued, "It would have meant my execution. That means nothing to you?"

She let out a scoff and dropped the accent she'd used as a servant. "Yer jes 'nother stuff'd shirt."

Jocelyn's hand itched to slap her. "He is a good man, innocent of any crime. How can you be so cold?"

Raw hostility rolled off the girl. "Ye rich nobs care 'bout nothin' 'cept yer fancy clothes and fancy parties while mos' o' England goes cold and 'ungry. Well, we 'ave a right to a good life, too."

"Who is involved in the plot?" Grant asked, still pacing behind the girl.

Emma clamped her mouth shut.

A calculating glint brightened Grant's eyes as he glanced at Jackson. "Do you know where her lover lives?"

"Yes, I do." Jackson said as if he found delight in his word. "I followed her there."

Grant rounded the chair and stood in front of Emma with his arms folded. "Good. Let's go rough him up a bit, get him to talk."

"No!" Emma said.

"We have no qualms about getting reluctant prisoners to tell us what they know." Grant's eyes took on an unholy glint.

Jocelyn shivered. Was he bluffing or in earnest?

"No!" Emma pleaded, all traces of insolence gone. "Don't 'urt him. He's not really involved—jes 'elpin' 'em wit a few things. Peter's not gonna to shoot anyone."

"Where are they going to try to kill the prime minister?"

Her chest heaved. "Promise to leave my Peter ou' o' it."

Grant got into her face. "I promise not to beat him to death while he's chained and helpless. That's all you get from me."

Still she hesitated.

Jocelyn watched the scene with the same fascinated horror one watches a carriage accident.

"This is pointless," Jackson said to Grant. "Let's go get him. Between the two of us, we'll get him to tell us everything." Jackson pulled out a knife and started fingering it.

The savagery in his expression sent a chill through Jocelyn. Dealing with the dregs of society must take its toll. Either he bluffed like a master or he truly enjoyed his work.

"No!" Emma let out a sob. "I'll tell you." She sniffed. "They're goin' to shoot th' prime minister and cabinet members when they 'ave supper tomorrow night."

Jocelyn's blood rushed out of her head with a roar. Sickened at the sight of such calculating hatred, such ruthlessness to destroy innocent lives, Jocelyn hugged herself.

Jackson choked.

"What?" Grant said, his face pale. "The entire cabinet, too?"

309

"Where?" Jackson demanded.

"I don't know," Emma said. "All I know is that the Freedom Fighters will storm th' room and shoot ever'one."

"Freedom Fighters?" Papa asked.

Emma hugged herself. "That's what they call themselves. They wanna new gover'ment—to 'ave the freedom t' get educated and 'ave proper jobs."

For a moment, Jocelyn's resolve cracked. Those desires were understandable. But their approach would never grant them their wishes. And it was so ruthless, so terrible.

"Who is their leader?" Grant demanded.

"I don' know," Emma said. "I don't get invited t' official meetin's; I only went wit' Peter to meet with his contacts. They said it was 'appenin' tomorrow night, but I don' know where."

Jackson let out an expletive that burned Jocelyn's ears. She cringed. Jackson glanced at her. "My apologies, miss."

Grant said, "We can find out where easily enough now that we know it will be at a dinner party tomorrow night. The Secret Service will know the prime minister's schedule. Or we can wring it out of Peter, which would be more fun." His dark glee mirrored Jackson's a moment ago. Surely he was bluffing, just as he'd been bluffing when he grabbed her in her father's study.

Jackson seized Emma by the elbow and hauled her to her feet. "It's irons for you."

Emma's eyes opened wide. "If you take me away, Peter'll know some'in's wrong. I'm s'posed to meet 'im tomorrow. If I don't, 'e'll suspect their plan's revealed."

"That's all right. You can stay in gaol tonight. I'll come for you in time to take you to meet him."

She lunged out of the chair and almost made it to the door when Grant caught her. From behind her, he pinned her arms with his. She struggled against him and finally gave up with a cry of fury. Grant, to his credit, held her firmly but never roughed her up unnecessarily.

Jackson fished a small pair of shackles out of his pocket and fastened her hands behind her back. While Grant held onto one of Emma's elbows, Jackson turned to Papa.

"Mr. Fairley, I regret any difficulty all of this may have caused you."

Papa regarded him steadily. "Give my regards to Richard Barnes." His mouth curved in a faint smile. "We were old friends once but..." He shrugged. "I'm sure he had no difficulty believing the worst of me."

Grant's expression turned pensive.

Jackson spoke, "Sir, it wasn't Barnes's idea. A criminal I arrested named you as the head of the conspiracy. He said you planned it as a way to ensure you became the new prime minister."

Papa thought that over and ran a hand over his hair. "That softens the blow. But if he didn't hold a grudge, well, he might have been less likely to believe the word of a criminal." He shook his head. "I don't want the position that badly, I assure you."

"We know, sir," Grant said.

Jackson glanced at Grant. "Meet me at the Brown Bear?"

Grant nodded.

While Jackson took Emma away, silence descended upon the room, as stifling as a dense fog. Jocelyn collapsed in a nearby armchair. Aunt Ruby, no doubt, would call for some chocolate. But all Jocelyn wanted was to throw her arms around Grant and burrow against him, buoy herself with his strength.

Standing in the middle of the room, Grant drew himself up and faced her father. "Sir, I—"

Papa waved him off. "It's all right, son. I know you were following orders, or something of the like." But his expression remained troubled.

"That's exactly what I was doing." Grant paused. "Sir, Barnes had good reason to suspect you. Not only did an informant name you as the leader of the conspiracy, but when I searched your study, I found a partially burned piece of paper with the words rifles and prime minister and meeting written on it—probably another clue Emma placed. And then, when I approached you outside the Palace of Westminster, I saw someone put a note in your pocket, so I picked your pocket and found mention of a meeting."

Jocelyn almost asked about that. But maybe she didn't want to know where Grant learned to pick pockets.

Papa frowned. "I remember that day. Someone nearly ran me over. Then you appeared, and that night, I found a strange note in my coat pocket. I had no idea how it got there or what it meant."

Grant nodded. "He must have known I was watching you and placed it for me to find. Brilliant, actually, the way he made it look so discreet."

312

"Upon my word." Papa looked thunderstruck. "They've been planning this for weeks." He ran a hand over his face.

Sitting next to her father, Jocelyn said, "In spite of the clues Emma and others placed, Grant investigated diligently and became convinced you were innocent. It is to his credit that he was so thorough. He cleared you even when Bow Street believed you guilty."

"I know." Papa glanced at Jocelyn. "I know." He stood and offered his hand to Grant. "England is in good hands with people like you watching over her."

"Sir, for what it's worth to you, I think you'd make an excellent prime minister." Grant shook his hand. He cast a quick glance at Jocelyn and headed toward the door.

She leaped to her feet. "I'll see you out." She all but raced after Grant.

Grant walked with long, swift strides toward the door. Jocelyn had to trot to keep up with him. Stiffly, he said, "You don't have to see me out."

"I want to."

At the front door, he turned. His grim expression softened. "You did well tonight. Admirably so."

She smiled hesitantly. Now that her father was truly safe, and the authorities knew how to protect the government leaders, her heart lightened so much that she just had to tease him a little. "I'm glad I was on hand. You wouldn't really have hurt Emma even if I hadn't been there, would you?"

He reared back, scowling. "Of course not. She was unarmed and half my size. And I've never harmed a woman, even those who deserve it." His scowl faded.

"Except when I attacked you. Threatened you. I..." His usual scowl faded and true remorse took its place.

Softly she said, "You didn't hurt me."

"I manhandled you and threatened you. I felt so guilty about that—I've never done that before." The confession seemed to take him by surprise.

Smiling, she stepped closer. "I know."

"I'm sorry."

"I know. And I only brought up Emma because I like ruffling you a little. You're so tough, and you pretend you despise everyone. But you have a true code of honor, a defender of the weak and innocent, and even women."

A half smile toyed about his lips. "I'm beginning to think you are neither weak nor innocent."

She looked him straight in the eye. "I'm innocent of having designs on you."

"None?"

"Only if you would call wanting to show you that I have grown..." she moistened her lips. Did she dare confess her love to him? She recalled her battle cry; bold and determined. "Only if you believe that I have grown to care for you, and hoping you have grown to care for me, is a design." She leveled a steady gaze at him. "You can trust me. I wish I could prove that to you."

An expression she could only describe as shattered overcame him. He swallowed. A long moment passed between them. Alternating vulnerability and helpless anger shadowed his silver-gray eyes. He touched her cheek with more gentleness than she thought he possessed, yet another layer to his complexity.

His fingers traced a little path down the side of her face. Warm tingles trailed after his touch.

His hand fell away. "I have nothing to offer you." He left.

With head bowed, she stood hugging herself. Her heart shriveled like a plant long denied water. The only moisture she craved was an outpouring of Grant's love. Even a trickle of acceptance and affection would suffice.

But his heart was a sealed well.

Chapter 27

Grant caught up to Jackson at the Brown Bear, the pub across the street from the Bow Street office where they held criminals arrested after-hours to await their hearing with the magistrate in the morning.

Jackson chained Emma White with the others and left her under the watchful eyes of the guards. Her bravado drained out of her and she slumped against the wall like limp cabbage.

"You ready to go get this Peter?" Grant said.

"No!" Emma wailed.

Jackson grinned darkly. "Let's go."

They headed through the streets on foot, reveling in the thrill of the hunt. Grant's senses sharpened, magnifying the scuttling of rodents, clanging of bells, horses' hooves, voices, laughter, dogs barking, cats hunting, and other sounds and sights of London at night. A member of the Night Watch followed their progress until they passed out of sight.

At a ramshackle row of dwellings, Jackson confidently led the way to a door. They crouched, guns at the ready, listening. All remained still. Voices murmured next door, but no sound or light emanated from the place they watched.

Jackson moved in a blur, smashing through the door. Grant darted in behind him. A cry of alarm sounded from the corner of the room. In a broken down bedframe, a figure struggled against entangling bedcovers. Grant and Jackson stood over him.

Grant cocked his gun. "Peter, I presume?"

The occupant let out an expletive. "Emma squealed, did she?"

"Only after considerable pressure. How did you know?"

Peter's cockney was so strong that Grant had to translate in his head. "I told her my name was Peter."

"Would you rather we call you by a different name?"

A pause. "No, Peter'll do."

Jackson took up the conversation. "Well, Peter. Would you like to get dressed first or shall we haul you down to Bow Street in your skin?"

Another pause. "I'll get dressed."

They waited, guns still ready while "Peter" drew on clothing.

Jackson's voice broke the silence. "We know about the conspiracy to assassinate the prime minister and his cabinet, and we know it's tomorrow night when they meet for dinner."

"I don't know nothin'," came Peter's reply.

"Who else is involved?"

A soft laugh. "I'm not so weak."

He made a lunge. Grant leaped, knocking him to the floor and landing on the man's back. They grappled for a moment, but Grant twisted Peter's hands behind his back and fastened them with handcuffs.

Jackson leveled his gun at their prisoner. "Try that again and I'll blow off your head." An empty threat, really, since they needed information.

Peter made a final twisting struggle but with his hands pinned, and Grant sitting on his back, he was powerless.

Grant got off Peter. "Sit up. We're going to have a little chat."

Glaring the whole time, Peter twisted around until he sat upright. Grant searched through the room until he found a flint box and lit the lone candle. The flickering candlelight cast distorted shadows throughout the room, illuminating a surprisingly young man with wild hair.

"Your Emma is in our custody," Grant said. "What happens to her is entirely up to you. She doesn't seem to know much. You can set her free by confirming that her involvement never went beyond placing a few scraps of paper for me to find. And if you provide us with the names of your co-conspirators, you might only face deportation rather than execution." Not that Grant had the power to carry out such promises, but this Peter might not know that.

"And if I don't?"

"She will hang along with the rest of you."

Peter laughed mockingly. "I don't know nothing. And even if I did, I wouldn't tell the likes of you."

"Even at the peril of your life? And hers?"

"She's nothing to me."

"Liar." But Grant wasn't so sure. The man showed no concern for his lover. Still, he might be bluffing.

Again came the mocking laugh. An idea came to Grant. He grabbed him and hauled him to his feet. "Maybe a day or two in gaol will loosen your tongue."

With Grant manhandling the prisoner, and Jackson keeping his gun ready, they took the prisoner to the upper floor of the Brown Bear pub.

"Peter!" Emma cried. "I was so worried 'bout ye."

"You stupid wench," Peter snarled. "You told them."

"No, I ..." she trailed off, clearly hurt by the verbal attack. "I told them nuthin'."

Grant decided to play them against each other. "She told us it was tomorrow night," he said helpfully. "When the cabinet has dinner together."

Fury twisted Peter's face until he resembled a gargoyle. "You witch! Shut your trap!"

Her eyes filled with tears. "But they said they'd 'urt ye. I was only tryin' t' protect you. I didn't tell 'em what time or 'ow the Freedom Fighters was gonna to do it—"

"Stop talking!" He lunged for Emma and kicked her where she sat, chained and defenseless.

She screamed. Grant leaped onto him and dragged the twisting, kicking beast off the helpless girl.

As Jackson and one of the guards dragged him off and chained him to the wall, Grant checked the girl. She sobbed openly and her face was already starting to swell.

Grant stared at her in mingled disgust and pity. "Why would you protect a scoundrel like him?"

"I...I love 'im. 'e loves me." But it came out sounding like a question.

Peter strained against his shackles. "I never loved ye, ye stupid twit."

Shock and disbelief crumpled Emma's face. Pity overcame Grant for the girl who'd been duped. How well he understood that kind of pain. A new fury for this Peter boiled in Grant's gut.

"But, you..." She let out a sob. "Peter?"

He rolled his eyes and sat shaking his head.

Her chest heaved as she gasped and tears formed in her eyes. "Ye...ye lied to me? I gave ye ever'thin'..."

"Should've killed you to keep you quiet."

She recoiled. Agony crumpled her face. Everyone in the room fell silent.

Bitter rage took over her features. Through quickly-swelling eyes, she looked at Grant and said in slow, deliberate, perfect Queen's English, "I want to make a deal."

Grant exchanged glances with Jackson. Though technically only a magistrate could make those kinds of deals, Barnes would likely go along with Grant's recommendation. He crouched next to her. "What do you propose?"

"I go free. Completely. The rest of them hang."

"Only if what you know is valuable enough."

"The main conspirators' names are George Smith—"

Peter's expression of disbelief turned to terror. "Emma, shut yer trap!"

She sat calm and still, un-intimidated by the screams of rage from her former lover. "John Hamilton. Frances Martin. And Peter's real name is Joseph Carter."

"Emma!"

Still speaking clearly, her accent genteel, Emma said, "Joe Carter is not just the person who learned where the cabinet would be having dinner, he's one of the main leaders of the Freedom Fighters." She shot Peter—Joseph Carter—a sneer of triumph. "I'm not as foolish as you think, *Peter*. I keep my ears open."

Grant almost quoted the famous line by Congreve, *Heaven has no rage like love to hatred turned, Nor hell a fury like a woman scorned.*

Carter raged, "I'll kill you, you—"

"Silence!" Jackson roared.

Carter fell quiet. Even the guards took a step back.

To Emma, Jackson said, "Your cooperation is appreciated, Miss White. I will speak with the magistrate about setting you free once we have confirmed you are telling the truth."

Grant interjected. "Why were you leaving evidence that Mr. Fairley was involved?"

Comfortable in her role, Emma said calmly, "If he's in jail for murdering the cabinet, he couldn't be put in as new prime minister, and Redding was too weak to take the role. The king hasn't been coroneted yet—and he's a wastrel."

Jackson started pacing. "They're trying to create anarchy—no leadership, no government."

The horrible reality sank into Grant. "That's just what happened to the French. And it paved the way for Napoleon."

Jackson nodded grimly. To Emma he asked, "Is there anything else you can tell us?"

Her eyes unfocused, and then darted back and forth as if searching for missing memories. "They have another weapon, something besides guns, but I don't know what."

Joseph Carter said, "Stupid slut, I'm going to wrap my hands around your neck—"

Grant stood over the man and pointed his pistol at him. "You are a traitor and a murderer. If you open your mouth again, I will kill you right here, right now."

Carter clamped his mouth shut.

They questioned Emma further, but she'd given them

all she knew. Grant ordered her wrist shackles removed, although he kept her ankles restrained just in case.

Before he and Jackson departed, Grant said to the head guard, pointing at Joseph Carter, "If that treasonous insect opens his mouth, or if he attempts to escape or to harm another prisoner, shoot him."

The guard nodded. "With pleasure, sir."

The entire sordid affair left Grant feeling soiled. Odd, but such events didn't used to leave a stain on him. He went home, stripped off his clothes, and sponged off until his skin was raw. Clean at last, he laid on his bed and quieted his mind. But instead of drifting in the realm of calm, his thoughts returned to Jocelyn. She'd been composed and brave tonight, unexpected qualities in women but he'd come to expect them in her. Still, she continued to impress him—her strength and courage, her no-nonsense way of dealing with tragedy and unsettling surprises. She hadn't even shrunk from the darkness within him.

Her smiling face led him to visions of loving and being loved. But that was only a sweet dream. He refused to let his darkness extinguish her light.

Chapter 28

Jocelyn awoke with the words she'd overheard at the house party running through her mind. If Emma White were the only co-conspirator in the household, who had she heard talking about Lord Liverpool, and sacrifices, and destroying innocent men? There had been two speakers, both male. If only she'd discovered who they were!

She grabbed a dressing gown and raced to her father's room. It stood empty. His valet gathered up clothing and straightened the room.

"Where is my father?"

"Gone down to breakfast, miss."

She tore downstairs and burst into the breakfast room. Papa sat reading a newspaper and sipping tea. At her approach he raised his brows. "Haven't you spent enough time in a state of undress?"

"Papa, I just remembered something I heard at the house party. Late one night, the night Grant saved me from my fall, I overheard two men talking. I can't remember everything they said but one of them mentioned Lord Liverpool. They said something about sacrifices and destroying innocent men."

He lowered his paper and stared in open shock. "Who?"

"I don't know. It was dark and they were speaking softly."

He let out his breath slowly. "Where was this?"

"Near the main staircase, somewhere towards the library, I believe."

He ran a hand over the top of his head, a familiar gesture of pensiveness.

"How sure are you?"

"Well...they were speaking very softly, little more than a whisper, but I'm certain they were male, and their words were very clear."

"If they were in the main hall, it's unlikely they'd be servants." Her father verbally reviewed the list of guests. "None of them would be interested in murder, especially not of this magnitude."

"I know, but I have no other explanation for it."

Her father closed his eyes before getting up to pace. "Dawson has mentioned on more than one occasion that I ought to allow him to spread rumors about Lord Liverpool and call into question his morals as well as his methods. He has also suggested we could throw doubt on Mr. Redding's reputation as well. It would make my appointment more likely—assuming they actually call for a vote of no-confidence against Lord Liverpool." He paced. "It's possible what you heard was a conversation regarding that."

Jocelyn ran what she could recall of that conversation through the context of an appointment to the position of prime minister, rather than through a murder plot. It was possible. But if they were mistaken, and there were others involved in the conspiracy, lives might be lost.

A servant stuck his head in. "Your coach is ready, sir."

Her father touched the side of her shoulder. "Don't worry, princess. We'll get to the bottom of it. I need to get to the House. Later..." He paused. "Do you really like Lady Everett?"

Jocelyn blinked at the sudden turn in the conversation. "I do. Do you?"

"Yes, very much. You know, I actually think I might be falling in love with her. Me—at my age."

"Oh, pish. You're not so old."

"How would you feel about her as a stepmother?"

"I think I would like that very much. If you recall, I am the one who started inviting her here."

He smiled. "True enough." He kissed her cheek. "I've invited her to join me at the opera tonight."

"Lovely. I'm happy for you, Papa, truly I am."

Alone, Jocelyn sat smiling, pleased that her father and Lady Everett finally seemed to be admitting their long-standing friendship could be more. But she didn't have the luxury of indulging in pleasure just yet. That conversation she'd overheard continued to roll through her mind.

Who had been speaking that night? And why hadn't she been bolder and lit a lamp or something, anything to have learned their identities? Papa might be right, but Jocelyn couldn't rest until she put her mind at ease.

Perhaps she ought to speak with Grant about it. Normally, she knew better than to engage in such unseemly behavior as to contact a gentleman. But Grant cared little for social conventions. And this was part of the conspiracy, which gave her some license.

At a secretary desk, she sharpened a pen and went to work. She began and crumpled up four notes. Each time, she began with too many courtesies the likes of which he wouldn't appreciate, or, considering how things were between them presently, even read. She began the fifth one by getting right to the point.

Grant,

Remember the conversation I overheard at the house party? The parties involved must be more extensive than we presently know. I will be at home today if you wish to discuss this further, or have me repeat what I overheard.

I am always your

His what? Love? Humble servant? Obedient servant? How does one end a note about murder plots to a man one loves but who has not accepted her love?

Jocelyn let out a groan and penned the words

friend,

Jocelyn Marie Fairley

She snorted. "Friend" didn't begin to explore the relationship she wanted with Grant. But at least if he could think of her as someone he could trust, he might learn to think of her as more than a friend eventually.

She snorted again. And horses might sleep hanging upside down as bats. Who was she fooling? Grant would never trust her. Aunt Ruby was right; he was too angry and cynical. Too wounded.

But a wounded man needed a healer, not a judge. And she loved him. She would not turn her back on him just to soothe her hurt feelings. Besides, giving up on him and feeling sorry for herself made it worse, not better. She'd stay focused. Bold and determined.

She sealed the letter and held it toward the butler. "I need you to see that this is delivered post-haste, Owens. Send only a trusted runner."

He nodded gravely. "Yes, miss. Right away."

A vague apprehension crept over her; every servant seemed to develop sinister motives. "On second thought, I'll deliver it myself. Have a coach ready to depart as soon as possible."

To ensure it didn't fall into the wrong hands, she could send one of her aunt's servants to deliver the message to Grant.

She dismissed Owens, tucked the note inside her shift, and hurried upstairs where she raced through her morning ablutions.

However, as she donned her gloves in the foyer, Aunt Ruby arrived. "We need to talk."

Delight and relief at her aunt's timely arrival scattered her apprehension. "Yes. Can we talk somewhere else?"

Ruby blinked. "Of course. Care for a trip to the confectioners? I have a terrible sweet tooth."

"Sounds lovely."

Inside Ruby's carriage, Jocelyn told her aunt everything about the conspiracy, beginning from Grant's behavior in her father's study when she thought he was an intruder, to her fears this morning.

Ruby listened without interrupting, her eyes wide until Jocelyn had finished talking. "And now you suspect all your servants." She stated it as a fact.

"They are the most likely, although the men's speech I overheard suggests they were educated, but why would they help members of the lower classes bring down the government? What could they hope to gain?"

"No, I agree, that doesn't make sense. Well, if it's your Grant that you need to see, we'll go there straightaway ourselves. I remember his address from when I invited him to dinner."

327

"Aunt! We can't call upon a man in his rooms!"

"We aren't. We'll simply wait in the carriage while my footman delivers the message." She rapped on the roof and called out an address.

"Yes, missus," the coachman called in reply.

Ruby settled back into the squabs and gave Jocelyn her full attention. "What happened last night in the conservatory?"

Jocelyn stared out the windows. Those events seemed days ago instead of only hours. She sighed, letting her head rest upon the pane. "He thought the reason you left us alone in the conservatory was so we could trap him into marrying me by claiming I'd been compromised."

"Oh, dear. That's not exactly what I intended. I simply wanted to give you some privacy so he could kiss you and be reminded that he does, in fact, like you and needs you in his life."

"He told me about the woman who broke his heart." Pain lanced her chest and tears blinded her. "She used him very ill." A sob wrenched out of her, carving a hole through her chest.

Aunt Ruby gathered her into her arms and held her in a motherly embrace.

Jocelyn rested her head against her aunt. "I'm sure he cares, Aunt. But how can he ever trust after something like that?"

"I know he cares, sweeting. I can see it in the way he looks at you, and in the way he tries not to look at you."

"What do I do? What if I'm not pretty enough or slender enough or smart enough or—"

"Stop right here." Ruby pulled away and put her hands on either side of Jocelyn's face. "Pretty and slender

328

are only wrapping—it's what catches a man's eye. But it's what's underneath that earns his love. Besides, you are much more than merely pretty—you are lovely. And thin? Ha! Who wants a thin wife when he can have a wife with so many delicious curves?" She uttered the last word so lustily that Jocelyn stared. And blushed.

Aunt Ruby chuckled. "Trust me, you'll understand. And he appreciates your curves. He tries very hard not to look, but he does. And his eyes say it all; he wants to eat you up like candy. Don't worry about it, sweeting. He wants you aplenty. Sooner or later, if he's not completely the most foolish, brainless man who ever lived, he'll come to his senses and see that he's better off with you than alone."

The carriage pulled to a stop in front of a plain yet respectable dwelling. Aunt Ruby held out her hand. "Give me your message."

Jocelyn fished it out from where it still resided in her shift underneath her stays, and handed it to her aunt. She called to the footman riding on the back of the carriage and instructed him to deliver it and wait for a reply.

Jocelyn's heart thumped at the thought of seeing Grant again. Despite her fatigue last night and the draining effect the events had on her, she still hadn't slept well. Instead, she fantasized about Grant touching her, kissing her, declaring his love for her.

Of course, that was in between fantasizing about making that merciless Isabel pay for her sins. Isabel being motivated to seek revenge on the enemy who assassinated her father, Jocelyn could understand. But to pretend to love a man, and then cast him off so brutally, mocking his love and using it to lead him to torture and slow death, it was beyond unconscionable. It was heartless.

Surely Grant would see that Jocelyn bore no resemblance to Isabel, that she offered a true love freely and without guile.

Aunt Ruby patted her hand. "Don't give up on him. That he opened up to you is very encouraging. Be patient. Someday he will shower you with all the love in his heart. I suspect he has a vast reservoir of love waiting for you."

Jocelyn smiled sadly. "I hope so. But with a man like Grant, I'll probably never hear sweet words of love, nor flowery phrases. I'd be lucky to get a brutish phrase such as, 'I'm probably making a mistake, but marry me, wench.'" Even that was probably too romantic.

Ruby laughed. "Would that be enough?"

Jocelyn rested her forehead on the window. "Yes. It would be enough."

If she had to wait years, she'd give him time to accept her love. The love he would offer her in return would be worth the wait.

Chapter 29

Grant enjoyed a breakfast at home unlike any he'd had in longer than he could remember. Apparently, Maggie had left at the crack of dawn to buy supplies and had outdone herself creating a feast. For one.

He glanced at the other side of the table, envisioning a smiling, lovely face across from him, her eyes the color of a cloudless, summer sky—eyes soft with genuine love.

But could he truly recognize genuine love? He'd thought he'd found it in the past, but that was a convincing counterfeit. And since then, he'd become the most unlovable person he knew. Was what he saw in Jocelyn's eyes the real thing?

He thought back. His brothers all seemed happy, married to surprisingly decent women. Each couple freely exchanged loving glances that certainly mirrored what he'd seen in Jocelyn's expression. And it bore little resemblance to the false adoration, the feigned passion Isabel had poured on him. The idea that a good woman, a woman like Jocelyn, would love a closed up lout like him was almost laughable. But it had been there last night, and at other times. He recalled her arms wrapped around him as he poured out his grief. He'd felt safe. Truly safe. With Jocelyn.

Could he accept her offering? Did he dare hand her his heart and trust that she'd keep it safe?

He was too broken to make a woman happy. She'd soon see how little he had to offer and give up on him.

Although, she had backbone. She'd proven herself calm under pressure and met every challenge face on, all with that dignity and composure he'd come to associate with her. And that smile. Cheeky wench. She certainly took delight in teasing him.

A life with her taunted him, a tantalizing dream. He visualized waking up with her in his arms, basking in her smiles across the table, sharing his thoughts with her, listening to her animated voice as she spoke of fairies and elves. He would certainly spend fewer nights creeping about London in search of a fight if she were waiting for him. She seemed to view him as a rogue Runner, a defender of the law, a protector of peace. But really all he wanted was an escape from his own loneliness and misery.

Perhaps he'd sought that escape in the wrong places.

Jackson arrived, grinning. "I thought I smelled food."

Grant gestured. "Take a seat. I have a cook now. She made enough for three."

"A cook, huh?"

"Eating all my meals at taverns lost its appeal."

"I can see that." Jackson made short work of the remaining food.

Sipping black coffee from a cup he didn't know he owned, Grant let him eat, then asked, "Is there any special reason you're here?"

Jackson grinned and polished off a sausage. "Besides your charming company? Barnes wants to see us."

Clark appeared and said with more formality than usual, "There's a footman all dressed up in livery here. He delivered this and is waiting for a reply. If you are available, the person who sent this is waiting outside to speak with you."

He handed Grant a creased and folded piece of stationery sealed with wax but bearing no seal, with his name written on it in a decidedly feminine hand with neat, even letters. The faint scent of flowers and vanilla wafted from it.

Jackson stared in rapt attention. "That smells like the perfume Miss Fairley wears."

Grant resisted the urge to leap at Jackson's throat. "How would you know?"

Jackson held out his hands in surrender. "I have spent a little time in her company. From a very respectful distance."

Grant scowled at him and turned his attention back to the note but not before he caught a brief flash of amusement crossing Jackson's features. Upon breaking the seal, Grant read the note. She'd signed it "friend." Were they friends? Could he view her as a friend? Trust her as a friend? She'd certainly supported him last night as a friend. But he wanted to do things with her that went far beyond a platonic relationship.

Returning his focus to matters at hand, he read her note a second time.

"She's reminding me of a conversation she overheard at the house party. Emma couldn't have been the only one there involved in the plot."

Jackson asked Clark, "She's waiting outside?"

The boy nodded. Grant and Jackson rose and followed the footman to a carriage waiting in front of the main door. Two figures sat inside. Wasn't that the carriage belonging to her aunt? Bonnet-framed faces peered out of the windows. Jocelyn and her aunt, Mrs. Shaw, waited.

Pleasure drummed his heart at the very sight of Jocelyn's face. She was beautiful in a serene, wholesome way, so unlike the mysterious seductiveness of Isabel. He squelched his admiration of her sweet beauty and the light that emanated from her. Ruthlessly, he suffocated the way she'd curved into his back and held him while he unmanned himself with memories of false love and betrayal. And he shut off all memories of her wearing only a dressing robe over a shift, her sash tied at her natural waist to show off her voluptuous curves, her golden hair spilling down her shoulders and back, the way the ends had brushed against her swaying hips as she led the way upstairs. He most especially refused to recall her calm and wisdom during events that would have sent other females into hysterics.

He swore and mastered his thoughts more completely. The case. She wanted to discuss who was in on the plot to assassinate the prime minister and cabinet. There. That helped.

A footman opened the door for them. As Grant got in and slid over to make room for Jackson, he glanced at both of the occupants.

Jocelyn spoke, "My aunt knows everything, as of a moment ago, so you can speak freely."

Grant stumbled over the fact that Jocelyn had revealed the conspiracy, but she'd probably needed to tell her aunt something to win her cooperation today. And it wasn't exactly a secret from the Fairley family any more. Looking discomfited, Jackson sat next to Grant.

Mrs. Shaw eyed Grant with new light and not a little suspicion. She probably thought he had pretended to court

Jocelyn in order to investigate her father. But even he wasn't that ruthless. He would never sink to Isabel's level.

He turned his attention to Jocelyn. Her eyes fixed trustingly on him. Trust. She trusted him.

Did he deserve her trust?

Could he trust her?

"Here is everything I remember." Jocelyn's gaze darted from Grant to Jackson and back again. "It was late and I was ascending the main staircase in the hall. I heard two low voices, male, but very soft, speaking. One said, something about the prime minister. The other said, 'Sacrifices must be made, but I don't like your plan.' And then something about innocent men being destroyed."

Grant sifted through her words, searching for a deeper meaning but couldn't find any. "What were the names of all the guests?"

She recited several names, most matching his memory. During the interchange, Mrs. Shaw remained quiet, watching them as if she viewed a diverting stage performance.

When Jocelyn had finished naming the guests, Jackson shook his head. "None of those were names Emma White said were part of the conspirators. But she might not know everyone involved."

"Or they might not be leaders, just others who are helping," Grant mused. He turned his attention to Jocelyn. "Everyone else involved so far were of the working class. Could the men you overheard have been servants?"

She tried to recall their words, their voices, but only ghostly threads remained. "No, I don't think so. Their accents seemed too refined."

"Gentlemen, then."

"I believe so."

He glanced at Mrs. Shaw and then leaned forward to get closer to Jocelyn, searching for signs of distress in her expression. "Do you feel you are in danger?"

Serene blue eyes fixed on him. "No, only now I don't know who to trust. That's why I decided to deliver this message in person."

Grant nodded. "I'll ask Emma White if she knows who they are."

"Will she tell you, do you think?"

He smiled grimly. "She's proven surprisingly cooperative, once she learned her lover was just using her."

"No," Jocelyn gasped in true distress. "She was certain he loved her so much."

Quietly, he said, "She was. But he didn't."

Her brow furrowed and she stared downward, then met his gaze, searching his face for ...what? She already knew the ugly truth of his past.

Her uncertainty and the almost desperate way she looked at him tugged at his heart. His heart. The heart that had slowly clawed back up to her light, like a ghoul escaping a grave and seeking a new life. Could his heart—could he—truly have a new life? With her?

She opened her mouth to utter some apparently burning question, but stopped, casting a glance at her aunt and Jackson. Jocelyn's brows drew together and she twisted her gloved hands in her lap.

Against his better judgment, he touched her hand. "If I learn of anything, I'll let you know. But for now I think you're safe assuming your servants are loyal."

"I want to go with you to talk to Emma."

"No. Out of the question."

"She might talk to me. Please." She turned her hands over and squeezed his.

"I don't think she will; she has a healthy resentment for people of your class."

"As the son of an earl, you technically outrank me," she reminded him.

"Not if you consider the company I usually keep."

"I resent that," Jackson said, but his eyes glittered with humor.

Grant tried again. "She's only helping us because we've offered her a deal, and it suits her sense of revenge." He softened his voice. "Go home where you're safe. We'll take care of it. By this time tomorrow, it will all be over and the threat to the prime minister and his cabinet will be averted."

She squeezed his hands more tightly, her eyes pleading. "Please be careful. I would be heartbroken if you got hurt." Sincerity emanated from every word. She truly meant it.

Heartbroken if he got hurt. He'd given her so little, and yet, somehow, inexplicably, she cared for him. Perhaps even...loved him. He met her gaze but didn't have to search deeply to find the truth in her eyes. She loved him. She truly loved him—a genuine love, not the counterfeit that had nearly destroyed his body and his heart and his soul—until Jocelyn breathed healing life into him. Did he dare accept her gift?

He offered her a faint smile and touched her cheek. "Friend?"

She gave a sad half-laugh. "Friend."

He and Jackson got out of Mrs. Shaw's carriage and watched it roll away until it disappeared in the maze of

London's streets. A renewed reason to keep England safe seized Grant—not to feed his hunger for action or for a misplaced revenge against criminals who broke the law and preyed on the innocent—to keep Jocelyn and her family safe.

"She's worth it," Jackson said softly.

Grant studied Jackson's face.

A new intensity appeared in the Runner's gaze. Jackson pointed his chin in the direction of the coach. "She's worth giving up your freedom, your bachelorhood. I trust her. You should, too." Shoving his hands in his pockets, Jackson headed in the direction of the Bow Street Office.

Grant stood rooted to the sidewalk as Jackson's words echoed in his ears. *Worth it. Trust.*

Perhaps.

But for now, he had a task and it wasn't to agonize over whether or not he had a future with Jocelyn Fairley. He caught up to Jackson and they strode to Bow Street, each lost in thought.

The Bow Street Magistrate's office was abuzz with Runners coming and going. Grant and Jackson found Barnes in his private office in the corner of the building. He ushered them in and closed the door.

Without preamble, Barnes spoke. "The prime minister and his cabinet are having dinner at Lord Tierney's home at seven o'clock. The Secret Service has replaced most of the staff. They'll privately evacuate the cabinet after they arrive. When gunmen storm the place, agents will act."

Grant shifted. "If the service doesn't take prisoners,

we may not learn who are all the members of this Freedom Fighters group, and they may plan another strike."

"I am well aware of that. I've been leaning on Carter but he still won't talk. I have Runners searching for the others Emma White named, but we haven't located them yet."

"What do you want us to do?" Jackson asked.

"Climb a roof. I'm having all the Runners patrol the area but I need sharpshooters to take up positions on nearby rooftops and keep watch. Maybe you'll see something the others miss."

Grant eyed him. "What do you suspect?"

Barnes shook his head and made a circle with his hand. "Something about all this feels off; we're missing something. And Carter mentioned something bigger in the works." He let out a grunt of frustration and shook his head. "Keep your eyes open. A plan of this scale wouldn't rely on a few men with guns."

Once they'd completed reviewing their plans in detail, Grant loaded and checked his most accurate rifle and went to his assigned rooftop to keep watch. In addition to whatever might have set off Barnes's instincts, Grant would also take out any targets that fled the building after the agents arrested the anarchists.

But the rooftop was already occupied by another gunner, probably a so-called Freedom Fighter. The other man wore the coarse clothing of a fishmonger and had a long, red mustache and mutton chops. Clutching his rifle, he paced along the edge of the building, unaware of Grant.

If the gunman were on the roof instead of inside the building, then the Runners' plan had a major flaw that would get everyone killed. What, then? Did they plan to set fire to the house and shoot people who ran out?

Falling into a crouch, Grant crept to the other man and hefted his gun. He called out, "Let me guess, you're a Freedom Fighter."

With a cry of surprise, the gunman turned. His craggy face revealed years of exposure to sun and wind.

"Don't move," Grant said, his rifle poised.

The ginger-haired man froze.

"What are your orders? Shoot people as they run out of a burning building?"

Freedom fighter, who smelled strongly of fish, clutched his gun with blackened fingers. He clamped his mouth shut.

Grant cocked his rifle. "Answer me or I'll shoot."

The ginger swallowed, saying nothing.

Words the anarchists spoke came back to him. *Something bigger. A weapon.* Setting fire to a building wouldn't be considered a weapon. Horror crept over Grant. Not fire. An explosive?

"Are they setting off a flash powder explosive?"

The gunman's expression turned to surprise and Grant could almost hear him ask, *How did you know?*

Instead, the ginger hefted his gun and pointed the barrel at Grant. As the man's fingers squeezed the trigger, Grant fired. The other man crumpled onto the rooftop. Grant ran back down the way he'd come up.

He had to warn them. The sharpshooters positioned on the rooftops would be safe, but the Runners and Secret Service agents, not to mention the government leaders inside the building, were in danger.

In the alleys, Grant dodged children, carts, dogs and piles of refuse as he raced to the ground floor of the house where the dinner party was about to commence. He burst in through the kitchen door. A surprised cook and a familiar-looking, grim-faced agent stood in the kitchen.

Grant shouted. "Get everyone out of the building! They have explosives. Where is the prime minister?"

"They're still inside." The agent rushed out of the room with Grant on his heels. "Explosives!" the agent yelled. "Evacuate now!"

They raced to the east side of the house where agents were escorting the government officials out a door they'd cut into the wall which led to the house next door, a plan that might have worked if the Freedom Fighters were simply going to storm the house during dinner or even set fire. But now, there was no way to know when they planned to set up the black powder explosive.

Out of the corner of his eye, Grant caught the figure of a slender young man wearing the livery of a footman. His arm blurred in swift motion. A flash of light blinded Grant. All the world dissolved into a deafening blast. He floated, weightless, into darkness.

Chapter 30

The butler approached Jocelyn where she sat staring at a letter she'd begun to write to her youngest brother, Jesse, who was attending school at Eaton. Her letter to Jonathan lay completed, awaiting sealing. The butler cleared his throat, and the page came into focus.

Dear Jesse,

Her thoughts whirled around so quickly that she hadn't gotten past the salutation. She lifted her head and acknowledged the butler.

"Yes, Owens?"

"Miss Fairley, the parlor maid who got arrested last night is here begging to speak with you."

Jocelyn set down her pen and capped the ink. "I'll see her."

The butler hesitated for a split second before bowing, "As you wish, miss."

Katie slipped in with a feather duster in hand but halted when she saw Jocelyn. "Sorry, miss. I'll come back later."

"Katie, how is your sister?"

Katie smiled. "She and the little ones are right happy, miss, thanks to you."

"I'm glad to hear that."

Katie turned to exit but stopped. "Beggin' your pardon, miss, but is anything wrong? You look worried, if you don't mind me saying."

"I am worried. But I'm sure all will be well, soon enough."

Katie nodded and stepped out.

Moments later, Emma came in wearing the same clothing she'd worn last night. She spoke in controlled tones and accent. "Miss Fairley, before you throw me out, please let me apologize. Your father seems a good man, and it would have been terrible if he had been blamed for...what they were planning." She bowed her head.

Gone was the angry, defiant girl who hated her employers. In her place stood a broken young lady.

Wrapping her shawl more tightly around her shoulders, Jocelyn stood. "Yes, he would have. And I'm hurt that you were willing to plant evidence against him. But you did it for love, and probably because you sympathized with their cause."

"Yes, miss," Emma whispered. Something indescribably sad passed over her features.

"Thank you for coming to me, Emma. I accept your apology."

Emma's mouth quirked in a sad smile. "I also came to get my things. I don't deserve to work here, not after what I did. But I have a friend who can help me find a new position."

"Before you go, please tell me; were any other members of the staff helping you? Were any others in our employ involved in this Freedom Fighters group?"

"No, miss. I were the only one. Why, if you don't mind me asking?"

"I overheard someone talking about the prime minister and wanting to destroy innocent men. This was at the house party."

Emma shook her head. "I'm sorry, miss. I don't know anyone in either this house or your country house who were involved." She paused. "Do you want me to find out anything more?"

"No, you'd better not. I don't want you to do anything to arouse their suspicions. These are dangerous men and might hurt you if they think you're no longer an ally."

"What do you care if they hurt me?"

"I don't want anyone to get hurt."

Emma turned that over. "Katie told me what you did for her sister and the little ones."

"Katie is a fine girl."

"You are, too, miss." She turned to leave, but stopped at the door. "Are you in love with that Amesbury fellow?"

Taken aback at the personal question by a former maid, Jocelyn stared. But last night, they'd discussed Emma's personal life, so perhaps it was only fitting. Some inner instinct whispered that her answer would matter a great deal to Emma, and possibly to the outcome of the conspiracy.

"Yes," Jocelyn said is a soft voice. "Yes, I love him very much."

"Is he the fellow you were talking about last night?"

Jocelyn nodded. "I think he does love me, deep in his heart, but he's been gravely hurt and he's slow to trust. But I won't give up on him. He's worth waiting for."

"What if he don't love you? What if he's only using you?"

"He isn't. He's not that kind of man. I've seen what a brave and good man he is."

Emma leaned against the door jam, her mouth pulled

to one side. "There is something more going to happen tonight. I heard talk of some kind of weapon, a big one. I don't know what it is, but if your man and the other constables go there expecting only men with guns..."

Alarm blasted through Jocelyn's veins. "We have to warn them."

"I've told them already."

"What precautions are they taking?"

"I have no idea."

Moments later, she slipped away, leaving Jocelyn frantic with worry. A dozen times she made up her mind to go to Bow Street and beg Grant to leave the peacekeeping to the Runners, but he would resent her interference. He was an able man, he didn't need a worried female getting in his way. Twilight had already enshrouded the city which meant the dinner party would probably begin soon. Grant may already be there, getting into position to apprehend the conspirators and protecting the prime minister. If only she knew something that would help them!

Jocelyn changed for dinner but her anxiety had smothered her appetite. She paced in the dining room awaiting her father, hardly noting the smells of food.

When Papa arrived for dinner, he took a single glance at Jocelyn's face and immediately went to her. "What is it, princess? Are you concerned about the events occurring this evening?"

"I'm so worried about Grant. If he should be hurt..." her throat closed off her words with a squeak.

Her father took her into an embrace. "I know. But

he's a capable young man. I'm sure he knows what he's doing."

She clung to her father, praying that Grant would be safe. If only she could help in some way. Remaining safe at home while Grant put himself in harm's way seemed a poor way to show her affection. Her love.

"I'm having dinner with Lady Everett before we go to the opera. Are you all right?"

"Yes, of course. Have a lovely evening."

He hesitated. "Do you want to come with us? There is space in the box."

"No. Go on. I look forward to a quiet evening."

He kissed her and left. Jocelyn ate dinner alone and wandered into the library in search of something to take her mind off the danger Grant faced. But the smell of books only reminded her of that moment in the country library when he'd trapped her with his arms on the ladder and that undeniable attraction sizzled between them.

A sudden blast shook the house. "Good heavens," she exclaimed. "Was that thunder?" She parted the curtains and peered out, but the sky remained clear. Long fingers of sunset spread outward from the west and cast buildings into silhouette.

Like an approaching ocean wave, screams and cries of alarm grew louder and closer. Over the rooftops, a black cloud boiled. Not a cloud. Smoke.

All at once she knew: the weapon.

Grant.

Jocelyn raced outside, winding through streets and alleys until she reached the area producing smoke. Smoke hung over the neighborhood, stinging eyes and throats. As

Jocelyn raced nearer, the collapsed wreckage of a house came into view. She knew that house. One of the members of the cabinet, Lord Tierney, lived there. Jocelyn attended a ball there every Season. This must have been the house where the cabinet was scheduled to dine and where the conspirators planned to strike.

Had the prime minister gotten out safely? The cabinet?

Grant?

She ran toward the ruined structure. "Grant!" she screamed.

A man blocked her path. "Stay back. It's still collapsing."

"Is Grant Amesbury out? Is he safe?"

The man shook his head. "Don't know 'im."

Another form reached her. "Miss Fairley?" Jackson, his face grimy with dirt and sweat, stood in front of her. "Stay on the other side of the street." Jackson joined a loose ring forming on the perimeter, watching as if awaiting their moment to act.

The odor of black powder stung her nose and watered her eyes. Cries and screams echoed in a confusing raucous. From next door, a large group of armed men stepped out, forming a protective barrier around men huddled together. The familiar faces of Lord Liverpool, Lord Tierney, and other cabinet members made up the center of the cluster. Armed guards hustled the government officials into waiting coaches.

But what of the brave Runners and agents who'd saved them? What of Grant? He was not among the guards.

She wanted to scream at the men standing outside the crumbled building to do something, to stop waiting around and to find Grant, but smoke lingered like a caustic blanket. Two men ventured toward the collapsed building, but the thick smoke drove them off.

Unable to watch any longer without doing something to help, Jocelyn pushed through the rapidly forming crowd toward Jackson. He stood, tense and expectant, his eyes so trained on the scene of the disaster that he didn't seem to notice her presence. Her nerves bunched, anxious to leap forward. She wiped her burning watering eyes and nose, and coughed. She searched for Grant's familiar form. Where was he? So many people stood nearby that he could be anywhere.

As the last of the smoke cleared, members forming the ring around the building broke and climbed cautiously among the rubble. As sunlight faded, the concerned, or possibly merely the curious, brought torches and lanterns, holding them aloft so others could see their way.

Grant was not among the helpers. Rescuers lifted shattered timbers and collapsed stone fireplaces as they searched for those still trapped inside.

A male voice called, "Amesbury? I'm coming for you. You hang on, understood? That's an order!"

Jocelyn glanced at the man but in the dim light could barely make out his form. Whoever he was, he believed Grant was in the rubble which meant he was caught in the explosion. Underneath the wreckage. Trapped.

He was not dead. He lived. He had to. He'd survived war, capture, dozens of fights. Surely he'd survive this. He knew how to protect himself.

Of course, if he'd used his body to shield another, the way he'd used his body to shield her when she'd fallen....

No. He was alive.

Every nerve screamed to search for him. She leaped forward and ran to the nearest heap of broken brick. "Grant?"

Black powder burned her nose. Using all her strength, she picked up pieces of brick and plaster, digging her way through. She rolled back something the size of a stone. A low moan caught her attention.

"Grant?" Encouraged, she clawed through.

She found a warm hand that clutched at her. A hoarse cry came from underneath the pile of bricks. Frantic, she continued removing broken remnants of the house.

"Help me!" she shouted. "I've found someone!"

Light appeared, and others helped. Volunteers unburied a living man, with blood seeping from his face and his arm crushed. A stranger.

Disappointment burned in her tears, but she blinked them back. If one man had been buried and survived, others would, too. Within moments, the highborn worked alongside jarveys and pickpockets as dozens worked to rescue the fallen. Three more men were carried from the heap, two alive but one dead.

Not Grant. He was alive. He was alive. She sang that mantra over and over in her head. Only vaguely registering pain in her arms and hands, she continued removing anything within her strength to lift or roll out of the way. Her heart jumping at irregular intervals, she worked at clearing away the wreckage.

A carriage and galloping horses' hooves clattered to the scene. "How many are still missing?" someone shouted breathlessly as if he'd just arrived.

"Nine that we know of." It sounded like Jackson's voice.

"Grant Amesbury?"

No reply. Jackson must have shaken his head.

The other swore. "Find him!"

Jocelyn kept up the work, praying Grant was alive and unharmed. He might not be hurt, only trapped. It was possible. Anything was possible.

As she focused on clearing the area, she fell into a state of calm where her fear faded. Her back ached and her fingers were fiery, but on she searched. She would not give up, could not give up, until he was found. Others arrived, calling out names, but she tuned them out.

A male voice she did not both identify frantically yelled, "Let me through! My brother's in there!"

Jocelyn stayed focused on digging, lifting, dragging. Her fingers left darkened smears on everything, but she kept at it. Grant was alive. He had to be. She had only to find him and then everything would be all right. He'd be safe. She'd have another chance to prove to him that she loved him truly. Somehow she'd convince him to trust her.

As she pulled away yet another broken pipe, she found something. A boot? She tugged gently, but it stuck fast. She felt along the boot, finding a leg.

She called, "I found someone!"

Others rushed to assist her and soon uncovered the lower half of a man lying on his stomach. The rescuers lifted a broken table from on top of him. More light arrived. Dark clothing, including a wool coat littered with dust and debris, covered his broad-shouldered back. A large piece of plaster lay over his upper shoulders and head.

Jocelyn dropped to her knees and pressed a hand to his back. "Grant?"

A helper lifted off the plaster to reveal the fallen man's dark hair dusted with white and small rocks. He lay motionless. Dark liquid concealed his features, but she knew the shape of his face.

Jocelyn gently placed both hands on his head, one on his cheek, and bent over, listening for signs of life. "Grant." It came out half a prayer, half a sob.

Please, please answer.

Chapter 31

Grant lay entombed in a silent world of darkness. Unable to move, a weight slowly crushing the life out of him, he fought to stay conscious. Breathe. Look for light. Stay awake. Pain shot through him every time he coughed, and blackness threatened to drag him under. He fought back to consciousness.

Faces passed through his mind—his family, friends long gone, comrades-at-arms. As if it were moments ago, the final taunting words hurled by the liar whom Grant thought he'd loved returned as she'd revealed her cruelest possible vengeance.

He'd loved her—an explosive, passionate love fed by her too-good-to-be-true charm and allure. But she'd never cared for him. She'd lied to him, used him, betrayed him, cheerfully delivered him to the French butcher and left him to suffer and die. He'd vowed never to let another woman use him again. Better to be alone than allow his heart to be torn out and shredded again. His misused heart had shriveled to a blackened, hardened, stump.

Until he'd met Jocelyn. She offered a pure, unselfish love that had grown so slowly he almost hadn't detected it. When, exactly, she'd gone from being the annoying daughter of his prime suspect to a lady who occupied his thoughts and a large part of his now-living heart, he couldn't have said. But she patiently loved him, waiting for him to trust her.

Unconsciousness hovered nearby, offering an escape

from pain, from life. If he succumbed, if he let go and left this life, he'd never see her, never hold her close and bask in the wholeness of being with her. Jocelyn had opened him up to a new world. He was a better, braver, nobler man for knowing her.

For too long, he'd allowed anger and bitterness to cut him off from the very people he should have turned to when he'd been so deeply wounded. When Jason died and Grant had blamed Christian for the fatal dare, Grant had shut himself off from his family, failing to give and offer the support and comfort that he should have found with them. He'd closed up even more when he got home from the war. He'd denied himself the healing he would have found from those who truly cared.

The darkness returned, singing like a siren's song. He fought against it. He wasn't ready to die. He had denied himself the love of a genuinely giving, loving woman who, for some unexplained reason, seemed to love him—even the darkest part of him. She'd shone her light into all those dark places and chased out the monsters lurking there, leaving him as close to a state of peace as he'd ever known.

If by some miracle he ever saw Jocelyn again, he wouldn't squander their time together. He'd accept the gift of her love and let her show him how to love her in return. He had a few ideas of his own. The weight on his back pressed down on him, cutting off his breath, and the darkness called again. His body slipped into numb weightlessness.

No. He wasn't done yet. Jocelyn. He had to get back to her. He had to tell her and show her that he loved her. The truth crept over him like a sunrise. He loved Jocelyn.

He loved her—not like the volatile chemistry he'd felt with Isabel. No, his love for Jocelyn came as a warm tenderness and a desire to bring her happiness.

He loved her.

He tried again to move, to breathe, but whatever pinned him, and searing pain, kept him immobilized. He swam in a world of gray where feeling slipped blissfully away, promising a permanent release of all pain, all sorrow.

Light. Voices. Air.

Pain.

"Grant." From a distance, Jocelyn's voice called him.

He battled his way toward her. Gentle hands rested on his hair, his face.

"Is he alive?" asked a familiar voice. Christian?

"Grant!" Jared, or maybe Cole.

Did he imagine his brothers' voices? Where were they? Where was he?

"Grant. Please come back to me." Jocelyn's panic-laden tone pulled him into awareness.

He opened his eyes and drew a full breath. Shards cut into his cheek, but he could finally breathe. Sweet breath. Such relief. Of course, breathing hurt like the devil, but the pleasure of filling his lungs overrode discomfort.

Jocelyn let out a sound that might have been a sob or a laugh. Opening his eyes, he reached for her. She enfolded his hands in hers. All the words he longed to say jumbled around in his head, none finding their way out of his mouth. Poorly illuminated by a nearby lantern, her face hovered inches from his. He turned his head as far as he could to get a good look at her. He devoured the sight of her—her face smudged with dirt and soot, her hair mostly

354

falling out of her hairstyle, her torn and filthy clothing, and her blackened and bleeding hands.

Memory returned in a flash. The explosion. He'd been buried. Jocelyn had clearly helped dig him out—because she was loyal and true. All the pretty words he should have said to her left him, and he said the first thing that came to mind.

"Daft woman. When are you going to stay home when I tell you?" He tried to scowl but it came out as a feeble smile.

She laughed and cried and fell over him, trying to embrace him where he lay, unaware how much her weight hurt. Through gritted teeth, he moaned.

She shot upright. "I'm sorry! I should have known you were hurt."

"It's not bad but your crushing me isn't helping." He squeezed her hand to soften his words.

She leaned in close to his face. A tired, welcoming smile curved her delicious mouth and a decidedly playful light touched her eyes. "What would help?" Did he imagine the provocative tone in her voice?

He had a few ideas what would help.

A male form fell to his knees next to Jocelyn. "You gave us a scare."

Cole, as dirty and rumpled as Grant hadn't seen him in, well, ever, eyed Grant, his expression grave. Next to him Jared stood pale-faced. Christian stood a few paces back. All his brothers had the haggard faces and torn and dirty clothing of soldiers on a battlefield. His brothers. They'd come to search for him. To find him. To help him. Just as they always would have if he'd allowed them to be there for

355

him. Just as they always would in the future—not because they owed him but because they were his brothers. He'd been a fool to isolate himself from his family. From love.

Grant pushed himself up on his elbows and tried to breathe through pain. Several hands reached out to help him rise. He sat, gasping and holding his ribs. One of those hands gripped his shoulder.

Cole shook his head. "When I heard what happened, I knew you'd be here. I vow, I nearly died when I heard you were caught in the explosion..."

Jared's smile shone eerily white in his streaked face. "Naw, the devil doesn't want Grant in the fiery pit just yet."

Christian stood apart, clearing his throat quietly. Grant almost smiled. Christian always was a soft-hearted boy. But that he'd become emotional over a dark soul like Grant... a humbling realization, actually. Grant clasped Cole's hand, then Jared's. Jared threw his arms around him, careful not to aggravate his sore ribs. Then he clapped him on the shoulder. Grant winced.

Jared's mouth twisted to a wry grin. "We're still not even, though."

As a current of memories tripped through is mind—Jared in prison, his raw back crisscrossed with lash marks, of cutting him down from the gallows, the battle to bring him back from near death—Grant gave him a grim smile. "I'll hold it over your head for the rest of your life."

Jared clapped him on the shoulder. Grant groaned.

Christian met his gaze, nodded, and picked his way through the rubble to Barnes who came up to stand behind Cole. "Is anyone else missing?"

"No," Barnes said. "Everyone is accounted for now."

Nodding, Christian glanced at Grant and offered a tentative smile before turning away.

Grant lifted his head and offered Richard Barnes a wan smile. "You really ought to stop rescuing me."

Barnes gestured to Jocelyn. "She beat me to it this time. I'm much obliged to you, miss. I'm Richard Barnes, at your service."

"Jocelyn Fairley. A pleasure."

"Fairley? Ah." He held out a hand to Grant. "A couple of doctors are here. Let's have one of them check you. Both of you." His gaze flicked to Jocelyn.

As Grant took his hand and hauled himself to a stand, gritting his teeth in pain, Jocelyn slipped underneath his arm and wrapped one of hers around his waist, carefully avoiding his sore ribs. "Lean on me. I'll support you."

He studied her for a long moment, finding only concern and pure, open affection in her face, her eyes. "Yes. I believe you will."

Her soft smile warmed every cold part of his body, even his heart. Once the doctor examined and treated them, they bade farewell to their friends and family.

Cole gestured. "Come to the house. Let Stephens examine you."

Grant put an arm around Jocelyn. "I'll see her home first and then come."

After glancing at Jocelyn, Cole nodded. "Take my coach. I'll get a ride home with Jared."

Inside the coach, Grant sat next to Jocelyn. If she considered the possible taint to her reputation caused by riding in a closed coach with a man, unchaperoned, she gave no indication.

Casting an anxious gaze over him as if reassuring himself he were unharmed, she touched his hand. "I can't tell you how frightened I was...."

She blinked several times. A tremor went through her body, but in typical Jocelyn fashion, she pulled herself together. But she didn't need to do that alone anymore.

He put an arm around her, careful not to aggravate his injuries, and pulled her against his chest. He wrapped both arms around her. "I..." he took a deep breath but cut it short as fiery pain shot through his ribs. "I thought about you when I was trapped. I couldn't see or hear, could barely breathe. All I kept thinking about was you."

She rested her head against him. "I am so relieved you are safe."

"You shouldn't have come. You might have been hurt."

Fiercely she said, "Just try to keep me away."

Smiling at her stern tone, he kissed the top of her head.

She pulled away enough to look him in the eyes. "I know you are reluctant to accept me, and I know you find it hard to trust. I promise I can be patient, but I must tell you now that I have the chance; I love you."

He brushed her loose hair away from her face. "Curse me for a fool, but I love you too."

Her eyes shimmered with moisture but she smiled. Then let out a half-laugh, half-sob. "Why, Grant, that was a surprisingly flowery sentiment, coming from you."

"That's probably all you'll ever get."

She smiled as if she knew better. And in reality, such expressions might come more freely now. He lowered his head and kissed her. The unrestrained passion that he poured upon her, and that came from her in reply, took the strength out of his limbs. As he kissed her over and over, her arms encircled him protectively, possessively. Warmth and comfort filled his entire being. They kissed in a world of silent bliss, and all coherent thought fled except the sweet knowledge that he loved her and that she truly, deeply, genuinely loved him. That was all he ever wanted, all he ever needed.

Chapter 32

Jocelyn sat in the morning parlor on a settee next to Grant. In the morning's harsh light, every cut and bruise on Grant's face stood out in glaring testament of the horrific events of the previous night. She swallowed, reliving how close she'd come to losing him, and thanked her maker for preserving his life.

Her father sat opposite them next to Mr. Barnes, the Magistrate of Bow Street. The two of them exchanged guarded, uncomfortable looks at each other.

"We tracked down and captured all the leaders of the Freedom Fighters," Mr. Barnes said. "And we rounded up about a dozen others who were helping them. They were all working class, and a few cutthroats, all claiming they wanted a better England."

Jocelyn shook her head. A better England by committing treason and murder and leaving the country without leadership sounded like a prelude to another tyrant like Napoleon seizing control. She shivered.

"None were in the upper classes, then?" Papa asked.

"None." Mr. Barnes gave her father a weary stare. "I wouldn't have had you investigated without just cause. And I did everything to be discreet, which is why I enlisted Amesbury's help."

"I understand." Papa held out a hand. "I'm sorry about the way things turned out between us."

"I am, as well." Barnes took his hand and then arose.

"I have a number of criminals to process at Bow Street, so if you'll excuse me, I bid you all good day."

After they said good-bye and Mr. Barnes left, Jocelyn gave into temptation and slipped her hand into Grant's. He curled his fingers around hers. His eyes softened and an affectionate smile curved his lips.

"Well, that rather wraps it all up," Papa said.

Jocelyn still couldn't believe the ruthlessness of trying to kill the prime minister and the cabinet, nor the way they'd planned to do it. If Grant hadn't acted when he did...

She rested her head on Grant's shoulder, so grateful he'd been spared, and that he sat with her now, that she could hardly speak.

Her father smiled softly at her. His gaze lifted to Grant. "You're lucky to be alive with only a cracked rib to show for being buried in the wreckage."

"I am indeed." Grant kissed the top of Jocelyn's head. "And I have your daughter to thank for that. I don't know how much longer I would have lasted."

He toyed with her bandaged fingers, spreading them out as if to remind himself of what she had sacrificed to search for him.

A mother-bear-type of protectiveness overcame her. "It's fortunate those criminals are in custody. Every time I think about what they tried to do, including what they tried to do to you both, it makes me want to hunt them down myself."

Grant tightened his hold on her and exhaled. Then grinned. Grant was grinning. At her. She gaped at him. If she hadn't been sitting down, the sight might have taken the strength out of her knees. If ever there were an appropriate time to swoon, this would be it.

"You're so fierce," he said.

She barely recovered enough to say in an exaggeratedly warning tone, "That's right, I am. Don't cross me."

"Yes ma'am." With a slight chuckle, he lifted her hand to his lips and kissed it. Moving slowly so as not to aggravate his injuries, he put an arm around her.

Grant, holding her, grinning, chuckling, kissing her hand—it seemed a beautiful dream. She hoped never to awaken.

"May I assume that you will shortly be asking to speak to me in private about my daughter?" Papa asked, his eyes still warm.

"Er, yes sir."

Jocelyn let out a happy sigh and snuggled in closer to Grant's side. "Does it have to be in private? After all, it is about me."

Her father smiled indulgently and focused on Grant's face. "Well?"

Grant paused. "Do I have your permission? Sir?"

Her father thought it over. "Are you going to continue to run into buildings that have explosives?"

"If it means saving lives, yes sir, I will. But Barnes and I agreed this would be our last case together. He suggested that I might need to spend my time on more pleasant pursuits. And I agree." He traced Jocelyn's hand.

"And you have the means to make my daughter comfortable?"

"I do. I live simply because I have few needs, but I

have a goodly portion tucked away that will keep us fed and comfortable. And I own several houses, both in London, and in the country that I let out. We could take residence in any of them. I promise she will never lack."

"Then I only want to hear one thing: do you love her?"

Grant swallowed, drew a deep breath. "Yes, sir. Very much."

Tears sprang to her eyes and she lay her head on his shoulder. She'd hardly dared hope she'd hear him say those words out loud. But he'd said them twice.

"Jocelyn?" her father asked.

"I love him with all of my heart, Papa."

Her father's eyes conveyed a tenderness that exceeded any she'd ever seen from him. "Very well. You have my blessing."

Jocelyn sprang up and ran to her father, hugging him and kissing his cheek. "I love you, Papa."

"Be happy, princess."

"Oh, I can't wait to tell Aunt Ruby. She'll want to hear all the details. And start planning the wedding."

At Grant's wince, she returned to him and resumed her position. "Not a big wedding, just our family."

He nodded. "Family suits me."

She smiled knowingly. "Yes, family suits very well." Then a thought struck her; she was being far too easy on Grant after all he put her through. "Wait." She put her hands on her hips. "You haven't actually asked me to marry you."

He smiled again. "Very well, you demanding wench, will you marry me?"

Pure joy bubbled out of her. "Yes, you grumbly, gruff man. I will."

Another perfect grin came in reply.

She let out a dramatic sigh. "I don't know if I'll ever get used to that. But I hope to have the opportunity to do so." She glanced at her father. "Should we hold off a few weeks, perhaps to allow time for a double wedding?"

Her father's face softened. "I have not yet asked Lady Everett for her hand. You approve, I presume?"

"I do. And she'll make a fine prime minister's wife."

He turned pensive. "I've decided to remove myself from candidacy and step down from the House of Commons."

She shot out of her seat. "What?"

"Like your Grant, I've decided to turn my attention to more pleasant diversions."

Her Grant. She liked the sound of that.

Papa continued. "In pursuing a political career, I was attempting to fill a void. But I've found a way to fill it. And..." he chewed his lower lip. "I recently learned that my supporters were overzealous. Nothing is worth that."

"What happened?"

"One of them was spreading rumors about my opponents, casting doubt on their characters. It would be dishonorable to take the position only because my competition had been unjustly removed from consideration."

Jocelyn thought back. "Is that what I overheard at the house party about ruining innocent men?"

"It is. They were planning to besmirch the characters of both Lord Liverpool and Mr. Redding so I would be viewed as the most obvious replacement."

"Was it Mr. Dawson?"

He hesitated. "Perhaps it is better you not know. I don't want you to think poorly of anyone."

"Please, Papa."

He held up a hand. "I feel strongly about this."

Papa was right; she probably ought not know who had concocted such an underhanded plan or it would surely color her opinion of that person.

Jocelyn settled back down next to Grant. "I'm disheartened that they'd stoop to such an underhanded scheme."

"As am I." Papa said. "But at least we can rest assured they were not involved in the conspiracy. As you see, I have more than one reason not to advance my political career. And Lady Everett mentioned how much she's always wanted to visit Italy. I envision a lengthy honeymoon—if she'll have me."

"Oh, I'm persuaded she will happily have you."

All Jocelyn's efforts to help her father achieve his political goals, all those dinner parties, the ball, it all faded away to meaningless tasks. But then, perhaps they had served a purpose after all; they had brought her father and Lady Everett together. And they had brought Grant into her life. He was worth all her efforts.

She touched Grant's cheek, admiring the strength in his jaw, the contours of his face. His gaze remained focused on her, so soft, so warm. Love shone there, clear and un-shuttered. However did she earn the love of this handsome, remarkable man?

His mouth curved into a true smile, soft and intimate. "How soon can we marry?"

Giddy over the sight of his smile, she said, impishly, "Well, the banns must be read, so at least two weeks..."

A devilish glint came into his eyes. "Not with a special license."

"But those are difficult to get."

"My brother is an earl." His mouth curved wickedly.

"Ohhhhh. How about tomorrow?"

"I'll see what I can do."

As if forgetting that her father sat nearby, or perhaps not caring, he kissed her again, giving her another taste of all the pent-up love he'd saved for her.

She'd never been so happy.

Epilogue

Grant shot a wry smile at Jocelyn and patted her hand resting on his arm. With his chest puffed out in pride, he led her toward the drawing room of the Tarrington London House.

Tonight would be the first time they'd paid any social call since their wedding last month. Reluctant to share even a minute of Jocelyn's attention with anyone, he'd grudgingly agreed to attend a family dinner. Jocelyn had been gracious about having a former prostitute for a cook, and Maggie's culinary skills had kept them content, but perhaps they ought to step outside the house once in a while.

Turning to her, he touched Jocelyn's cheek, leaned in, and kissed her softly. "You look beautiful, love."

Her warm smile turned sultry. "You look delicious." She nuzzled the hollow behind his ear.

He laughed uneasily, battling the desire to drag her off into a dark corner and mess up her perfectly coiffed hairstyle. "Lusty wench. Are you giving me an excuse to take you back home, or maybe even just back to the coach?"

She grinned unrepentantly. "Do you need an excuse?"

"No." He grabbed her as if to throw her over his shoulder.

Chuckling, she swatted his hands. "Behave yourself. We promised your family we'd dine with them tonight. We can leave early, if we wish."

"Oh, I wish," he said breathlessly.

She kissed him quickly and made a point of turning them both toward the open doorway. At the entrance, he stopped. His family, people he loved most in all the world—next to Jocelyn of course—gathered in the comfortable room filled with lamplight and candles.

Cole stood near the mantel with his wife, Alicia, whose figure had already returned to the shape it had been before she gave birth to their baby. Dressed in evening wear that would put Beau Brummell to shame, and comfortable in the center of attention. With his eyes glittering, he delivered the punchline of his story. "So, I said, 'With friends like that, who needs pirates?'"

Everyone laughed.

A chuckling Jared, looking as much like Cole's twin as ever, right down to the cut of his tailcoat, sat with his arm around his wife, Elise, who snuggled in against him.

"Did you tell them we had more cutlasses in the ship?" Jared asked.

Cole chuckled. "I should have."

His youngest brother, Christian, and his wife of only a few months, Genevieve, sat on a settee together, his golden head close to her auburn curls, their hands intertwined. Christian caught Grant's glance. His little brother nodded a greeting. Then he gave Grant a full grin. Grant wondered what kind of unholy pleasure the pup was enjoying.

Odd, but sometime over the years, Grant had stopped wishing for Christian's demise, half-heartedly or otherwise. He'd even sprang to action several months ago to protect Christian when a vengeful lord had tried to kill him.

Somehow defeating a villain together had allowed them to call a ceasefire, even a reconciliation of sorts. He'd actually stopped blaming Christian for Jason's death. Christian's dare had been a simple childish challenge, not the work of a heartless blackguard. Grant had forgiven him, even when Christian hadn't truly been to blame.

He'd even relinquished his rage at Isabel. She must have felt justified in taking revenge against the assassin who killed her father. He couldn't truly blame her motivation.

Grant had never felt more at peace. It was all due to Jocelyn's soothing, optimistic influence, no doubt.

His twin sisters, Margaret and Rachel, sat next to a window, Margaret's husband nowhere to be seen. The bounder was probably out with his mistress or gambling away his fortune. With any luck, he'd drink himself to death and spare Margaret the pain of a life with the lout.

Rachel, who'd long ago embraced her spinsterhood, waved a copy of her newest book about herbs at Margaret. Rachel let out a scoffing noise. "...not that Cambridge would be open-minded enough to allow a woman to give a lecture in their hallowed halls."

"One day they will," Margaret said.

Mr. Fairley and Lady Everett stood behind the settee occupying his youngest brother. It was considerate of Alicia to include Jocelyn's father and stepmother-to-be at the family gathering. Mr. Fairley and Lady Everett stood close enough to touch, their heads together, murmuring softly, possibly discussing their upcoming marriage, an event that Jocelyn seemed to view with great joy.

Cole's gaze lit on Grant. A grin lightened his expression but he quickly covered it with mock solemnity. "Grant and Jocelyn. Welcome."

The murmur of conversation died down. Instead of calling out greetings, everyone went silent as Cole poured glasses of champagne and handed them around to everyone.

He raised his glass. "To Grant, who saved England, and to Jocelyn, who saved Grant."

Everyone toasted. Grant gaped, then scowled. "Saved England," he muttered, shaking his head. "What rot."

But as he gazed at Jocelyn who smiled at him with a purer love than he'd ever dreamed, he had to admit Cole was half right. Jocelyn had, indeed saved Grant.

Author's notes:

The murder plot in *The Suspect's Daughter* was inspired by a true event in England known as the Cato Street Conspiracy, which thankfully, was averted largely in part due to an undercover Bow Street Runner whose name I never learned. This event happened in 1820, the same year my book takes place. In my original story plot, Mr. Redding, the contender no one believed was a contender, was meant to be the bad guy—the brains of the plot to kill the prime minister and cabinet, and to frame his most likely replacement to get him out of the way so Redding would be the new likely choice as prime minister. But the more I delved into it, the less likely it seemed that a wealthy, powerful member of the British upper class would risk so much, unless it were personal, and it felt like too big a plot to be personal. It seemed more and more likely that a member of the repressed lower classes would be behind a plot of that magnitude, which is how it happened in real life events. So *my* conspirators are more like the real ones.

In the Cato Street Conspiracy, there was no black powder explosive used—I invented that for the purposes of this novel.

Also, in my story, the Magistrate of Bow Street is the purely fictional Richard Barnes. I could find very little about the real magistrate at that time, and I wanted to have the liberty of him having a backstory interwoven with Grant's, as well as with Mr. Fairley.

As far as I know, there was never any discussion of casting a vote of no confidence on the Prime Minister of England, Lord Liverpool. I invented that for purposes of my plot. Lord Liverpool's term lasted until 1827 and was the longest-serving Prime Minister of England.

I hope you enjoyed *The Suspect's Daughter*, book 4 of the *Rogue Hearts series*. To keep informed of new releases, read fun tidbits about the Regency Era, and to find sneak peaks and deleted scenes, please stop by my website **www.donnahatch.com**

You can also follow me on the sites:

Amazon author page
Facebook author page
Twitter page
Goodreads page